How Bridge McCoy Learned To say I love You

(An Off Center Love Story)

by

Robert K. Swisher Jr.

OPEN TALON PRESS

PUBLISHED BY
OPEN TALON PRESS

EDITORS: Sheila Awalt

COVER DESIGNER: Samantha Fury
PRINT FORMAT: Samantha Fury

Library of Congress - In Publication Date

Swisher, Robert K, 1947 -
TROUT FISHING FOR BODIES: A novel / by Robert K. Swisher Jr.
Summary: mystery, humor, satire
ISBN is 978-0-9979096-5-4
LCN is 2020913864

OTHER PUBLISHED NOVELS BY ROBERT K. SWISHER JR.

Historical Fiction: Trade and E-book
Published by Sunstone Press
The Land
Fatal Destiny

Contemporary Western Fiction: Trade and E-book
PUBLISHED BY SUNSTONE PRESS
How Far the Mountain
The Last Narrow Gauge Train Robbery
The Last Day in Paradise
Love Lies Bleeding
The Man From the Mountain

Literary: Out of Print
Published by Samisdat Press - Canada
American Love Story

Young Adult: Trade Only
Published by Echo Press California
The Weaver
Published by Sunstone Press
Only Magic

Humor: E-book only
Conversations With the Golf God

Mystery Series: E-book and Trade
Bob Roosevelt Mystery Series – 4 novels

Contemporary Fiction: E-book only
Hope
A Circle Around Forever

Trade and E-book
Published by Open Talon Press
Vent
Grammar Nazis Are Not Always Rite, Right, Write
Vent Revisited
The Lonely Cowboy
How Bridge McCoy Learned to Say I Love you
Short stories and poetry in literary journals, articles in outdoor magazines.
Reviews by Publishers Weekly, Best Sellers, Library Journal, and many others.

How Bridge McCoy Learned To say I love You

Dedication:

For the little girl from
Omaha
Please Don't Grow Up

Chapter One

Bridge McCoy was in a deep dilemma. Something had happened to him that although wonderful in many ways, was also terrible and gut wrenching, and should never happen to a man of his age. He would wake up at night with his mind flooded with so many questions he would tumble out of bed and pace around muttering over and over to himself, "Why me? Why me? What have I done that I should be inflicted once again?"

Bridge decided he should confide in his best friend Stoops, but he did not know if he had the courage.

****

Bridge McCoy had a hard time getting any place fast. It wasn't because he was crippled or had a disease. It was because when he walked he took two steps forward and then one step backward. He hadn't walked this way his entire life. One evening, without any kind of warning, his wife handed him divorce papers. "How can you buy me gold and diamonds?" she asked, "when you're a lousy writer and will die in poverty?"

"A lot of good writers die in poverty," Bridge replied truthfully, which were the last words he ever said to his wife.

The next morning, feeling lower than gum stuck to the bottom of a table, he got out of bed and walked two steps forward and one backward. When he tried to walk normal his legs refused to move.

At first it frightened him. Was it a nervous disorder that would spread throughout his whole body and in time make his head spin around in circles? Was it worms? Was it a sexually transmitted disease that even the hippies hadn't discovered? But Bridge did not go to the doctor. He was enrolled in the VA at the time and figured if he went they would only tell him to come back in six years and then they would give him a penicillin shot.

In a couple of weeks, Bridge grew to like his way of walking. It was surprising how many things in life he had overlooked until he started taking one step backwards. It did make it hard for him to dance, but he had never been into dancing anyway. It also made it hard for him to run, but Bridge had given up on exercise - the infantry had cured him of that problem. To Bridge, exercise was for people who wanted to live to be about six hundred years old, be embalmed with granola oil, and come back to life when there were no more saturated fats.

****

Large dark clouds were building over the mountains to the north of Lost City, which, because it was monsoon season in the high desert of southern New Mexico, would probably dump about two inches of rain, but since no one in the area grew cotton, beans, or corn, it didn't do anything but run off into the arroyos and make the weeds grow. It helped people who had homes with grass yards, but Bridge figured people who planted grass yards in the high desert should be flogged and banished to Iowa. He hoped if there was such a thing as reincarnation, the yard loving people would come back as sheep with no teeth.

Bridge and his best friend, Stoops, were headed to the This Isn't Heaven Bar to drink their breakfast - a morning Bloody Mary. Bridge was taking two steps forward and then one backward. Stoops, looking like an old Jesus Christ on welfare who had given up on saving souls, was walking backward one step at a time. It made him feel like he wasn't walking next to a cowboy who could really screw up the two-step. It also enabled them to keep up a conversation. They could also see in front and in back of them - almost like a paranoid four-legged praying mantis with one gimp leg.

On their way to the This Isn't Heaven Bar Bridge and Stoops passed several dreadlocks looking for a brush and trying to remember if soap had been invented, two street bums scavenging for cigarette butts, three ladies who looked like the circus had left them behind, sixteen pigeons that did not bother to get out of the way and had to be stepped over, four broken wine bottles, two broken beer bottles, six piles of dog poop, and four Chicanos who were trying to figure out a way to walk since their pants were belted around their knees.

The This Isn't Heaven Bar was the local hangout for bikers, Chicanos, old hippies who had given up on peace and love, construction workers, bums, cowboys, tourists who had gotten lost, and the occasional suit who just wanted to slum it for a while - the chapel for all of those with the faith of Nothing Can Save Me Now. It had been open since the town was a boomtown in the 1890's, and had never had any major renovations. Inside was always the color of a wet Seattle day without the rain and smelled like a not so clean horse stall. The wooden floor was so cracked anyone with less than a four-inch-wide heel would fall through the cracks. The building itself was about forty feet long and twenty feet wide, with a long wooden bar extending down the right side complete with over a dozen non-matching stools. Behind the bar was a mirror that had last been cleaned shortly after the Mexican War, a long shelf with any cheap whiskey you could think of, and a collection of sweet booze that tasted like cough syrup that was for college night - college night being very popular for people who liked to watch coeds get drunk, take their blouses off and dance on the pool tables while shouting, "I'm educated, I'm educated."

Squeezed in a dark corner was a jukebox that from ten in the morning until closing time spewed blues, western, Spanish, and heavy rock. Normally the music was so loud it was impossible to hear what a person was saying who was sitting a quarter of an inch away, although most of the conversations weren't very stimulating anyway. On the wall was an unlucky mounted buffalo head that hadn't been dusted since he got shot. Years earlier, some Einstein had put red lights in the buffalo's eyes. The lights flashed on and off, on and off, on and off, twenty-four hours a day - no one ever took the time to unplug the lights and let the poor buffalo sleep.

The animal rights people had protested such inhumane treatment of a dead animal, but the bikers had told them to back off or they'd sic their pit bulls on them. The animal rights people, realizing no animal was going to put their life on the line for them, prudently turned their efforts toward easier game - mainly anyone who wore leather shoes and backpackers who ate beef jerky. Everything in the bar, including the patrons, had a yellow tinge from all the cigarette smoke - the cops in town having better things to do than enforce the no smoking law. The barmaids were always down and out young girls in various stages of undress and decorated with the latest in tattoos and body piercings.

"You look worried or bothered. You're not your normal sarcastic self," Stoops said to Bridge with a tone of concern to his voice as they neared the This Isn't Heaven Bar.

"I don't want to talk about it," Bridge replied curtly, although he really did.

"Why not? I am your best friend. In fact, I might be your only friend," Stoops said.

"You might laugh at me," Bridge replied.

"I would never laugh at your problems," Stoops said, which was an outright lie.

Stevie Ray was on the jukebox singing a song about how he had a hard time counting his money now that he was dead when Bridge and Stoops walked in - Bridge two steps forward and one backward and Stoops just backward. Plastic, a sixty-year-old longhair, living on disability money, who really had nothing wrong with him but had played his cards right, was sitting at the end of the bar drinking a beer and smoking. He hollered, "When you going to learn how to walk, Bridge?"

"When the world starts learning from its mistakes," Bridge hollered back over the blare of the jukebox.

"You'd better start taking three steps backwards," Plastic coughed his four packs of Camels a day cough. "Nobody learns from their mistakes unless they get caught."

"Buy Plastic a beer on me. He thinks he's a philosopher this morning," Bridge yelled at Gloria the barmaid.

Gloria was in her early twenties, pretty in a beat-up sort of way, and grunted in reply to Bridge as she went to get Plastic's beer. Her two-inch spiked hair, dyed in three even rows of green, blue and orange, looked like it had been set in place with airplane glue.

Bridge and Stoops sat at the bar. Gloria leaned over the bar in front of them. She was wearing a low cut sleeveless black T-shirt and no bra. The T-shirt read, 'At least They Are Not Balls.' Her nipples were pierced with brass loops. Through the shirt, her nipples looked like the butt end of two angry hornets with a tack stuck in their butts. Her arms were completely covered with colorful tattoos of dragons and motorcycles and about fifteen men's names that had been tatted over. Her ears had so many earrings in them her neck seemed to sag. Her black eyeliner looked like it had been put on with a paintbrush and it made her hazel bloodshot eyes look about as big as pie plates.

"I think you need a ring in your nose," Stoops said to Gloria in jest.

"Up yours," Gloria said. "It's not a good day."

"Two Bloody Marys, with horseradish, onions, olives, celery, and anything else with food value you can toss in," Bridge said.

"You want a salad, go to a restaurant," Gloria snapped.

"It's a bad Harley day," Stoops said as Gloria walked away.

"She's lonely," Bridge said, almost succumbing to tell Stoops his dilemma, but he did not. With that thought, Bridge was overcome with a sudden and deep pang of sadness.

Bridge constantly had pangs of sadness - a weakness he tried to hide. It seemed to him loneliness covered every person he met like a wet shawl. It wasn't like he wanted to feel people were sad, but he did. At times he could almost convince himself that most people were sad was only in his head, but then he would look at the world and know he was only kidding himself. The only people who weren't sad were either simple or so stupid they didn't know they had feet. Sadness was the building block of all things. It was the need for a painter to paint and the need for a writer to write. It was endless. Birds didn't sing because they were happy, they sang because they were sad - poor misguided birds anyway.

Gloria set the two Bloody Marys in front of Bridge and Stoops. They looked at them like two stray hungry dogs that had just had two medium-rare steaks placed in front of them, and they were so surprised all they could do was drool and wonder what the catch was - generosity in this modern world is hard to believe.

Bridge and Stoops clinked their glasses together. "To crabs and herpes," Bridge said, "the safe sexual diseases of modern times."

They drained the drinks in four large gulps. "Two more," Stoops hollered over the sound of the jukebox. Johnny Cash was singing something about how he liked prison.

Gloria was talking to Plastic whose eyes were riveted like

magnets on her pierced nipples. "Why didn't you tell me you guys wanted two? I could have made them at the same time, inconsiderate jerks," Gloria protested.

"Yeah, what's wrong with you guys, anyway?" Plastic yelled, trying to play Prince Valliant.

"You," Stoops yelled.

"Just wondering," Plastic replied. "Nothing personal."

"She is a looker, but I'd sure hate to be her old man," Stoops said, watching Gloria splash together the Bloody Marys like she was about to slop a pen full of hogs.

"She likes women," Bridge said. "After sleeping with at least a thousand men, she thinks men only want her for her body."

"Why don't you tell me what is bothering you? I miss your hour-long blasts at whatever is normal in the world," Stoops said.

Bridge gave Stoops a needy look, thought for a moment, but then shook his head. Gloria set the Bloody Marys in front of them, scowled and headed back toward Plastic.

Stoops glanced at his reflection in the dirt-fogged mirror hanging over the bar. Stoops was six feet tall and one month away from turning sixty. He was as thin as a toothpick. He always wore Levi's and pullover shirts that he got from the used clothing store. His clothes hung on him as if they were embarrassed. He had a long gray ponytail that reached his waist and a white bushy beard with no set form - the left side was longer than the right. His moustache hung over his lip, so when he talked you couldn't see his lips move, which in a lot of ways was good, because he didn't have any teeth. His eyes were black, so black it took a certain light to distinguish the iris from the pupil, but they were merry, merry in an old pirate sort of way and he knew more jokes than a priest knows sinners. He had been a smuggler for most of his life, not counting the times he was in prison, which was over twelve years. But he had been a smuggler with principles, he told himself. He only smuggled pot. One day Bridge told him he had listened to too many old Willie Nelson songs and there was no honor among thieves except in songs and on TV. Stoops, after some deep thinking, responded, "You really know how to ruin a man's self esteem."

Stoops, having been raised in El Paso, Texas, knew the border like the back of his hand, but now with the drug cartels with their guns, and killers, and with all the border patrol and politicians paid off, the old days of shorting a few friends were over. All the money he had made in his life had gone to lawyers. Stoops only smoked an occasional joint now, normally when he was trying to get in the pants of some old hippie tourist that believed marijuana cured everything from buck-teeth to cancer, although to him marijuana's only purpose was to get high and make a few bucks. He and Bridge had known each other for years. They had met in a bar in Santa Fe and instantly became good friends, although Bridge never got into the dope business with him. Stoops had done his last stint in a Texas penitentiary hoeing beans and watermelons, and when he got out, with no money and nowhere to go, he had called Bridge, who was in Lost City. Bridge had told him, "Come up here to Lost City. It's about the only place in the world you will fit in. There are so many old hippies living here marijuana is the main cause of pollution, and because you were a smuggler they'll make you a hero and maybe even make a statue of you and put it in the park."

"I've been shit on enough a little pigeon shit on my head won't hurt my feelings," Stoops had said.

Stoops slept on the floor of Bridge's gallery for a month and now did odd jobs to pay for a small adobe house that was heated with wood. He swore he would never go back to the border - he didn't want to die in jail. There wasn't enough money in the world to make him die in jail. He'd told Bridge once, "Hell, Bridge, I never meant any harm. It shouldn't be against the law anyway."

"Yeah, but in most states it is," Bridge said.

Bridge had a way of knowing the real world. He did not live in illusions or dreams or myths. Being in a war has a way of getting rid of a lot of the gray in life. But Bridge knew Stoops was a good guy, a little lost most of the time. But who wasn't? Bridge felt like Stoops' older brother, even though he was younger. He also knew Stoops carried an unusual amount of sadness on his shoulders but was never a feel-sorry-for-me guy - or needy "sympathy-needing punks" as Bridge called them.

Stoops took a sip from his Bloody Mary. "It's funny how you end up someplace and really don't know how you got there," he said distantly.

"You got here on a bus," Bridge said.

"You're born and one day you wake up and you're almost sixty," Stoops said, ignoring Bridge's attempt at humor.

"I think we were hatched," Bridge said. "And although we are all a bunch of stupid birds, we have the illusion we are really mankind."

"You should have been a Buddhist," Stoops said. "They think everything in life is an illusion."

"In America, all Buddhists have a car, normally a sports car, and their beggar rice bowl is a bank vault and the only illusion they have is that they are a Buddhist," Bridge stated, not hiding his dislike for all organized religions. Although, he did understand that they all served a purpose and a belief in something was good. Bridge didn't really believe in anything, but what he really hated were people who went around spewing their beliefs like they were right and everyone else was wrong. What is right? What is wrong? Shit.

"I heard you picked up an odd job," Bridge said after another drink from his Bloody Mary.

"I'm helping a guy tile a kitchen," Stoops replied, finishing his drink and standing. "You should tell me what is bothering you this afternoon at Bill's. I promise I won't laugh."

"I'll get these," Bridge said, adding, "Maybe I will tell you this afternoon."

Stoops headed out the door.

There was a group on the jukebox, which was not The Doors, playing "Light My Fire," but it sounded like they had lost all their matches.

In a few minutes a Merle Haggard song blasted through the bar. Most of the time Bridge hated music - white blues guys crying, black blues guys wishing there weren't so many white people in the audience, cowboys crying because their balls hurt from their Levi's being so tight, rock and roll boys whining, bluegrass people wishing they could learn to not sing through their nose, opera people wondering how to get the cob out of their ass, folk singers trying to invent more things to protest from their living rooms in Malibu, Mexican singers with an accordion that would not stop playing. Bridge wished some very wise man would invent silent music.

Bridge finished his drink, put enough money on the bar for the bill and a two-dollar tip. "Here's enough to polish your nipple rings," he called to Gloria.

"Sorry I was in such a bad mood," Gloria called back.

"What are friends for but to bitch at," Bridge replied.

Bridge two-stepped forward and one backward towards the door. "All the lonely people," he said to himself, feeling a pang of sadness sweep over him - a pang of sadness that had nothing to do with his dilemma. "All the poor, lonely, sad, people."

Chapter Two

The clouds had vanished and the New Mexico sun was on its quest to inflict mankind with skin cancer. Bridge grew depressed as he looked up and down Bullard Street. He remembered when he had first moved to downtown, besides the This Isn't Heaven Bar there were only two other stores open. One was a head shop and the other a military surplus store. The head shop owner made a living selling pipes, papers, and bongs to hippies that lived in the mountains, while the military surplus store did well because many of the local people were into killing deer and elk and dressing like Rambo. The other stores were boarded up or had their windows broken out. Any open space on a wall had been covered with the local Chicano gang's graffiti - symbols so obscure nobody really knew what they meant, but Bridge figured there wasn't a turf war going on in a city of ten thousand people, unless they were fighting over who could sell pot to their grandparents. At the time, Lost City got about one thousand tourists a year - mostly people who went through town on their way to the Gila Wilderness to look at the Indian ruins and go to the hot springs, or hunters hoping to blast a turkey, deer, or elk into their freezer. Now, thanks to the Chamber of Commerce and the Arts Guild, and, much to Bridge's chagrin, also himself, the number of tourists numbered over twenty thousand a year. The fact he had gone back on a promise bothered him immensely.

The one-time hardware stores, grocery stores, railroad worker opium dens, butcher shops, bars, and pawnshops were now galleries, antique stores and combination studios and galleries. There was even a store selling organic home products, which Bridge thought was water. There was an Italian restaurant that the owner had moved from New York because he got tired of saying to customers, "What da fuck ya want?" There was a Chinese restaurant about to open on the corner. It was going in next to a brewpub. The brewpub served salads, which completely lost the ambiance of a brewpub for Bridge and he refused to enter the establishment. It was almost as bad as a bar in the mid-west selling sushi and not hard-boiled eggs and pickled pig's feet.

All the stores in the downtown art district were painted bright happy colors like a poor improvised town in Mexico, the Mexican people having reasoned gringos might like buildings painted red, yellow, blue, green, orange and mustard. To them it was gaudy and completely out of character, but who could figure out the stupid Americans anyway. Most of the buildings' new owners were people from California - the California people having made a fortune selling their old Beach Boy albums. "We'll have some guy from San Diego here soon with a burro and a large sombrero taking pictures of tourists," Bridge grumbled under his breath. But even his gallery, the Why Am I Here, was painted a burnt orange with a red chili red around the windows. "Life is nothing but a dichotomy," Bridge cursed to himself.

Bridge didn't feel like going to his gallery, so he two-stepped forward and one backward toward Vivian's coffee shop, the Wake Up Or Die. The coffee shop was across the street from Bill's Restaurant and Libations that had recently opened by three gay men after an expensive restoration. Bridge had always wondered why gay people always seemed to have a lot of money. Stoops tried to solve the question one day, stating, "They don't have any kids."

"We don't have kids and we're broke," Bridge had replied, shooting Stoops' idea to wherever bad ideas go.

Outside of the Wake Up Or Die were cute little metal tables and chairs that wished they were in Paris. There were also about one hundred dogs - Lost City having more dog lovers than any other town on the planet. A person was not a real dog lover unless he or she owned at least three and spent four hundred dollars a month feeding them, bathing them, getting them pills for their tummy aches, walking them, and carrying commercial garbage bags around to pick up the dog poop. But, it did give people a good reason as to why they were poor, and people could talk about fleas and heartworm. The town's leash law stated a leash could only be ten feet long, but people couldn't afford them after buying so many garbage bags, so the dogs meandered around like their owners with lost looks on their faces and wondering where they were. Bridge didn't own a dog. He figured a dog wouldn't pick up his poop, so why would he pick up a dog's poop. But he did realize dogs must be smarter than people, and if there was such a thing as reincarnation, coming back as a dog might be a good thing, especially if he had connections and could come back to Lost City and not some farm in Missouri where he would have to make his keep by treeing raccoons all winter.

A few tourists and several locals sat at the cute little tables. The tourists talked to each other about how quaint and different Lost City was. The locals were telling each other how if they ran the world everyone would have pot brownies in their cupboards, six pair of sandals, and fifty foreign movies. It was easy to tell a tourist from a local in town. The tourists wore sunglasses, and the men always wore socks with their sandals. The locals bought their clothes from the discount rack at the army surplus store and normally had so many tattoos on their arms they couldn't lift them anymore.

Bridge went inside the Wake Up Or Die. The coffee shop was one large open room that had big windows with panes of unleaded glass set above them. Plants hung in the windows, normally needing water, but for the plants it was a good life - they didn't have to worry about hail or frost or being pissed on by dogs. Used sofas and tables and chairs were scattered haphazardly about that for some reason gave the impression they were exactly where they were supposed to be. The wood floor creaked comfortably as a person walked. The walls were covered with a local artists' paintings that exhibited for a month. Normally the art was not great, but good, and the painters were always happy to see their stuff on a wall and even occasionally sold one - at which case they would go into shock and dream about going to New York and showing in a gallery that sold Andy Warhol's garbage. There was a large magazine rack that held magazines ranging from *High Times*, to *Body Piercing*, to *Building Environmentally Friendly Homes* from dragonfly wings and discarded toilet paper. If a person wanted to read *Newsweek*, *Time*, or *Christian Science Monitor* they had to go to a doctor's office. If they wanted to read *People* or *Vanity Fair* they had to go to an upscale warm spring's spa that was several miles outside of town.

In the far corner was the coffee bar that served every frothy coffee known to man, hundreds of organic teas, and, for three dollars, hard-sweetened bread that in the old days would have been dried bread with sugar and cinnamon sprinkled on it. Along a narrow corridor which led to the bathroom were five computers. If you bought a cup of coffee you could use a computer for seven days and seven nights. After that you were out of there unless you bought another cup of coffee. There was also a bookcase filled with games and puzzles, checkerboards, and, for the intellectually advanced, chessboards.

The Wake Up Or Die was packed as usual with its normal clientele, some of which were artists, bikers in leather discussing over a double cappuccino how the head on their Harley was getting warped, a few gallery owners reminiscing about New York and how they wished they could get an over-priced bagel that tasted like exhaust, a few street bums who would sweep the sidewalk for a cup of coffee, a couple of poets who couldn't spell rhyme, several college kids doing their homework, and a guy who had told everybody he was from Nigeria who was on one of the computers sending out e-mails to half the world begging for money so he could buy Bolivia.

Bridge two-stepped forward and one back over to Chris the barista. Chris wore his dyed blue hair in a crew cut. He had silver loop earrings, a tongue stud, and tats that were supposed to make him look like a gay Hawaiian warrior. He would normally lisp around his tongue stud something like, "Oh Bridge, you should try the chocolate mousse, truffle, vanilla cream coffee with just a few sprinkles of dried marmalade on the top."

But, since Vivian, the source of Bridge's big dilemma, owned the coffee shop, Bridge would nod his head politely and reply, "No thank you, black, the strongest you have, will be fine," when he really wanted to scream, "Give me a cup of normal coffee!! What is wrong with the damn world!!? Jesus Christ!! Coffee, just a cup of black coffee!! Only poodles should drink that frothy crap!!"

Chris started to pour Bridge a cup of black coffee when Bridge said in a tone copying a tourist from Washington State. "You know, Chris, I think I want a double chocolate, vanilla, sour cream, frothy, with raspberry sprinkles on top and only an inch of froth, understand, no more or no less, one inch."

Chris was so shocked, his mouth dropped open and his tongue flipped up and down several times crashing his tongue stud so hard against his teeth it had to hurt. "Bridge," he said with admiration, "you have finally come out of the dark ages."

Bridge replied, "The path to enlightenment is sometimes very mysterious."

Chris went to making Bridge's order as if he was the chef at a five-star restaurant. When he handed Bridge the concoction he was overflowing with so much pride, Bridge had to step back from the force field. "On me," Chris said proudly as if he had converted a Christian to atheism.

"Where's Vivian?" Bridge asked looking at his coffee like it was a stool sample he had to carry around the VA hospital for two days to find a nurse that wasn't sleeping or talking on the phone.

"She went to her Pilate's class."

"Hasn't anyone heard of sit-ups?" Bridge scowled and two-stepped forward and one back toward an empty seat by the far window. He passed a table where two lesbians were arguing because one of the partners had caught the other partner looking at another woman. At another table, four men, all dressed in black slacks, white shirts, black penny loafers, white socks, and Jimmy Cagney black hats, were waving their arms around so wildly while discussing something Bridge figured they must have been from France and had watched the Blues Brothers one too many times. In one corner a young woman, who looked like a college freshman, was writing in a journal with a contented smile on her face. Poor thing only the young and those about to die know contentment, Bridge thought.

Bridge sat and looked at his coffee before tasting it. "Who ever thought man would ever make coffee that tasted like a milkshake?" he muttered disdainfully.

He then looked out the window. A cluster of bicyclists peddled by with their black spandex pants, yellow spandex shirts, and yellow helmets they reminded him of goldfinches that had forgotten how to fly and were discussing hemorrhoids.

Bridge rubbed his forehead and suddenly felt weary. It had happened to him for his complete life. He would be fine, at least a passable fine, and then a deep weariness would fall over him. It was like he was suddenly covered with invisible mud, mud that sucked all the power out of him, mud that did not want to kill him, but only wanted to knock him down, kick him in the gut, bust out a few teeth then laugh at his plight and leave. Bridge looked at the coffee, knowing he could not lower himself one more time and take another sip, and then rested his head on the table. Sleeping at the Wake Up Or Die was ok as long as the sleeper did not drool, fart, or wake up screaming, "Mommy, mommy, save me, you didn't tell me life would be this hard."

"So weary," Bridge murmured. "So weary. So troubled."

And then his sleeping mind went on its own journey, which wasn't hard to do, as Bridge's mind went on its own journeys while he was awake. The journey was like a low budget documentary film, grainy with a bouncing camera, and the sound never in sync with the speaker's lips.

Bridge's dream documentary: The first Indians, or Ancient Ones, who lived in the area of Lost City did not always have a good time. No matter what the history books say, it was a screwed up business staying alive as a primitive. Being truly organic, and long before vaccinations, their normal life span was around 38 years. The Ancient Ones were hunters and gatherers and did not give a hoot about gold or silver or copper - money was of no importance to them. They lived in caves on the sides of vertical cliffs where they constructed mud dwellings. The paths leading to their homes were so steep and treacherous they would have made a mountain goat blanch. The Ancient Ones drew up ladders behind them at night. They didn't hike up vertical cliffs to sleep for fun, they hiked up because there were other Indians who wanted to kill them for many reasons - the land, the water, the game, the fact their women were prettier than theirs, their god of the rocks, bushes, sky, and moon was better than the Ancient Ones god of the rocks, bushes, sky, and the moon, or just for the hell of it. In the end, the Ancient Ones vanished - some say they went to Mexico, others with big vocabularies say they were "assimilated into other tribes," which really means the men were killed and the women were raped. The Indians that did the killing were Apaches, who are now poor unfortunate savages because they in turn got killed by the United States, now the brutal savage, but will one day also be the poor unfortunate ones that will get killed, probably by ten billion little yellow men who are angry because the United States is hiding the Dalai Lama - sympathy has a way of changing. But there is one truth, which is, nobody feels sorry for the winner, and, so far in history, there has never been a peaceful winner.

The Apaches were not as nice as the Ancient Ones, they said screw this hiking up cliffs just to get some shuteye, they were not hunters and gatherers, they were warriors and thieves. They fought any tribe that fit their fancy at the time, stole their food, took their women and children, and then went home and had a big orgy with a lot of food - a trick they had learned from Genghis Kahn.

This was all well and good until one day a few Spaniards happened to blow into the area. They had already wiped out the Aztecs and stolen all their gold, and the King and Pope were on their cases to go find more gold. The pesky Spaniards who couldn't smell a pork chop grilling did smell gold and silver close to the city which was not yet a city, which made all the priests so happy they wanted to save the world and the Pope so happy he got a mistress. Over the next couple of hundred years, the Indians, Spanish, Mexicans, and the new United States did everything in their power to kill each other - the Indians wanted the land but everyone else the gold and silver. Of course, the upstart normally wins, and the white city fathers blew in and discovered the city that had not been a city but now would be a city. They called the city Silver City. They wanted to call it Let's Ruin The Environment, but no one at the time knew how to spell environment, and the ones in power, like those today, really didn't give a damn about the environment anyway. They opened up big silver mines, exploited the Indians and Mexicans and whatever stupid Spaniards had hung around, and imported Chinese workers to whom they would not have to pay the lousy wages they paid everyone else - they would just send them back to China when they could no longer work. They also funded lobbyist that would fight any attempt to make a company pay a livable wage.

The city fathers were making so much money they built huge brick homes on the hillsides like homes from back east - thus starting the tradition of moving from an area and then trying to make it look like where you moved from. The homes were so big that to keep them warm it took at least fifteen fireplaces, and in no time at all they had stripped the mountain slopes of all its trees, which made the wives of the city fathers wonder where all the birds had gone. They then built a small downtown. They had their own bank, their own bars, and their own whorehouses - they didn't know about coffeehouses yet - their own bakeries, and meat shops, and harness shops, and all those other nice things that make a downtown. They then created a slum named Little Dog Hill. Mostly Mexicans lived in Little Dog Hill. The Indians slept on the edge of town, the Indians being the first hippies, but they didn't know it at the time or they could have cornered the market on peace signs and hash pipes and not wasted their time making blankets and carving flutes. The Chinese slept in their opium dens.

Then someone smarter than even the city fathers created huge mining conglomerates and one bought all the mineral rights and water rights for hundreds of miles around. While digging for gold and silver, the conglomerate discovered the largest copper deposit the world had ever seen, and since pennies and telegraphs were a big thing at the time, they were off and running.

The city was now on the map. It had a railroad, a playhouse, a small college and was so big it even needed cops, mostly because the rich guys who controlled the town needed someone to pay off. More and more houses were built, and the slum, Little Dog Hill, was expanded. But, as all fairy tales go, the price of copper dropped - somebody rigged the market. The brick homes went to ruin as the rich owners split for some other area that needed to be discovered. The people living on Little Dog Hill said, "Same old shit," and didn't move because they didn't have the money to move and if they did move it would be to just another Little Dog Hill. They did rename the town Lost City, which seemed more apropos.

Lost City stayed this way for many, many years until Bridge - Bridge escaping from Santa Fe - Bridge in his old truck and his typewriter and a thousand bucks in his pocket - Bridge after his divorce - Bridge looking for a place that was stuck in time and would not change. Bridge drank at the This Isn't Heaven Bar, ate the cheap Mexican food, didn't join a gang - he was the wrong color - and wrote and wrote and wrote, and some of his books were published.

Bridge groaned, shook his head and woke up with a look in his eyes like he had been turned into a vegan. He raised his head slowly. He looked around and remembered he was at the Wake Up Or Die. The two lesbians looked at him as though they were afraid to ask if he was ok. He gave them an "I just had a bad dream look" and smiled.

They tried to smile back, but smiling at a man was very difficult.

Bridge took a deep breath and muttered to himself, "I am the one who messed it all up. Poor Lost City, I am so sorry. Without me you would still be a ruin, a glorious shell of your once self, a sleeping decayed falling down monument to the folly of man, but enjoying your slumber, enjoying your old age. But now, now you are an up and coming art town, a town that will be restored and glorified - a town that will be paved and polished - a town that millions of people will want to come and see just to say they have been there. Before long we will have a taxi, and a tour company, and a Chamber of Commerce that will put out glossy brochures. We will even have tour buses, and tour guides, and traffic jams, and the taxes will go up and I will have to move to Yugoslavia and start drinking homemade vodka. I am so sorry, so very very sorry."

Bridge stood. He did not feel weary anymore. He felt guilty. He looked at his disgusting cup of double chocolate, vanilla, sour cream coffee with raspberry sprinkles and froth on the top. "It's all your fault," he screamed at the coffee. "It's all your fault."

Every conversation in the Wake Up Or Die ceased. Every startled eye turned toward Bridge. The air hung still, not a fly buzzed, not an espresso machine wheezed. "The world is ruined, we're all ruined, and all because of fancy coffee!!" Bridge stormed, his face turning as red as a half-ripe beet. "Frothy coffee is the cornerstone of destruction, the barometer of deceit and capitalism. Coffee is supposed to be black and strong and bitter - bitter like life, fuck, fuck, shit, fuck!! Something so good and simple, so filled with the essence of life, and what do we do, we screw it up, we take anything that is good and we froth it up, we make life into pudding, an illusion, a dream, we put raspberry sprinkles on it. Where is the mystery, the deep dark mystery?" Bridge had to stop, he was gasping. Even though he had stopped smoking, thirty-four years of smoking had taken its toll.

A lady, reading a philosophy book, looked at Bridge gasping for breath, stood and said softly as if she had just fallen in love for the first time, "Beautiful, beautiful, that is the most beautiful spontaneous poetry I have heard in years.

A deep collective sigh spread through the Wake Up Or Die and a wino who had come in merely to get out of the sun started clapping. Soon every biker, tourist, lesbian, gay man, punk rocker, college professor, hippie, and artist were all on their feet applauding and chanting, "More, more, more."

Bridge, knowing that perfect timing is the key to any performance, gave everyone a disgusted artist look and then two-stepped forward and one backward out the door toward his gallery. The applause only grew stronger the further he distanced himself from the Wake Up Or Die. Finally the people had to stop clapping because their hands hurt and several of them had to go to the bathroom. The lady in the corner who had been reading philosophy started crying.

Chris shook his head and commented to a customer, "I should have left the raspberry sprinkles off of his coffee. The shock was more than he could take.

Chapter Three

Bridge was oblivious to the people he passed as he hurriedly two-stepped forward and one backward to his gallery. He had to find sanctuary from frothy coffee with raspberry sprinkles on the top. In his agitation he kept missing the lock hole with the key to the door of his gallery. He did not even look at the words he had painted on the outside wall of the store. There was a great review from *Publishers Weekly* - "Bridge McCoy writes movingly of the various peoples and places of the west and does not gloss over the cruelties of nature or man in his novels."

But his favorite was a rejection letter from an agent on a novel of his that was now in its fifth printing. "I do not feel that your manuscript is ready for publication, and if it was published, there would be nobody stupid enough to read it."

The book had sold over 40,000 copies. The rejection made people laugh. It made Bridge want to shoot the agent, especially since the rejection should have said no one, not nobody. There was also an eight-by-twelve glossy photo of Bridge stuck to the wall with his best 'I am a lost writer' look, pity me, I drown in my folly.

Bridge finally got the door open and two-stepped forward and one backward into his gallery. "Safe," he said with deep relief.

Bridge took a deep breath. The Why Am I Here was sanctuary to him. It was a Catholic cathedral, a Mormon tabernacle, a Jehovah Witnesses conversion, a Kwanzaa tom-tom, a Buddhist temple without the fat guy, a Tibetan monastery without all the bells and prayer wheels and silly red robes. To sum it all up it was safe at home plate, a hockey goal, a three-point shot, a hole-in-one, somebody buying you a drink when you were broke.

Bridge locked the door behind him. His gallery was four hundred square feet with two large front windows. In one window hung two elk antlers he had found years earlier when he was into killing Bambi. Right by the door was a table with a fifty-year-old Navajo rug covering it, a book for tourists to sign, and a cheap calculating machine that would even add tax. Without it, Bridge couldn't have added five and three. There was a gas heater across from the table that was older than the hills that during the winter kept the store at about 40 degrees. Behind the table was an old kitchen chair he had found on the corner. How it got there was a mystery. Stoops said it had run away from a terrible home. The walls of the store were painted white, and any protrusion was painted a burnt orange. The floor was an earth brown. He didn't really like the burnt orange, but Vivian had picked it out, and relationships have to have concessions. On the walls were what Bridge called contemporary western paintings - paintings of horses, buffalo, hawks, local landscapes, prints of Indians, and four Santos an artist made who was thinking about becoming a monk, but not until after the Burning Man convention in Nevada. On tables scattered around the store was a beaded Indian dress and some very nice jewelry boxes made from walnut wood that came from the local mountains. Rolled up on the floor were two large Navajo rugs from the 1940s. Everything was lighted by track lighting he had bought when another gallery had gone out of business. The store was comfortable, the colors blended into each other like each painting, or piece of art, or rug, were in reality a part of each other, a part of the wall, a part of the whole and not just itself, which to many people in town was their goal in life - to become one with everything - but which Bridge knew was a crock. Ask Jesus or Allah or any of the heavyweight religious guys.

In the middle of the gallery was a hand carved table with spurs for drawer pulls. Placed lovingly on top were Bridge's seven books that were still in print. He sold more than the publisher did and, being the author, he did get them for 50% off of cover. To his satisfaction he sold an average of two thousand copies a year. He autographed any book he sold and put in a bookmark - which of course had his e-mail address, web-site and phone number on it. Bridge, to his deep grief, knew artists were capitalists, maybe more than most people because it was a personal thing, and there was nothing one could do about it unless the artist lived off of a trust fund. Destined to be a capitalist, he had created over the years a nice mailing list, developed post cards, and people from all over the world had read his books - not many people from all over the world, but enough to make him feel good at times. He also spoke at regional writing clubs and libraries - normally trying to tell the people if anything in life don't be a writer unless you can embrace poverty.

At the back of the gallery was a metal door that opened up to what at one time had been a beer cooler. The gallery was originally a liquor store. The cooler now held, imprisoned in typewriter boxes, Bridge's six unpublished manuscripts. At times they hollered from their confinement, "Send us out, Bridge, find us a home or at least get us a beer." Bridge always kept a paper copy of his unpublished books. He felt closer to them than their files on his computer.

The rest of the cooler was filled with boxes of typing paper, printer cartridges, a box of rejection slips, and a trunk containing his original copies of manuscripts - some so old they had been done on a typewriter. There were also piles of his poetry he had written when he was younger - the drivel that college freshman write. There were also copies of his published books.

At the very back of the gallery was a separate room with no windows. The room was about ten feet by ten feet. Bridge lived here. It was his living room, den, and bedroom. He had a cot, a small table, and a bookshelf filled with books - he read everything, chick lit, mysteries, literature, history, science fiction, westerns, biographies, but he would not stoop to self-help books.

In four cardboard boxes were his clothes. There was a small bathroom with no shower, and a small electric refrigerator big enough for a pack of processed cheese, mayonnaise, lunchmeat, and a six pack - all the necessary ingredients of life. Vivian, out of the grace in her heart, let him take a bath or shower at her house.

The most important thing in the room was his computer, or quill and inkwell, as he called it. Bridge was working on a book now, but he had no idea where it was going or why he was writing it. In the trade, when a writer is just writing they call it, practice, which in all truth really means lost.

His mother had told him once that if you put more sex in his books he would sell more. Being a dutiful son, he had tried, but his sex scenes were always boring. He couldn't get over the modern man's plight of not knowing what foreplay was, which, in one way, was good - if men were more romantic Chick Lit writers would have to get a real job. His sex scenes were always a wham bam thank you ma'am type of thing. The most romantic part being, "with the golden aura of love still in the air the couple went off to McDonalds and shared a double cheeseburger with everything and a large fry followed by an apple fritter and a smoke."

Bridge stood by the window and looked across the street. His gallery was on Texas Street and directly behind the This Isn't Heaven Bar. The stacked-up crates of empty beer bottles behind the bar waiting to go to the dump were always an inspiration to him, the discarded remains of those down and out, those destined to never live the American dream. He knew that soon other gallery owners would be stopping by to say hello. It was a morning ritual. On cue, Rainy Day, from the gallery to his left, knocked on the door. She had a gallery called the Sunbonnet that was painted bright cannery yellow. Rainy Day was a plein air painter, which is a fancy word for people who paint outside - they don't want to simply say we paint outside. Rainy Day spent days and days in the mountains painting. Her latest work was a painting of mosquito bites titled, The Beginning of West Nile Disease. Rainy Day was single because she couldn't find any man in town her age who liked to hike, most of the men were into sitting at the bar and talking about what they did before they moved to Lost City. Rainy Day had bubbling blue eyes, white short hair, and dressed in early L.L. Bean. She was always in a hurry to go someplace. She rushed around town like whatever she was about to do had to be done instantly. She and Bridge would talk occasionally - normally about where she was going to go camping. Bridge would try and not be sarcastic. The outdoors to him was why man had invented houses and towns.

Bridge opened the door. "I don't want to come in, I was just seeing that you are still alive," Rainy Day said.

"According to my feet I am," Bridge said.

Rainy Day smiled and rushed off to wherever she was rushing off to.

No sooner had Rainy Day departed than Gertrude came to the door. Gertrude's gallery was to the right of Bridge's. She named her gallery Gertrude - it was easy to remember - most artists are not good at long term memory, which has nothing to do with Alzheimer's. Gertrude painted huge paintings of important dead people - writers, thinkers, painters. Bridge laughed to himself thinking she painted them because they couldn't write or think anymore. Gertrude also excelled in paintings of man's way of ignoring poverty, hunger, war, and any other topic that has plagued mankind forever. But her best selling painting was of the This Isn't Heaven Bar of which she had sold at least a thousand prints. "I am just seeing if you are ok?" Gertrude asked.

"In what sense of the word?" Bridge asked.

"Ok with the fact the town is changing?"

"No, I am not ok," Bridge said with a frown.

"Get over it," Gertrude replied and went to her store.

Gertrude, contrary to Bridge, belonged to every group she possibly could in town from the Chamber of Commerce, to the Arts Council, to the film association, which specialized in bringing films into town nobody could figure out what they were trying to say. The fact no one spoke French, German, Italian, Greek, or early Latin had nothing to do with it. Bridge would tell her, "Gertrude, why do you want to belong to all those orginazations? You're not only ruining the town, you're messing with your own time."

Gertrude always replied, "Time is change," which meant nothing to Bridge but meant a great deal to Gertrude.

A few seconds after Gertrude left, Sergeant walked by. Sergeant was an ex- marine, Vietnam Vet, with three Purple Hearts. He moved to Lost City from Florida. Bridge and Sergeant never talked about the war, the hell with it, it was over. Sergeant sold paintings that were swirls of color, dreams living on canvas. He also sold wooden figures - some angels, some stars, some little girls and boys - with quaint sayings painted on them that made people sigh and looked good in bathrooms, which is the only place in our modern world most people take the time to think.

Sergeant was tall and thin and had eyes that, although steady in their gaze, looked past a person to a world he kept secret. He kept his hair short, not for the old Marine in him, but because he was bald and three or four long hairs hanging down your back doesn't exactly put one in the longhaired group. He drove a 1962 Volkswagen bus with over 300,000 miles on it and had sixteen girlfriends. For some reason, Lost City had a shortage of men - gay men were in abundance but were not exactly the woman's woman type of thing. Sergeant had named his gallery The Beginning Of A Rainbow and most of the time he still thought he was in Florida but somehow he couldn't find the beach.

Sergeant said, "Good morning." Old marines don't talk much.

"Same to you," Bridge said.

Running perpendicular to Texas Street was Yankee Street. On the Corner was a Greek eatery named Sally's that was owned by Rudolph and Rebecca, a couple from San Francisco who had grown tired of smog, traffic, the smell of fish, and the fact the Forty-Niners couldn't win a game if they had to and men's clothing stores only sold clothes in shades of pink with everything else in leather. The store was painted bright red. Rudolph and Rebecca were into causes, California having about every cause there is, and even some causes that are not causes yet, but will one day catch on if for no other reason than they originated in California. Bridge ate at Sally's occasionally even though he really wasn't into pita bread and hummus and anything else that hinted at being Greek, he'd heard too many things about Greek men that he couldn't get out of his head.

Rudolph was in his early sixties, always wore a hat and dark sunglasses and, being true to his California roots, ingested every drug known to man. Bridge figured Rudolph down deep really wanted to be a mob boss but the fact he was a Liberal got in the way. Rebecca was a grief counselor, which was a good job for her - anyone from California has to have been exposed to more than the normal share of grief. Rebecca was a pretty lady in her late fifties who never wore a bra. People going to grief counseling need a good dose of nipples.

Next to Sally's was a two-story brown building where on the second floor were six small artist studios. Bridge, in all the years, had never gone up to visit with the artists, most of them old hippies who had found a place to die and whose last wish was that bell bottoms and gaudy shirts would come back in style. He did wave and say hello, but since karma, and astral projection, and tarot cards were not his cup of tea, there really wasn't much to talk about.

Across the street from Sally's were four galleries painted like the rest of the downtown, bright green, orange, purple, and something between mush and oatmeal. They all had exotic names: The End Of War, Art Beyond Words, Love Is Only A Painting Away. They sold the gamut from jewelry to pottery to paintings. The owners were transplanted hippies that had found a place they fit in. Bridge would go over occasionally when they were having an opening so he could eat good cheese, gulp down a few free beers, and discuss arty subjects.

Bridge's favorite gallery on Yankee Street was owned by a man nicknamed MeJoe - no one really knew his real name. MeJoe owned a gallery called All Art Is The Same In The Dark which to him it was. He was blind and sat in his gallery wearing sunglasses and holding his white cane like at any moment he would jump up and pummel something, which was possible, as MeJoe never smiled. His smile was a perpetual scowl. MeJoe didn't like anybody unless the 'anybody' was a customer. He normally didn't talk to any other gallery owner. If someone tried to strike up a conversation with him, the only response they would get was a stern, "Fuck off."

MeJoe was in his mid-sixties and thinner than a broom handle. He only wore white cotton pants, white socks, white tennis shoes, a white long-sleeved cotton shirt, and a white straw hat. His clothes were always spotlessly clean. People figured he had to have at least fifty sets of the same clothes. He shaved his head and his eyebrows and did not have a beard or a moustache. His skin was almost pink, like he lived underneath a tanning lamp that was turned up too high, and he wore no jewelry. He lived above his gallery and didn't ask anybody for any help. How he went to the store or paid his bills, no one knew, and no one had ever seen him anywhere else but his store. A few people thought he had magical powers and just made things appear in his room - things like pork chops, soap, razors, and the occasional blind whore. No one knew where he had come from, any of his history, or even where he got the art that hung in his gallery. The amazing thing was that MeJoe painted his own paintings and never spilled a drop of paint on anything. He could see in his mind's eye the painting. He knew what he painted and saw it brighter than if he could really see it. But he never signed his own name, making up a name for each piece of artwork. It was not an ego thing. He just really didn't like artists and hated the fact he was one. All of his paintings were of the sky, majestic clouds, bigger-than-life suns, and never had a shadow in them.

When tourists were interested in a painting in his gallery, he would point his white cane at the one they were talking about and say, "That one is my favorite."

For some reason, he outsold everyone in town. One day, ignoring a stern, "Fuck off," Bridge asked MeJoe, "MeJoe, how do you sell more art than anyone else?"

MeJoe, in a chance moment of kindness, answered, "Art is in the eye of the beholder, and if you can't see, who gives a fuck. Now fuck off and don't ever bother me again, dick-head writer anyway. Who in the fuck do you think you are thinking you can make any sense out of life with words?"

What was different about MeJoe, more than anything else, was the fact he had two friends, Me and Joe, who lived in his head. So in all reality there was MeJoe, Me, and Joe, all walking around in the same body. MeJoe would stand in front of his store carrying on full-blown conversations with himself. At times Me and Joe would debate so radically MeJoe would punch himself in the jaw. "Take that, Joe," Me would say, hitting Joe.

"Take that, Me, you jerk," Joe would say, hitting Me.

No one ever tried to stop the fight when Me and Joe were fighting, mainly because it was hard to figure out who had started it.

Bridge turned from the window and two-stepped forward and one backward toward his desk. Halfway there he felt he should open the door and take the closed sign out of the window, but he didn't. He sat at his desk and did not turn on his quill and inkwell. He stared at the dark screen - a vague reflection of his face came from behind it. His hair was light brown and hung to his shoulders. He was 5'9" and a little over 170 pounds with a slight beer gut. He was in his late-fifties and an army brat. Living from army base to army base, Bridge had never really had a childhood friend - a circumstance he figured that had helped make him stand-offish, lonely, and, in his younger years, searching desperately for love. But Bridge did not use his upbringing as an excuse for how he was, he figured he could have just as easily been born a pigeon instead of a human being, and, many times in his life, he wished he was a pigeon - getting a grip on being a human was a lot harder than pooping all over park benches.

Bridge normally wore baggy short pants, hiking boots, and solid black or white T-shirts. He hated T-shirts with slogans on them. He wished everyone that wore them would be turned into a billboard. His green eyes always seemed masked. Something he really didn't like but couldn't help. He did not have an earring, tattoo, or wear jewelry.

There were worry lines on his forehead and around his eyes from years of too many strange thoughts. He did try to smile as much as possible even though most of the time he didn't feel like it. Many people considered him snide and sarcastic, but, for reasons they could not figure out, they liked him.

Bridge had done his duty in Vietnam, real duty, infantry boy, not quite the muster of a marine, but close. When he was nineteen years old he received his Dear John letter from Kay, his girlfriend at the time, love of his life, I will never forsake you, and all that stuff.

Dear Bridge: It is too tough on me going to all the parties at college and worrying about you being in a war...blah, blah, blah. I will always hold you in my heart.

The letter devastated him and left him feeling like cold oatmeal. He had opened his soul to Kay and she had abandoned him. He swore he would never fall in love again - love was nothing more than a deceit.

The war left him feeling sad, lost, disillusioned, and with a deep distrust of all governments, anything in power and slightly off kilter with everything and anything. He did know that there was nothing in life that he wanted to possess. He had no desire to own a home, two tons of jewelry, or a fancy car. He wanted to live his life. The problem was he did not know what track he should follow with his life.

After the war, and trying to discover who or what he was, he became a hippie for several years. He tried a few drugs, but quit. What was the purpose? Even without dope his feet were two feet off of the ground most of the time anyway.

He dropped out of the hippie life because he couldn't take the constant stream of philosophy, plus he liked soap, and being around hippies made him feel like an alien - Buddha and healing crystals were lost somewhere with empty AR-15 spent cartridges. But he liked his long hair. There was something free about the wind blowing through his hair. Being a hippie also did not quell his feelings of being lost and disillusioned. If anything it only made them stronger, and free love was not love, it only led to a deeper loneliness.

After the hippie stint Bridge tried college for several years but flunked out - the thought of being an accountant or a professor or running a business seemed useless to him. Once again he could not discover what he wanted to be.

While in college he did start writing poetry, but it was so bad even he couldn't understand it and Bob Dylan had already cornered the "What the hell are you saying" part of the market.

Then, with a burning desire to be alone, having not found a reason for his life, he got a job on a ranch and for years he worked on ranches all over the west. He didn't consider himself a real cowboy, life had to be more than horses, cow shit, pick-up trucks, and how far a person could spit a glob of tobacco juice, but he did love the land and the solitude, even though he felt like he was spending his life in a bubble that floated along in no set direction. He kept his hair long, which at first was confusing to the other cowboys, but Bridge, being a veteran, had no qualms about fighting, and when he did get in a fight, he did his best to hurt anyone that had instigated the fight. Willie Nelson got the cowboys off of the 'I want to beat the shit out of a long hair,' bit. Hell, some cowboys now have earrings - funny how life changes.

Bridge had always had the urge to write more than poetry and one day he started writing a novel. When he was finished the novel was so obscure even Timothy Leary wouldn't have been able to figure out what he was trying to say, so he burnt it, but Bridge did discover being a writer was as good an excuse as any in life, and in all truth it beat the pee dunk out of being a cowboy, and for some reason beyond his comprehension, even though still sad and lost, the bubble disappeared - he had found his calling in life. He would be a full time writer - being slightly off kilter is a plus for the writing profession.

He stopped working on a ranch and moved to Santa Fe when it was still quaint and affordable, before the realtors and jet-setters discovered it and drove all the poor people out of town. Over his own advice he fell madly in love, told the girl he didn't want to do anything in life but be a writer and did not give a hoot about material possessions, she agreed, they got married, and all his sadness and hollowness drifted away. Over the next several years he wrote several novels about the vanishing west, collected rejection letters from publishers, tended bar, mowed yards, the normal 'I want to be an artist' life.

After his divorce, once again disenchanted, broken-hearted, completely disillusioned at what Santa Fe had become, (the mecca of the rich and famous), off kilter more than normal, and vowing for sure he would never fall in love again, he discovered Lost City.

Ten years earlier Bridge McCoy had wandered into Lost City

looking for a place that was as far away from Santa Fe charm as he could get. He wanted to live in a place that was rustic and cheap - a place that was real - a place that would never change.

Lost City is surrounded to the east and west by huge open expanses of ranch land and nestles at an elevation of 6,000 feet at the base of the Gila Wilderness. Locals laugh because to get to Denver you drive downhill. Bridge had an idea that he could make a living if he opened a store and sold only his own books - maybe not a good living, but enough to eat beans and tortillas and not have to get a job. The only problem at the time was that he had not had a book published and did not have enough money to self publish a book - this was before Amazon but, Bridge figured, what the hell, that's why there are dreams, plus, for a reason he did not know, Lost City made him feel he had found a place he belonged - a place being off kilter was no big deal, which was evident as no one said a word about the way he walked.

Lost City, at the time, was in a deep depression. Its ten thousand people were a mixture of Hispanics, whites, a few Chinese, and a lot of old hippies. The hamburger joints, car part shops, and other small town businesses were barely staying open. The small university in town had gone from 3,000 students to 1,000. The copper mine outside of town had closed and the main source of income was welfare. Somehow Bridge ended up downtown, which took up six blocks and looked like a ghost town. The majority of the buildings were boarded up. The streets were bumpy and potholed, and on each corner were old lampposts that were never turned on but still worked. "Hey Bridge," the old buildings said to Bridge. "If you are quiet you can write all you want. Rent is nothing. There is a cheap bar and Nancy's Cafe has burritos that are so big you can make three meals out of them."

The old lampposts that still worked but were never turned on said to him, "We like resting at night. It's nice to look at the stars."

The bumpy and potholed streets explained to him it was a relief not having things on their backs all the time. And Bridge said, "Thanks, boys. Having been in a war and tried my hand at being a hippie, a college student, and a cowboy, and trying to write books is a pretty confusing thing at times, especially when you top it off with a twice-broken heart. All this killing, and peace, and love, and get along little doggie, is enough to get a man down. And truth be known,

I have never really gotten a grip on it."

"You have to promise us that you won't try and change us," one old store, being the spokesman for the lampposts and pot holed filled streets said. "We don't want to be remodeled and turned into fancy bars, or galleries, or barbershops, or bookstores. This old age isn't that bad if people would just let us die in peace. And the streets want to stay bumpy and potholed and the old lampposts don't want to be turned on."

Bridge said, "I promise, one Santa Fe in the world is enough. I will do my best to not let anyone remodel you, pave the streets, or mess with the lampposts. But you know how it is. Those pesky realtors are as thick as flies on a summer cattle herd and about as blood sucking as leeches in Vietnam. If they get wind of Lost City and think they can get rich, they'll be in here quicker than hookers to a gold rush town."

And then the old buildings, the old lampposts that still worked, and bumpy pot- holed streets all with menacing voices told Bridge, "If you ever go back on your word, Bridge McCoy, we will haunt you forever. You can run, but you cannot hide."

Bridge took their threat very seriously and had never done anything on purpose to improve the town. He did not join the Arts Council or the Chamber of Commerce and always was very vocal against change. Of the two things Bridge wanted, one was for everything to stay the same. The idea of being stuck in a time warp appealed to him. The other was he never wanted to fall in love again - never - never - never.

Bridge rented an office building, named it the Why Am I Here, sold his truck, vowed he would never own another polluting vehicle and got rid of his watch. What is time anyway? And he wrote and mailed out manuscripts.

Now, he had placed seven novels with small publishers, received good national reviews on several of them, and made enough money to buy several pairs of shorts, three T-shirts, and a pair of boots, and be called at times, 'author,' a term he did not really like, as it made him feel like a doctor who had forgotten his name, all except Doctor. He sold through his store about two thousand copies of his books a year, far more than the publisher. He had written six more, which had been all rejected by publishers and agents as being too obscure, which did not bother Bridge, as he figured people who lived in New

York and Los Angeles were the ones who were truly obscure.

But now there were more than a few people in town who had visions of making Lost City another Santa Fe - most of which were realtors - every small city has its Judas. Bridge hoped they would all get run over by a city garbage truck, not killed but mangled enough they would be in the hospital for at least twenty years, which Bridge knew was not a nice thought, but by then he would be dead and all the people who wanted to turn Lost City into another Santa Fe could choke on their ten dollar a glass wine, seven dollar beers, blue corn tortillas, opera, turquoise rings the size of diesel trucks, and houses that needed a $50,000 dollar addition so the cat would not feel closed in and go on a bummer - hairball puking, no ball fetching, self-centered creatures anyway.

But Bridge knew he was partially to blame and felt terribly guilty after promising the old buildings, lampposts, and potholed streets he would never do anything to change the town. To his relief they so far had done nothing to him in retaliation for going back on his word. It was by pure luck a newspaper in Albuquerque heard about a writer in Lost City selling his own books and wrote an article about Bridge. It doesn't take long for artists to sniff out cheap rent, and within a few months of the article most of the old stores had been rented. With the artists came an influx of hippies, Liberals, fortune tellers, palm readers, tattoo artists, gays, retired professors, the cult of tongue studs and 102 earrings, and other fringe people from around the country, but, as things go, everyone got along - New Mexico has always been diverse and accepting - it might be something to do with red and green chili or the high content of mercury in the water.

Bridge locked his gallery door. He had had enough of saying hello to the other shop owners and he turned on his quill and inkwell.

Chapter Four

Bridge read a few paragraphs of the novel he was working on and leaned back. It was boring, had no plot, once again no sex, and his characters were unbelievable. He was about to start typing when there were three loud bangs on the door. He knew it was Vivian. Vivian didn't knock, she banged on the door like a gorilla that knew you had a bundle of bananas, and if you didn't open the door she would beat it down, take all your bananas and give you a few thumps on your head just for the fun of it.

Bridge two-stepped forward and one backward toward the door and, even though Vivian was his dilemma, he smiled.

Vivian always wore long, very colorful dresses, glass beaded bracelets around each ankle, sandals, a plain silver ring on every finger, four toe rings, three silver loop earrings in each ear, and a leather cord with three knots in it around her neck. Bridge never asked her what the three knots signified, figuring it had some cosmic meaning he couldn't care less about. And although Bridge did not do drugs, Vivian smoked enough pot to keep the largest cartel in Mexico into caviar and bean dip. She had never gotten over her Haight Ashbury days. Vivian had left San Francisco because she said all the good men had turned gay. She was originally from Wisconsin and moved to California when she could no longer take cheese balls and perch and the endless talk about the Green Bay Packers. She now owned the coffee shop in town, named the Wake Up Or Die, having stolen enough money from one of her old boyfriends who had been a dope dealer and was now doing fifty years under the Rico laws. They had never really caught him, but since there are now more snitches than sparrows in America, it was an easy case.

Vivian was into slam poetry readings, save everything from snails to ringworms, war protests, legalizing pot, and still read *Mother Earth News*, but liked greasy hamburgers and fries with salt. She drank coffee from opening time in the morning to closing time and talked so fast her words were almost Morse code. She liked tequila straight, saying anyone who screwed up booze with any mix should drink water. She was a big blocky woman, about 185 pounds, and had waist-length graying hair that she wore in two long braids. Her face was oval, almost moon shaped and devoid of wrinkles. Her complexion was like soft marble. Bridge told her she would have been a German milkmaid. Her hands were big, her fingers short and stubby, her hips swayed like an ocean wave when she walked, her breasts were large enough for six women, her lips were full, and her teeth crooked but beautifully white. She would say, "This is how I am, if you don't like it, tough."

She didn't wear makeup, something about chemicals and only whores wore makeup, although she had slept with at least five hundred men during her life. The thing that had attracted Bridge to Vivian, beside the fact she didn't have tattoos, no diseases, and shaved under her arms, were her pale blue eyes. To Bridge, Vivian's eyes reminded him of children. Vivian meant no harm to anyone, anything, or any creature. She was about the only person he had ever met in his life that in many ways was still a child. But, anyone who believed dancing around a fire naked with fifty other middle-aged people was the way to find grace had to be a child. Plus, Vivian was also the only woman he had ever gone with who, when she was talking about them as a couple, she always said "we," meaning Bridge and her, and not, "I" want or "I" need. She had gotten over the self-centered hippie me, me, me, me crap in her late twenties after eating mescaline that was laced with speed. She also talked like a sailor when she got angry, which was not often, because if she was really angry, there weren't three bikers, two Chicano gang members, or a police officer who could have whipped her. She told Bridge when they started getting serious, "You ever go out on me and don't tell me, Bridge, I'll put a beating on you so bad your nose will end up on the back of your head."

She was always doing fundraisers at the Wake Up Or Die - clothes for the homeless, food for the poor, money for people who could not afford to pay their doctor bills, money for kids to buy school supplies, money to get dog's balls cut off, canned goods drives for the mission, birdseed drives for birds, rubbers for elk to control herd population so there wouldn't have to be a hunting season. The causes were endless. There was no charity or good cause she would not put her whole large body, childlike eyes, and grating voice into. Vivian was a kindred soul and kind to everyone she met.

Vivian was peering through the window, not smiling. Bridge opened the door, decided he might as well put the open sign up in the window and left the door open. Vivian brushed by him. Her long flowing dress of green, blue, orange, purple, red, and burnt sugar looked like a mixed up rainbow that was looking for some rain. Bridge had no sooner turned when Vivian, not quite angry but slightly perturbed, said to him with the speed of fifteen cups of coffee, "What do you mean spouting poetry in my shop without letting me know first so I could make up some flyers? I could have sold at least twenty cups of coffee and some of those god-awful breadsticks I was stupid enough to buy."

"It was one of those moments of glory that cannot be controlled," Bridge said.

"I didn't know you were a poet," Vivian smiled, with a tiny trace of admiration in her voice, no longer peeved.

"I have many talents, one of which is not poetry," Bridge replied.

Vivian's smile gave him a momentary shot of warmth in his troubled mind.

"Chris told me you ordered a double chocolate, vanilla, sour cream frothy with raspberry shavings on top. I really came by to see if you were feeling well or if you were coming out of the closet," Vivian said, genuinely concerned, "but if you are coming out of the closest, and give me a disease, I'll wring your neck."

"That reminds me," Bridge said, completely ignoring her question. "I had a strange thought last night."

Vivian almost wished she had not come over to check on Bridge. At times when he had strange thoughts he would rant and rave for hours, not making any sense to anyone but himself. It always helped if they were at a loud bar when he was attacked by a strange thought he wanted to expound on, then nobody could hear him. It was like watching a wind up pantomime act with a spring that would never run down. Plus, Vivian didn't believe half the bull Bridge got excited about anyway. She had learned in her life men were easy to entertain and also very easy to ignore.

"What was the thought?" Vivian asked cautiously.

"What is it called if a gay man goes straight?"

"I don't know," Vivian answered.

"It is called going into the closet," Bridge smiled.

"You are sick," Vivian said.

"I have to agree," Bridge said.

"It's Friday, which you probably don't know, and Jackson is playing at the bar in Woodsmoke. I was wondering if you would like to go," Vivian asked, which Bridge knew was a loaded question, but yes it was true, he had no idea what day it was.

"I'd love to," Bridge replied. It was one of those appeasement of women things that men have to do, or it was the last aftershock of drinking a double chocolate, vanilla, sour cream coffee with raspberry shavings and froth on the top.

"I'll pick you up at seven," Vivian said and started for the door.

"I need a hug," Bridge said to her back, trying not to sound needy.

Vivian turned, smiled, and put her arms around Bridge like a Grizzly bear would hug a human smeared in bacon grease, squeezed so tight he had to fight to not fart and then let him go.

"Thanks," Bridge said, feeling better with the great and large warmth of Vivian surrounding him like a not so gentle mist.

"Everybody needs ten hugs a day," Vivian said.

"Why ten?" Bridge asked.

"What do I look like, the answer lady?" Vivian replied tersely. "It's just ten, there is nothing else to it, Bridge. Don't make simple things so damn complicated. That's why you are so messed up in the head. People can say boo to you and you think they are trying to say something else. Boo is boo, ten is ten."

Bridge knew better than to open his mouth. She was right. He always put more into things than there really was, but he still hated it when other people were right - it just didn't seem fair, damn, Bridge was the only person in the world who was supposed to be right - smart people anyway - jerks.

Vivian once again headed for the door, got to the door, stopped, turned, pointed her finger at Bridge and said, "Remember, next time you do poetry you let me know so I can send out flyers."

"The next time I do poetry will be when all the people from the East and West Coast blow out of this town and take their Marvin Gaye, Jimmy Buffet and Beach Boy albums with them," Bridge said.

Vivian shook her head and headed back to the Wake Up Or Die.

"Vivian, you have such a great heart," Bridge said to the empty door, turned and two-stepped forward and one backward back to his computer.

He had no sooner sat when a couple walked in with a daughter who was about twelve years old. Bridge two-stepped forward and one backward and stopped behind the table by the door. The couple smiled at him. He said, "Hello," in his best salesman manner, and sat. Bridge didn't normally get into conversations with customers, only if they started the conversation. The girl stopped by the table that displayed Bridge's novels, one of which was a young adult book titled *Only Magic* and had a paint horse on the cover. The girl was thin, dressed in blue short pants, dirty tennis shoes, and a wrinkled white blouse. She had long blond hair, kind of scraggly, and blue eyes topped with blond eyebrows. With longing in her eyes she looked at the book with the paint horse on it - all young girls, no matter if they live in the Arctic, dream about owning a horse. Glancing at her parents, and by the little girl's clothes, Bridge knew they did not have a lot of money. How could anybody in the modern world with kids have any money?

The parents walked around the store looking at the paintings. "You can pick up the book," Bridge told the girl.

She smiled shyly at him and tentatively picked it up.

"That book has been used in several schools," Bridge said. "It's a story about a wild horse in Colorado and a young girl from California. They both dream about each other. I wrote it over ten years ago."

The girl held the book to her chest, as if she was afraid to open it - if she opened it, the story would escape. She fidgeted slightly and then looked at the cover.

"Can you read?" Bridge asked.

The girl nodded her head shyly.

"Open it and read a few lines," Bridge said.

The girl smiled but shook her head and clutched the book

tighter to her chest.

The parents walked up behind the girl. "What do you have?" the mother asked disapprovingly, giving Bridge a sideways glance like the girl was doing something wrong.

Bridge could see weariness in the mother's eyes.

"He wrote it," the girl said, pointing at Bridge.

"You should put it back," the mother said. "We have to be going."

"What's your name?" Bridge asked the girl.

"Lisa," she replied timidly, giving her mother a sad look and still clutching the book to her chest.

"Bring me the book, Lisa, and I will give it to you and sign it."

The parents seemed shocked. Lisa bounded over to Bridge, a big smile on her face, and held the book out with both hands. Bridge signed it, 'Lisa, a dream story, follow your dreams,' although he did not believe in dreams. He put his card in the book and handed the book back to Lisa, "You write me and tell me what you think after you have read it."

Lisa smiled and the family started to leave. At the door, the mother turned, gave Bridge a soft look, and said, "Thank you," Bridge smiled.

Bridge gave away a lot of books, and he always wondered if the people read them. He had a feeling Lisa would. A warm feeling filled his heart as he two-stepped forward and one backward back to his computer, back to his sanctuary, back to the rutted roads, and cheap rent, and cheap beer, and graffiti, and rich dark coffee so dark it was bitter and made a person scowl when they drank it.

About to type, Bridge thought about the first time he saw Vivian. He had not wanted to fall in love. He had vowed, swore, begged, and beseeched to never fall in love again. There had been a few cases of lust, but lust did not hurt a person or cause a broken heart. Living alone, he did not hurt anybody and nobody could hurt him. He was his own master.

Bridge was disgusted with the news a coffee shop was going to open in town. But, he decided to attend the grand opening, only because the Wake Up Or Die was giving away free coffee. Approaching the front door, Vivian was standing in front saying hello to everyone. She was wearing a dress with so many colors on it made the gay rights flag look drab. Seeing Vivian, Bridge was blasted so hard by love at first sight he took one step forward and two backwards, which is not a good way to get anywhere, could hardly breathe and felt like his complete world had been swallowed by a black hole. After Bridge recovered and made it to the door, when Vivian said hello to him, all he could do was nod his head. He got his free cup of black coffee, sat in the corner, and could not take his eyes off of Vivian. He was both elated and afraid. That afternoon, back at his store, he paced around the room laughing at times and moaning at times, "Why me? Why me?"

But true to his spirit, it was not he who made the first move. The thought of asking Vivian out on a date scared him to death. There was no way he wanted to ever get hurt again - love was nothing but a thorn

Bridge laughed, remembering the first words they had said to each other.

Chapter Five

Vivian was sitting in the corner of the Wake Up Or Die drinking an iced coffee. The iced coffee made her feel stupid. It had never made her feel that way before, but now it did. She told herself it was part of Bridge rubbing off on her. Coffee was coffee, it was supposed to be black and hot and bitter; its only purpose in life was to keep a person awake. Farmers, cowboys, construction workers, truck drivers, people who worked hard, and people in the military drank coffee, everybody else should drink tea, and when they held their tea cup they should stick their little finger out and talk about world politics and how the empire is crumbling and bitch about how soft the biscuits are. Then they could go to the wine bar and swirl their wine around, still sticking their little finger out, which by now would have a cramp in it, stick their nose in the glass like a whooping crane poking around for a minnow, and tell everybody that all the tannic acid in the tea they had been drinking had ruined their taste buds, giving them an excuse to gulp their wine down so they could have another one. In all truth, they only wanted to drink wine to get pie-eyed like the lower class beer drinkers.

"Bridge, you bum," Vivian half laughed to herself, then grew somber, almost melancholy, and murmured, "I don't think you really know how much you mean to me."

She got up and tossed what remained of her iced coffee in the trash can, commenting, "A sacrament to the folly of man."

Vivian strolled through her shop, nodding and smiling at

customers and those just hanging out, past the computers, past the bathroom and to a blue door, which she always kept locked. It wasn't because there was anything valuable in the room, but because it was her room, her private space. Nobody came into her room, not even Bridge. When she was in her room, everybody had orders not to bother her unless someone had died in the store.

Vivian unlocked the door, went inside, and then locked it behind her. The room was twelve by twelve and had one small window. The window was no more than two feet by two feet and was set so high on the wall Vivian could look over the roof of the building across the street. The window would not open. It had been painted so many times it was sealed shut. The window was covered with two white lace doilies. A stained glass hummingbird hung from a piece of fishing line from the curtain rod. The doilies had been her mother's and the hummingbird her grandmother's. Both her mother and grandmother had lived hard lives on a small farm in Wisconsin, outliving their husbands. They never griped about life or circumstances. Both had also died in horrible pain from cancer. It was a part of Vivian's life she had never really gotten over - good people should die without suffering. It made no sense, and Vivian, with every ounce of her heart and strength, just once in her life wanted to find some aspect of life that made sense - so far she had failed. All she really saw in life was sadness.

The room was furnished with a full-length brown suede sofa, with a varnished stump for a foot stool a hippie who lived in the mountains had given her for six months worth of coffee - a cup a day only. Vivian, although big hearted, was not a fool. The walls were eggshell white. There was one framed print on the wall that the sofa faced. It was of a dark-haired girl looking at a robin sitting in a tree. The girl's face was calm and peaceful as if the robin were God. Vivian had had the print since she was in her twenties. It had cost her two bucks at a flea market in San Francisco. At the time, she had been dating a guy who had eaten so much acid he had convinced himself he could walk on water. His plan was to walk on water, become a prophet, and have half of San Francisco begging him for his wisdom. Of course, it would cost $19.95 per bit of wisdom. He went to the pier on a Sunday while six million people were out strolling around and telling each other how lucky they were to be in San Francisco. He did take one step on the water before he drowned. He could not swim. Vivian always figured if he was that stupid he wouldn't have been a good prophet anyway.

Next to the sofa was an old Victorian lamp with a red, blue, green, yellow, orange, and purple beaded lampshade. The beads were in no set pattern. When the light was turned on, tiny colored fairies came to life on the white walls - fairies that did not know sadness, pain, grief, need, want, or desire - just little flashes of twinkling color that only gave smiles and warmth.

Vivian plopped down heavily on the sofa. A thin sliver of light came through the window and danced off of the hummingbird. She could almost hear its stained glass wings buzz.

Vivian reached under the sofa and pulled out a small wooden box. Inside she kept her stash and pipe and disposable lighter. What was life without pot? What was life to Bridge without his Bloody Mary in the morning and his beer at night? Vivian put a pinch of pot in the bowl of the pipe, lit it, and inhaled deeply. After all the years of smoking pot, when Vivian died, old freaks could roll up her hair, smoke it, and think they were smoking the best Humboldt in the country.

Vivian took two more hits and put the pipe away. She turned on the light. The fairies flew from the red, blue, green, yellow, orange, and purple lampshade. During the daytime they were not as bright, but translucent and delicate. They danced on the wall, the floor, her large hands, her face, and on her dress. They crept delicately into her mind and behind her eyes. "Sometimes I wish I had never been born," Vivian sighed, feeling like crying, but not, and looking at the print of the little girl and the robin. "I wish I was small and delicate and my hands were tiny with long thin fingers," she said. "I wish my face was pretty and I didn't look like a sack of potatoes."

The fairies danced. Vivian took a deep breath and shut her eyes. "Sometimes I wish Bridge would tell me he loved me, even if he didn't, just tell me he loved me."

"I wish I didn't feel hollow most of the time - hollow and empty and useless and not trapped by life."

Vivian opened her eyes. The red, blue, green, yellow, orange, and purple fairies danced only for her. They did flips and circles and pirouettes like little girls in their first ballet class. The girl gazing at the robin smiled at her. The lace doilies over the windows moved from an invisible wind. The hummingbird buzzed. "Bridge, you

come off like such a tough guy that hates everything and everyone. But I know you, you are just as lonely as the rest of us and probably sadder. But you are not sad for you, you are sad for people. I really don't want to love you. I have been lonely so long
I don't know if I can take the pain if you leave me."

Vivian thought about all the men she had known in her life. She knew she had never really loved any of them. They were merely objects that she used to try and feel needed and in love, but it had never worked - loneliness cannot be fooled.

She remembered the first time she had seen Bridge. It was her grand opening and she said hello to him as he two-stepped forward and one backward for his free cup of coffee. She felt like she was fourteen, her heart raced, her face felt hot, and she wanted to grab him, kiss him, and tell him all her secrets. All during the day she could not get him out of her mind and the deep loneliness she always felt was not as strong.

Vivian shut her eyes once again and she could feel the red, blue, green, yellow, orange, and purple fairies caress her body, soft delicate touches like butterfly wings, and she smiled - ever so slightly, she smiled.

Chapter Six

It was five o'clock and Stoops was at Bill's Restaurant and Libations waiting for Bridge. The three men who bought the building, Bobby, Jeremy, and Colette, had put more than a million dollars into renovations. At first they envisioned a bar and restaurant for gays only. They developed a menu consisting of cute finger foods, pasta dishes with pink pasta, and sandwiches with exotic names that only gay people would know. What they forgot was that Lost City was three hundred miles in any direction from any major town and the only thing in between were large ranches. It is a matter of truth, to be "contraire" with *Broke Back Mountain*, most cowboys aren't gay - their horses and cow dogs and a few cattle might be, but not cowboys.

When the bar was done, the three men proudly hung their gay rights flag outside and waited for the drag queens, and dykes, and lesbian couples, and gay couples to flock in with big smiles on their faces like they had finally tamed the west. But, fifty gay couples at tops living in Lost City does not make a million-dollar restoration turn a profit, no matter how many overly-sweet drinks they drink or how much ceviche they gobble down like starved penguins frantically holding their breath and chasing ice fish.

On opening night, when the band, The Triple Dykes and Their Bitches, only drew in twenty-five people - one poor gay man could not find a companion for the night. To add insult to injury the patrons of the This Isn't Heaven Bar stood on the street and whistled and barked at the people as they went into the bar. The gay owners, being good businessmen, knew they would have to be cordial to straight people or they would lose their asses. So, dejected, but practical, they moved the gay rights flag from hanging over the front door to a more subdued place - it was tacked to the wall over the bathrooms. What they didn't think about was that most straight people didn't know that gays even had a flag - most people think flags are for democracies, and communism, and dictators, and third-world countries that need an identity to be able to steal money from the UN. The men also came to realize that the majority of people in Lost City did not really care if people were gay or not - if they really cared, they would have lived in a part of the world filled with Baptists. The owners got rid of the pink pasta and such and put chicken strips, hamburgers, French fries, steaks, and roast beef sandwiches on the menu. They did not get rid of the cute finger food. Immediately, business boomed. All the art community came - the wine list was superb and they could talk about dryness, body, fruit flavor, and all that nonsense. The Chamber of Commerce people came because the inside was so nice you could show off your expensive clothes and Rolex watch. The mayor came, and all the other city officials, because the people that went to Bill's Restaurant and Libations were not felons and could vote. And the tourists came because it was just like all the bars back home. The patrons of the This Isn't Heaven Bar even started coming over once in awhile - it was nice to get a mixed drink in a real glass and to be able to carry on a conversation without screaming over a jukebox. They apologized to the owners for their behavior during their opening, saying, "It was nothing personal, we just thought you didn't like us because none of us are gay. We bikers go through a lot of shit too - the friggin' Hell's Angels gave us a bum rap. We are really just a bunch of fuzzy rabbits who like leather and chains and passing our girlfriends around."

The owners smiled, understanding leather and chains, and accepted the apology but under their breath mumbled, "Straight motherfuckers anyway. They can really mess up a nice thing."

The owners started making so much money they took three gay-only cruises a year, sixteen trips to San Francisco, and even hired two straight bartenders and one straight waiter - enough being enough. They had a band every Friday night, ranging from country, to folk, to jazz, that packed the people in. But they never did hire The Triple

Dykes and Their Bitches again - they all had looked like construction workers from Vermont who would kick the pee dunk out of their grandmother if she looked at them the wrong way.

Bridge two-stepped forward and one backward into Bill's Restaurant and Libations. He had made up his mind he was going to tell Stoops his dilemma. Bridge liked Bill's, even though it was too clean, too orderly, too polished and the mauve walls with velveteen shadowboxes over the windows didn't hit his pleasure spot. But they had a great selection of beer, the bartenders made a good mixed drink, and, unlike the This Isn't Heaven Bar, you could use the bathrooms without feeling like you were going to catch cholera or, at the least, a mild case of the plague. Plus, the owners treated him nice, and at times when he forgot to pay the bill, they never chased him down the street with a ball bat. When he came in next time they would come up to him, smile, hand him the bill, and say, "Bridge, you're so silly."

The tables at Bill's Restaurant and Libations were over four feet tall and each had four chairs around them. Bridge liked them because if an obnoxious drunk fell off one, he normally knocked himself out, and a few patrons would carry him outside and toss him in the street, where several of the hundreds of unleashed dogs in town would take turns pissing on him, which would wake him up and he could stagger over to the This Isn't Heaven Bar and puke in their bathroom.

Bridge did not know many of the people sitting in Bill's. But by the way they were dressed he knew they were tourists, just as if he took a trip to Washington D.C. all the locals would know he was from New Mexico. Bridge knew people from New Mexico are easy to pick out of a crowd - after several years their skin starts to turn a light shade of turquoise and they smell like green chili.

Bridge sat at the table with Stoops. "You're still ugly," Stoops said.

"They pay you for putting in the tile?" Bridge asked.

"Cash," Stoops said with a big grin.

"Good, you can buy. Vivian and I are going to Woodsmoke tonight, and I'm a little short. I haven't sold a painting or any of my books in two weeks."

Stoops' grin vanished.

Bridge laughed.

"Bastard," Stoops smiled.

"You only say that because you like me," Bridge said.

Frauline, the waitress, started for their table. She was in her mid-thirties, had long blond hair, blue eyes, was a little plump, but in a pleasing way, and was from Germany. She had only been in the country for a few years. Bridge liked Frauline, although he couldn't for the life of him understand her. She was always smiling. There was no such thing as a bad hair day, she just smiled. At times, for some weird reason, Frauline reminded Bridge of a cute little dog that always wagged its tail and to which people talked baby talk to – "you are so cute, you little cutesy wootsy." Even if you popped the little bastard on the head for stealing an egg roll off of your plate, it would look at you and wag its tail. Even if Bridge was in a bad mood, which was about every day, when he saw Frauline he had to smile.

Frauline stopped by the table, bubbling smiles and good will. "The usual, Bridge?" she smiled, showing off her straight and perfectly white teeth. The usual being a Tecate beer from Mexico with a lime and a cold glass. Bridge knew having a cold glass with a beer was kind of a sissy thing, but everyone has to show their feminine side at some time. It really didn't mean he wanted to start wearing eyeliner.

"Yes, thank you," Bridge said. It was hard to say, "Of course, you dumb ass," to a smile.

Frauline smiled at Stoops. "I'd like a Budweiser," Stoops said, adding, "and how is your day?"

Frauline frowned, and her blond eyebrows sagged. "My cat got run over," she said sadly, but instantly her frown was replaced by a smile and she chirped like a happy little bird, "Now he is in cat heaven and doesn't have to suffer anymore." Without another comment, she bubbled toward the bar to place the order.

Both Bridge and Stoops did not know what to say. Happiness has a way of shocking people. After a moment Bridge cleared his throat and was about to talk when Frauline brought over the two beers, smiled as she set them down, and then went to another table to take an order and give away some more happiness.

Bridge poured his beer in the glass, squeezed in some lime, and then he and Stoops clinked bottle to glass. "To dead cats," Bridge said. "May they rest in peace and harmony, and, if there is reincarnation, may they come back as a bird and see what the other side is like."

They both took a large swallow. Bridge looked around the room as if he was being followed by two Mormons on their mission. He looked at Stoops. "Stoops," he whispered. "I have to tell you something. Something so serious I don't know what to do."

"Your ex-wife wants to get back together," Stoops whispered back.

"No."

"A publisher wants to publish the last book you wrote. The one that is so complicated and obscure you don't even know what the hell you were trying to say."

"No. This is really serious."

"You are going to buy a car."

"I'll never buy a car again," Bridge stormed loud enough to make three tables of tourists look at him for a moment - breaking up their conversation on how they wanted to buy most of the mountain north of town and open up a combination tennis facility, spa, and drug rehabilitation center for rock stars and porn queens.

"Sorry I mentioned car," Stoops said.

Bridge took three deep breaths. Cars, trucks, buses, anything with a motor had a way of throwing him into his ugly side, especially environmental freaks who drove cars – double-headed idiots, they could take their rubber shoes and plastic belts, which were made from petroleum, and figure out who was really polluting the world. Whoever it was, it was not Bridge. Bridge would not own a car. He'd ride in one, but he sure as hell wouldn't own one - a trick he learned from the Amish.

"Tell me what is so serious," Stoops said, leaning forward in the universal sign of, 'I am your friend and I am going to listen for at least ten seconds before I butt in and tell you my problems, you inconsiderate jerk for wanting me to listen anyway.'

Bridge took another swallow of his beer, pursed his lips, scratched his head, looked Stoops directly in the eyes, and, as though he had to force the words out because they were stuck in his throat, whispered so low no one else in the bar could possibly hear him, "I am in a serious dilemma, so serious I don't know what to do. I feel like my world is caving in around me."

Bridge stopped, took a deep breath to settle his nerves and in a cracking voice whispered, "Stoops, I have fallen in love, but I can't tell the person I have fallen in love with I love you. Whenever I start to say I love you all I can get out of my mouth is I, I, I, I, Lo, Lo, Lo, Lo, and then I start to choke like there is a giant meatball stuck in my throat."

Stoops jumped out of his chair with a look on his face like he had just seen his grandmother naked and hollered over and over again like a stuck record, "What? What? What?" while waving his arms up and down like he had taken some cheap acid and thought he could fly. He then jumped up and down several times in a very bad impersonation of a pogo stick. By now, Bobby, Jeremy, and Colette, the three gay men who owned Bill's, the bartender, Frauline, all the tourists, and a couple standing on the street were all looking at Stoops and wondering if maybe they should toss a bucket of water on him to calm him down. Stoops finally cleared the what, what, what, out of his throat and screamed like a fifty-year-old lady who has just learned she is pregnant. "Love!!! My God, Bridge!!! Don't you know any better than to fall in love?"

Stoops then fell back into his chair and slumped as if all his bones had dissolved and the only thing holding him up were his dirty clothes. He grabbed his beer as if it was the Torah to an Arab and drained it in two large gulps. He then looked around frantically for Frauline, and called out, "Two beers, please, quickly, my friend has gone bonkers on me."

"I'll never tell you anything again in my life," Bridge told Stoops after Frauline had brought the beers. She was so in shock she did not even smile.

"Don't give me the old bruised ego bit," Stoops said.

The bar went back to normal. Everybody had something to talk about - the idiot who thought he could fly and his friend the idiot who had fallen in love. "Poor bastard," both the men and the women and the gay people said to each other.

Stoops, almost recovered, leaned towards Bridge once again. "Tell me who you have fallen in love with, Bridge, I promise I won't freak out again. My old heart couldn't take it."

"You really promise?"

"Yes."

"Cross your heart and hope to die."

"Bridge."

"No, cross your heart and hope to die."

Stoops crossed his heart.

Bridge nodded and spit out his troubles like he was hammering out the words on his computer. "I am in love with Vivian but I don't know how to tell her and I don't know if she loves me and don't know if I should tell her even though I am in love with her and I don't want her to laugh at me and I don't want to get hurt and I don't know if it would work out and it makes me feel wonderful and terrible and terrified and all in all pretty confused and messed up."

"What's the problem?" Stoops said. "You have always been messed up."

"Be serious," Bridge scowled.

Stoops looked up at the ceiling. He narrowed his eyes. He pursed his lips, he scratched his head, he hummed, he rubbed his chin, he pulled on his beard, and he drummed his fingers on the table.

"What are you doing?" Bridge demanded.

"I'm looking serious," Stoops said.

Bridge shook his head.

"I thought everyone got over this love thing when they were about ten," Stoops said. "After that, it is just lust and monetary gain or somebody else's wife."

"I'm screwed," Bridge lamented.

"You're screwed," Stoops agreed.

"What can I do?" Bridge almost cried.

"I'll think about it," Stoops said.

Bridge forced a smile but felt no relief. Stoops' thinking was suspect.

Frauline bounced over grinning from ear to ear. "You two had us worried," she said with relief. "Two more?"

Bridge nodded. Frauline headed for the bar.

Stoops looked at Bridge seriously. "I'm really glad I don't have your problem. I'm broke. I don't have many clothes. I don't have any teeth. I don't have any insurance. I've spent so much time in the joint I don't have social security. But, thank God, or Buddha, or Jehovah, or Allah, or Martin Luther King, or the IRS, I'm not in love."

"Life always throws you a curveball when you least expect it," Bridge said and rubbed his temples.

"No, life throws you love," Stoops said, but down deep Stoops wished he was in love.

Chapter Seven

Bridge and Stoops had two more beers and tactfully avoided the topic of love. Then Bridge, with no relief from his problem, two-stepped forward and one backward to his gallery. He shaved, stripped down and took a sponge bath, which for some strange reason always made him feel like a prostitute in some sleazy bar in Mexico. He put the same clothes back on, but he did change his underwear and socks and combed his hair. He then went and stood in front of his store. All the other stores were closed now. The normal gallery hours were eleven in the morning until four - six hours of hard labor was enough for any artist to take. The exhausting schedule was the main reason most galleries weren't open on Sunday and Monday. Bridge was open every day - except for Bloody Mary breakfast and the four o'clock beer with Stoops. Of course sometimes the four o'clock beer turned into an all-nighter and breakfast lasted all day. Bridge was not stupid though, he always left a note on his door stating - 'If interested in art or a book come to the This Isn't Heaven Bar or Bill's Restaurant and Libations and ask for Bridge, or look for the guy with twenty-seven empty Tecate beer cans on the table with a lime tree growing out of his left ear.'

Four mangy dogs scampered down the middle of the road and did not even slow down or look sideways as they went by Bridge. It was like they were on their way to a dog-only poker game that would have Pomeranian strippers.

On Yankee Street, MeJoe came out of his shop. He was waving his cane around madly and yelling. "What do you mean the Democrats will save the world?" Me shouted.

"It was you Republicans who screwed it all up," Joe shouted.

"Don't call me a Republican, you jerk," Me shouted. "I am an Independent."

"Independent, Independent, what the hell is an Independent?" Joe screamed.

"We are the only smart ones of any of you," Me screamed back.

MeJoe was turning a bright red instead of his normal pink, and Bridge wondered if he should go over and break up the argument before Me or Joe got hurt.

"Independent hell, you're one of those Liberals who think they can save the world as long as we all feel sorry for everybody and take care of anyone who can't take care of themselves. Life isn't fair and all that crap and anybody who has done any good in their life should feel guilty," Joe screamed louder.

Bridge started to two steps forward and one backward across the street to break up the argument when MeJoe suddenly hit himself in the head so hard he crashed to the sidewalk cold stone out. Bridge didn't know if it was Me or Joe who had tossed the punch, but whichever one did it was one hell of a roundhouse right. Bridge went back to his store. When MeJoe woke up, one of them would apologize and feel bad. It was one good thing about Me and Joe, they never carried a grudge.

Vivian drove around the corner in her 1973 two door Saab that was belching black smoke thick enough there was no environmentalist for two miles who would survive. The car had needed rings since 1986. It had so many dents, it looked like it had been through two dozen hail storms in Minnesota, and it had white, blue, and yellow daisies painted all over it with house paint. Several months ago, a freak who lived in the commune outside of town and was called My Feet Don't Touch The Ground had offered to paint Vivian's car. Bridge liked the rust himself, but Vivian had told My Feet Don't Touch The Ground to go ahead paint it. But she had forgotten to stipulate what she meant by paint. Strangely, Vivian liked the paint job, even though the paint had run and all the flowers looked wilted. When Bridge started to protest, Vivian had given him a 'shut up, stupid man' look, and said, "What do you expect for five joints?"

Vivian stopped and Bridge crawled through the driver's side window. The door had lost its ability to open when Nixon finally told the truth. It took Bridge about a minute to unscrew his body and get situated in the seat. When he was done he smiled at Vivian like he had just climbed Mt. Everest. Vivian was wearing a bright orange dress, had freshly braided her hair, had splashed on enough lavender oil for every old hippie chick in California, and her eyes were sparkling their 'I am only a child' magic. Looking into her eyes, Bridge wanted to blurt out, "Vivian, I love you." But all that came out was "I, I, I, Lo, Lo," and Bridge started to choke.

Vivian gave Bridge a strange look but said nothing. Finished choking, Bridge smiled and said, "As usual, you look stunning."

Vivian leaned over and kissed him on the cheek and whispered, "I like the way you lie."

"It isn't a lie," Bridge said truthfully.

He wanted to tell her he could feel the beauty she had inside of her. He wanted to tell her, her aura was shimmering gold like a perfect sunset. But since he didn't believe in inner beauty and all that aura mumbo jumbo, or at least he told himself he didn't, he kept his mouth shut.

Vivian drove out of the downtown arts district, leaving Bridge's comfort zone behind. Away from the orange, red, green, mustard, and oatmeal painted stores - away from the world of paintings and carvings and books - away from the world of gays, politics, dog's rights, and save a llama for your karma - away from the world of organic food and coffee shops. Vivian drove into the real world - the real world that to Bridge surrounded the arts district like a blood sucking tick. The world of car lots, fast food and cash-checking rip off joints - the world of furniture stores and attorneys - the world of billboards and stop and speed limit signs - the world of trailer parks, over-priced gas, and hotels with Internet access and a hot tub. The world of after work bars that reek of toil and weariness. The world of rent a movie, let me take you to another world, your world sucks and you know it, rent me, I will make you feel, I will stop your boredom and your weariness, I will show you what love is, all for only five bucks. The world of car part stores and Sears and hardware stores - the world of telemarketing centers - buy this, it will end your misery - buy this, it will make the world a better place - buy this, your wife or husband will love you forever - the world of cell phones and all night convenience stores - the world of dentists, doctors, hospitals, secretaries, janitors and mechanics - the world of cops, courthouses and judges. The world held together by the glue of minimum wage. What do you mean you don't have any loyalty? God damn you I pay you $7.65 and hour. $7.65 you white, chink, nigger, Chicano, wop, grease ball, slave. Don't you understand I own your ass? You'd better learn loyalty or I'll fire you, and you and your wife, and kids, and grandmother, and grandfather, and aunt, and uncle, and dog, and hamster, and goldfish, and cute little bird can all starve for all I care. You should get down on your knees and kiss my feet for giving you a job.

Bridge watched it all go by and was deeply saddened. Every store had in its guts a person or persons who only wanted to see the clock hit five so they could go home. Go home and worry about bills and clothes and children. Go home and have a few minutes or seconds of, 'It's all right, it's not good, but it's all right.' And then go to bed and get up in the morning and start it all over again. Isn't life grand?

Vivian turned onto Highway 152 and headed north into the mountains. The side of the mountain was dotted with big expensive homes. To Bridge, the homes that were nestled into the pinion and juniper trees were trying to hide - hide their pretentiousness, hide their vulgarity. When Bridge had moved to town there were no homes on the side of the mountain. It had been ranch land. Now there was California, Wisconsin, Minnesota, Oregon, Washington, New York, New Jersey and Florida dotting the mountainside like little cities. Normally only two people lived in any of the large houses, which was probably nice, as they only had to see each other once a week.

Woodsmoke was seven miles up the mountain on the edge of where the pinion and juniper trees thinned out and the pines took over. It was an old mining town that's claim to fame had been gunfights, whorehouses, white men killing Indians, Indians killing white men, and white men killing white men. There was never really enough gold to get killed over, but even a little gold is a good enough excuse. Now mostly doctors owned homes in Woodsmoke. Land that couldn't grow a weed and was nothing but rock was $35,000 an acre. There was also a hotel hidden by trees that rented out cabins. But the rent was so high only Arabs could afford to stay there.

Woodsmoke was now famous for its bar, that also had a bar menu, and a connecting upscale restaurant. The building was an adobe building that had been built in the 1860's. The inside was darker than most people's hearts. The bar did not have a name - it was just called The Hole. From the outside it looked like a small version of a dilapidated Alamo, minus Davy Crocket wondering how he had gotten himself into such a mess and knowing truthfully that Texas was really a shitty place to die. At The Hole the freaks living in the mountains rubbed shoulders with tourists and those who could afford the twenty-five dollar steaks. The freaks could because of the pot they grew on government land. In the winter, both the bar and restaurant had large fireplaces that gave the place an old time homey feeling complete with wood smoke drifting through the rooms, as the fireplaces had not been cleaned in years and did not draw properly - thus the name of the town. The walls were decorated with photographs of old miners, most of which had died poor, and paintings of bar room nudes - nudes that looked down at the people and tried to tell them being a whore was not all it was made up to be and if they had it to do over again they would charge three times as much and save at least half of it so they could move to California and open up a bed and breakfast. At the end of the bar, sitting on a stool, was a life-sized fully dressed mannequin of a drunken Indian holding a beer can. His head rested on the bar. He had not moved in over sixty years, content to let life go by and do whatever it was going to do. Tourists had their photographs taken with the Indian, and to their surprise he didn't even charge them a dime. An Indian organization from out of state had protested to the management several years earlier that the mannequin was detrimental to the Indian people. The owner of the bar, a cowboy, had said to the leader, "If you want, I'll paint half of his face white and we can call him a half breed and then both the whites and you Indians can try and sue me."

After three weeks in a smoke lodge pondering the problem, and out of peyote, the leaders of the organization decided it wasn't worth the hassle and went to the bar, had a few drinks, toasted their drunk buddy and left. The last anyone heard, the organization had moved to Arizona and was trying to unionize the Navajo ladies who wove rugs and trying to get slot machines into religious ceremonies.

On one wall of The Hole was a huge buffalo head. But unlike the buffalo at the This Isn't Heaven Bar his eyes did not blink on and off, on and off. They just stared vacantly at the painted nudes and photographs of miners as though he was wondering how he was dumb enough to get shot and have to spend eternity on a bar wall.

Bridge liked the bar, it was a drinking bar - dark and gloomy with an occasional fight, it really didn't put on any pretensions. It was a carnivore bar, a deer hunter's bar, a loud raucous bar. People bitched about the service being slow, but the drinks were never watered down and the beer was cold. Bartenders came and went like horse stall flies. Most of them were from out of state out to see the west and left when they found out the west was normally not much different from where they had come from and it was more likely to be poor in the west when everything was expensive and the wages so low. The two ladies who were waitresses at the bar had been there for years. They had heard every come-on known to man, and rushed around with worried and drawn looks on their faces that let everyone know they really didn't want to be there but there was no place else to go unless they wanted to work at Walmart, which was notorious for having lousy tips. Friday and Saturday nights, a band played in the bar. Since the bar itself took up over half of the inside, and the rest were tables, there really was no dance floor, but people still danced around the tables and if it was too crowded they went outside and danced in the street. Next to the bar was a new building that had been built to look like a mid 1850s opera house complete with private sitting balconies above the main floor. In the winter folk singers sang at the opera house. The folk venue had not changed since Bridge was a hippie. He figured all folk singers should only be allowed to eat at missions and play in ghettos for free. If they did play in ghettos, the residents would look at them like they were stupid and say, "What is that shit you are playing, man? We want to hear something you can dance to. Honkey motherfuckers, what the fuck do they know about being poor?"

Vivian parked in front of The Hole and got out. Bridge did not slide across the seat to get out, but extricated himself through the window like a slightly overweight contortionist who knew his life with the carnival was over and he was going to have to get a job selling overpriced wheelchairs to only people with Medicaid.

Bridge took Vivian's hand as they entered the bar and squeezed it slightly - he normally would not hold hands. Vivian gave him a quizzical look and smiled. It was still early and the only people in the bar were two men dressed in camouflage expounding on the best way to skin a deer. Bridge didn't know either of the men, so he gave them his 'I'm a tough guy' nod. They nodded back with a look on their faces like they wished Bridge had four legs, brown hair, a long nose, antlers growing out of his head, and they could make jerky out of him. There was a new bartender behind the bar who looked like he had just ridden a raindrop in from Seattle - his skin was the color of ivory soap and Bridge wondered if his feet were webbed. Bridge and Vivian headed for a table for two in the near corner that would face the band and was by a window. From the window, the view encompassed several rolling mountains that always reminded Bridge of sleeping bears although he had never seen a sleeping bear. Bridge held out a chair for Vivian to sit. Vivian gave him a very confused look as she sat - almost an 'I let you sleep with me so why are you being nice? It must be you want to do something kinky. Is it something you saw in a dirty magazine you sly devil you' look.

"It's nice for you and me to be able to be alone once in awhile," Bridge said.

"We are alone when we make love," Vivian said.

"That's different," Bridge said.

Vivian smiled as Terry, one of the waitresses, walked up to the table. Terry was in her mid-forties, tall and slim, tiredly attractive, with hair that was bleached somewhere between peach and dirty white. At last count, she was on her 68th boyfriend, all of whom she had met at The Hole and had promised to take her to Phoenix and change her life. She had five kids and had stopped trying to figure out who the father of each one was.

"Is sleeping with your boyfriend the same as going out alone to eat dinner?" Bridge asked Terry.

Terry, who was not one of the brightest birds in the world, chewed on her pencil like she was taking an exam to get her G.E.D. and answered. "My new boyfriend is into having people watch when we do it, so no, it is not the same," she smiled.

"Interesting," Bridge said, giving Vivian a 'see I am not always so stupid' look, which is a hard look to give to a woman more than once in a man's life.

"I'd like a shot of the cheapest tequila you have," Vivian said, "and forget the lime and salt."

"Would you like a water chaser," Terry asked.

"Do I look like a fish?" Vivian said with a smile.

"No," Terry said seriously. "You look like a Cancer to me. Your face is oval and I can tell from your vibes the moon is always dancing around in your head."

Bridge ordered quickly. "I'll take a Corona with lime and a glass." He did not want to get Vivian started on a 'what is your sign' kick? Sometimes she could go on for hours. My moon has been in Saturn while my feet have been in hot bath water and my mind is somewhere on Pluto, even though it is not a planet now, and my nose and teeth have been in Haley's comet and that is why I'm going to go to the organic food store and buy a lot of fresh vegetables and let them rot in the crisper because I won't have the energy to even peel the stuff.

"What, no Tecate?" Vivian said, looking confused that Bridge was going to drink a Corona, but at least she was distracted from the intricacies of outer space.

"Life is all change, one must jump at times into the unexpected to test his or her true grit," Bridge said. "And what better way to jump into the unknown than to try a new beer?"

Vivian shook her head but was smiling.

Bridge looked deeply into her blue childlike eyes. They pierced the bar dimness with a thin ray of golden light. A light that was simple and pure. The ray went into Bridge's eyes. It spun through his brain and flowed slowly through his veins and made his fingertips and toes tingle. It spun a web of warmth around his heart. Bridge sighed silently. Words, a single letter at a time, tried to escape from his throat. "I, I, I, I, I, I," he stammered, "Lo, Lo, Lo," but the rest of the words started to choke him like he had tried to swallow a whole meatball without chewing. He grabbed his throat and tried with all his might to go on, but all he could stammer was "I, I, I, I, I."

His face turned red and perspiration formed on his forehead.

"I what?" Vivian asked, looking confused but concerned. "Are you ok? Do you have gas?"

Bridge started to turn darker red, and Vivian jumped up and started pounding on his back. The thumps were so hard they sounded like tom-tom signals warning all the tribes the caca had hit the fan and hoping they understood that leather shields with totems painted on them do not stop bullets.

Bridge coughed and spat out, "you," and stood so Vivian couldn't beat on him anymore.

The word love went back down Bridge's throat, back to his heart - unheard, but safe.

"What's wrong with you, Bridge?" Vivian asked, sitting back down. "You look like you just swallowed a bug."

"I think at times a bug has swallowed me," Bridge said, also sitting back down and wiping his face with a napkin.

"That is a different concept, you should put it in one of your books instead of all that vanishing land and contemporary western hogwash you love to write about. One day you are going to have to understand people don't give a rat's ass about the land unless they can buy and sell it."

"No. I understand completely," Bridge said, but wondering how he choking and feeling like a bug had swallowed him suddenly turned into a discussion of his writing style.

Terry set the Corona and shot of tequila down on the table. "You two going to eat," she asked, "or is Vivian just going to beat on you all night?"

"I think he inhaled a bug," Vivian said.

"Any reason is a good reason to beat on a man," Terry smiled.

"I would like a small Buffalo burger with green chili and fries," Vivian said.

"Me too," Bridge said, "and one more beer and another shot."

The burgers at The Hole were about the size of pie plates and when cash was short, which was most of the time for most people in Lost City, a Buffalo burger could be stretched into three meals. The fries had to be eaten right away, because if they were taken home, the grease on them would set up and they were almost impossible to cut even with a serrated knife. An ingenious old hippie who lived in a teepee outside of Woodsmoke put wicks in the end of the fries and used them for candles.

Vivian picked up the shot. Bridge poured his beer in the glass and squeezed the lime into it and dropped the lime in the glass. It was a habit of his. When he hit twelve limes in the bottom of the glass he usually figured he had had enough. The fact he could no longer talk and had been to the bathroom eight times really didn't factor into the equation.

Vivian and Bridge clinked their glasses together. "To life and liberty and trust and all those other fantasies," Vivian toasted and inhaled the shot like it was only an illusion.

Bridge took two swallows of beer.

Pill, last name unknown, came into the bar but completely out of character he was not wearing his sign. He spotted Vivian and Bridge, ambled over to the table and stood looking at the two like a lost puppy dog looking for a home. People in Lost City never asked if their company was wanted, it was almost a secret code of honor to butt in. Bridge and Vivian liked Pill, so Bridge didn't tell him to get his rude ass out of here and go find his own friggin' table. "Get a chair and join us," he said instead.

Pill slid a chair over from the next table and sat. He was from Texas, 44 years old, over six feet tall and no more than twenty inches around at the widest spot. His brown straight hair hit him at his belt. He had brown eyes that constantly darted from side to side like an old gunfighter who knew one day he was going to get shot. He talked slowly, like a good Texan should, said y'all and ma'am and howdy and seemed to know everybody in town. He had three changes of clothes, which consisted of three pairs of Levi's, three brown shirts, three pairs of white socks, and one pair of hiking tennis shoes and a frayed army coat he wore in the winter. Pill spent most of his time camping in the mountains. If he wasn't in the mountains, he camped out at Vivian's coffee shop, she would not let him pitch his tent next to the espresso bar. He had a fifteen-year-old Toyota truck crammed with all his belongings - besides camping gear, most of his belongings were boxes of every prescription drug known to man and several cases of peanut butter and unsalted crackers. The drugs came from a friend in Texas. Pill would not sell them, but if a person had the shits, headaches, nose bleeds, falling-out hair, hemorrhoids, restless leg syndrome, couldn't get it up, saggy tits, wrinkles, short fingers, big toes, depression, anxiety, backaches, the urge to kill five thousand people, a cough, a pimple, no appetite, too much appetite, gas, indigestion, heartburn, cancer, or a broken heart, Pill would give them something for it. One day, in a roundabout way, Bridge asked Pill if he had anything for people who had fallen in love. Pill gave Bridge an exasperated look and said, "There is nothing known to man that cures that malady."

All Pill mostly ate was peanut butter and crackers. He had eaten so much peanut butter his skin was a roasted brown. He was also highly educated, articulate, and read constantly. He had started living in the woods in 1969 after taking five hits of Sunshine Acid in Austin, which turned out to be a very bad trip. He had witnessed his brain dripping out of his skull through his left ear while a deep booming voice told him to go build an ark in New Mexico with only an axe and to start wearing a sign stating the end of the world was only six billion years away. Somewhere in the hills was Pill's ark. He would never tell anyone where it was, or even how far he had gotten to its completion, but it did make him very nervous mankind had only six billion years to live. When he came to town, he wore a billboard like he was advertising for a car lot, only the billboard stated in bold letters - **THERE IS ONLY SIX BILLION YEARS LEFT FOR THE WORLD.** The sign should have stated - **THERE ARE ONLY SIX BILLION YEARS LEFT UNTIL THE END OF THE WORLD** - but no one had the heart to tell Pill.

Pill could only be around people for short periods of time. He would be talking, suddenly look lost, and then run to the mountains. He might not be seen for a month or two but then one day would show up again. People wondered how he made enough money to buy gas for his truck and the truckloads of peanut butter until it was discovered he was drawing disability from an acid overdose, which now no one could do - there were so many burnouts the agency was running short of money and had to give it to more needy people - like stressed out bankers and CEO's who had to go to jail for six months after stealing Florida. All the old burnt out acid-heads living at the mission, after hearing the news, fell into a deep depression for six weeks. All the burnt out people who called themselves artists, but didn't know the difference between red and blue, were telling each other six billion years was not really that far away.

Vivian leaned across the table and hugged Pill. Pill smiled and then shook hands with Bridge. People in Texas shake hands like men should, a firm grip, not so firm to break a few fingers, but still firm. Most people in Lost City shook hands like their hands were made out of Jell-O. Lost City was also filled with the huggiest people Bridge had ever known. Men hugged men, women hugged women, women hugged men, everybody hugged dogs. Bridge did not enjoy being hugged by men, or for that matter, not many women. The only thing he figured a man should hug was his wife or girlfriend or the commode.

Terry came to the table with the beer and another shot. "You want the usual, Pill?" she asked.

Pill nodded his head. The usual was an order of fries and a glass of orange juice. Unless someone else was buying, then it was a steak sandwich, salad with blue cheese dressing, and a double shot of the best bourbon in the house. Old hippies have a way of knowing the angles.

"Pill," Vivian said, sounding like a marriage counselor, "you should go get you one of those young hippie chicks and take her to the mountains with you. I think you need to get laid."

Pill shook his head no so hard it looked like his neck was a spring and said, "Are you kidding me. I lived down all that hippie stuff years ago and I really am too old to get crabs. Besides, incense gives me a headache and anyone who believes in the third eye, astral projection, previous lives, or reincarnation can go live in India and snort curry for all I care. Peace and love and wow man are for young people and politicians who never get elected."

"That's a good statement. I like that," Bridge said.

"I'm only trying to help you," Vivian said to Pill, giving Bridge a dirty look. Bridge wondered why women always wanted to help men. He figured it was really because they couldn't help themselves, but he had never been brave enough to tell any woman that. He might have been stupid during many phases of his life, but he was not that stupid. He did know that the only thing men really wanted to help women with was to take their clothes off. He had always considered himself a male chauvinist pig - a fact he was not really proud over, but what the heck, you have to go with what you are. At one time in his life he wanted to start an international club called Chauvinist Pig's Unlimited. The Unlimited he did not really understand, but it sounded important, and mankind was obsessed with important titles - king, queen - the royal term, not one for a gay person - CEO, president, doctor, Department of Sanitation Executive Director, principal, on and on and on. The charter for Chauvinist Pig's Unlimited would state a woman had to be able to cook, clean, make love at any time, knit, darn socks, not bitch, never go through menopause, and have a job that paid at least $65,000 a year so her husband could afford to play golf, go fishing, or, if he was an artist, not have to work. But when Bridge started doing preliminary research, he discovered that no matter a man's beliefs, most men were so afraid of women they didn't have the nerve to join his club. They mostly went to the bar with their buddies and talked about how their wife was the best thing that had ever happened to them since their mother, although nine-tenths of men don't like their mothers - it is a genetic trait they pick up from their fathers.

Terry brought the food to the table and Bridge noticed the bar was beginning to fill and was getting noisier. Friday night in da da land he called it. Tonight all the problems of the world would be solved. If I was king there would be no war, no famine, no disease, no bellybutton lint, no big corporations that own the entire world, everybody would be rich, there would be no discrimination, not even against stinging insects - poor biting pests are just doing their own thing anyway and you want to swat them. No religion. No cars. No planes, nothing with an engine, mankind can walk, no boats, no cats, no dogs, and no chipmunks - peanut eating pee brains anyway. No inner city, everybody would live in an outer city. After all the problems of the world had been solved, everyone would get down to the serious business of picking someone up and getting laid. I am so glad I met you, you might be the love of my life, but first may I ask you a few questions? Do you have AIDS, sweet thing? Do you have hepatitis C, darling? Do you have herpes, love child? Have you had unprotected sex within the last ten minutes? Are you a chronic liar, gorgeous one? If the answer to any of these questions was yes, good luck. If they were all no, then let's go get it on, and in the morning we can both hope we never see each other again.

Bridge ate one of his fries and wondered why his mind was so screwed up. He glanced at Vivian, who had already eaten half of her hamburger and most of her fries. She was not into dainty eating. She inhaled her food - more than two chomps on a bite was one too many. If a person glanced away from Vivian for more than a few seconds when she was eating and then glanced back, the plate would be empty. It was a disappearing act even Houdini could not have copied. She even ate the cute little garnishes that cooks put on plates thinking they are making a piece of art. The things that taste like dirt and are only good for snails.

Bridge ate another fry and took a bite of his hamburger. Vivian was done and took her plate and set it on the bar. She hated dirty dishes in front of her. In fact, she hated dishes and didn't own any at her house. She ate off of paper plates and used plastic silverware and tossed them in the garbage when she was done. Bridge was going to tell her once that she was being very wasteful, and paper products and plastic were bad for the environment, but when he thought about it, everything was bad for the environment - especially people.

Vivian came back with another shot of tequila and winked at Bridge, who winked back. Vivian had many winks. There was a wink when she wanted Bridge to look at something she was looking at. There was a wink when she was just winking and did not know why she was winking but just felt like it. There was the wink of an inside joke that only she and Bridge knew. There was the wink of 'let's get out of here before I get pissed and kick the snot out of that lousy so and so.' The wink Bridge liked best was after Vivian had six shots of tequila and meant 'take me home, you over the hill stud you. I am going to get naked and smother you with my 185 pounds in the best love making you have had since the last time you slept with me.' But Bridge had to get her to her house quick when he got that wink. If he was not fast enough, Vivian would have a few more shots and all he got that night was a good earful of snores or a, "Not now Bridge, wake me up in the morning," which in the morning, Vivian, feeling like 185 pounds of rotten fish, would get up, throw up all that cheap tequila, which is not a good prelude to mad passionate love making, and Bridge would go home wondering why during most of his life his timing had always been bad. Stoops told him once it must be his karma.

Bridge told Stoops to stick his karma up his nose. If there was such a thing as Karma Stoops wouldn't have had to do a total of twelve years in the joint and Jesus would not have been crucified.

Bridge finished his hamburger and Vivian took his plate to the bar and brought him another beer. Pill had only eaten about six of his fries. He would pick one up and take tiny bites off it - chewing each bite slowly. But anybody who ate as much peanut butter as Pill did, when they got a real meal, probably enjoyed savoring every last bite.

Pill reminded Bridge of a condemned man who was going to make his last meal last for twenty-two years.

More people came into the bar, most of which Bridge knew but really didn't want to talk to. He really didn't want Pill sitting at the table. All he really wanted to do was tell Vivian he loved her. Bridge knew for a fact he was not a reincarnated Romeo.

A man nick-named "Professor" entered the bar, looked around, saw Bridge and ambled over to the table. So much for a quiet night with Vivian, Bridge thought but said, "Want to join us, Professor?"

The Professor found a chair and sat opposite of Pill, after first, of course, getting a hug from Vivian. Bridge did not stand up. He and the Professor shook hands. The Professor, being from Oklahoma, was like Pill and knew how to shake hands, although at times Bridge did not know if he trusted the Professor, as the Professor at one time had been an attorney, but he had given up the profession after making a zillion dollars defending dope dealers. He was now on his fifth college degree. Pill was so engrossed with eating a fry he didn't look up. By the look on his face it was almost an orgasmic experience. The Professor was in his late forties, and had short brown hair just showing the beginnings of white. His hair was always nicely cut - some things an attorney can never give up. He had kind blue eyes, another good trait for an attorney - especially when they say, "I know we won the case, but the fact you are not going to get any money is because I, your God-given attorney, have charged you enough that even after the settlement you still owe me more money," give them the blue kind eyes look and blame it on the law.

The Professor was around 5'9", close to two hundred pounds and built like Santa Clause. His shape had something to do with his love of barbecue and total disdain for salad or vegetables.

No one ever asked the Professor what his five degrees were in because they knew the only reason he was really going to school was to date young women. He used to bring young women to parties, but everybody told him he had to stop because a girl constantly giggling and talking about how tough freshman algebra is was more than anyone could take. He then tried to date women his age, but they all called him a pervert. If he had been into eighteen-and-nineteen-year-old boys they would have called him a gay artist and everything would have been perfectly ok.

"How's the new book progressing?" the Professor asked Bridge.

Bridge and the Professor usually talked about old books and writing and traded books back and forth. They mostly read obscure writers who had written about the west. They weren't into anything mystic or supernatural. Living in the west can get rid of a lot of the mystic and supernatural - that is, unless you are an Indian or a hippie.

"I should finish it within the next three hundred years, which by then I might be famous," Bridge replied.

"I'm thinking about starting a book," the Professor said, which he had been saying for the past eight years.

Bridge did not make a response to the statement. Everyone he knew was going to write a book and the book was going to be the best book that had ever been written. It was going to be the best book ever written because it was about their lives. Bridge did not tell people the only reason their life was important was because it was their life, but to most people it would be a very boring book - except, of course, for a few relatives. But the relatives would only want free copies and wouldn't read more than ten pages before falling asleep for fifteen years.

"What will it be about?" Vivian chirped in. She had a way of extending conversations that Bridge wanted to get out of. It's a couple dilemma thing.

"I think I'll write about the art world in Lost City. It is a place that the world should know about," the Professor said, sounding profound and literary, which for a professor is easy to do - for a writer it's tough as hell.

"Everyone would think you are crazy and should be locked up," Vivian said.

"It's just an idea," the Professor replied.

"Well, get a real one," Vivian said in her pragmatic way. "And for God's sake, if you do start writing, don't write the drivel Bridge writes about and put some good, down to earth, grunting grinding sex in it. Not 'he looked into the pools of her eyes and could imagine every shadow that lived in the curves of her voluptuous body' bullshit. Lord, write a book for real women, women like to screw just to screw just like you dumb men. If a man ever told a woman the lines that are in most of the romances today, all they would get for their effort would be laughter."

"Have another tequila and tell me what you really think," the Professor smiled.

"That's a good idea," Vivian said, got up and went to the bar, returning with another shot.

Pill finished his last fry, looked at Bridge, looked at Vivian, looked at the Professor, shook his head like he didn't know where he was, then got up and almost ran out of the bar. "I guess we are buying," Bridge said.

"He can only take people for so long," Vivian said in a kindly manner.

Pill did not stop running until he got to his truck. He started the truck with trembling hands and drove toward the mountains while his mind repeated with machine gun speed over and over again, "there is only six billion years left for the world, there is only six billion years left for the world."

The band came into the bar lugging amps and mikes and their guitars. "Oh good, the music is about to start," Vivian said happily. Old hippie chicks never get over music.

The Professor saw a lady who had just moved to town and didn't know anything about his perverted side. Not even saying goodbye - a lawyer trait - he headed for her faster than a Mac truck driver who had eaten twenty bennies and could only holler, "Whoopee, you car driving runts, I'll smash you like a bug if you get in my way."

Bridge took a swallow of beer and wished he had a set of earplugs. Vivian looked at him. Her face was glowing tequila, her lips were smiling, and her childlike eyes bore into his green faraway eyes. She reached across the table for Bridge to take her hand and Bridge held it - her hand that weighed three tons from all the silver rings. He put her hand to his lips and kissed it gently and smiled. Words letter by letter formed in his heart and made their way to his throat. "I, I, I, I, I, Lo, Lo," he whispered without choking.

"What?" Vivian asked with her gleaming childlike eyes, leaning closer to him.

"I, I, I, I, I, Lo, Lo, Lo," he whispered lower yet, still without choking.

"What?" Vivian asked again, softly, expectantly, matching his whisper.

"I, I, I, I, I have to go to the bathroom," Bridge said as a meatball stuck in his throat.

As he got up, he could see a momentary shadow of sadness creep into Vivian's face and he felt sad, but then she smiled at him and winked and he winked back. "Bridge, you're such a heartless jerk," he said to himself.

Chapter Eight

The band was called Jackson and The Open Doors. Why Jackson had named his band The Open Doors, no one really knew. Why do some people get tattoos all over their face? Why do some people eat bean sprouts? Why do some people think that by driving a biofuel car they are really helping the environment? It takes more energy to produce the biofuel than if they were driving a gas car. Why do some people have twenty kids? Why do countries have wars over religion? Why do some women not shave under the arms? Why are the majority of men stupid? Why does everything in life only go in a circle? Why? Why? Why?

For whatever reason under the sun the band was called Jackson and The Open Doors. Jackson had been blessed with a voice like an old time minstrel, but he did not have to wear pointed shoes, ridiculous pants, cut his hair in a pageboy, play a mandolin one string at a time or worry about getting his head cut off if the king did not like his music. Jackson played an assortment of his own songs - all mellow and tender. Half of the women in town were in love with him. They could picture Jackson singing a lullaby to them as he nibbled on their elbows. Barbara, Jackson's wife, and a writer for the local newspaper, ignored all the women swooning over him. She had been married to him for sixteen years, and any spouse of any type of artist, after hearing a song ten million times, or a poem sixteen thousand times, or proofreading a five thousand page novel six times, somehow gets tired of it all. Barbara had figured out that being married to an artist was in all reality just being married. She would normally listen to one set when Jackson was playing, then go home and enjoy her solitude. She had never told Jackson she really didn't like guitar music and really wished he played the piano.

Jackson and his two band members, Roach and Clip, said hello to everybody and, since they weren't as famous as Dylan or the Rolling Stones, they had to set up their own equipment. For some reason, Jackson, Roach and Clip looked like brothers. They all had long wavy brown hair. They all had long brown beards and moustaches. They all wore Levi's, collared short-sleeved shirts, and sandals. It might have been from practicing so much together. They say a man and woman after living together for a long time start to look like each other. Maybe it is the same rule for bands. To Bridge, the band looked like a younger version of the three guys that had made several billion dollars selling cough drops.

Vivian watched The Open Doors setting up. She had a look in her eyes like anyone who could play music was two notches higher on the totem pole than most people. To her writers were in the middle of the pole, which didn't bother Bridge, as he figured most old hippies had lost the ability to read somewhere in the early 1970s, and if they could read, there was no way they would remember any of it anyway.

When all the equipment was set up the band members went through the ritual of tuning up their instruments. Roach did not have much to do since he played the bongos, and Clip didn't really have to work much harder, as he played the bass guitar. Jackson strummed out a few licks, tweaked the strings a little, and then all three of them headed to Vivian's table. Bridge was still standing in line with thirty other guys to go to the bathroom. The Hole had only one commode in the men's room for a seating capacity of two hundred - most of the locals went outside and pissed on the side of the building, but Bridge was too self conscious, and besides, in the dark he might hit his feet.

When it was his turn in the bathroom, it took Bridge longer than most people, as he had to two-step forward and one backward several times, each time taking shorter steps so he could get close enough to the urinal.

Jackson, Roach and Clip drank copious amounts of coffee at Vivian's - having been musicians for many years they used to snort coke, but now that they were all in their mid to late fifties coffee did the trick. They had figured out they liked their teeth, plus two bucks a cup beat one hundred bucks a gram. Also, no matter how much coffee you drank, you wouldn't go to jail. For Roach and Clip, both of whom were single, the closing time line had changed from "Hey baby, want to come over to my place and snort a line?" into "Would you like to come over to my place and have an espresso? I even have decaf."

God bless the wisdom of age.

Jackson, Roach and Clip sat, but not before they all got a hug from Vivian. "Where'd Bridge go?" Jackson asked.

By now the bar was packed and the noise level from everybody talking all at the same time and not listening to anybody else was about the same pitch as the right engine on a Boeing 707.

"He is getting at the age where it takes him a long time to pee," Vivian said.

Neither Jackson, Roach or Clip smiled - they were also getting to that age. The next age would be the drip age no matter how many times you shook it.

"Bridge seems to have something bothering him," Roach said to Vivian.

"I've noticed it too," Clip said. "He seems remote and distant."

Jackson nodded his head - being the lead singer he was the sage and really didn't have to talk much.

"There is always something bothering Bridge," Vivian said, "he's a writer; everything to him is always dark and mysterious and screwed up."

"Never thought of that," Roach said.

Roach, being the bongo player, did not really question life. Life was just one bong on a bongo to the next - bong bong bong, bong bong bong, bong bong bong - bonging through life was a good thing, which is one reason Roach always had a smile on his face - more people should try bonging.

"I think Bridge is sensitive," Clip said. "He tries not to show it, but I think he cares too much and at times his caring puts a heavy weight on his shoulders."

"How can you care too less?" Jackson asked.

"I don't think you can care too less," Vivian said. "But a lot of times I couldn't care less. Some people aren't worth caring for at all, at which time I don't care at all, which is really zero caring and not caring too less."

Jackson wished he had kept his mouth shut. Clip wondered what was in the tequila Vivian was drinking. And the whole idea of caring less, too less caring, little caring, and zero caring completely flew over Roach's head - bong bong bong, bong bong, bong.

Bridge two-stepped forward and one step backward through the crowd. "If I played country, you could dance," Jackson said as Bridge stepped up to the table.

"If you played country you'd be living in Abilene and have a raw steak hanging from a cord around your neck and you'd be saying howdy and y'all," Bridge said.

No one at the table offered to give Bridge their chair.

"Have you heard the new CD by Donovan?" Vivian asked Jackson.

"It's great," Jackson replied, looking animated.

"I thought Donovan had turned into a banana and was living in a tree in Jamaica," Bridge said.

Jackson, Roach, Clip and Vivian all gave Bridge a dirty look. Musicians don't like to hear negative comments about other musicians, even if they are intended to be funny, that is unless the other musician has stolen one of their songs or slept with their wife.

Just then, Stoops walked into the bar. Vivian and the band were discussing the major reasons why the Pope should decree Jimi Hendrix a saint, and since Bridge was not a musician or a music lover, they were ignoring him. Bridge saw Stoops and two-stepped forward and one backward toward him, wondering as he did if there was a saint for heroin, and if there was, he or she couldn't be that much of a saint, because they would be nodding all the time and drooling all over their nice white outfits.

"What's been going on?" Stoops asked Bridge.

"Since I saw you, I have taken a sponge bath, changed my socks, drank three beers and eaten a hamburger," Bridge replied. "The excitement has been so intense I might have to go on heart medication."

"I have contemplated your problem, and I think you should tell Vivian you love her," Stoops said.

"I've tried twice. But every time I start to it feels like I am choking on a meatball and I can't get the words out," Bridge frowned.

"It's because you are afraid you will get hurt again," Stoops said.

"Well duh," Bridge commented.

More people entered The Hole. It was so crowded now there were no seats left at the bar, or at the tables, and to move down the aisle was like trying to catch the subway in New York. Although there was one major difference - a person did not have to worry about getting mugged at The Hole. "I wish you would fall in love," Bridge said to Stoops.

"It's hard for a man with no teeth to find a woman who thinks he is attractive," Stoops said pragmatically but also sadly.

"You could move to the swamps in Louisiana," Bridge advised. "Louisiana is famous for bad teeth."

"No, they'd just call me a Yankee and hang me," Stoops replied.

Bridge took three gulps of his beer - parts of sentences from hundreds of conversations banged off the walls and ceiling. The words buzzed in Bridge's ears like angry bees that could not find their hive, "taxes, nice boobs, nice butt, war, maybe I should have a screwdriver, I'd love to take that one home, she's married, who cares, I am going to Rome for my vacation, I need new tires, my boss is a dirt bag, when is the friggin' band going to start playing, someone keyed my car, do you have a joint, I have to go to the bathroom, she is such a bitch, I don't like beer, I don't like wine, pot should be legal, I used to nail her in high school and now she is married to a banker and won't even look at me, stuck up, rich bastard, damn cops, republicans, democrats." The words buzzed louder - fragments, incomplete sentences that would go on forever. They bombarded Bridge - loud buzzing words trampling all over each other - hoping to be grasped by another human being and not washed out by the other words - not left incomplete - not destined to only be loud. Bridge could visualize the words traveling through space like radio waves and on some distant planet people with sixteen legs, twenty-four arms and five brains, with a life span of over thirty billion years, and the ability to travel the entire length of space in a few seconds sat listening and saying to themselves, "I know mankind is stupid, but this really takes the cake. Thank Plutonium they only have six billion years left. What a nightmare they must go through."

"Hey Bridge, what's wrong with you?" Bridge heard but did not respond.

Stoops grabbed Bridge's arm and shook him several times.

Bridge shook his head and blinked, looked at Stoops in a faraway fashion and mumbled, "Those people with sixteen legs and twenty-four arms are a lot smarter than we are."

"This love thing really has you screwed up," Stoops said and made his way through the crowd looking for a woman with no teeth.

The band started to play, and Bridge headed for his table. Hopefully Vivian was saving a seat for him - out of sight out of mind is a very truthful statement in this modern world.

Two gay men Bridge did not know were sitting at the table with Vivian. Bridge could tell the men were gay because one of them had purple eyeliner on and they were holding hands. Bridge hoped they were shaking hands gays and not huggy huggy type guys. He sat. "This is John and Joan," Vivian introduced Bridge to the two men, two women, man woman, woman man, or whatever they were. Thankfully to Bridge they did not extend their hands to shake or get up to hug. At times life can be good, Bridge thought. "They are from San Francisco," Vivian said. "They are thinking about moving here and opening a cafe selling organic vegetarian egg rolls and soy-based drinks."

"Interesting," Bridge said, wondering if they might do so good they would put all the steakhouses in town out of business and the Mexican restaurants would have to take the hamburger and chicken out of their tacos.

As soon as Vivian was done with her introduction, she, like all the other women in the bar, put all her attention on Jackson and The Open Doors. Jackson was singing some sappy love song about caring and devotion and you are the only light in my eyes. He should be playing at the senior prom for a high school, Bridge thought - all chiffon, high heels, and rented tuxedos and brains the size of dried peas. Jesus, what a depressing thought, Bridge thought on and tried to drive the image out of his head but couldn't. It stuck on the inside of his skull like it was glued with super glue. He remembered his high school graduation. He was so in love with Kay he tried to tie the laces of his slip-on shoes. Tonight was going to be the night. After the prom they were going to rent a room and do it, as it was called then. Of course, those were the days when most girls made it through high school without doing it - their breasts were almost flat from heavy petting, but it still was not doing it. Now at sixteen, they have not done it, they have been fucking for two years, the hell with the heavy petting, get to the point - none of this waiting for true love and I am saving myself, I want to be pregnant by the time I am eighteen. Don't you know the world is going to end in six billion years?

That night at the prom Bridge did dance, although he felt like every eye in the world was looking at him and every mouth in the world was laughing at him. After the dance, Kay and he went to a party and then rented a room. But they found out that four quarts of cheap beer, four shots of vodka, four shots of gin, and one shot of rum does not a romantic evening make. All Kay said in the morning was, "If we did it last night, it is really not such a big deal."

In between having the dry heaves, Bridge had to agree.

Jackson ended his song. The women of both genders clapped. The men looked at each other like don't you dare clap and ruin my reputation. Vivian smiled at Joan, who smiled back. Bridge looked at John with his 'what the hell do these women think' look, which John returned - immediately forming a bond between the two. Vivian sighed, "He has such a beautiful voice."

"Yes he does," Bridge agreed truthfully, although he would have used the word nice instead of beautiful.

Jackson started playing a more upbeat song. Three cowboys came into the bar, all cowboy hats, boots, Levi's and silver belt buckles the size of hubcaps. The gay men swooned.

Vivian leaned over and planted a big kiss on Bridge's nose. "How many shots have you had?" Bridge asked.

"Five, I think," Vivian winked and gave him a sly look.

"I'll buy you one more." Bridge grinned his sexy grin.

"You're such a romantic," Vivian smiled.

Terry brought John a beer and Joan some red drink with three cherries in it that looked like something a grandmother in Georgia would drink while sitting on the porch when it was one hundred and five degrees and the humidity was 98%, which is a good reason for Georgia to stay in the south and not move west and bring its maladies with it.

Bridge ordered another beer and Vivian a shot. Terry winked at Bridge knowingly. Lost City being a small town, there are really no secrets. The only way a secret could stay a secret was if a person told it only to himself or herself.

Vivian gulped the shot down and her face took on a whole new look. Oh, oh, Bridge thought. It was the dancing look. Women have a strange desire in life to make men dance. Not dance on the end of a string, which is normal and men are used to, but dance - dance like tango and waltz and two-step and fox trot - all those dirty degrading words.

Vivian looked at Bridge, knew he did not want to dance, looked at Joan, Vivian didn't want to dance with her, looked at John, who without saying yes or no got up and took Vivian's hand and they started dancing. Not so much together, because Vivian didn't dance with a partner, she danced with herself. She danced to dance. Vivian loved to dance. Her whole body would absorb the music and every ounce of her 185 pounds would move to the music. Bridge loved to watch her dance. She was graceful and beautiful. 185 pounds of pure music, she would swirl and turn and her dress would swing out away from her sending its bright colors like strobe lights around the room. People would stop talking and watch her dance. The band members would get caught in her web of joy over their music. Sometimes they would get so transfixed they would play the song three or four times. When Vivian danced, Bridge loved her the most. At times he even wished he could dance. Vivian would tell him, "Bridge, don't you understand that just because you can't dance a lick people don't give a hoot? You dance to dance. Stand on your head and wiggle your toes for all I give a damn, you are afraid to take a chance, get over it."

Bridge would only look at her and say nothing, thinking to himself, "Why won't I dance?"

The music ended. No one in the room had seen John dancing. They had only seen Vivian. Jackson said with admiration in his voice, "Thank you, Vivian, for dancing. The world needs more dancers."

Vivian sat, joy and contentment radiating from her perspiring face, while people applauded, not for the music but for Vivian's dancing.

Bridge leaned over and kissed her on the forehead. She smiled. Joan whispered to John, "Next time, you dance with me or you can go home alone."

Even the gay life is not heaven.

Vivian headed for the bar. Bridge knew a wild night of sex was headed out the window. He shrugged his shoulders, smiled, and muttered to himself, "Such is life. Dance on, pretty one, dance on.

Chapter Nine

Stoops, after not finding any women in the bar without teeth and drinking eight beers, staggered over to the table. Vivian was still at the bar. He stepped up close to Bridge, leaned over and whispered in Bridge's ear, "Did you tell her you love her?"

Bridge shook his head.

Stoops sat in Vivian's chair. "Somewhere in life is a woman who would think a man with no teeth is sexy," he said.

"Stoops, this is John and Joan," Bridge said. He hated it when people did not introduce other people.

John nodded at Stoops. Joan smiled and said to Stoops, "If you were gay, having no teeth would be an asset."

Stoops said, "I like your eyeliner."

Joan giggled. John gave Stoops a 'don't mess with my woman' look. Stoops wondered what a possessive gay man was called and came up with Male Chauvinist Piglet.

"Where is Vivian?" Stoops asked Bridge just as Jackson started playing another song.

Bridge looked around the bar and Vivian was not hard to spot. She was dancing on the bar with a shot of tequila in each hand. The people, instead of hooting and whistling at her, were all quiet - once again caught in the web of her dancing.

"I think Vivian loves you," Stoops said to Bridge.

Bridge ignored him.

"If she loved me, I would tell her I loved her," Stoops went on.

Bridge still ignored him.

The Professor walked back to the table. Stoops got up. "You can have my chair. The conversation around here is only one sided," he said to the Professor and disappeared into the crowd.

"Some people talk too much," John commented.

Bridge ignored John also.

The Professor sat.

"I guess your pursuit of the new woman in town has ended in failure," Bridge said.

"She told me she didn't like attorneys or anything to do with higher education. She said the law is only for the rich and higher education only makes people use big words which, in all truth, they really don't know the meaning of. But it is strange. I feel deeply attracted to her."

"What is she doing in New Mexico?" Bridge asked.

"She is on a quest to walk every rock wheel in the state and find her center. She said that rocks talk to her, and they have within them all knowledge known to man, and somewhere in New Mexico is the rock of all rocks, the heavy of rocks, the rock that will tell her all of life's secrets and set her free, making her one with the universe."

"What is real knowledge?" Bridge asked, watching Vivian dance.

"I think you have to die and ask God that question," the Professor replied. Terry came by and the Professor and Bridge ordered another beer.

The song ended and Vivian drank her other shot, was helped off of the bar and headed for the table. The Professor saw an empty chair and brought it over to the table. Vivian took several deep breaths and winked at Bridge, but it was an 'I have had eight tequilas' wink, which is a wink when the eyes are starting to cross, the pupils are doing somersaults, and the brain has become nothing more than a gray sponge with all common sense wrung out of it.

Vivian looked at the Professor. "I had a strange thought while I was dancing," she said, which came out more like, "IIIIII, haaaad, aaaa, straaaangge, thouuught, whiiillle, I III, waaas, dannnncing."

Tequila has a way of elongating words, normally two shots away from where it completely wipes out the ability to say words and communication becomes grunts and moans.

"Yes," the Professor said. "What is the thought?"

"I had the realization that of all the creatures on the face of the earth, ducks, and only ducks, don't fight. They squabble, but they don't fight," she slurred.

John, Joan, Bridge and the Professor all pondered the statement. Ducks don't fight. Ducks don't fight. Ducks don't fight.

"I'll be a son of a bitch," the Professor said after awhile.

"I'm so confused," Joan said, reaching for his purse and finding refuge by grabbing his eyeliner.

John didn't know what to say.

Bridge was trying to think if he had ever seen ducks fight. He had fed them in parks, he had seen them in zoos, he had seen them on TV, he had blasted them when he was a duck hunter, but it was true, he had never in his life seen a duck fight. They quacked, they swam, they squabbled, they flew in V shapes because they didn't know what a W was, they pooped everywhere, but they did not fight. "Jesus Christ, what a revelation," Bridge hollered and jumped up from the table like he had just won the lottery.

Insights in life always filled Bridge was tremendous amounts of zeal. "Ducks don't fight," he hollered again.

By now, no one in the bar was sober, so they didn't pay any attention to Bridge, which didn't bother him, as no one had ever really paid much attention to him anyway

He sat back down. His eyes were glowing with their new knowledge. His brain was swimming with a truth. He grabbed his beer like it was the last one in the world and gulped it down.

"You know, that would make a good master's thesis," the Professor said nonchalantly like most overly-educated people speak when they really don't know what they are talking about.

"The big question is, why don't ducks fights?" Bridge said barely above a whisper, his mind already delving into the many possibilities and reasons.

"Maybe it is because they are too stupid to fight," John said. "Can you think of any other creature that is as stupid as a duck?"

Once again the group pondered a question - more stupid than a duck...this is a tough one...

Vivian was the first to come up with the right answer. "Mankind is stupider than ducks," she slurred.

Everybody nodded their heads in agreement. The Professor stated, "Man is the only creature on the face of the earth that truly knows they have screwed everything up and can rationalize their behavior by saying, 'Well hell, it's too late now, might as well buy a few more cars, get another electric heater, a wood stove, sixteen bread makers, a Lear jet, and a gas generator in case the bottom falls out.'"

"If we could isolate the gene that makes it why ducks don't fight, we could implant it in human beings and there would be no more wars," Bridge said.

"We'd mess it up and all that would happen would be that women would start laying eggs and growing down feathers on their boobs," the Professor said.

Joan giggled.

John gave her or him a look that said, "Why don't you grow up or I'll have to go home and duck slap you a few times?"

"I like the feather bit," Bridge said.

The band started playing another song. Terry brought the Professor and Bridge their beers. "You didn't order me another shot?" Vivian slurred to Bridge in a tone that Bridge knew meant he was an inconsiderate man who couldn't eat a hotdog without spilling mustard down the front of his shirt.

Bridge almost answered, "In all truth, Vivian, I really think you have had enough," but telling Vivian she had had enough would be a big no no. So he shrugged his shoulders, smiled wryly and said, "I'm sorry," got up, went to the bar and brought back two shots.

Vivian gulped one shot down. She blinked several times, her eyes rolled back in her head, and then she closed her eyes and shook her head like a Saint Bernard with water in its ears. Bridge had seen it all before. John and Joan looked concerned. The Professor had also seen it and gave Bridge a knowing look. The knowing look being, 'no matter your hatred of cars, Bridge, soon you will be driving Vivian home and hoping she does not puke all over the car, but at least if she does you will not have to clean it up, as it is her car.'

Vivian stopped shaking her head, opened her eyes, and shot down the other shot. The shot glass had no sooner left her lips then her head crashed to the table with a resounding echo like a huge pine tree biting the dust and headed for plywood heaven. Her arms hung down from her sides like a napping white gorilla that was wondering why nobody liked him when it was not his fault he was white. Terry came over. "Do you think she needs a pillow?" she asked Bridge and handed him the bill.

Bridge paid the bill. "Help me get her to the car," he told the Professor.

"It will take more than two of us," the Professor said - at times an education is useful.

Bridge looked around the room, saw Stoops talking to the mannequin Indian at the end of the bar, and hollered at him, "Stoops, code three, help, help."

Stoops knew that a code three was Vivian was drunk. He apologized to the Indian about having to leave and break up their discussion of black holes.

Vivian was 185 pounds of limp tequila-filled flesh. With Stoops under one shoulder, the Professor under the other, and Bridge pushing, only with Bridge pushing two steps forward and one step back, the four of them looked like a cross-eyed caterpillar trying to find a tomato plant. They huffed and puffed outside. It took them fifteen minutes to get Vivian into the passenger's side through the driver's side door. When they were done, Vivian looked like she had melted. Her body had no form. It was merely a colorful blob of whatever blobs are made of. As Bridge shut the door, Vivian rolled her head and muttered, "Why do I love him so much? Bullshit writers anyway."

The Professor and Stoops were already headed back to the bar. After so much work, they needed another beer. Bridge looked at the blob of Vivian bathed by the brilliant starlight. He looked at her face, which looked like it was trying to drip away and become candle wax. "Oh Vivian," he said. "Is there even such a thing as love? Looking back on my life I don't know if I was ever in love. What is love? Do I love you or am I only confused at what I feel for you? Sleep well, lady. Maybe the only time we are really worth anything is when we are unconscious."

Chapter Ten

After paying the bill Bridge drove down the mountain toward Lost City - at times, one must do things they do not want to do. The city lights looked like a black ocean covered with shimmering clear plastic bottles. The bottles would soon make their way to the far corners of the world and be someone else's landfill problem. Since he did not have a driver's license, Bridge drove barely under the speed limit, which, for Lost City, was unusual - most people being from other parts of the country like L.A., Frisco, Seattle, Denver, and New York drove sixty miles an hour in a thirty-mile-an-hour zone and gave other drivers the finger for going so slow. Not in a hurry, stupid bastard. What the hell? A rerun of Donald Duck is on TV and if I miss it, the next time I see you I'll run over you - stupid local, why don't you move to where I came from.

Bridge hated to drive. Driving, to him, was blasphemy. Why driving a car was different from riding in one, he really didn't know. But it was different.

Bridge drove through town. All the slave businesses were closed except the fast food joints, which were doing a great business on grease and salt, and made Bridge crave a cheese burger and an order of fries.

Vivian rented a one-bedroom dilapidated adobe on Little Dog Hill, which was no longer the lone refuge for the Mexicans the original city fathers had screwed over so royally. It was now home to a lot of old hippies. Most of them had lost the ability to think and were still reliving a Grateful Dead concert they had attended in the 1970s. Wow man, it was almost bliss, I just can't get it out of my mind, far out, groovy, my life is complete but where do I go from here.

One thing had changed recently on Little Dog Hill now that Lost City was being advertised as soon to be one of the best little towns to retire to in the whole wide United States, small run- down houses that a few years earlier a rat would not want to live in were now selling for one hundred and fifty thousand each, and being New Mexico, the realtors were calling them cute fixer uppers, with great views, and best of all, filled with New Mexico charm, which really meant you will have to fix the plumbing, the wiring, the roof, the walls, and the floor, so your one hundred and fifty grand will turn into six hundred grand for which within five years you will only lose about four hundred thousand and wonder why you moved to the land of enchantment anyway. The realtors also didn't mention the infestation of scorpions, Black Widow spiders, and the fact most of the people on Little Dog hill owned dogs that, if they get off their chain, would ripe a person's face off.

Bridge parked in the driveway to Vivian's house. Vivian's house was easy to find, as the last time the weeds had been cut in the front yard was when Poncho Villa finally had the revelation somewhere along the line he was going to get shot and lose out on all the book royalties, and movie rights deals, so he had better steal more money from the poor. A bandit has to do what a bandit has to do.

Bridge shut off the car, put the keys in the ashtray, leaned over and kissed Vivian on the forehead, which was not an easy thing to do, as her head was listing to the side, her tongue was hanging out of her mouth, and she was snoring so loudly Bridge thought she might wake up the neighbors. There was no way in all of creation he could get Vivian into her house by himself, so he locked all the doors to the car and got out. He looked through the window to make sure Vivian had not stirred, felt warmth in his heart looking at her snoring, now slobbering face and whispered, "I, I, I, Lo, Lo, Lo," and choked on a meatball.

Little Dog Hill was only a few blocks from Bridge's store. Most of the houses on Little Dog Hill had some form of fence, the rule of thumb being that most poor people only steal from other poor people. Each house Bridge passed greeted him with a chorus of dog barks, which Bridge answered with, "Shut up, pea brain, before I jump over that fence and crap on your sidewalk."

The dogs would normally stop barking, knowing that human crap is the worst crap there is, and since their sense of smell is ten thousand times stronger than ours, it would really be a bummer.

Bridge walked by the galleries and peered through several of the windows. Inside, the paintings were sleeping. Some of the paintings were dreaming hopeful dreams, 'Tomorrow will be my day. Some rich guy from out of state will buy me and take me to where the water supply is not running out.'

Other paintings were having nightmares that the artist would want to take them back to their studio and flop more paint on them because the artist had been attacked by another round of inspiration. "Please," the paintings pleaded. "Don't you understand I like the way I am, flaws and all, it's me, damn it, it's me, people always want to change everything."

Bridge went into his gallery the Why Am I Here and only turned on one light. The paintings on the walls seemed to blink, saw it was him and went back to sleep.

Bridge went to his living room, den, and bedroom, did not turn on the light and turned on his quill and inkwell. The computer screen hummed and buzzed, flipped through its jargon of systems before it could be used and then the screen turned blue and illuminated the room like the inside of a submarine. At times, at night, when Bridge was writing he felt like he was in a submarine - a submarine that would never come up for air again - a submarine that would prowl the depths of the oceans for so long that the captain and crew would forget that they were from a world that had stars and trees and daytime. Bridge thought maybe his books were in all reality submarine torpedoes - torpedoes that would never be fired, afraid to be more than they were, safe in their cold long tubes, safe not being read.

Bridge stared into the blue screen. He could not see his reflection, but he saw Vivian's face. Not a drunk and drooling Vivian, but Vivian looking at him with her child like eyes, and he could hear her say over and over again, "Why do I love him so much? Bullshit writers anyway."

"Love, much, bullshit, anyway, writers, do I, why?" Bridge

muttered.

He shut his eyes and leaned back in his chair. The steady hum of the computer filled the room - the hum of a non-living heart - uncaring, unfeeling, unknowing except to dits and dots and electricity and facts it did not understand or comprehend - the brain for the brainless - the dream for the dreamless - the inspiration for the uninspired. "Inspiration is work," Bridge muttered almost angrily, "it's not a gift, it's work. It's a farmer plowing his field. It's a truck driver driving his truck. It's a garbage man day after day picking up mankind's trash. It's a clerk at an all-night convenience store. It's a wino sleeping in the gutter. It's a mineworker. It's a whore and a drug addict. It's everybody and everything - poor sad inspired world."

Bridge opened his eyes and Vivian was still looking at him. He shut his eyes again, took several deep breaths and sighed.

Bridge opened his eyes. Vivian's face did not look at him from the blue screen of the computer. The screen was empty. "Maybe in all truth we are the illusion," Bridge muttered. "We are the maker of dreams, but now our dreams control us and we have forgotten what came before the dreams."

Vivian's words came to him one more time. "Why do I love him so much? Bullshit writers anyway."

Bridge got up, quickly two-stepped forward and one backward out the door and headed back to Vivian's house.

Chapter Eleven

Vivian was not in her car. The living room light was on and the front door was wide open. Bridge hurried to the door - a front door open in the wee hours even in the best of neighborhoods is not a good thing.

Vivian was sitting on the sofa holding her head and moaning. If the moaning could have been deciphered, it would have said, "Dear God, I promise I will never do this to myself again. If you let me survive, I will only drink soy milk and energy drinks."

Bridge eased onto the sofa. Vivian looked at him with her bloodshot childlike eyes. "Why didn't you tell me I had had enough instead of buying me more?" she almost begged.

Bridge patted her on the knee. "Don't, any movement makes me feel like I'm riding the biggest wave in history," Vivian groaned.

Bridge had to smile. It is a strange human trait, but any time someone does something to themselves that is overindulgence and they are suffering, everyone always thinks it is funny.

"How do you feel?" Vivian asked Bridge.

"I feel fine. I only had six beers."

"Jerk. I need someone to suffer with me. Suffering alone isn't like suffering with another person. Mankind embraces sympathy. Don't you know that?"

Bridge smiled again knowing Vivian never wanted anyone to feel sorry for her.

Vivian moaned, held her head, and moaned again.

"What are you doing here anyway?" she asked in between moans.

"I was worried about you."

Vivian took her hands away from her face. Looking at Bridge, her bloodshot childlike eyes softened. "Thank you, that is very considerate," she said softly.

"Would you like me to get you something, tea, a Seven-Up, anything?"

Vivian stood but had the balance of an overly-filled water balloon. Bridge started to help her. "No, no, don't touch me," she said, adding, "but if you want to do something for me, I'd like you to sleep on the sofa while I suffer in my bed. At times it is nice to know that somebody is in the other room."

Vivian made her way to her bedroom like an out of balance bowling ball.

Bridge made sure she made it to her bed and went back to the living room. He looked around the room. It was a nice room, warm - there were pictures of relatives on the mantle above the fireplace, a few prints of mountain scenes, and a vase of plastic sunflowers. Bridge turned on the kitchen light, turned off the light in the living room and lay on the sofa. Vivian's snoring drifted through the house like an overweight mouse. Bridge shut his eyes. "Why do I love him? Bullshit writers anyway," filtered through his mind.

"Oh Vivian, maybe lovers should only be friends. Friends don't need or want, they only are."

Bridge opened his eyes and gazed into the pale comfort of the room. The snoring grew quieter - the snoring of a friend. He smiled and fell into a comfortable sleep, a sleep with no dreams, only warm wispy shadows that whispered, "All is well, all is well, for now all is well. You have a friend in the other room, she might be shit-faced on tequila, but she is a friend."

The sun was shining when Bridge woke up. At first he did not know where he was, but then it dawned on him. He two-stepped forward and one backward to Vivian's bedroom, but she was gone. Vivian was an old trooper when it came to tequila, and when it came to her coffee shop, the world would end before she would not open on time - time being six a.m. sharp, and sharp meant sharp. She was not like a lot of old freaks who would miss work with a lame excuse. What, me work? I am part of the universe. I am the center. They forget there is no center to the universe. The universe is constantly expanding and does not have a round edge. Space is not a circle. Wake up. There is no center. There is only slightly off center. Put your brain cells on that riddle for awhile.

Bridge headed for the Wake Up Or Die. The coffee shop had its normal one hundred dogs out front wishing their owners would give them a cup of coffee, but, since caffeine was bad for people, they were out of luck. They were stuck to eating vitamin fortified dog bones, dog food with broccoli and spinach in it, and taking one a day vitamins. Several of the radical dogs were planning on killing their owners, running away and taking up a life of crime. They wanted to rob butcher shops and eat a few real bones before their owners made them turn into granola dogs.

Inside the coffee shop was the normal assortment of people. Chris looked at Bridge cautiously as Bridge went in and approached the counter, but before he could order, Chris said with a stern voice, "Only black coffee for you. You had me worried last time, and besides, I think your poetry sucks."

"Is Vivian around?" Bridge asked, not offended by Chris' statement. He knew his poetry sucked.

Chris did not answer his question but said, "She said you made her drink ten shots of tequila last night and tried to take advantage of her." He smiled and added, "You should have known to cut her off at six, Bridge."

"Story of my life," Bridge replied.

Bridge got his black coffee and sat at a table by the window. He liked to watch people as they walked by. Why, he didn't know, because he really didn't like people. Most of the time, Bridge didn't consider himself a person. He was an it - a non-entity - a mass of cells and blood vessels that should really have been a rabbit or a fish or a snail - something that without thinking or knowing had a purpose - the purpose being life. Ask a rabbit if it really cares if there is heaven or hell? Ask a fish if time is of big importance? Ask a snail if salt really makes him paranoid?

Bridge sipped his coffee. It was good. Dark, hot, almost bitter enough to make him scowl. Who would want to start the day with a smile? About the only thing he missed about his cowboy days was cowboy coffee. Heat the water, toss in some coffee, let the water boil until the coffee screamed to be saved, pour it, and let the grounds settle before drinking. It had enough caffeine to jolt a whale, bitter enough to get one straight with the world.

Stoops walked into the coffee shop looking like the last time he had slept was when a Baptist minister shut up.

He got a cup of coffee and joined Bridge. He slurped his coffee several times - drinking coffee with no teeth is harder than one thinks. "How was your conversation with the stuffed Indian?" Bridge asked.

"I like him," Stoops said. "He never butts in and he is a great listener."

"Too bad he's not a woman," Bridge said.

"It's too early to laugh," Stoops said, looking into his cup of coffee like it was a mirror and there was no way he was the fairest of them all.

"I don't think I'm ready for breakfast at the This Isn't Heaven Bar today," Bridge said.

"Me either," Stoops said. "We can resume our normal life on Monday."

"Why? Are you going to church on Sunday?"

"No. Believe it or not, I met a lady, and she wants me to take her to the Indian Ruins."

"I'll be damned," Bridge said, truly amazed.

"After you left last night she came up to me and told me she could tell I was a kindred spirit and by my aura she knew I am a reincarnated medicine man. We are going to have lunch before we go."

"You are a kindred spirit," Bridge said, "but the medicine man thing is a little over my head."

"I'd hate to come back as anything in life," Stoops said.

Vivian came over to the table. She was wearing a red, white, and blue dress that put the American flag to shame. Her complexion could not have been smoother and her eyes were sparkling. Bridge and Stoops were truly amazed. "You look like you should be on the cover of an organic cereal box," Bridge said.

"I took ten aspirin, took a shower, chewed on sixteen mint leaves, drank four Sprites, puked six times, and I now feel better than puffed rice," Vivian said with a big smile.

Just then a lady dropped her cup of coffee and Vivian rushed off to get the mop - coffee and mops in a coffee shop go together like biscuits and gravy to a farmer, or to a vegan celery and lettuce, or to a wino anything with alcohol, including aftershave and spray deodorant.

"If you ever tell Vivian you love her and move in together, you will have to get a job to be able to afford all the tequila she can put down," Stoops said.

"If it comes to that, there will be a prenuptial tequila agreement," Bridge said.

Stoops finished his coffee and got up. "I have to go clean up and try and look like a medicine man," he said.

"Learn a few Indian sayings like, 'take em off blouse, medicine man can only heal pale face woman who is naked,'" Bridge said.

With Stoops gone Bridge went back to watching humanity walk by the window. He saw four bikers go by wearing leathers and spurs, three girls with purple hair, four skateboarders, two cops, several tourists, three Chicanos with snakes tattooed on their right cheek, a priest, two winos heading for the mission and a free lunch, and a local realtor with ten people following him who were trying to figure out how to buy the town, rip everything down, bring in an ocean and some seals and make Lost City into another Carmel, complete with an over-priced golf course and fifteen actors who really couldn't act but had good connections.

Bridge finished his coffee and headed for his gallery. He figured brushing his teeth would be a good thing. After last night, and the coffee, his mouth felt like the way Vivian should have looked.

Bridge put up the open sign, left the door open, turned on all the lights, put the newspaper by the computer, and then cleaned up. The toothbrush is a great invention - ask anyone who was born before the 1800s - a yucky mouth for one's complete life would be harder to take than either a Republican or Democratic National Convention.

Bridge sat and opened up a blank page on his quill and inkwell and started to write.

Dear Vivian: Being that I have never been good with the spoken word, I am going to try and write what I feel for you. I, I, I, I, I, I, I, I, I, Lo, Lo, Lo. Bridge tried three times to write I Love You, but he could not do it.

Gertrude came into the store. "I have to tell you something," she said to Bridge with a concerned look on her face. "Within a week the city is going to replace all the old lampposts that still work with new lampposts that look like old lampposts."

Bridge felt weak, he felt ill, he felt like a failure. He could not talk. Gertrude went back to her gallery

"The old lampposts will try and kill me," Bridge lamented.

He turned off his computer and went outside and stood by an old lamppost. "We know," the lamppost said like Bridge was a traitor.

Bridge wanted to say something, how sorry he was, it was not his fault, but the lamppost said to him, "Go away. We trusted you. We should have known better. But for your information, we are going to go from wherever the city takes us to the mountains and start a commune.

Bridge turned despondently and went back to his computer. He typed, Dear Vivian: How can a traitor love?

Chapter Twelve

It was getting close to four o'clock in the afternoon and Vivian still felt like a spring daisy. Bridge would be two-stepping forward and one backward to Bill's Restaurant and Libations soon and she was looking out the window for him. She had been thinking about Bridge stammering I, I, I, I, Lo, Lo last night. He had been trying to tell her something. He had held her hand. He had pulled out the chair for her to sit. What did he want to say?

Bridge had sold three of his novels during the afternoon. It always made him feel good to sell a book even after the news about the lampposts. He would like to sell a million books, but since only 20,000 people a year visited Lost City, Bridge figured he was a long way from the *New York Times* best seller list.

He had had a strange thought after selling a novel to a lady from New York City, which had had nothing to do with his selling a book, but the thought was, if there is no true love, there is still a feeling that could be called love - love is unrecognizable - love is indefinable - love may not be, but it still is. After going over and over his thought for close to an hour and not being able to decide if it had merit or not, he worked on his novel for awhile - a fictionalized character does not have to answer questions, and even if he gets a headache, he does not feel it. Fiction is a good thing.

Barbara, Jackson's wife of Jackson and The Open Doors, came to the store right after lunchtime, which reminded Bridge all he had had to eat all day was a cup of coffee. Barbara was originally from

Princeton, New Jersey, and had graduated from Princeton. How New Jersey ever got a place that was nice was beyond Bridge, but Princeton was nice. Barbara had a degree in English and Creative Writing - each of which to him seemed weird. English was English and any writing was creative. But then Bridge figured to a creative writing professor his or her idea of creative writing was what creative writing really was and every other professor's interpretation of creative writing was merely poop. A professor would not dare say another professor's opinion was shit.

Barbara was a pretty girl with short blond hair and amber eyes, and she talked with a rhythmic educated voice that, if one listened closely, still contained traces of Princeton. She liked wine, all the little finger foods that go with being from Princeton, the fancy spices on food like thyme, and she really didn't understand the west. She thought cattle grazing permits in the National Forest should be illegal and that ranchers who kill wolves that had destroyed fifteen thousand dollars' worth of their cattle should be sent to prison for 10,000 years. Bridge never got into discussions with her over anything to do with ranching - having worked on a ranch, he knew what a tenacious life it was. He also hoped Barbara never decided to move to Idaho, Wyoming, or Montana and state her ideas about cattle permits and wolves. All three states have people that hunt Liberals and taxidermists that would be more than happy to mount their heads. To some, Barbara's pretty little blond head would look great over the fireplace next to a bear or mountain lion head.

Barbara worked as the assistant editor and a feature writer for the local paper called Let's Turn Lost City Into A Political Hotbed. The LTLCIAPH, for short, was distributed all over southern New Mexico, El Paso, and parts of Arizona. There were articles about bird watchers, artists, people who protected wolves - sharp fanged little suckers - and articles about local, city, and state government, normally negative. When has any government been positive? There were articles about the stars, natural healing, foot massage, articles on the immigration problem, articles on restaurants, new gallery openings and closings, articles on green building materials from cow pies to paper adobe bricks, and articles against all wars. Why can't people get along, just because man has enjoyed killing each other since the beginning of time, and on and on and on? The paper made money like most papers through advertising. Most of the advertising was by realtors, which Bridge thought was vulgar and children should not be allowed to read. It also sold a lot of advertising space to artists, which normally showed a painting by the artist and had the artist's inspirational statement. Bridge figured most artists were so full of inspiration they should have taken up the cloth. The LTLCIAPH was Lost City's connection to itself. The paper was not quite Liberal, not quite middle of the road, but more like an over the hill old hippie to whom life had taught a few things and who now knew he wasn't always right - bummer - no utopia - better roll a joint and contemplate oblivion - maybe the real world will go away and I can live in my illusions.

Bridge liked Barbara and at times wished some of her education would rub off on him, but osmosis does not seem to work with education. Barbara and Bridge would talk about books and writing. There are zillions of musicians in the world, so it is easy for them to find someone to B.S. with. There are a lot of writers, but most of them are afraid to come out in public - light and air scare them. Neither light nor air scared Barbara or Bridge. Barbara wrote all the time, and instead of saying, "I think I am going to write a book," she *was* writing a book - miracle of miracles.

Bridge figured with her education and ability to spell and punctuate correctly she might have a chance to hit the big time, and he told her what Vivian had told him - put some good old time grunting sex in your book.

"But Bridge," Barbara said. "I am writing a nonfiction book on the evolution of the Vinegar Beatle."

"Don't they have sex?" Bridge asked.

Today Barbara was in a huff. When she walked into the store, her face was flushed and her blue eyes were little pinpoints of fire. Bridge hoped it was a temporary thing, as he figured Barbara was too young to have hot flashes. Before Bridge could even say hello, or nice day, or what do you want, Barbara blurted out angrily, "Did you hear on public radio this morning that the state of Texas voted down marijuana use for chronically ill people?"

Bridge started to reply again, but his lips were too slow.

"It just seems too unfair and heartless," Barbara said, but she had lost her fire and looked like she would cry.

"They could move to Colorado or they could buy illegal pot like they have been doing for years," Bridge said.

"Legal pot in Colorado is nothing more than corporate greed," Barbara said bitterly. "And if they get caught buying pot in Texas they will go to jail."

Ever notice people with a cause always seem to have an excuse why their cause will not work under whatever current law or opinion is at the time current - current is a word that changes daily - it's a strange word. What is current today might not have been current yesterday and might not be current tomorrow - no wonder there is no true communication in the world. Who the hell knows what anyone is really trying to say?

Current bastards anyway.

Bridge knew there was no end to the question, or an answer, so he tactfully said, "I have no idea what people who want medical marijuana in Texas should do."

The tactful answer did not work. It more than did not work, it backfired. "You heartless oaf," Barbara stormed. "Don't you have pity or compassion for the dying?"

Bridge was stunned. Oaf was a big cuss word for a lady from Princeton. It was drummed into Princeton people to never lose their cool and stoop to the level of a non-Princeton person. Ivy League schools are still into that crap. Not like West Point or Annapolis - they have guns and ships to keep a person in place. In Princeton talk, oaf is more demeaning than calling someone a Harvard grad.

Bridge regained his composure. "We are all going to die, Barbara. I really don't think it's a matter of having pity or compassion. It's a part of life."

Bridge didn't really know if he believed what he said, but it sounded good and had the desired effect. Barbara relaxed. "I'm sorry for calling you an oaf," she said.

"Thanks," Bridge replied, adding, "I didn't see you at The Hole last night. You normally go and watch Jackson play his first set."

"I'm doing an article on a lady who just moved to town who thinks rocks talk to her, and right now I am having a difficult time finding any rocks to interview to corroborate her story," Barbara said.

"The Professor tried to put the move on her last night," Bridge said.

"Good luck, that one is colder than stone," Barbara grinned.

Bridge didn't think the statement was funny, but he smiled - half of life is placating.

Barbara suddenly got serious. Not serious 'dying people can't smoke pot legally.' Not serious 'cattle should not be able to eat the people's grass.' Not serious 'what if a few wolves make a rancher go bankrupt,' but serious serious. "Rumor has it that you are in love with Vivian," she said, "and that you can't find the nerve to tell her."

"Who told you that?" Bridge demanded, visualizing ringing Stoops' neck like Stoops was a chicken - there were feathers flying everywhere, Stoops' eyes were bulging out, his arms were flapping madly, and his legs were jerking uncontrollably.

"A tourist came into the office to buy some papers and told me about some idiot he had seen at Bill's Restaurant and Libations who had fallen in love. I knew by his description the idiot had to be you, and as far as I know the only lady you are going out with is Vivian," Barbara said.

"Did the tourist leave town?" Bridge asked, trying not to show his anxiety. What if Vivian had heard?

"Yes," Barbara said.

Bridge took a deep relaxing breath.

"Why can't you tell her you love her?" Barbara asked, giving Bridge the old you can trust me look.

"I don't know," Bridge answered truthfully. "It's very complicated."

"That will teach you to fall in love, you oaf," Barbara said and started for the door, saying with her back to him, "I have to go find that talking rock."

"Do me a favor, will you?" Bridge asked. "Don't tell anyone."

"I'm going to put it in the paper," Barbara stated matter-of-factly and went out the door.

Bridge two-steeped forward and one backward around the store for several minutes. It could have been called pacing, but it was more like jerking. Would Barbara really put it in the paper? She would never do anything like that. Maybe? Who knows what a woman is going to do? He then went back to his novel - not so much because his mind was settled, but because his legs were sore from all the jerking, and most of the stuff he wrote did not take a lot of thinking and not thinking was good.

****

From the Wake Up Or Die Vivian saw Stoops go into Bill's

Restaurant and Libations. She went to the bathroom, made sure her hair looked nice, splashed a little cold water on her face, and dumped a half a bottle of Visine in her eyes even though they were not bloodshot and headed over to Bill's.

Stoops was sitting at a table and Vivian was surprised as he looked animated. "You look better than you have looked since you got out of the joint," she said, joining him.

"I had lunch with a lady who thinks I am a reincarnated medicine man," Stoops said, like medicine man rhymed with stud, hunk or lover boy.

"Is she pretty?" Vivian asked, even though the only medicine man she wanted to know was the guy who sold her pot.

"At my age, with my looks, the main thing is she is alive," Stoops laughed.

Vivian smiled.

"Want a shot of tequila?" Stoops asked and winked slyly.

"Want a punch in your eye?" Vivian winked back.

Frauline came over, all smiles and bubbles and happiness. "The usual?" she asked Stoops.

Stoops nodded. Frauline smiled and bubbled.

"And for you, Vivian?" Frauline asked.

"I'd like a glass of ginger ale with a squeeze of lime in it, please."

"Must have been a rough night," Frauline smiled, walking off to get the drinks and leaving a trail of bubbles behind her.

"She is an Alka-Seltzer to life," Vivian said.

"I like the please bit," Stoops said.

"Try it some time, you might find out how powerful of a word it is."

"Me no need please, me medicine man," Stoops grinned.

"You'll think medicine man when this lady sees your shriveled up sixty-year-old wampum pouch," Vivian chided.

Stoops didn't see anything funny in the statement. He would have much rather they kept talking about the power of please.

"I want to talk to you seriously," Vivian said.

Oh no, Stoops thought, first Bridge and now Vivian. They both must think I am the answer man. What do I know? I've spent one fifth of my life in the joint, which is not the place one learns wisdom or contemplates the reason for love. Why don't they ask me how to make a shank or raisin wine?

"I'll listen to you seriously," Stoops said, trying to give Vivian his serious look, which is hard to do for a man with long hair and a beard when nobody, not even the mirror, can really see his face. Stoops should have given Vivian his hairy look.

"I am in love with Bridge," Vivian said, not sounding happy about it but more like she had an in-grown toenail.

Stoops did not jump up and down or holler. He pulled on his beard, rubbed his head, scratched his neck, pulled on his moustache, and finally replied, "Tell him."

Frauline smiled and bubbled over with Stoop's beer and Vivian's ginger ale.

"If you loved someone and did not know if they loved you would you tell them you loved them?" Vivian asked Frauline.

"I love everyone," Frauline replied - smile, smile, smile, bubble, bubble - and headed for another table.

Both Stoops and Vivian shook their heads.

"I think it is easier to hate someone than to love them," Stoops said.

Vivian sipped on her ginger ale and thought back on her life.

She was born in a little town in Wisconsin - all German and potatoes and fish and sausage. She was always lonely. She never knew her father. He was gone before she was five - leaving with no see you later, I love you, hope you have a good life. Vivian's mother worked at the cafe. Vivian did not really remember going to school - school was just school, and being a big blocky girl, she was mostly ignored. Being ignored did not make her bitter even though it increased her sadness, but it made her search within her heart for things that were good. While other kids were going to parties or football games, she read. She read mostly science fiction - tales of distant worlds and distant stars. Her dream growing up was to one day get on a spaceship and just go. Vivian's mother died when Vivian was eighteen. They had never been close or shared mother-daughter things, so Vivian, although feeling sad for her mother, was not crushed. There was a small inheritance, and three days after the funeral, Vivian packed a bag and bought a bus ticket to San Francisco. She never looked back. Wisconsin was farther away than any spaceship could ever take her. In San Francisco, she first lived in an apartment with six other people on Haight Street - free love, acid, mescaline, sex, and clap. She sold flowers in the park. She worked at bookstores. She waited tables. She drove a cab. She made tie-dyed dresses and shirts. She beaded necklaces and rings and earrings. She walked in every protest movement there ever was - save the whale, save the beach, save the gays, legalize pot, legalize prostitution, stop the war - it was endless. She finally stopped after she developed flat feet and fallen arches. One morning, after her boyfriend had been sentenced to fifty years on the RICO laws - he was trying to supply all of North America with pot so he could put a down payment on Peru - Vivian was sitting on the steps to her apartment, which in San Francisco was cheap, only $2,400 a month. She didn't miss her boyfriend - if he would have quit when he was ahead he would have been fine, but gold watches and fancy cars had had more allure than the old hippie peace and love and simplicity. Vivian looked down the street she lived on. Cars were bumper to bumper. The color of the air was somewhere between green and brown with a tint of yellow. People were shoulder to shoulder on the street and none of them were smiling. It seemed to her that her life had passed her by - she was stuck in some old Janis Joplin song - and Vivian suddenly realized hippies would grow old now and that social security, savings, life insurance and hospitalization somehow had become good things, not just manipulations of the government. She realized that unless she wanted to die in a mission or in the gutter it was time to get her act together and make some money. The next day Vivian took her boyfriend's money, got in her car and started driving to wherever to find a new life. First she went to Portland - the same. Then Seattle - the same. Denver - the rocky mountain air was greener than San Francisco. Santa Fe - please. Sedona - the center of the vortex, crystals and bells and jeep tours just didn't seem to be the elixir of life. Phoenix - she didn't have an East Coast accent. And then Lost City - home away from home - old hippies, artists, bikers and Chicanos - safe. She rented an old building and started her coffee shop. At first she did everything herself, and then she hired people. Her shop now made her close to fifty big ones a year. She had a savings account. She had insurance. She even had a credit card. She paid taxes. She did not have a cell phone - there are some things in life that people with principles cannot stoop to. But even with her shop and all the people that came in, Vivian, for a long time, did not really make any true friends. She had many acquaintances - people she talked to and joked with. She went to parties and movies, but she did not have a true friend. She realized everything she had done in her life was a search to not be sad.

One afternoon, sitting at the window of her coffee shop before it was open, Vivian felt lonelier than she ever had her entire life. Not lonely enough she wanted to cry or go find a shrink, but lonely enough she knew all she really wanted in life was a good friend - someone she could laugh with and joke with, someone who would not judge her or tell her what to do and once in awhile give her a hug. She didn't want a man to stick his tongue in her ear and tell her the same old bullshit he had told every other woman in his life, she just wanted a friend.

The first time she really noticed Bridge was the day of her grand opening. As she said hello to him her heart fluttered, and being a big woman, she had a big heart, and it was a big flutter. Over the next few days she found out he was a writer, and everyone said he was obnoxious, snide, and very vocal in the fact that he did not want Lost City to become another Santa Fe. If you wanted another Santa Fe, move to Santa Fe - Jesus Christ. A few people who had read his books did say that he wrote feeling books. She also knew he did not date and that he was the only guy who bought black coffee at the coffee shop. But even with her fluttering heart, Vivian did not go to Bridge's store and say hello.

One morning, Bridge went to the coffee shop, got his black coffee and sat at a table by himself. He was in a dark and gloomy mood - one of those 'I don't want to be bothered by anything or anyone' days. Vivian went over and without being invited sat at the table with him. The first words Bridge spoke to Vivian were, "If I wanted company, I'd ask for it." Even though he knew he had fallen in love with her at first sight.

The first words Vivian said to Bridge were, "Fuck you, you sarcastic fuck."

Bridge smiled. They had been friends ever since.

But now, to her, being friends had become love. She loved Bridge but was afraid to tell him. Afraid he did not love her.

"Vivian, Vivian," Stoops said. "Are you ok?"

Vivian looked around Bill's. Looked at the gay couples and the tourists and several people she knew. She looked at her glass of ginger ale. "This stuff should be made illegal," she said, stood and started to leave, adding, "Tell Bridge to come over tonight and I will fix him dinner."

"Your message will be delivered with the utmost secrecy," Stoops said and asked, "Do you want me to tell Bridge about our conversation?"

Vivian shook her head.

Too bad, Stoops thought.

Chapter Thirteen

Stoops was on his fourth beer when Bridge two-stepped forward and one backward into Bill's Restaurant and Libations. He waved at Frauline as he sat. Frauline knew it was his Tecate with a glass and a lime wave. "I saw Vivian and she wants you to go over tonight. She will make you dinner," Stoops said right away, long term memory not being one of his strong points.

Frauline bubbled over to the table with the beer.

"Do you have a boyfriend?" Bridge asked Frauline.

"Are you kidding me?" she replied. "Why do you think I am so happy all the time?"

She smiled and bubbled back toward the bar.

"How did your lunch go, old medicine man?" Bridge asked Stoops.

"She thinks that when I was a medicine man I was so powerful I could communicate with all the animals."

"I didn't know you could speak turtle and rabbit and rainbow trout," Bridge said.

"I've got the turtle and rabbit down, but the trout is hard for me to grasp. Every word ends with a gurgle which I can't seem to be able to do. It's an oriental R thing."

"What is the lady's name?" Bridge asked while pouring his beer.

"She won't tell me her real name, but in her new life she has taken on the name of Organic Muffin. She believes that if every person in the world ate one organic muffin a day all the ills of the world would go away."

"I had a guy come into the store today and inform me that owls are really aliens who are spying on us."

"Anything that lives on mice and rodents couldn't be much of a threat," Stoops said.

"I think you really like this Organic Muffin," Bridge said.

"I do. It's strange, but having lunch with her I realized how lonely I am," Stoops said.

"I hope it works out, Stoops."

"Me too."

Bridge knew Stoops was serious, and he hoped for the best.

Sergeant came into Bill's, but with none of his sixteen girlfriends. He saw Stoops and Bridge and joined them at the table. Frauline bubbled over. Sergeant ordered a shot of Jamison and a dark beer. Stoops tried to whistle, which with no teeth sounds more like a plugged-up vacuum, and said, "Now that's real drinking, none of this beer drinking stuff."

"You can't afford to even sniff Jamison's," Bridge said.

"Did you hear that a guy from Texas has bought the abandoned building at the end of Bullard? He is going to remodel it and make more gallery space," Sergeant said.

Bridge cringed.

"He is also going to open an organic bakery and a vegan restaurant," Sergeant continued.

"No wonder he is getting out of Texas. I bet the Cattle Association has a hit out on him," Stoops said.

"Why is it that most of the new people that come to art towns are vegetarians?" Bridge asked, trying to get the idea of a new building in town out of his mind. His brain was screwed up enough over this love thing he really did not want to push it too far.

Neither Stoops nor Sergeant had an answer, which was really fine with Bridge - no answers in life are about par. Frauline brought over the beer and shot, and before she could leave Sergeant shot the Jamison down, took a drink of the dark beer, closed his eyes in ecstasy, sighed, opened his eyes, and grinned.

Bridge remembered his whiskey days. But being a cowboy at the time, it was Jack Daniels. Jack Daniels in the whiskey rankings is like Folgers coffee to an imported coffee bean. God, it was almost a nightmare. He couldn't even smell the stuff now without wanting to puke.

"I heard Vivian had too many shots of tequila last night and you had to drive her home," Sergeant said.

In small towns, even a thought can start a rumor - being true or not is of no importance.

"If I had money," Bridge said, "I would move to Mexico and start a cheap tequila distillery, and by cheap I mean it would be the Tokay of tequilas. I'd call my tequila, Vivian's Dance All Night Until You Barf. It would be the number one seller to college freshmen in the country, causing a population explosion, and make so much money I could buy an island off the coast of Maine, start my own country and tell my friends they could live there only if they bought one of my books. Then I would be a best seller in my own country. When the news got out about my best seller I would be on public radio and I would explain that Vivian's Dance All Night Until You Barf tequila is really the secret- to-living-forever-potion the stupid Spaniards were looking for in Florida until they got all turned around and ended up in New Mexico and Arizona and started the land grant controversy."

"That's really a good idea," Stoops said.

"I like the population explosion," Sergeant said, which is a normal statement for someone with sixteen girlfriends.

Four of Sergeant's sixteen girlfriends came into Bill's, saw Sergeant was sitting with Bridge and Stoops, and went and got their own table, letting Bridge and Stoops know that they were only Sergeant's women. Sergeant took his beer and headed toward one fourth of his harem.

"How does he have so many girlfriends?" Stoops asked.

"He tells them all how lovely they are, how nice they are, and how each one of them has a place in his heart," Bridge said.

"And they believe it?" Stoops said.

Bridge shrugged his shoulders. "It's a lonely world."

Rudolph, the co-owner of Sally's restaurant, came into Bill's Restaurant and Libations and sat with Bridge and Stoops. Rudolph always smelled like hummus and grape leaves, which didn't really bother Bridge, as it was a lot better than a lot of people in town who smelled like dog poop.

Bridge liked Rudolph, even though he was from California.

Like most people from California, Rudolph smoked so much

pot his lungs were barbecued, and he believed the only reason the country was messed up was because there were Republicans and all of them had been lousy actors. Also like most Californian's he could remember every injustice that had happened to man since the Revolutionary War - the first injustice being America won the war and had to start looking out for themselves. Bridge always figured it was tea's fault and if coffee had been popular at the time there would have been no war - no one was dumb enough to toss good coffee into the ocean. Another reason for the Revolutionary War was George, Jeff, and Ben were trying to cut in on the tax thing themselves - being already rich they were greedy and figured the normal citizen was dumber than a pig, as, at the time, most people couldn't read, so what was the Constitution and Bill of Rights to them? Ignorant common people deserve to be told what to do and pay taxes - all you have to do is let them bitch. They can't seem to figure out that bitching never changes anything. It still rings true today - give the common man sports, a car, a mortgaged home, two weeks off at Christmas, and let them bitch about the government and they are happier than the guy who shot George Wallace.

"Where's your wife?" Stoops asked Rudolph.

"I think she is going to leave me and be one of Sergeant's girlfriends," Rudolph grinned.

To live in California, one has to figure that your wife is going to screw around on you. It's all that salt water and the fact most of the women are fake blonds and have plastic boobs and bikini lines.

"Did you hear about the guy from Texas who is going to open a vegan restaurant?" Bridge asked.

"Vegan bastards anyway," Rudolph snarled.

Even restaurant owning Liberals hate other restaurants.

"I also heard that the city is going to pave Texas Street," Rudolph said.

Bridge was taking a swallow of his beer and started choking, but not on the beer. His face turned almost purple, he gasped several times, and his eyes watered. Now both the lampposts and old asphalt would want to kill him.

Rudolph looked alarmed and started to get up to pound on Bridge's back, but Stoops said, "Don't worry about it, every time Bridge hears the word pave he has a small fit."

"He must have fits when he hears Arlo Guthrie sing," Rudolph said.

Bridge swallowed, wiped his eyes with a napkin, and took several deep breaths.

"Why do they want to pave over anything that has character?" he asked to himself more than to Rudolph and Stoops.

Neither of the three had an answer - paving is a very deep and serious question in the United States. If it were at all possible, the contractors would pave over all the cornfields in the mid-west, the wheat fields in Kansas, and the lettuce, tomato, grape, bean, celery, artichoke, berry, and on and on and on fields in California. Who needs food? All we need is pavement. They would also want to pave every mountain that has the audacity to want to be more than flat - independent stupid mountains anyway trying to be bigger than anything else - you need four inches of pavement on your bloated heads.

"The next thing that is going to happen in town is someone is going to put in a parking lot," Bridge snarled.

"A guy from Chicago just bought the empty lot by the Catholic Church and is going to put in a parking lot," Rudolph said.

Bridge started to gasp and clutched at his throat.

Both Stoops and Rudolph ignored him.

Within thirty seconds, Bridge had regained control of himself. During his attack, Stoops had ordered Bridge another beer and Rudolph ordered a glass of red wine. Bridge hoped the wine was from Italy - it would serve a Californian right.

"I don't think you could live in a big city," Rudolph said to Bridge, "you'd choke to death."

"He couldn't work on a highway crew," Stoops said.

"I was born one hundred years too late," Bridge lamented and took a long pull on his beer.

"If it was a hundred years ago, you'd be bummed out because the town was putting in wooden sidewalks," Stoops said.

"Wooden sidewalks are the culprit behind paving," Bridge said, slightly agitated, but thinking about Stoops' statement.

"Maybe you just like to gripe," Rudolph said. "You just gripe because that is all you really know how to do."

Bridge wanted to say, "Who made you two shrinks?" But Stoops and Rudolph might be right, which, if they were, he would have to start being nice all the time and would have to invent another Bridge

McCoy. He might even join a committee and start campaigning for new sidewalks, a new dog catcher truck, more stop lights, more police, since modern man can't take care of himself, a noise ordinance downtown, and to top it off, be like Santa Fe and have a building code - everything has to look as if it is made out of adobe and be painted camel shit brown.

Bridge shook his head, ripping the lewd thoughts out of his mind. "I don't gripe just to gripe," he said passionately. "I gripe because the more Lost City gets paved and the more things change, the sooner Lost City becomes like any other city."

"So?" Rudolph said.

"So!! So!! So!!" Bridge erupted, "So!!"

Not even taking another drink from his beer, Bridge got up and two-stepped forward and one backward as fast as he could out of Bill's, muttering all the way to his store. "So, so, so, so, so, so. So don't you understand we have to be unique? Someone someplace has to be unique. Everyone wants to be like everyone else. Are we all nothing but a large herd?"

"Volatile guy," Rudolph said after Bridge had gone. "Doesn't he understand one cannot stand in the way of change?"

"Someone has to," Stoops said.

Bridge sat in his living room, den, and bedroom. In his mind, a huge black smoke belching pavement roller was flattening asphalt all over Lost City. People did not even bother to get out of its way. They cheered and applauded as it neared them and then still cheered and applauded as it rolled them into the asphalt - leaving in its wake thousands of flat people imbedded in the black asphalt with smiles forever smeared across their faces.

The next image that entered his mind was a parking lot. Only it was not flat, but a level-by-level parking lot that was so tall it made Jack's beanstalk look like a dwarf. Lines of cars stretched all the way from California, New York, and Florida just to park in the magnificent parking lot. As the cars inched along, they passed miles and miles of signs. **SEE THE NEW WORLD OF LOST CITY. ALL THE OLD HAS BEEN TORN DOWN, PLASTERED, PAVED, SCRAPED, AND PAINTED OVER. GUESS AT WHAT IT WAS AND GET FREE PARKING. WAS IT A CITY? WE HAVE CHANGED IT ALL. NOW IT IS COMPLICATED. NOW IT IS NEW. NEW, NEW,**

EMBRACE THE NEW. NOW THERE ARE TRAFFIC JAMS AND CRIME AND POLLUTION. BE HAPPY. WE ARE ALL THE SAME. SEE THE NEW WORLD OF LOST CITY.

Then, in Bridge's mind, cucumber slices and chopped cabbage soaked in organic soy sauce with a dab of ginger and all rolled up in a tortilla suddenly sprouted arms and legs and two eyes and a mouth. The mouth was saying, "Save a cow, save a chicken, kiss a fish, down with white meat, we only need animals for manure, veggies for the world."

And then old street lamps that still worked and were now living out the rest of their lives in a commune suddenly came to attention. One of them started screaming, "We will not die like this. Old has dignity. Old Lamps unite."

The old lamps formed into ranks and marched to the arts district of Lost City. They marched up to the new lampposts that looked like old lampposts and screamed at them, "You are too young to know what true light is, you cheap imitations of us."

The young upstarts said to the old lampposts, "It is not our fault the city replaced you with us. We really wanted to be placed around a park. It would be a nicer life being pissed on by dogs than having to look at humanity all the time."

The old lampposts did not know what to say and marched back to their commune.

Bridge remembered Vivian had invited him to dinner. Thinking about dinner his stomach started to growl and he wondered how he had survived so long when most of his sustenance was beer. He decided beer must have many redeeming qualities that a good marketing agency was missing out on.

Bridge took a whore bath, rinsing the washcloth several times. He even changed his short pants and shirt, ran a brush through his hair several times, and dabbed on a splash of Old Spice. Old Spice always reminded Bridge of his grandfather.

His grandfather had been a farmer who had never gotten more than ten cents a head in his complete life. He worked sunup till dark, drank gin like he invented it, fought in World War II, got out, never bitched or told stories or cried about it, went on with his life as a farmer, married, had three kids, two of which died young, and died in bed at 86 from lung cancer. Bridge would never forget when his grandfather was on his deathbed and his grandmother told Bridge,

"Go fill your grandfather's pipe, but don't pack it too hard. He is too weak to pull on it."

Bridge stood by the bed-ridden old man in the bedroom that smelled of lost causes, and he looked at the pale wrinkled face, which smiled a crack of a smile. The old head rose up from the pillow like every millimeter was pain. Bridge handed his grandfather the pipe, lit the stick match for him, and held it on the bowl as the old man lightly puffed. Three puffs and his grandfather's head fell back, the pipe clattering to the floor. Bridge picked up the pipe like it was an angel. He held out the pipe to his grandfather, who shook his head. The old eyes looked at Bridge. The thin dry blue lips barely moved. The words were a pained whisper. "We are only smoke, Bridge. Do no wrong that is hateful."

The eyes shut. The old man's breathing barely made his chest move. The shallow raspy breathing was only smoke. But the smoke was powerful, and good, and simple, and it was the first time Bridge felt a deep sadness, a sadness that had never gone away, and he realized his grandfather was right, man is nothing but smoke - identity, form and substance are only temporary illusions - no more than a puff on a pipe.

After the funeral, his grandmother gave Bridge his grandfather's Old Spice. Do no harm that is hateful. Bridge had never succumbed to hate. He might dislike things, he might despise things, but he had never hated - hatred was ignorance. He did not hate the men he killed during the war.

Bridge two-stepped forward and one backward towards Vivian's coffee shop. "I will tell her I love her tonight," he told himself.

Vivian had gone home after talking to Stoops. She normally closed the coffee shop herself, but Chris could do it. He would mess something up - not count the money drawer right, leave something unlocked - but so what? There was always some screw-up in life and it really didn't seem to change much. How can the screw-up of life change a screw-up?

Vivian took a shower, washed her hair, dried it and braided it, brushed her teeth, sprayed on enough lavender perfume to odorize ten flower shops and put on a long dress she had just bought at the second hand store. The dress was covered with red, orange, and yellow hibiscus flowers. She normally wore a bra, but she did not put one on, knowing Bridge was a boob man, which didn't bother her.

Everybody in life had to be something. Vivian liked cowboy butts, in which Bridge was lacking, but such is life. Win one, lose two. The loses never seem to match the wins. Vivian had never cheated at life except when she took her old boyfriend's dope money, but as everything can be rationalized, Vivian figured stealing from a dope dealer was not really stealing. How can stealing from a thief be stealing?

Vivian was about to turn on the radio but decided not to. She'd give Bridge a break tonight. Vivian went to the kitchen. She set out the paper plates, paper napkins and plastic utensils on the table. People made fun of her, but to Vivian, paper plates and plastic utensils always reminded her of a picnic, and picnics were happy. People smiled, kids ran around, dogs barked, people ate chicken, potato salad, and watermelon, the flies buzzed, the ants bit, the men drank beer and talked about whatever men talk about and think is important, and the ladies drank tea and lemonade and talked about important things - grandchildren, who was having an affair, and aunt so-and-so who was going crazy and would have to be sent to the home soon.

Vivian got a pound of thick sliced bacon out of the refrigerator and took four eggs out of the carton. She loved bacon and eggs for dinner. At times she bought organic eggs, but eggs that cost as much as steak made her angry. She felt organic food was good, but it was a rich person's folly. Poor people didn't go to the organic co-op unless they were buying food with food stamps, just like rich people didn't go to Walmart, saying with a turned up nose, "I never go to Walmart, it is such a classless place."

Try being poor - poor people don't go to Macy's or Rodeo Drive or spend twenty bucks for a piece of cheese from Yugoslavia and spread it on crackers that cost sixteen bucks because the caraway seeds were hand-picked by the lowest paid people on the face of the earth.

Vivian got four potatoes out to make hash browns. She peeled and thinly sliced and then chopped them up. Vivian then went out onto her back porch. The back yard was small, no more than twenty feet by twenty feet, and surrounded by a wooden fence that was leaning in about every direction possible but still had not fallen down. For some reason the fence reminded Vivian of a squad of happy drunk soldiers, although she had never seen such a thing. She did not know that soldiers do get drunk a lot but are never truly happy - killing people is not a happy business. The porch was covered and there were two chairs and a tree stump for a table. Growing in the middle of the yard, surrounded by weeds over two foot tall, was an apple tree that had not been pruned since Geronimo figured out it was better to work for Buffalo Bill than live on the reservation. The tree produced about a dozen apples a year that would not even have made last place in a state fair in Iceland. There was a path worn through the weeds a herd of cattle would have been proud of that led to a hummingbird feeder that hung from the tree. At the base of the tree were a few rotting apples that the ants were methodically getting rid off - poor non- unionized ants, working so the whole community can survive and not worrying that Joe ant has a nicer car than Frank ant - stupid misguided ants, maybe some day they will get it together and learn capitalism - more for me, none for you, more for me, none for you. Elect me, I am for the people, even though I wear $2,000 suits and ride around in a limo, I am for the people.

Vivian went and fetched the hummingbird feeder, brought it inside, washed it and filled it with clear sugar water she kept in the refrigerator. She hung the feeder back in the tree, and even before she stepped away a hummingbird appeared, flew several times around her, seemingly infatuated by the hibiscus flowers, then hovered by her face for a few seconds in thanks and started drinking from the feeder.

Vivian smiled and sat on the porch. She liked her back yard. There was no order, no little flower beds, no potted pansies, no rocks stacked in piles, just weeds - true Mother Nature. To Vivian, there was beauty in weeds. They were tenacious, they were strong - they lived their own lives and did not need to be fertilized or watered. Weeds were what they were, ignored but proud, the destitute who did not cry for mercy, the workers of the plant world, the ones with scars and no teeth, destined to be pulled up and discarded, but they never strayed from what they were - weeds.

The sun went down behind the mountain. The blue sky turned a watered down red. "Red sky at night farmer's delight," her mother would say in one of her rare moments of communication. A slight breeze slipped through the yard and departed - not even a memory. The hummingbird flew to the depths of the apple tree - safety in the brittle branches. Vivian sighed, suddenly feeling lonely, and remembered the first date she and Bridge had gone on.

Vivian, in a moment of weakness, asked Bridge if he would like to go to the mountains. She sensed he liked her but was too afraid or too shy to ask her to go anywhere, so she took the initiative. Bridge said yes. They did not hike. Two steps forward and one backward would make a one-mile hike three miles. They parked by a small stream that in any other state but New Mexico would have been called a dribble, but since over one million people have been killed over water in New Mexico, anything that is wet is sacred ground and not to be taken lightly. The only water people in the west have not been able to figure out how to kill each other over is rainwater.

Sitting by the dribble, with Bridge over three feet from her, Vivian felt relaxed for the first time in a long while. On the ride to the dribble Bridge had not bored her with endless talk about his life. He had not touched her on the knee or shoulder when they did talk. Mostly he had just looked out the window like Vivian did not exist, but it did not bother her - for some reason she felt safe and secure, and for some reason she knew Bridge would never burden her or try and control her. For over one hour sitting by the dribble neither Bridge nor Vivian said a word to each other. Neither of them was shy. Neither of them was nervous. It was just that there was nothing really to say and merely being together was enough. They sat by the dribble and listened to the wind in the pine trees, watched squirrels, water spiders, swatted a few mosquitoes, saw a mother robin feeding a little one, heard but did not see ravens, saw a buzzard so high in the sky he was a mere dot, and then they looked at each other and smiled. "Thank you," Vivian said.

"For what?" Bridge asked.

"For the silence."

"Maybe in truth that is all there really is," Bridge said, and he kissed her on the forehead like an older brother kisses his younger sister.

Vivian knew then that she loved Bridge. They then went to Vivian's house. She drank tequila. Bridge drank beer. They flirted, hinted, laughed, drank more tequila and beer, petted, drank more tequila and beer, and when the time was right they fell asleep in each other's arms on the sofa.

When she woke up, he was gone. No pawing help me I need you. No yanking on her clothes, just gone, but not gone - a warm two steps forward and one step back tranquility remained.

Vivian heard Bridge knocking on the front door. Even after being together for over two years he always knocked. She got up. It was dark. The stars were dancing. She went to open the door, saying to herself as she turned on the lights, "Thank you for the silence."

Chapter Fourteen

Bridge two-stepped forward and one backward into the house, then, looking at Vivian, he whistled and said, "That is one great dress," adding in jest, "Do a hula for me."

Vivian, always on cue to dance, danced a wonderful hula for several minutes. There was not one ounce of her 185 pounds that did not glide, slither, or jiggle.

When she was done, she bowed to Bridge, smiled, and headed for the kitchen. Following her, Bridge commented, "Vivian, you can really shake that whole thing. Not part of a thing, but the whole, whole, whole thing. If Don Ho was not dead, you could move to Hawaii and make a fortune dancing."

"I spent a month over there years ago and got so sick of people telling me, 'island living mo' better for you.' I wanted to move to Alaska and live with the Eskimos."

"That bad?" Bridge asked, slightly taken back.

"Hawaii is the only state in the union where matchmakers arrange marriages between tour buses. They even have a daycare for young tour buses and a retirement community for older tour buses. There are so many tour buses the last I heard there was a movement to try and limit all tour buses to only one offspring, the theory being they have to let the top end die off to control the population. The tour bus matchmakers are fighting it, saying there can never be enough tour buses and to limit a couple's number of offspring would be an affront to Mother Nature."

"There is a group in town that wants to try and route tour buses through Lost City," Bridge said sarcastically.

"It would be good for the coffee business," Vivian said, setting a cast iron frying pan the size of a garbage can lid on the stove.

Bridge was perplexed. How could he be against something that would benefit the person he loved even if he had never told that person he loved them? Why are there always two sides to everything? Damn double meanings in life anyway.

"Maybe one or two tour buses a year would not be bad," Bridge said, knowing he really did not mean it, but love has a way of making people say things they really don't mean.

"Bridge McCoy, don't lie to me. If you saw a tour bus in town crammed to the gills with people wearing Bermuda shorts, you might shoot the driver," Vivian said.

Bridge did not respond. It's hard to argue with the truth.

Vivian carefully placed each slice of bacon in the frying pan. She liked her bacon flat, not all scrunched up and crinkled, and she always put it in the pan before she turned on the stove. She then stepped back from the stove and looked at the pan of bacon. Bridge two-stepped forward and one backward until he was beside her. "Beautiful," they both said in unison, admiring the pan of bacon.

"If someone painted that I would buy it," Bridge said.

"If the animal rights people find out we are eating bacon they might picket the house," Vivian said.

Vivian turned on the stove and set the flame low. She cooked bacon slowly. Within a few seconds the bacon aroma filled the air. "If bacon didn't smell so good pigs would have had a better chance in life," Bridge said.

"The Jewish people give them a break," Vivian said.

"That's what carp balls will do to you and having to wear funny little hats and bob up and down while you are praying like a heron with a spring caught in his throat," Bridge said, opening the refrigerator and getting out two beers. He opened them both and handed one to Vivian. They clinked cans together. "To bacon, hibiscus flowers, hula, and the plight of the pig," Bridge said.

After taking a swallow of the beer, Vivian gave Bridge a surprise hug that was so hard his eyes bulged. "Tonight, big boy, I want to get naked," she said.

"You can get naked right now and cook the eggs," Bridge said, squirming out of her embrace before he had to go to the doctor for three broken ribs and a ruptured right eye.

Vivian studied her bacon like Picasso studied under-aged women. Looking at her, surrounded by the smell of bacon mixed with a lavender field, Bridge felt like his complete being, his self, his center, even though there is no center, were all in love with her. Even though he did not know what love was, he was in love. Bridge felt the words I love you forming in his throat and start to inch toward his vocal cords. "I, I, I, I, Lo, Lo, Lo," he stammered.

"Don't give me that bug caught in your throat stuff again," Vivian said.

Love you slid back down Bridge's throat.

Vivian flipped the bacon one more time, scooted it to one side of the pan and put the hash browns on the other side. Bridge watched her and said to himself, "I, I, I, Lo, Lo, Vivian," and silently choked on a meatball.

He then wondered how after five hundred boyfriends she had never gotten married. Even old hippie chicks with their love of independence have a breakdown sometime - normally after eating acid or mescaline when they love every living human on the face of the earth. Bridge took a swallow of beer. Vivian turned and faced him. "I thought about cooking naked for you, but I don't want to splatter grease on me. That would not be very sexy."

A vision of a naked woman covered with pig grease and hash browns zipped through Bridge's mind and he had to agree, but he figured there was some kinky freak somewhere that was into pig grease.

Vivian carefully took the bacon out of the frying pan and, without bothering to drain it, put it on a plate. She flipped the hash browns and then cracked each egg as meticulously as a surgeon sewing up a heart after a heart operation.

Bridge looked at the eggs. All four eggs were perfect - no broken yolks. The hash browns were crisp. Life was in order. There was no paving to be done in Lost City, no tour buses, no fancy cars, no new stores and no new lampposts. There were only hash browns and bacon and four perfect eggs.

Soon they were eating. "There is nothing better than a mega dose of cholesterol at night," Bridge said. "Who gives a damn if it's the good kind or the bad kind - bring on the grease, down with veggie burgers and turkey bacon, stinking impostors anyway."

The paper and plastic dishes in the garbage, Bridge opened two more beers. "Let's sit on the back porch," he said.

There was a quarter moon and no clouds. The lights from downtown did not wash out the stars. Two bats swooped and darted above the houses eating some poor bugs that had never bothered to wonder about their existence, and in not wondering had never realized they had been alive, or that they were now being digested in the gut of a bat.

Vivian had brought her pot pipe and taken a few hits. They were sitting a few feet apart. In the moon and starlight, everything had the complexion of light gray marble. Even Vivian's colored hibiscus dress was shades of gray.

Bridge looked at the dark outline of the apple tree and the night sky. "I looked at the stars about every night when I was a cowboy," he said. "But you know, it's funny, I only know the North Star and the Big and Little Dipper. I can't name any of the other constellations. They are just stars, if stars can be called just."

Vivian looked up at the stars. "In San Francisco you don't really see the stars. You know they are there, but then after awhile you really don't think about them. The building lights become the stars. But even though you don't think about the stars, down deep you miss them - something is missing that shouldn't be missing. Building lights and car lights have no mystery. The stars are nothing but mystery."

Bridge smiled.

"When I was in the war, and looking at the stars, I always thought it strange that people who wanted to kill me were also looking at the stars, and I felt we were both filled with the same wonder," he said.

"Maybe the UN should have all their meetings outside at night," Vivian said.

Bridge smiled again.

"Why do you fear change so much, Bridge?" Vivian asked.

Bridge took a drink of the beer. What to say? How does one explain something they really can't put into meaning? Words are never enough. Feelings are never enough. What is change but constantly saying goodbye?

Bridge took another swallow of beer.

"Tell me, Bridge," Vivian said, not commanding, not imploring, only wanting to know more about him.

"I don't know if I can answer that question, Vivian," Bridge said, talking more to the apple tree and stars than to Vivian.

"I won't hurt your heart, Bridge. I might slap you around a little or knock you in the eye, but I won't hurt your heart."

Bridge smiled to the darkness and said softly, "I guess I don't like change because I'm comfortable here. I was never comfortable my whole life until I moved here to Lost City. This town is like a respite to life. It's like the world forgot it existed. It's more a mirage than a reality, more a shadow than an image. It's a place for malcontents to not be malcontents. It's a home for the homeless."

"It will change, Bridge," Vivian said. "No one, no thing, nobody can stop change."

"I know, but I don't have to accept it. I wouldn't know who I am if I did."

"Do you know who you are?" Vivian asked.

Bridge grinned ruefully. "I am nouns, adjectives, adverbs, pronouns, and made-up characters that tap dance in my head. I am chapters and titles and page numbers. I am novels that nobody will ever read but that have sustained me. What else I am, I have no idea, but it does not bother me, and in the long run it does not really matter. In fifty years, no one will know I was ever alive."

"Why do you like me?" Vivian asked, but as soon as she asked it she wished she hadn't. "Why do we need?" she thought.

Bridge turned and looked at the gray marble glow of her face. Vivian was looking at him, but the dark hid her childlike eyes. But even with the dark, Bridge felt the deep intensity of her need to know. "I like you because I feel that in many ways you are still a child, and when I am with you I feel like I am with a rainbow. I suppose it is very selfish of me."

The words made Vivian warm, even though she did not feel like a child. She felt inadequate and overwhelmed with life most of the time. She felt that no matter what good a person did, it was never enough. "Thank you," she said, and she wanted to tell Bridge she loved him. She wanted to tell him he made her feel warm and happy, but she could not. She reached over and took Bridge's hand and held it lightly. "Let's make love," she said.

"It would be my pleasure," Bridge replied.

They stood, still holding hands, and went to the bedroom.

The happy drunk soldier fence bowed with their leaving. The stars winked, and the moon smiled, and somewhere in the distance tour buses and paving machines started their engines.

Chapter Fifteen

Vivian was snoring. Not a grating honk, honk, honk type of snore, but a quiet and contented peep, peep, peep, peep, snore. Bridge lay in bed gazing into the darkness of the ceiling. The moonbeams crept through the window like shy ghosts. Bridge had slept with his share of women in his life - from whores during the war, to hippie chicks, a few wives, and, after closing time screws that only left him feeling empty. With Vivian there was no great passion, no great need, no grunting and groaning like cattle, but gentle - gentle like warm rain. Her plump body was like tall summer grass, cool and comfortable between the toes. When they were done, Bridge found rest - rest like a mountain stream running through his brain - leaving him in a dream state that was more real than life.

Bridge rolled over and looked at Vivian's sleeping face. Her eyelids moved slightly - dancing to music only she could hear. "I, Lo, Lo," he whispered, choked on the meatball, and put his arm around her.

Vivian stirred but did not awaken - peep, peep, peep, peep.

When Bridge woke up, Vivian was gone. He remembered Stoops was not going to meet him for breakfast. Bridge two-stepped forward and one backward to his store. He passed on the way the normal array of bikers, old hippies, and the usual parade of one hundred dogs wondering how they had been destined to have to live in front of a coffee shop.

Bridge did the normal early morning wake up America thing. He combed his hair and brushed his teeth and wondered if Colgate really cured every mouth disease known to man. He then headed for the This Isn't Heaven Bar.

Sunday morning at the This Isn't Heaven Bar - the gathering place for the hung over slugging down Bloody Marys like they were communion hosts - Christ's blood and soul disguised with cheap vodka and tomato juice - Lord have mercy, Christ have mercy, Lord have mercy.

Plastic was sitting at the bar and had two empty glasses in front of him. He was on his third Bloody Mary. There were close to a dozen people scattered around the bar who made zombies look good. The jukebox was blasting "Sunday Morning Coming Down," and Bridge wished he had a large bucket of Kentucky Fried Chicken. He sat next to Plastic. Plastic looked at him. Plastic's eyes were so bloodshot he could have picked up some extra change being the red light of a traffic light. "Where's Stoops?" he asked.

"Stoops met a woman who thinks he is a reincarnated medicine man. They had a date last night," Bridge said.

"Me make big magic. You get naked," Plastic grinned.

Gloria looked like she had not slept in sixteen weeks, although her pierced nipples did a good job making sure no male really looked at her face. "Bring me a Bloody Mary," Bridge ordered, adding, "You don't look like you can stand up for long."

"Thanks, Bridge. I didn't sleep last night."

"I couldn't tell," Bridge said.

"If she wasn't into chicks I think I could fall in love with her," Plastic said sadly as Gloria trudged to do her duty.

"There is always something in the way of true love," Bridge said.

Gloria brought Bridge two Bloody Marys. "One is on me for being so thoughtful," she said. At times life does have its upside.

Bridge paid her for two. Gloria tried to smile, but Bridge could tell smiling made her head hurt.

Bridge gulped down the first Bloody Mary. Hell, he'd already had bacon and eggs the night before. He then slurped down half of the second one.

"When God invented man, He said to Himself, Self, these poor bastards are going to have to invent alcohol quickly or they won't be able to take all the suffering I am going to throw at them," Plastic said.

Stoops sat by Bridge. "The best laid plans of mice and men," Bridge said, seeing a look of disappointment on Stoops' face.

"Organic Muffin, who think Stoops be big powerful reincarnated medicine man, turn into woman who like tie up Indian, whip with black whip, and make the Trail of Tears seem like a tea party," Stoops said, adding, "Kinky sex to me is doing it on the floor."

"I had a girlfriend once who was a vegetarian, and carrot juice was her weak point. A glass of carrot juice and she would moan over and over, 'plant me, plant me,'" Plastic said.

Gloria brought Stoops two Bloody Marys and left without saying anything.

"I really thought I might have found a soul mate," Stoops said as sadly as he could. People who have done time in prison lose the ability to sound sad or whiny - sad and whiny is for the normal man with a good job, insurance, vacation time, and a locked in pension. They can whine because their wine is bitter, their steak is not cooked the way they like it, or their salad was not crisp enough. Their wife can whine because the maid forgot to dust behind the commode and her nails are brittle.

"Nobody has a soul mate," Bridge said.

"You do," Stoops said.

Bridge looked at Stoops cautiously and asked, "Who?"

"Do your feet fit a limb?" Stoops said.

"Who is my soul mate?" Bridge asked again, slightly peeved.

"Vivian, who else," Stoops said.

"No doubt," Plastic added.

"What do you mean no doubt?" Bridge asked.

"When you two are together, anyone can see how much she feels for you," Plastic said.

"Bridge can't," Stoops said.

"What do you mean I can't?" Bridge asked Stoops, trying to ignore Plastic's comment, but it stuck in the back of his mind like a lamprey on a Lake Michigan lake trout.

"You can't see how much Vivian really likes you?" Stoops said.

Johnny Cash's, "I Walk The Line," blasted out of the jukebox.

Bridge listened to the words and finished off his second Bloody Mary. Two guys started to play pool. Between the lyrics, the sound of pool balls crashing against each other, and Plastic and Stoops telling Bridge Vivian really liked him, Bridge felt like he was the ice cube in his drink - all wet and cold and even though he was surrounded by vodka and tomato juice he couldn't drink any.

Plastic got up to go to the bathroom. "I'll tell you what I will do," Stoops said, "I'll go tell Vivian that I know you love her but you are too shy to tell her yourself."

"I don't need any of that old French guy with the big nose stuff," Bridge said.

"How about the Three Musketeers? I'll poke you in the ass with a sword all the way to her house and make you tell her."

"Maybe she should tell me first," Bridge said.

"Men always tell women first that they love them," Stoops said, and added, "then the woman can tell the man to go fly a kite if they want to. It's a power thing."

"Women just don't understand how tough it is to be a man," Bridge said.

"I wonder if medicine men in the old times liked to be whipped by a pretty woman wearing a black deerskin dress?" Stoops asked.

"Medicine men were probably into younger women," Bridge said, glad to be off the subject.

Plastic sat back down. "I heard that a group of investors from Dallas bought the old Elks Club. They are going to make it into a French restaurant and take one floor and turn it into a ballroom for ballroom dancing."

Bridge started to gasp and clutched his throat. Stoops and Plastic ignored him. What are friends for?

"French restaurant," Bridge finally blurted out. "Two slices of white asparagus with a wedge of baked potato and a piece of fish the size of a dime for forty bucks."

He took three deep breaths. "And ballroom dancing. Ballroom dancing. My God, the town might as well become a cruise ship."

"That's a good idea," Stoops said. "Then all you gallery owners could have gangplanks leading to your door and give away drinks with colored umbrellas stuck in them."

Bridge held his throat.

"It would bring a lot of good-looking babes into town," Plastic said.

Bridge started to turn blue.

"I could open a bikini shop and make a fortune selling suntan lotion," Stoops said.

Bridge coughed.

"Then we could open an escort service for all the old men who the last time a woman slept with them was when Dean Martin stopped drinking," Plastic said.

"And the ballroom would be perfect for the Captain's Ball," Stoops said.

"We could rent tuxedoes and dresses," Plastic said.

"The hell with you guys," Bridge wheezed.

"Happy Sunday morning to you too," Stoops said.

"You idiots forgot sandal rentals, lounge chairs on every corner, and gay guys wearing white pants and shirts delivering towels," Bridge stormed.

"And duty-free booze," Plastic said, ignoring Bridge.

Bridge got up and disgustedly two-stepped forward and one backward out the door. Stoops and Plastic did not notice him leaving - they were caught up somewhere between martini bars, swimming pools, and wet T-shirt nights.

Bridge made his way to the Wake Up Or Die, passing as he did a Hummer with California plates. He figured they were getting ready for the revolution. Then there was a Jaguar with Arizona plates and a Toyota from Oregon.

All the out of town plates did not help Bridge's disposition.

Chris was in a sparkling mood, which only gay men can be in, and smiled at Bridge like Bridge was his long lost brother.

"What the hell are you smiling about?" Bridge scowled to Chris.

Two ladies with shaved heads were standing to the side of the counter waiting for some frothy coffee that only Lassie would like. They were wearing matching camouflage skirts, combat boots, and black T-shirts. They gave Bridge a look that he took to mean, 'You can't talk to a gay man like that, they are very sensitive.'

"You two must be in the Italian army," Bridge said to them and then smiled.

They both looked away, angry that Bridge did not recognize the uniform of the underground movement to stop men and women from going together.

"I think you needed another Bloody Mary this morning," Chris said, still smiling.

"I need a rudder and a foghorn," Bridge said, "and a double shot of espresso made from the most caffeine filled beans you have."

"You might as well buy a hit of speed, it's cheaper," Chris smiled.

Bridge wondered if Chris was related to Frauline but dismissed the idea. Cruise ships can really screw up a sane man's way of thinking. Bridge gave Chris $4.00 for the espresso, which always made him cringe, because the espresso cost him one beer out of his life, but he figured begrudgingly there were some sacrifices that had to be done in life to keep the old heart pumping faster than it should. What is mankind if it isn't jacked up and running around in circles?

Bridge wandered around trying to find a place to sit. The coffee shop was packed, philosophy and politics dripped off the ceiling like bird poop off of a telephone line. Bridge did not want to sit outside with the one hundred dogs, although the conversation might have been better. He saw one empty seat next to a lady. The lady saw him, smiled, and motioned for him to sit with her. Bridge two-stepped forward and one backward to her table. He had never met the lady. She was in her late forties or early fifties and was wearing a black beret. Her white hair was slightly longer than a crew cut. Her face was heavily wrinkled more from being outdoors than sitting around and fretting. Bridge figured she probably rode a bicycle everywhere and took nature hikes in the mountains to bother all the poor animals. She had a pleasing smile and teeth almost as white as Vivian's. Bridge sat. "I'm Lisa," the lady said, sticking out her hand to shake. At least she was not a huggy, huggy type of person.

"Bridge," Bridge said simply and couldn't think of anything else to say. What does one say to a strange lady when meeting? "I like your boobs. What a pleasing butt you have. I would really like to get you naked and forget all this courtship ritual stuff, and I really don't want to hear about how many husbands you have had, boyfriends who have screwed you around, or the story of your life, or how you ended up in Lost City and are thinking about becoming a real estate agent."

"I read one of your books," Lisa said, taking a sip from a black cup of coffee, which impressed Bridge. Another black coffee drinker - there is hope in life.

Bridge was always cautious when people told him they had read one of his books. The first thoughts that came to his mind were always negative - your characters are flat and shallow, your sentences are too long or too short, you don't use any semi-colons and what were you trying to say?

"What book did you read?" Bridge asked, which was really the only thing he could say.

"I read *The Land.* I thought it was both thoughtful and very insightful and I loved how you rounded out the cruelty and harshness of both man and nature so the reader understands that no matter what happens there is always some amount of good in the world and if we believe or don't believe in a supreme being or God it makes no difference as long as in our essence we try to be good."

Bridge pondered Lisa's words. For sure it was one great run-on sentence, which he appreciated. He was good at run-on sentences, but as to the deep meaning, he really had no idea. He wanted to tell Lisa his mother had written the book and he had only put his name on it.

"Man will gobble up all the land in time," Bridge finally said. "Every rock and bush will have a price tag on it. It seems if mankind can't put a price on everything in life, we really can't appreciate anything."

Lisa sighed, sipped her coffee, sighed again, sipped her coffee. Her face softened, the deep wrinkles around her eyes faded into an understanding smoothness. She sighed again and said with a smile, "You writers are so full of shit."

Bridge started laughing. Not a laugh that has to be laughed at times when a friend has told a really bad joke. Not a sarcastic laugh when something really dreadful has happened, and instead of crying or going into a deep depression for sixteen weeks, one has to chuckle. Bridge laughed a deep belly roll laugh. A har, har, har, har, har laugh. A laugh at himself, because, he knew, har, har, har, har, Lisa was right. Right on the old nail head - right as a punch in the nose - right as there are numerous gods in the world and they all hate each other. Numerous gods, give us a break, please? You can have all the souls, let mankind have matzo balls, pickled fish, brown rice, barbecue, steak, carrot sticks, Big Macs, tacos, crab legs, camel milk, spitted goat - let all stomachs be full - let the gods fight their own wars, coward bastards anyway using mankind as their pawns, and stupid pawns we are.

Bridge kept laughing. Lisa started laughing. Bridge laughed louder. Lisa laughed louder. All the people in the coffee shop looked over at them. At first they thought, rude people, how can they laugh with politics and philosophy dripping off the ceiling like bird poop? How can they take away our serious coffee shop musings? "Har, har, har," Bridge laughed on. "He, he, he, he," Lisa laughed on.

Soon, even if they did not want to, all the potheads, philosophers, bikers, lesbians, dykes, gays, cross dressers, and tourists started to laugh. The one hundred dogs outside looked in the windows and wondered how in the hell they were the ones on leashes? Vivian was in the back inventorying coffee beans and the ten crates of dried breadsticks she still had not been able to sell. Hearing the laughter, she went into the coffee shop. Chris was laughing so hard he was bent over with a gut ache. In the middle of a hard, har, har, har, Bridge saw Vivian, smiled ear to ear at her, stood, held his arms above his head like a place kicker that had made a field goal to win the game and hollered above the laughter, "Life is good. I have discovered the truth. I am full of shit."

"Full of shit, full of shit, full of shit," the crowd echoed.

Bridge two-stepped forward and one backward over to Vivian, who was the only person not laughing, she was more in shock - coffee was supposed to be a somber meditating thing, not laughing gas. Bridge kissed her on the forehead and then two- stepped forward and one backward out the door and back to his gallery.

Within three minutes there was no more laughter in the Wake Up Or Die. People just sat around in a daze wondering what had gotten into them and soon got back to politics and philosophy - but none of them delving into the philosophy of laughter, war and crime and genocide and other bad things being easier to debate. Embrace misery. It is our savior.

Bridge put the open sign in his window and left the door open. He looked at the paintings hanging on the walls. The hawks, horses, and beads seemed to smile at him.

He went back outside. MeJoe was standing in front of his store. This was unusual, as Bridge was normally the only person who opened on Sunday.

Gertrude came out from her gallery. There was a smudge of blue paint on her chin - a smudge of dreams. A smudge of 'this is my world, it is a good world. Let the world be what it is going to be as long as there is canvas and paint.'

Bridge waved at her. Gertrude called to him, "We all decided being open on Sunday is a good idea."

"Art is capitalism," Bridge said.

The other gallery owners were putting out open signs. Buy a piece of my being. Buy a gourd, or a painting, or jewelry. Buy what my heart, and toes, and fingers, and guts have created. We are not stone. We think. We feel. We are. We are the fringes of life. We are the geeks. We are what the tourists want to see. We are the lost in a world of the lost that does not know it is lost. Lost City - bring on the tour buses and the cruise ships and the paving machines. Bring on the Hummers and Jaguars. Bring on the ones who have ruined the places where they lived and will ruin where they live now. Bring on the higher rents and bigger stores. Bring on the smog from California, the snow from Nebraska, the guns from Detroit, the "What the fuck you want?" from New York. This is the west, lets ruin it, and to hell with let the buffalo roam and give me space, lots of space. I can massage away your open spaces. I can read your tarot cards and build a parking lot. I can make your coffee taste like there is no coffee in it.

Bridge two-stepped forward and one backward into his store and turned on his quill and inkwell. He sat just as a couple came into the store. They were in their late thirties. She was tall, pretty, nicely dressed and had on a Lady's Rolex. He was tall, handsome, nicely dressed and had on a man's Rolex. The Rolex - symbol of I have won. Bridge two-stepped forward and one backward to the table by the door. The couple smiled at him. Bridge smiled back. The lady stopped in front of the table where Bridge's books were displayed, looked at the books, looked at Bridge, and said, "I really loved your novel, *Last Day In Paradise*."

"Thank you," Bridge said.

The words made him feel warm, not happy, but warm, not I love you Vivian, but nice.

"Your book had a deep undertone of sadness to it," the lady said, "and your characters were lovely."

"I can't help the sadness," Bridge said.

"None of us can," the lady said and picked up *Love Lies Bleeding*, Bridge's Vietnam novel.

She bought three novels. Life at times is good even though we are all full of shit.

Chapter Sixteen

It was early evening and Bridge was outside. He had worked on his book all day and once again tried to write Vivian a letter telling her he loved her. The book writing went fine. The letter was a complete failure. The street was deserted when Sergeant came out of his gallery. Bridge waved at him and Sergeant walked over. "It's nice when the street is empty," Bridge said, looking at the back of the This Isn't Heaven Bar and the fifty or so cases of empty beer bottles.

"We all crave to be alone, but we also crave company," Sergeant said.

Old veterans seem to be cursed with puzzles. Number one being why did they survive? Was it fate? Divine intervention? Destiny? Or merely luck?

"Have you ever been in love, Sergeant?" Bridge asked, suddenly feeling sad as he watched a Styrofoam cup being pushed down the street by a slight breeze and thought, petroleum, we are surrounded by a sea of oil - bicycle tires, rubber shoes, cups, plates. The La Brea Tar Pits are nothing. We all will be fossilized in oil.

"I am in love with sixteen women," Sergeant said.

"And why do they love you?" Bridge asked.

"I have no idea," Sergeant answered and went back to his store to close up, go home, drink a few beers and ponder why sixteen women loved him all at the same time.

MeJoe came out of his store. Me and Joe were talking, but Bridge could not hear what they were saying. Bridge, having the desire to be told to fuck off, went over to say hello to MeJoe.

"Hey MeJoe, what's going on?" Bridge said like he was talking to an old high school friend - not the one who had stolen his girlfriend.

"Fuck off," MeJoe said, not caustically but a normal fuck off.

"It's a nice day," Bridge said, understanding every day in one way or another is a fuck off day.

"Fuck off," MeJoe said, now slightly caustic.

"He doesn't really mean what he is saying," Me said, apologizing for Joe.

"Yes I do, fuck face," Joe said.

"I have a problem and I need help," Bridge said, not believing what he had just said.

"Fuck off," Joe said. "Don't you understand English?"

"No, Joe, you shut up and listen to Bridge's problem," Me said.

"Do I have to?" Joe almost whined.

"Yes, it is only right," Me said.

One half of MeJoe's face seemed to pout and the other half smiled. "What is your problem?" Me asked Bridge.

Bridge didn't really want to tell Me his problem, but he had committed himself - damn commitments anyway. "I am in love with a lady, but I can't tell her," Bridge said.

"Then write her," Joe said.

"For once in your life you have some good advice," Me said.

"I tried to write, but the same thing happens to me. As soon as I am about to say or write I love you I feel like I am choking on a meatball and I can't get the words out," Bridge said.

"Come back in a few days and we might have an answer for your problem," MeJoe said, turned and tapped his way back into his store.

Two steps forward and one backward back to his store, Bridge felt like he had been talking to a washing machine and he wondered what had possessed him to even ask MeJoe for help - desperation is a strange thing.

Even though it was past closing time, Bridge left the open sign in the window. Open, I am open, come buy a book, a painting, a beaded dress. I am a painting dream, take me home and hang me on your wall. I am a book dream, take me home and read me and toss me in the trash. Bridge headed for his living room, den, and bedroom, but stopped in front of a black and white photograph of a Crow warrior that was taken over one hundred years ago. The Indian did not look at the camera but off to the left. His face was hard and his eyes held no emotion. Bridge at times figured the Indian had it figured out - life is only to be stoic.

Bridge two-stepped forward and one backward to his quill and inkwell and turned it on. Dear Vivian, he typed. What to say? What to do? I, I, I, I, I, I wallow in a land of in between and I cannot even be stoic. Bridge McCoy - Sunday Night.

Chapter Seventeen

It was 9 p.m. and The Wake Up Or Die had only a few customers - Sunday night coming down. People were home and getting ready for Monday. Monday, the day most people turn off their mind and bus, walk, bicycle, drive, fly, or crawl back to work. Chris was sweeping the floor and Vivian was cleaning the espresso machine. Vivian felt tired, not just physically, which could have been a delayed reaction from too many tequilas, several beers and making love, but also mentally. Her mind felt like someone, or something, had stuck an electric mixer in her head and whizzed her brain into undercooked gray scrambled eggs.

Finished cleaning, Vivian told the remaining people they had to go, as she was closing. They trudged out of the store like they had been kicked out of their comfort zone. The Wake Up Or Die was safe, a dream in the middle of chaos. Chris hugged her before he left. Vivian locked the doors and went around turning off the lights, leaving two on. She then went to her private room, turned on the red, green, blue, yellow, orange, and purple stained glass lamp. The fairies danced to life - not dancing to jazz or rock or country, but a Viennese Waltz - slow and smooth, with gentle twirls and billowing gowns. Vivian collapsed onto the sofa. Bridge thinks I am like a child, she thought. Who can be a child? Where is there room in life for dolls and tinker toys? Please, let there be room for dolls and tinker toys.

Vivian looked at the lace curtains and the dangling hummingbird. The fairies waltzed around the room. She thought back to last night. Bridge was always gentle when they made love. His touches were soft, almost tentative. There was no groping or hurry, no mad panting. It was almost like he was afraid, afraid to be close, but Vivian knew he needed the closeness.

The fairies waltzed. The silent music settled in the corners of the room like stardust. Vivian filled her pot pipe and was about to light it but put it back - her gray scrambled brain settled, rested, the yolks became whole, the whites circled the yolks, and the yolks and whites went back into the egg.

San Francisco, hippie heaven. Vivian smiled a smile that was not a smile, a smile that covered a grimace that was not a grimace but a sadness - all the lost people dancing and screwing and spewing philosophies that never had a chance in hell to become real. Did it make life a joke, or was life always a joke? What makes the puppet dance? The puppeteer or the puppet? And now another generation enters the world. Nose rings and tongue studs and tattoos, shaved heads and spiked heads, but still the same rap, the same dream - no war, no hunger, no injustice. Mother Teresa, where have you gone? You have been replaced by TV preachers that for only $19.95 will mail you a book that will bring light to the darkness. $19.95, a blessing that comes complete with a bookmark, and for only two bucks more, a cookbook explaining how to survive on faith - forget food when the end of mankind is only six billion more years away. Think about it children, only six measly billion more years. $19.95 now before it is too late - six billion years is only a blink in the eyes of God.

Vivian stood and started to waltz. One, two, three, turn, glide, twirl. Dance with me, Bridge. One, two, three. Why do we need love? One, two, three. We all go two steps forward and one backward. We look at life through the back of our head. One, two, three, turn, glide, twirl.

Vivian stopped dancing and watched the fairies. "My little friends," she whispered.

Large teardrops formed in her eyes and fell heavily onto her breasts - teardrops that the red, blue, green, yellow, orange and purple fairies flew into. "Bridge, make me a child, let me be your dream," Vivian cried softly.

She wiped her face with the hem of her dress and turned off the light.

She locked up the Wake Up Or Die. Down the street she could

see light coming from Bridge's store. She started to go to the store but stopped, looked at the light sadly for a moment, then turned and headed for home.

Make me a child.

One, two, three, turn, glide, twirl.

Chapter Eighteen

Stoops and Plastic ended up drinking all day, by which time they were both pie-eyed, and had completely examined any means of making money when the cruise ships started docking on the edge of town - something about 1400 miles of desert and mountains between Lost City and the ocean had never entered their minds. They went home, went to bed, and dreamed contentedly of being rich and having their pick of young ladies wearing bikinis who thought old over the hill hippies and ex-convicts were the bee's knees of men. Dreams have a way of messing up the reality of life.

All during the evening, and into the dark, Bridge had tried umpteen times to write Vivian a letter. Dear Vivian: I, I, I, I, I, Lo, Lo. Erase screen. Dear Vivian: I, I, I, I, I, Lo, Lo. Erase screen. Bridge wished he had one of his old typewriters. Then, in a fit of rage, he could rip the typing paper out of the carriage, wad the paper into a tight ball and toss it at the wastepaper basket, which, in the old days, he always missed - no catching basket, why don't you have hands? Bastard anyway.

Bridge then worked on his book, if typing three paragraphs twenty times and erasing them twenty times can be called work.

Bridge stood, saw it was dark outside, remembered he still had the door open and the open sign up and went to close the door.

He two-stepped forward and one backward outside, looked sadly at the old lampposts, who snubbed him, and was about to go back inside when the Professor walked around the corner, saw Bridge, waved, and came over.

Bridge wanted to talk to the Professor about as much as he wanted to type and erase three paragraphs twenty more times. But friendship is friendship, and for whatever friendship is worth, enemies can't hurt you, only those you trust get close enough to really bury the knife in deep – ask Caesar about his buddy Brutus?

"Burning the midnight oil," the Professor said.

"It's not midnight," Bridge said. "And we no longer burn oil. I am burning the nine o'clock electricity, which, by my wasteful use of electricity is adding fossil fuel gasses into the atmosphere that the hole in the ozone is gobbling up like a starving pig, causing it to get bigger. It would be a fit ending for mankind if we all died from skin cancer."

"My bitter snide friend, good to see you in form," the Professor said.

"What are you doing walking around town on Sunday night?" Bridge asked.

"I'm searching for the lady who talks to rocks. I think she might be on to something that has escaped mankind since the beginning of time."

"She has already dumped you before you had a chance to really get dumped," Bridge said.

"To dump or not to dump, that is the question," the Professor said in a bad impression of a plump Shakespearian actor who had taken too many acting classes and was now hawking at a carnival.

"You been drinking or smoking dope?" Bridge asked.

"Breathing the air is like smoking dope."

"It's also cheaper," Bridge said.

The Professor sat on the curb and Bridge sensed that, besides being half plastered, he was depressed. Bridge really wanted to go back to his computer and once again take a stab at writing Vivian a letter, if he was lucky he might get to I, I, I, I, I, Lov, but what does one do when a friend sits on the curb that might need company? Bridge sat next to the Professor. Not close enough that if someone they knew came by they would start a rumor that the Professor and Bridge had come out of the closet and were going to open a fabric store together.

"What are you bummed out about?" Bridge asked the Professor.

"I'm not bummed out," the Professor answered defensively.

Bridge, always one for thoughtful words, said, "Don't give me that shit, spill it or get out of here."

"The infantry taught you how to get straight to the point, didn't it, Bridge?"

"The infantry taught me a lot of things, not all of them good, but also not all of them bad," Bridge replied.

"I wasn't in the military," the Professor said.

"I know that isn't what's bumming you out," Bridge said, suddenly feeling a deep sadness for the Professor.

"At times I feel that life is really nothing," the Professor started like he was talking more to himself than to Bridge.

Maybe friends who did not have ears would be the best friends, Bridge thought. People could smother their no-eared friends with their problems, and when they were done talking, the friend with no ears would pat them on the back, smile, and the talker would feel better, relieved because he or she knew they were only talking to themselves anyway and that they had solved their own problems.

Bridge did not reply to the Professor, his thought had left his mind out of breath.

The Professor continued. "I have spent my complete life searching for something, but I really don't know what that something is. It's a hollow feeling in my gut that, no matter what I do, or find, or say, never goes away."

"Try being a writer," Bridge said but was immediately upset for saying it. He was supposed to be listening.

"I've tried being a writer," the Professor said. "I talk about it all the time. I see paragraphs and pages in my head, but then I don't take the time and do it."

The Professor then asked, "Why do you write, Bridge?"

Bridge thought for a few moments and then replied, "You have a hole in your gut. I have a hole in my complete body. I understand nothing. I comprehend nothing. Life is folly. Death is folly. And yet I feel that there is more. More of what, I don't know, but sometimes I can almost feel whatever more is. It's like my mind, or my fingers, or my toes, are one thirty-second of an inch from grasping it. But, alas, no cigar, no grasping, no ringer, no hole-in-one, no home run, no three-point shot, no nothing. I guess that is why I am a writer."

"When I was an attorney I thought I would help the poor and oppressed," the Professor said. "But I found out most of the people I defended were guilty as hell, so I changed my attitude and got rich."

"That's a step in finding out the reality of life," Bridge said.

"Then I quit and I figured the more education I got the smarter I would be and I would get on top of it all, thus the five degrees."

"That's a step in really getting all screwed up. Anyone that once a year has to dress up like a judge, wear a flat hat with a colored string hanging from it, and tell the graduating senior class they are ready for the world has to have lost it somewhere."

"Then I thought young chicks would help. I would submerge myself in young breasts and forget the world."

"It's the giggling and hearing stories about when they were young that gets on my nerves," Bridge said. "I'd like to be young again like I'd like to go back to war.

"And now I go to the bars looking for whatever I am looking for," the Professor said, sounding really bummed out.

"It beats the hell out of playing golf," Bridge said, although in truth he liked golf. It was something about the futility of hitting a round object with a flat object and hoping to defy a rule of physics by hitting it straight.

"I don't know what to do, Bridge. I really don't."

"I think you should really pursue the lady that talks to rocks. Like you say, she might really be onto something. I have known people who talk to walls. I have known people who talk to dogs and cats and horses, but neither walls nor dogs nor cats nor horses have seemed to help them any. Hell, rocks might be the true solution to life."

The Professor stood, relief smeared on his face like jelly on a peanut butter and jelly sandwich and said excitedly, "That's exactly what I thought. I have to find the Rock Lady."

Before Bridge could stand, the Professor ran around the corner hollering, "Rock Lady, Rock Lady, where are you? You are my salvation."

Bridge closed the door and took down the open sign. Taking two steps forward and one backward towards his computer, he said out loud, "Another thing about being older is you understand love is not salvation. It is a helping hand."

Dear Vivian: I, I, I, I, I, Lo, Lo, pause, erase. Dear Vivian: I, I, I, I, I, Lo, Lo, damn it, erase. Dear Vivian: I have only one question. Am I a rock?

Chapter Nineteen

Monday morning and a city crew were removing the old lampposts, while behind them another crew was putting up the new lampposts. Bridge, outside of his gallery, was the only one who could hear the old lampposts cursing at their abductors. "You bastards, take your hands off of me, you fucker, you don't know what you are doing, fuck face."

Bridge felt terrible, but rationalized communes were not such a bad place. They beat the hell out of staying in a Motel 6.

He went back inside, locked the door, and headed for his quill and inkwell. He had not gone more than five steps when Stoops tapped on the window. If Mondays are tough, try starting it by looking at a longhaired, bearded, no toothed, old pot smuggler looking through the window. Bridge opened the door. "Stoops, you look like a stray dog that not even a nun would feed."

"It has taken me years to cultivate this particular look," Stoops said.

"It's not ten o'clock," Bridge said. "What are you doing here?"

"I came by because I have some important news for you."

Bridge looked wary, unlike Friday, which is a good news day - any news on Monday nine out of ten times is bad news - life is chasing Friday.

"What is the news?" he asked.

"Vivian is telling everyone at the Wake Up Or Die she is pregnant and you are the father," Stoops said.

Bridge started coughing. He started hopping up and down. His arms flopped around like they were made from silly putty. "Wha, wha, wha, wha, what?" he stammered.

Stoops started laughing from every cell in his body. "Ho, ho, ho, ho, ho, ho, just joking, ho, ho, ho, ho, ho."

Bridge leaped at him, arms outstretched to grab Stoops' neck and wring the ho ho ho out of him.

Stoops ran out of the store, "See you for breakfast."

Bridge was so shook up it took him twenty minutes to calm down and get over the urge to go buy a pistol and shoot Stoops in the ass. There are some things in life that are not funny - number one being pregnant women over fifty.

Stoops and a man named Berry were in the This Isn't Heaven Bar. They were the only ones there. They were both nursing Bloody Marys. For a reason known only to some higher power the jukebox was not on. Berry was in his mid-seventies and very seldom came out to socialize - spending most of his time at home drinking wine. He was toothpick thin, clean shaven, and kept his sandy hair cut like a farmer in Iowa. His clothes hung on him like they were held up by wire, not flesh and bone. When he smiled, people didn't really know if he was truly smiling or not. His smile was like he was a professor who got a big chuckle out of handing students their failing grade. He had been a research botanist, traveled and lectured all around the world, and was published in all the high-ranking botany papers. Nobody in Lost City had ever read one, mainly because the only botany they cared about was growing pot. Berry now called himself a photographer, although he never carried a camera, telling people he took pictures in his mind, which to most people in town was normal. Who needs a camera anyway? About a year earlier, Berry had had a stroke that made him walk with a limp, and he had lost the majority of use in his left arm. But he did not want sympathy, and the stroke had not changed his attitude - his attitude for his entire adult life being that life in general sucked and all people, including him, were jerks and any good that came out of life was a pure accident. People called Berry, "The Old Grump," which Berry liked. But those that took the time to get to know Berry learned he was a very generous man and, like most of mankind, his grumpiness came from something in life that had hurt him so deeply he had taken on the grumpy persona to keep the majority people away. Bridge and Stoops liked Berry, mainly because they knew that if they got old they would be old and grumpy, and Berry was one of life's learning experiences on how to achieve one's goal - grumpiness is an art that must be studied.

Bridge two-stepped forward and one step backward into the bar. The old lampposts were now gone. The new lampposts tried to say hello to him, but he ignored them. Young upstart fuckers anyway. What the hell do they think they know? He was now over Stoops' not so funny joke about Vivian being pregnant, and he made a vow to himself he would get Stoops back. The Arabs say that there is no revenge after fifteen minutes. But what do they know? They have to pray three times a day and sneak around to drink booze.

"Berry, you sorry grump," Bridge said. "Where have you been for the past two months?"

Terms of endearment can be strange things.

"I went camping in Utah, if it's any of your business," Berry said, smiling his 'I gave you an F' smile.

"Did you convert to Mormonism?" Bridge asked, waving to Gloria for his breakfast Bloody Mary.

Gloria threw Bridge the finger.

"My seventh wife was a Mormon," Berry replied. "She had six kids, all from different fathers, but strange as it may sound, all of their last names were Young. It wasn't the kids that finally drove me away, it was hearing the word prophet two zillion times a day, and I don't think their choir is all that good anyway."

"How many times have you been married?" Stoops asked Berry.

"Twelve. Each marriage lasted one year. They all thought they could stop me from being grumpy, but they found out that down deep I am truly a jerk."

"Everybody has to be something in life," Bridge said as Gloria put his Bloody Mary down in front of him.

Gloria had her normal Monday morning look. She did not have dark circles under her eyes, she had black grocery sacks. Matching the sacks were four hickies on her neck that would have made Dracula jealous.

"I didn't know women gave each other hickies," Bridge said.

"I thought I would go straight, so I went out with a guy," Gloria snapped, rubbing her neck so hard her nipple rings jiggled, adding as she stomped away, "See what you male bastards do to us women."

"She is right about one thing," Berry said. "We are all male bastards."

"I am not the product of a mistress," Bridge said.

"You're still a bastard," Berry said.

"To bastards all," Stoops said, and the three of them clinked their glasses together and drank deeply.

"There is nothing sacred in life," Berry said out of the blue.

Stoops pondered the question as only an old convict can.

"There has to be something sacred in life," Bridge said. "I have no idea what it is, but there has to be something."

"Tell me one thing that is sacred and I will ridicule it," Berry said, once again smiling his, 'I just gave you an F' smile.

"That's good," Stoops said. "That's very good."

The Professor and a lady came into the bar. Seeing Stoops, Berry, and Bridge, the Professor ignored them and the two went to a far corner table.

"It must be the Rock Lady," Bridge said.

"Who is the Rock Lady?" Stoops asked.

"The one that dumped him at The Hole but who he has a deep infatuation over," Bridge said.

"Why do they call her the Rock Lady?" Berry asked.

Two questions in a row almost made Bridge want to scream, "What do you think I am an encyclopedia?" but he replied, "She talks to rocks and they talk to her and she thinks there is the big granddaddy of rocks somewhere in the area of Lost City that will tell her all the secrets to life."

"This is a great town," Stoops said.

"I ate mescaline years ago and sat in a stream for twenty-two hours talking to rocks," Berry said.

"What do rocks talks about?" Stoops asked, genuinely wanting to know.

Bridge motioned to Gloria for another Bloody Mary. Gloria smiled at him - it was either a mood swing thing or she had forgotten about her hatred for men.

"Most of the rocks in the stream in general were dumb, thus the old saying, dumber than a rock, but a few were really quite intelligent," Berry said. "But their main fear is that they will all be turned into gravel."

The answer seemed evasive to Bridge, but Stoops seemed

satisfied.

Gloria brought Bridge his other Bloody Mary.

"Hey Gloria," the Professor called from the corner table. "Are you going to take our order or not?"

"You order from the bar, you know that, you dumb man," Gloria stormed.

Mood swings at times are very quick.

"Two Budweisers and I'll pick them up at the bar," the Professor ordered.

Being from Oklahoma, the Professor only drank lousy beer - American, but still lousy beer, but it did go along with American lousy cars, lousy houses, lousy school systems, lousy wages for the common man, lousy hospital insurance, and, to shorten the endless lousy list, lousy politicians.

Gloria did her duty. The Professor picked up the beers and still ignored Stoops, Berry, and Bridge. Hoarding women should be a sin. And to be fair, hoarding men by women should also be a sin. Berry put money on the bar and stood. "I've had about all I can take of you two sick jerks," he said and shuffled out of the bar like only a person who has had a stroke can.

"Take it easy, Berry," Stoops called to him.

Berry did not answer.

"I like the old grump," Stoops said.

"I hope if I ever have a stroke it kills me," Bridge said, and then added, "I have a strange fear that Berry at times wants to kill himself."

"Me too," Stoops said, but they dropped the subject, even though the topic of suicide on Monday morning fit the mood.

Two old hippies who looked like they had not taken a bath or changed their clothes since Woodstock floated into the bar. Bridge waved at Gloria and paid his bill, as usual leaving a good tip. Gloria mumbled something that resembled thanks.

"I have to get out of here," Bridge said to Stoops. "Within a few minutes the hippies will be playing Doors songs. See you this afternoon at Bill's."

Two-stepping forward and one backward toward the door, Bridge called over to the Professor, "Salvation is one day short of six billion years."

"Not for granite," the Rock Lady answered as piously as a lesbian Episcopalian priest with four grown children from a previous marriage.

At the Wake Up Or Die one hundred dogs were looking in the windows wondering why their owners talked all the time about topics that really didn't matter - true life was bones, liver-flavored treats, and cold noses - stupid bipeds anyway.

Bridge two-stepped forward and one backward toward his store muttering under his breath, "Please, God, Allah, spacemen, whatever, let me die before I am crippled."

Chapter Twenty

Vivian saw Bridge heading for his store and smiled. There was something about his two steps forward and one backward that always made her smile. Vivian had been feeling stupid all morning for confiding in Stoops about her feelings for Bridge. What was she ever thinking? For all she knew, Stoops had blabbed the news all over town. She had decided that if Stoops did she would knock his gums out since he had no teeth.

The Wake Up Or Die was doing its normal brisk business. People were drinking cappuccinos, and Americana's, and espressos, the occasional out of touch one a cup of black coffee, and then of course there were always a few people who thought they were British and were drinking tea - some even with milk in it. It was a regular cornucopia of caffeine and tannic acid.

Vivian at times was amazed at the amount of coffee she sold, but then she figured the main reason coffee shops did a good business was it gave people a place to socialize where they figured there was no chance of getting their asses kicked by some drunk - coffeehouses not being known for brawls, screaming insults or puking - although political debates and bad poetry can make a lot of people inwardly violent.

Vivian got over feeling stupid for confiding in Stoops. She was going to have a free meal for the homeless on Wednesday, and since winter was closer than most people thought, not six billion years closer, but several months, she was asking for donations of scarves, coats, socks, and all the normal winter stuff most people own about fifty of. She had already put flyers around town stating in large bold letters - **GIVE UP SOME OF YOUR WINTER STUFF, YOU HOARDING CAPITALIST.** Six restaurants in town were going to donate everything from turkey, tacos, cheese sandwiches, mashed potatoes, miso soup, green beans, and refried beans to organic rice rolls and organic salad - not that the homeless were really into organic food, but everyone should live dangerously once in their life. Vivian was going to perk up gallons of Folgers coffee - Folgers being the coffee of choice for most street people - the fact being most street people don't have a coffee bean grinder on their necessary list. Also, during lunch, Jackson and The Open Doors were going to play. Right at the moment, ten volunteers were walking around town telling all the street people that Wednesday was their special day and to be at the Wake Up Or Die at noon. Most of the homeless hearing the news thought something must be wrong, as it was not Thanksgiving - Thanksgiving being the only day that people really gave a damn for them. The hell with those street people, they put themselves on the street, but since it is Thanksgiving toss them a turkey leg and some instant potatoes. Lord have mercy, Christ have mercy, pass the watered down gravy.

Vivian got a cup of coffee and sat in the corner. Pill walked in, saw Vivian and ambled over to her in only the way a Texan can amble who is wearing a sign that states - **THERE IS ONLY SIX BILLION YEARS LEFT FOR THE WORLD.**

The first thing Vivian said to Pill was, "No, you can't pitch your tent in here. I'm feeding the homeless tomorrow."

"But I am homeless," Pill said.

"I'm not serving peanut butter either," Vivian said.

"I'll help serve," Pill said, giving Vivian his 'there is only six billion years left for the earth' look, which in reality meant, would you give me a free cup of coffee before the end of the world.

"Go get yourself a cup of coffee," Vivian said.

Pill headed for Chris faster than a jackrabbit runs from a truckload of cowboys with shotguns. Vivian knew Pill would help serve - paranoid people are always caring - it's the main reason they are paranoid. Maybe it's the people who aren't paranoid that are really the scary ones. Only six billion more years and counting. Lord help us Jesus how time flies.

Vivian remembered the first time in her life she had really seen a homeless person. Being raised in a small town in Wisconsin there was no such thing as homeless. There were poor, but even the poor had a home. When Vivian went to San Francisco and saw for the first time true street people, she was appalled, but like anything else, seeing them every day the sharp edge of sorrow gets worn off. For years she didn't feel sorry for the homeless. It was not until she moved to Lost City and once again saw street people that she was overcome with their plight. Being older, she knew there was nothing that would solve the problem, but she could toss them a bone every so often, which to her big heart was a caring sorrow.

Pill took his sign off and sat by Vivian with a cup of coffee. "Thank you," he said.

"You ever been in love, Pill?" Vivian asked.

"No," Pill answered simply and decisively. "I could never understand it. People say I love you to someone. What does that mean? They say I love a cat, or a dog, or a movie, or a child, or a car, or a TV show. I just don't get it."

"Don't you want to be with women?" Vivian asked although she was in tune with the understanding thing.

"That's lust. I understand that completely," Pill grinned.

Three of Vivian's Feed the Homeless volunteers walked over. Francis, a green haired tongue-pierced college student wearing black Levi's, black high top tennis shoes, and a black T-shirt said, "Word is out all over town the dinner is for the homeless only and not vagabond hippies pulling off the old line 'I need money to feed my puppy.'"

Vivian nodded, and the three headed to wherever college students go who aren't old enough to hit the bars.

"You hungry, Pill?" Vivian asked.

Pill looked at her like it was a loaded question.

"Let's go to the house and I'll make you a peanut butter and jelly sandwich. I need to get out of here for awhile."

Pill gulped his coffee, crawled into his sign, and followed Vivian out of the shop as happy as a little kid whose mother was taking him to an ice cream shop. Peanut butter and jelly, if only life could be so simple. Would you like crunchy or smooth?

Chapter Twenty-One

Bridge worked on his novel for several hours while at the same time trying to get the dilemma of telling Vivian he loved her out of his head. It was worth the try, but the dilemma beat around in his head like a woodpecker on speed. Is love like a grub, hiding in the bark of our defenses?

Bridge had no idea where his book was going, but even in his dilemma he was enjoying writing it. "If I could take life this way I'd have it made," he said. But telling himself things during his life that he knew were rational had never panned out. Someone has to embrace poverty, he had told himself when he decided to be a writer, without artists, poverty would be a very lonely god. But he wondered at times if he should have embraced a few good paying jobs.

After working on the book, Bridge sat in the store for awhile, which was about as exciting as watching snails eat lettuce. Monday in the arts district of Lost City was always slow - unless three people are considered a crowd. Bridge decided he would go on a gallery tour. He hadn't been to any of the other galleries on Texas and Yankee Streets in a long time. He did decide he wouldn't go into MeJoe's, as he was not in the mood to be told to fuck off - Monday in itself is a fuck off. But he did remember that Me had told him he and Joe would talk over Bridge's love problem and get back with him.

Bridge two-stepped forward and one backward into the Sunbonnet gallery. Rainy Day, always looking outdoorsy, was sitting in the corner thumbing through a famous outdoor catalogue - the catalogue for those who really spend the winter in front of the fireplace. Who would go outdoors in seven-thousand-dollar shirts and three-thousand-dollar pants? Do elk, rabbits, quail, squirrels, or any other game animal really give a hoot what a person is wearing when they are blasted into the skillet or oven? Lord, even hunting is a fashion show. I killed this trophy elk wearing my double wool, stag buttoned, red hunting shirt, which I got on sale for only twenty-two thousand dollars, and I am proud to say that only the thread came from China. Now pass the elk steak and the bottle of 1952 Cab. Danielle Boone, eat your heart out - leather loving cutie that you were.

Rainy Day hugged Bridge, which reminded him that for two days Vivian hadn't asked him if he had gotten his ten hugs a day. There had been one lady tourist from Florida he wouldn't have minded hugging, but at the last moment he backed off, thinking he might have gotten an osmotic plastic overdose - plastic can be sneaky - it shows up in more things than people think and can cause blindness, acne, and male dysfunction. Females like plastic more than men do and in more cases than not they like men with male dysfunction because they know the men want them for more than their bodies.

"How's life?" Rainy Day asked Bridge.

Bridge had never understood the question, how's life? He wanted to say, "Besides war, famine, disease, world-class killing storms, racism, premature babies, slums, and the fact the world will end in six billion years everything is peachy keen," but instead he said, "Everything is fine."

Rainy Day smiled, knowing nothing is fine, but what the hell, everyone says it. "I was in the mountains over the weekend and painted one of the best sunsets I have ever done," Rainy Day beamed, walked over to the wall and took down a small painting and brought it back to show Bridge.

"Nice," Bridge said, in truth not liking the painting, but telling a painter you do not like one of their paintings is like telling your mother her meatloaf tastes like dog food. Rainy Day hung the painting back up. "How much do you want for it?" Bridge asked.

"I figure it's worth about eighteen hundred dollars," Rainy Day said.

If her painting is worth eighteen hundred dollars, Bridge

thought, my books should sell for about twelve thousand dollars each. Art is not life, it's a price war.

"Did Vivian tell you that she is feeding the homeless at the coffee shop tomorrow and that Jackson and The Open Doors are going to play?" Rainy Day asked.

"No," Bridge replied, slightly surprised.

"Lovers never really do communicate," Rainy Day said, not sadly but matter-of- factly.

"What do you mean by that?" Bridge asked, holding onto the hope that love was the epitome of communication.

"Bellies popping together have a way of getting in the way of communication," Rainy Day said with a sly smile.

Bridge wondered if that was only true for fat people. But if it was true, then a skinny couple with no bellies and protruding hip bones were in for a wordless relationship, which wasn't that bad. Talking too much always seems to get people in trouble more than keeping their big yaps shut. A man of constant sorrow has to be a big talker.

"How's your book coming?" Rainy Day asked.

Bridge wanted to say, "Books don't come, they are written or dictated but they don't come," but he said instead, "It is coming along fine," deciding that in all truth books do come, and adding, "Where it is going, I really don't know and I have no idea how I am going to end it."

Rainy Day seemed puzzled by the answer, which in all truth also puzzled Bridge. How does one write a book and not know?

"Have you been selling any paintings?" Bridge asked.

"I haven't sold a painting in six months," she said as depressed as a Cadillac salesman in a Lexus market.

"You will," Bridge said as a customer came into the store, giving him an excuse to leave. Painters who have not sold a painting in six months can sometimes talk about the injustice in life for at least three days - the fact the economy has gone in the tank, there really is no middle class left, and only the rich have any money has nothing to do with it.

Bridge then went to Gertrude's gallery. Gertrude was working at her computer. As usual she was in a good mood, not bubbly like Frauline, but good. "I know you don't want to hear it, Bridge," Gertrude said, "but I am working on a new advertising campaign for

Lost City."

"The Chamber of Commerce strikes again," Bridge said. "Is there nothing sacred in the world?"

"Of course not," Gertrude said. "After sixty years of being alive, you should know that."

"I am a pessimistic optimist," Bridge said and then asked, "What is your new campaign?"

Gertrude looked pensive for an instant then replied. "We are going to run ads in *True West Magazine* and other western publications playing up how we are part of the west."

Bridge was flabbergasted. His was the only gallery in town that carried western art, at which most of the other gallery owners were appalled - western art was not art - paintings of cowboys, Indians, horses, cattle, and beadwork was not art. A person had to be from anywhere but the west to be a real artist. Cowboys were just independent idiots who minded their own business and solved their own problems - criers in life get more sympathy. Help me, help me. It's not my fault. It's my parent's fault. They force fed me Rice Crispies and made me watch *The Walton's* and *Rin Tin Tin*. That's why I'm afraid of my shadow.

"At least you people are finally figuring out where you live," Bridge said, doing his best not to be sarcastic.

"We know where we live, Bridge," Gertrude said.

"What is your idea for advertising in redneck magazines?" Bridge asked.

"We are going to have a golfer dressed in an old west outfit swinging a golf club, and the heading will be 'Take A Shot At Lost City.' And we will list all the galleries in town."

Bridge was impressed, although he had no idea what golf had to do with art. I woke up this morning and the first thing I saw was a golf ball flying through the air. I was so delirious with life, and love, and joy, I decided to paint the entire ceiling of the Vatican, even knowing that the lead-based paint would make me go blind and I would hear voices in my head endlessly saying, "I told you to be a hairdresser."

"How many tourists do you think the ad will attract?" Bridge asked.

"Circulation for the magazines is over 400,000. If we get five percent, it will pull in at least 20,000 people, and since you write novels set in the modern west, you might sell two thousand of your books," Gertrude replied with a warm Chamber of Commerce smile.

Bridge's own books were his Achilles' heal. Bring on a small paving machine and a small tourist bus, Bridge would meet them on the edge of town and sell them his books and then make them turn around - that is, unless they wanted to buy him a Bloody Mary at the This Isn't Heaven Bar or a beer at Bill's Restaurant and Libations.

"That would be nice," Bridge said in a tone like selling his own books really did not interest him at all. He was a closet writer who only wrote for himself.

"There is something else I want to talk to you about," Gertrude said, giving Bridge her grandmother look.

Bridge normally said yes to a grandmother look, although it made him wary. "Yes, what is it?" he said, trying not to sound even remotely committed to anything.

"I have been watching you and Vivian, and I know she loves you," Gertrude said.

Bridge felt faint. He felt hot. He felt cold. He wished he was a woman, then it would have been normal. Trying not to sound like he was lying, Bridge said, "We are only good friends."

"You can't lie to granny," Gertrude smiled and shook her finger at him like he was in the second grade and if he screwed up one more time he was going to have to write on the blackboard - I, I, I, I, I, I, I, I - until he had to take a pee.

"How do you know she is in love with me?" Bridge asked.

"I know."

"But how do you know you know?"

"I know I know simply because I know."

"Oh God, Gertrude," Bridge lamented. "If only people were both sexes instead of man and woman, then we could just go through life loving ourselves."

"It is a bitch," Gertrude said, looking sad for a moment.

Bridge two-stepped forward and one backward toward Sergeant's gallery, The Beginning Of A Rainbow. He wondered if when a person really loves someone they emitted a scent that everyone in the world could smell except the one that they loved, but then he decided in Vivian's case it wouldn't make any difference, as she wore so much lavender perfume she couldn't smell it anyway.

Sergeant was writing sixteen invitations, one for each of his girlfriends, to go out to dinner. There was a take out Chinese place with a grand opening deal, and several of his ladies had been complaining about always having to eat hot dogs and only being able to afford drinks at happy hour. There really can be too much love or should be a law that from the second to sixteenth girlfriend they have to be anorexic. "How can I say I love you in sixteen different ways?" Sergeant asked.

"I can't figure out how to say I love you one time," Bridge said.

"Have you ever figured out why you wanted to open an art gallery?" Sergeant asked, looking at one of the paintings hanging on the wall like it annoyed him.

"Art brings happiness to people," Bridge replied, even surprising himself with his answer.

"You can't tell me when you opened your gallery your main desire was to bring happiness to people," Sergeant said, giving Bridge his 'I was in the military too' look.

"No. I wanted to be left alone to write."

"And sell books," Sergeant added.

"And sell books," Bridge begrudgingly conceded.

"Do you ever get tired of it?" Sergeant asked.

Bridge started to feel like he was a prisoner who was being interrogated by a guard who did not know how to say a long sentence, but he decided to answer anyway and replied, "I have to admit I enjoy it when somebody buys one of my books."

"Your armor isn't as thick as it used to be," Sergeant said with a slight smile.

"After awhile the dings get thin," Bridge replied somewhere between humor and irony.

Sergeant looked at his invitations and said more to himself than to Bridge, "I invite you to the hole in my heart. I invite you to my world of memories. I invite you to my losses. I invite you to quell my loneliness, if only for a moment, and show me warmth even though I cannot feel it. I invite you to, to, to, what, Bridge?"

"To continue," Bridge said and two-stepped forward and one backward out the door.

Bridge headed for the Love Is Only A Painting Away gallery, thinking, even war is an art and even without it life would still be hollow.

Lotus Blossom owned the Love Is Only A Painting Away

gallery. She had moved to Lost City from Washington State after gallery space rent cost more than a meal at the Space Needle and all the locals started to grow fins, develop webbed feet, and cut their marijuana with moss. She had a bumper sticker on her car that stated - RAIN FOREST LIVING IS ONLY GOOD FOR FROGS. Lotus Blossom looked like a pixie to Bridge. She wore her auburn hair short in a modified pageboy. She had a smile that would even make the head of the CIA smile and smoked non-filtered cigarettes from Mexico. She was around 5'3" and pleasing looking in a farm girl sort of way. Her skin was milky and her green eyes always merry and unguarded. Bridge had heard she had had many tragedies in her life, but they did not seem to weigh her down, and he felt she had a fragile caring heart. Her art was making masks out of gourds. Bridge figured every person on the face of the earth wore an invisible mask that even when they looked in the mirror they could not take off. Lotus Blossom's masks were intricately carved and decorated with the brightly colored tail feathers from parrots. The masks were beautiful, but there are thousands of parrots sitting in trees with a bare ass - even art is not fair. The masks ranged in size from a few inches to several feet. Her work was placed in galleries all over the west and had won many awards. She had been through several husbands, always seeming to have the ability to pick out men that only wanted to use her. She blamed it on water on the brain from living in Washington State too long. She now lived with a man named Seeds who bought high-end pottery in Mexico and sold it all over the west. He treated her like the princess she was and guarded her heart.

Lotus Blossom did not notice Bridge when he first walked in. She was sitting cross-legged on the floor intently taking the seeds out of a dried gourd, which Bridge figured was a good job for chipmunks.

The walls of Lotus Blossom's gallery were covered with her masks. Every eyehole seemed to peer directly at Bridge. It made him feel like he was standing in an African chief's hut, and the chief was pondering whether he wanted to boil Bridge in a pot with yams, or bamboo shoots, as he had wasted all his onions on a Presbyterian minister who while being boiled kept saying, "Save them, Jesus," when he should have been saying, "Save me, Jesus."

Lotus Blossom smiled at Bridge. "I heard Vivian is feeding the homeless tomorrow and you are going to recite poetry," she said, which was more news to Bridge.

"No," Bridge said. "I'm going to take a quick trip to Japan and teach them how to fry hamburgers and stop eating so much fish. I want to convince them they live too long and that heart disease is well worth a bad diet."

"Looking at your figure, you could use a change in your diet," Lotus Blossom said.

"Beer does not have any cholesterol," Bridge said defensively, wondering why women can always get away with telling men they look like hell, but men had better keep their lips still when it comes to how women look.

"Maybe it's too many olives for breakfast," Lotus Blossom said, setting her gourd down and standing.

"Gloria won't order celery," Bridge said. "She told me if I want fiber to go to the health food store."

"How's the book coming?" Lotus Blossom asked.

Two book coming questions in the last twenty minutes made Bridge's mind flip several times in his head, but instead of being a wise ass he answered, "The book is coming fine. It's the words that have me all screwed up. The buts and ands have all been easy. It's putting words with any meaning in between them that is difficult."

"You're funny," Vivian grinned.

"Thanks," he replied. "My over-inflated ego has been deflating lately and I need some down to earth encouragement."

Just then MeJoe stopped by the door. "Bridge, you fuck face," Me or Joe said. "Come out here, we have debated your question and want to talk to your stupid dumb ass."

Bridge did not know that asses could be stupid. They could be round or fat or flat, always cracked, but not stupid. Bridge smiled at Lotus Blossom and went outside. Lotus Blossom sat back down on the floor and started doing whatever a person does to a gourd to make it into a mask.

MeJoe was tapping his way toward his gallery, so Bridge figured he was supposed to follow. When Bridge went into the store MeJoe was sitting in a single chair that was placed directly in the middle of the store. There were no other chairs, which Bridge thought was inconsiderate, but inconsiderate people always held a warm spot in Bridge's heart. "Joe thinks anyone who can't tell the person they love that they love them should be castrated and forced to live in the Playboy Mansion," Me said.

"Tell Joe he is right," Bridge said, even though when he was younger he had been more into *Penthouse*. There was something about *Playboy* that was too squeaky clean - it had something to do with the airbrush.

"I didn't say that," Joe said. "Me is lying."

Me started laughing.

"There is really nothing funny about my situation," Bridge said and started two- stepping forward and one backward toward the door.

"Don't get carried away," Joe said. "I just thought the situation needed a little humor."

Bridge stopped, turned around and said, "I think at times that you are only faking that you are blind, MeJoe."

"Only the blind can truly see," MeJoe said and took off his sunglasses.

MeJoe had no eyes. His eye sockets had translucent skin covering them. "I was born with no eyes. I am not limited like the rest of you," he said and put his sunglasses back on.

"I guess there is a Thomas in all of us," Bridge said but in no way hinting at an apology for his statement.

"Me and Joe have given serious thought to your problem, Bridge, and we think you were probably hurt deeply in an earlier relationship and are afraid you will get hurt again. We think you should go see a hypnotist."

"That's a great idea," Bridge said. "Why didn't I think of that?"

"Because you are a writer who spends most of the time with your head stuck up your ass," Me said.

"Thanks MeJoe," Bridge said, truly excited - the dumb ass writer bit being true, so no offense was taken.

"Fuck off and get the fuck out of here and the next time you want advice write a letter to Dear Abby's ghost," MeJoe said.

Bridge two-stepped forward and one backward as quickly as he could toward the Wake Up Or Die. They had to have a copy of Let's Turn Lost City Into A Political Hotbed, or in short, the, LTLCIAPH, in which there would be at least twenty hypnotist ads plying their abilities, plus he had to have a talk with Vivian about reading poetry during the dinner for the homeless. Bridge did not volunteer for anything, or take kindly to being volunteered without his consent - there was something about volunteering for the infantry that had turned volunteering into a bad thing.

For mid-afternoon the Wake Up Or Die was doing a brisk business, every table was surrounded by people deep into political conversations. The majority of the people looked like they had been members of the circus but the circus train had left them behind - possibly on purpose. Bridge wondered how people could talk politics for eighteen hours a day without repeating what they had already said at least fifteen times.

Vivian was talking to Chris. Chris for some reason looked stressed out or he was having a bad tongue stud day. Bridge two-stepped forward and one backward over to them. They were in the middle of a conversation on how to arrange the tables for tomorrow's fundraiser. "Why don't you set the tables on the street? The homeless stink," Chris said like a flustered housewife who couldn't get the toilet bowl clean.

"It's not their fault they are dirty," Vivian said. "You set up the tables in the morning the way I told you to."

Chris gave Bridge a huffy look and went back around the counter. "They do stink," Bridge said to Vivian.

"Dirt is their red badge of courage," Vivian replied tartly, which made no sense to Bridge, but he thought it was a good line. He might be able to fill in the spaces between a few ands and buts in his novel with the statement.

"I understand you have been telling people I am reciting poetry tomorrow," Bridge stated flatly, about to refuse, but Vivian cut in, saying simply, "You are."

By her tone Bridge understood completely, he was. Simplicity is hard to argue with.

"How about some Dylan Thomas or Frost?" Bridge asked.

"I want you to read some of your crap," Vivian said.

Bridge didn't know there was such a thing as crap readers, but he supposed if people read tea leaves and chicken guts somewhere in this big expanse of mankind there had to be at least one crap reader. I see by your crap that your life is all messed up, but soon you will fall into a great fortune, but you will once again be broke because your new love interest is going to steal all of your money.

Bridge could see that Vivian was not in the mood for conversation or his company. Whenever she did a benefit, she put more work into it than if she was serving high tea to the Queen of

England. It's a tough decision where to put the plastic forks and knives next to the paper plate. Do they go on the left or right side? And how about the dessert spoon? Or to make it really complicated, paper or cloth napkins with or without a napkin ring. "I'll get my poetry together," he said and two-stepped forward and one backward toward the magazine rack to find a copy of the LTLCIAPH. He was lucky and got the last copy and went outside and sat at a table with four dogs tied to it. Their owners were inside verbally saving the world. The dogs paid no intention to Bridge. Bridge looked through the paper. The first page made him gag. There were photographs of homes with a picture beneath them of the realtor trying to sell the house. Words like cute, cozy, fixer upper, gracious, handsome, and wonderful dotted the page like disguised parasites. Bridge quickly turned the page as visions of going out and buying a pistol blasted through his brain. Then there were four pages of political opinions, followed by an article on global warming - after two million articles, people should be able to figure this one out, but car fumes can get in the way of solid reasoning. Then there was an article on yoga. For years Bridge thought yoga only concerned a dead funny baseball player. Then two pages of Taurus and Pisces and all the other signs made Bridge wonder if he should apply to the paper for a crap reading column. Finally, there was a complete page dedicated only to hypnotists. Bridge read each ad diligently - stop smoking, stop drinking, stop procrastinating, eat less, subdue pain anywhere in the body. How about a pain in the ass? Bridge thought. There was a dog and cat hypnotist, and to make it all even, one for birds. And finally one stating in bold letters - **ALL LOVE'S PROBLEMS SOLVED, STRICTLY CONFIDENTIAL, CALL OR COME BY.**

Bridge carefully tore out the ad and stuck it in his billfold. The four dogs looked at him like they were having organic doggy treat withdrawals. Bridge petted each one on the head and, even though it was early afternoon, two-stepped forward and one backward across the street towards Bill's. I wonder if there is a hypnotist that can make you drink more beer without gaining weight Bridge thought as he went inside.

Chapter Twenty-Two

An empty bar in the middle of the afternoon is a sad place. A gay bar might be sadder, as some say they take things more personally. The male bartender was reading *Cosmopolitan,* which, even for straight men, has better looking women than most men's magazines. Frauline was sitting at the bar watching TV. She brought Bridge a Tecate, glass and lime. "Care if I sit with you awhile?" she asked with a smile, but it was not her normal bubble, bubble, bubble smile. There was only one bubble.

"Of course," Bridge said, pouring his beer.

Bridge had never talked seriously with Frauline. People really don't talk to bar maids unless ordering booze, and food, is in all truth the sole purpose for conversation. People do talk to bartenders about everything - normally things they don't know a damn thing about, but they know the poor bartender has to listen and treat them like they are the Buddha of intelligence.

"I'm in a twixt," Frauline said.

Oh, oh, Bridge thought.

"I ate Chinese food last night and my fortune is bothering me."

Bridge knew the next thing for him to say was, "What was your fortune?" which he said.

"It said, 'Though ambition in itself is a vice, yet it is often the source of virtue.'"

Bridge wished it was a three-bubble day.

Since Bridge had not understood one word Frauline had said, to show he was not completely ignorant he said, "Would you say that again," and took a sip of beer.

"Though ambition in itself is a vice, yet it is often the source of virtue."

"So what is the problem?" Bridge asked, still stupefied.

"How are ambition and virtue related to each other?"

Bridge took another swallow of beer - still stupefied. He took another swallow - still stupefied. He took another swallow. He had to burp. "I think it means that anyone that is good, and gets rich, can spend their money doing good deeds."

Frauline smiled - one bubble. Her smile grew bigger - two bubbles. It returned to its normal contagious glow - three bubbles. Bridge smiled.

Frauline stood and a trail of bubbles followed her toward the bar. She returned in just a moment with another beer. "This one is on me for your help," she said and kissed Bridge on the cheek.

Bridge did not know what to say - a kiss and a beer. Life does have its moments of joy.

Bridge remembered a professor he had in college who told him that although in his opinion Bridge was dumber than a rock, he did have the gift for gab. When Bridge asked, "What exactly is the gift for gab?" The professor told him it was the ability for people who were ignorant to talk and have people believe their gibberish. "Is that what it takes to get tenured?" Bridge inquired, which had not been the only reason for his failing grade.

Bridge was looking at his free beer like he had just seen a smiling Virgin Mary come down from the sky and try and bless four Muslims, who, even though they were impressed, it did not stop from shooting holes in the aspiration with their M-16's set on fully automatic while screaming, "Don't take the dream of our virgins away from us."

Even the Virgin Mary can be coy and teasing.

John the Baptist would have clubbed the four men to death with the hipbone from a one-thousand-pound wild hog that had been stupid enough to run away from a Jewish settlement and move into a highly populated Christian area.

Stoops joined Bridge. "I just came from Vivian's. She told me you are reciting poetry at the dinner for the homeless tomorrow."

"I don't want to talk about it," Bridge said.

"Ignoring issues does not make them go away," Stoops said.

"At least it prolongs the agony," Bridge said.

Frauline bubbled over with a Budweiser for Stoops. Pill came in and sat at the table without bothering to take his **THERE IS ONLY SIX BILLION YEARS LEFT FOR THE WORLD** sign off. Pill looked like he had just seen a ghost to which he owed money to. "What wrong, Pill?" Stoops asked.

Seemingly out of breath. Pill wheezed, "I just talked to a girl who informed me there is only five billion years left for the world."

Stoops sipped his beer. Bridge sipped his beer. Pill started deep breathing to try and stop from passing out. "I think she is wrong," Stoops said.

"Do you really think so?" Pill pleaded. His eyes looked like the eyes of a wild horse that knew he was headed for an Alpo can.

"I know she is wrong," Bridge said.

Pill stood, ran outside, and started screaming at the top of his lungs, "Six billion years and counting, six billion years and counting, we have an extra billion more years to get it right."

The one hundred dogs tied in front of the Wake Up Or Die started howling in relief even though their owners were still paranoid.

For a few moments Bridge and Stoops did not know what to say. Finally Bridge couldn't take the twenty seconds of silence and said, "I'm going to go see a hypnotist."

"You're already hypnotized," Stoops said.

"MeJoe told me a hypnotist might be able to put me in a trance and when I woke up I could tell Vivian I love her," Bridge said.

"What if the hypnotist makes a mistake and you start telling everyone you love them?" Stoops asked - there is always a pessimist in the crowd.

"I'd try and be a hippie again," Bridge said. "Only I'd be into safe sex and have my own bong."

"You could bring tie-dyed T-shirts back, bell bottom pants, and Made in China peace symbols," Stoops said earnestly - some people are always looking for the angle.

"We could open a small store and sell them by the thousands when the cruise ships start stopping outside of town," Bridge said sarcastically.

"Plastic and I got over the cruise ship thing," Stoops said, sounding a little despondent.

"All great minds fail at one time or another," Bridge said.

"I wonder how much the hypnotist will charge," Stoops mused. After twelve years in jail he never stayed depressed for long.

"If we were in Africa, it would be a few chickens. If we were in Tahiti, it would be a goat. If we were in Jamaica, it would be a few joints. But since we are in Lost City, it will probably cost me two crystal rocks and about fifty bucks. The crystals to counteract the evil aura of money," Bridge said.

"It might work," Stoops said, "but I have heard that a person cannot be hypnotized if they don't want to be, and it is possible that even though you want to be hypnotized, deep down in your subconscious you might not really want to be hypnotized, so the hypnotist won't be able to hypnotize you. In which case it would be cheaper, at least two crystal rocks and fifty bucks cheaper, to just get off your lazy ass and tell Vivian you love her. Jesus Christ, Bridge, you can really make simple things complicated."

"Would you say what you just said one more time," Bridge said, having not been able to keep up with all of Stoops' hypnotizes.

"Tell her you love her," Stoops said.

"That's what I thought you said," Bridge said.

Then they smiled at each other, clinked their glasses together, and drank deeply.

Beer - without it there would be no reason in the world.

Frauline bubbled over with two more beers. "Frauline, if you were in love, would you have any trouble telling the person you loved that you loved them?" Stoops asked her.

"They would have to tell me first," Frauline smiled and bubbled away.

"Thanks Stoops," Bridge said. "You are a lot of help."

"No problem," Stoops answered just as the Professor walked in looking like he had been camping for six days and had forgotten to take a tent, sleeping bag, shaving gear, or matches, and to top it off, he had been kidnapped by two Martians who were looking for a good pot connection and only let him go when he told them to go to British Colombia.

Seeing him, Frauline half ran to the bar and had his beer sitting on the table even before he had finished sitting. Before drinking, the Professor rubbed the cold bottle across his red and feverish-looking forehead. He then chugged the beer, mumbling when he was done, "more, more, more," like he was a drunk rock singer who had finally figured out the reason the band was so loud was because he couldn't sing.

Frauline darted off and was back faster than the little engine that could with two more beers and left as quickly as she had come. Desperation, anger, frustration, any mental condition besides smiles Frauline avoided like hippies avoid working anywhere except an organic food co-op or a head shop.

"Been having a good day?" Stoops asked the Professor.

No response except the sound of beer being swallowed.

"Did the Rock Lady pour sand in your brain?" Bridge asked.

"Glug, glug, glug."

"It's nice when a man can take two ten thousand years worth of words and simplify the language to only one sound," Bridge said. "It would make it very easy to write a novel."

"Screenplays would be a snap," Stoops said.

"I need help," the Professor stated in desperation like a man who was about to be shot by a firing squad and had figured out in all truth he was scared to death - the death part not going to be much of a problem soon, nor, for that matter, the scared.

"My consultation hours are from four until midnight," Stoops said.

"It is four," the Professor said.

"Pour out your problems, unburden your soul, cleanse your heart, and buy me and my assistant a beer," Stoops said.

"My assistant and me," Bridge corrected.

"Last night I had a soul-searing experience that for the first time in my life has left me wondering what my life is all about," the Professor said.

"Two beers first," Stoops said.

The Professor waved at Frauline in the circular motion that in any bar in the world means, 'bring a round' - communication can really be easy. All the leaders of the world should just get together, wave their arms around in circular motions and then get drunk. It would solve a lot of political problems, but the radical Christians and the Muslims would get angry, but what the hell, they could have their own war while the rest of us partied ourselves to death.

Frauline delivered the beers, gave the Professor a worried look, and was about to say something but decided against it.

"Now you may continue, old troubled one," Stoops said to the

Professor.

"Last night I took the Rock Lady out into the desert to search for the rock of all rocks," the Professor said. "And suddenly she ran off into the darkness screaming, 'I see you rock of rocks. I see you.'"

"How big was this rock of all rocks?" Bridge asked.

"I didn't see any rock," the Professor answered. "But when I caught up with the Rock Lady she was down on her knees praying in some gibberish I had never heard and then she suddenly stood and ran off into the desert again. I looked for her all night and all this morning, but I couldn't find a trace of her."

"That's one way to end a love affair," Stoops said.

"I never slept with her," the Professor said.

"What kind of love affair is that?" Stoops asked, looking perplexed.

"Safe," Bridge said.

"Now my main problem is do I call the cops?" the Professor said. "Do I call search and rescue? Or do I let her wander around in the desert for forty days and forty nights looking for a rock that only she can see?"

All three of them drank some beer and thought, forty days and forty nights, hum, that is a good one. "I think she will show up," Bridge finally said. "I don't think it would be proper to stop her on her spiritual quest."

"For all we know," Stoops said, "there are invisible rocks all over the world that live in another dimension, and they are in truth our salvation, and the Rock Lady will come back with the answer to life for all of mankind."

"Sounds good to me," the Professor said cheerfully. But even though cheerful, Bridge sensed that the Professor was truly concerned over the Rock Lady.

The Professor finished his beer, stood and headed for the door, saying over his shoulder, "I'm going to go home and clean up. Thanks guys."

It was only as the door swung shut Stoops figured out the Professor hadn't paid his tab. "He didn't pay for our beers," he stammered.

"You charge too much anyway," Bridge said, tossed a few bucks on the table and two-stepped forward and one backward toward the door and the security of his gallery. He had his own quest to follow.

He had to find a poem to read to the homeless, who, he figured, did not give a damn about poetry and were more into gravy and potatoes.

Chapter Twenty-Three

Just as Bridge unlocked the door to the Why Am I Here the sun went behind a cloud and all the stores on Texas and Yankee Streets were bathed in a tarnished gold. For some reason, the stores reminded Bridge of the whore section of Amsterdam where the girls of the night sat by windows displaying their charms. See my breasts. Don't I have nice legs? By the minute, by the hour, young and old come to me and in me. I will only bring you emptiness. An emptiness that is not as empty as I am. Five bucks, ten bucks, all races welcome. Am I the used or the user? Am I the prayer or the altar? Flesh to flesh. My trade is your sin.

Bridge went inside. The slumber of dreams, he thought, looking at the art. The dreams of all the ages of man starting with the first etchings on cave walls. What makes a person want to express themselves beyond the boundaries of life?

Bridge two-stepped forward and one backward to the locker that held his manuscripts - his thousands of typed and scrawled words living Bridge's illusions tucked away in boxes. If there is no mystery left, then what is there Bridge questioned? Maybe the Rock Lady knows the secret. Believe in what nobody else can see. Manifest your own God, call Him Frank if you want. At least then there is a mystery. Frank, Frank, where are you? I am a believer, but please don't make me sacrifice my oldest son, and don't make me pray sixteen times a day and have my women wear shawls.

Bridge dug out the box that contained all of his poetry and went into the living room, den, and bedroom. He started reading. What gibberish. What audacity. Was my mind still filled with hopes? Was I at one time that nice? Where did the dreams go? Are they still alive, even though I no longer search for them? Are they covered with paving machines, ad campaigns, land developments, coffeehouses? Be snide, be sarcastic, hide your feelings. And love, where are you but lost in I, I, I, I, I, I, Lo, Lo, Lo. Could I say me love you, Vivian? Me love you more than anything else in the world. Do no harm that is hateful. I, I, I, I, I. Me, me, me, me, me. Homogenize the planet. Ambition and virtue. Six billion years and who really cares. Throw the homeless a turkey leg and let's go have a beer.

Bridge read about half of his poetry. Each poem was a memory. He felt his poetry was crap. Over forty years of crap - the crap changing from year to year. Every new thought only living long enough to be another thought. But art was not science. Art had no facts, no boundaries, no limits. Art schools and writing schools are bunk. How does one teach feelings? Technique is science. Art is? Art is? Art is? Art is what? Art is the blank canvas - the blank page - the uncut marble - a pile of unstrung beads - a sand castle that will soon be washed away.

Bridge turned on his quill and inkwell, watched it buzz to life, the little icons of red and blue and gold letting the electric blood give them substance.

Bridge started to type. His fingers typed words, but his mind went in its own direction. Why do we shun our poor like poverty is a disease?

When he was done typing he reread the work several times and decided not to make any changes. He turned off his quill and inkwell and two-stepped forward and one backward outside. It was dark. He locked the door to the Why Am I Here and headed slowly to Vivian's. As he walked, the dark seemed as thick as ink and settled into his bones. The stars did not twinkle like they did in nursery rhymes, but hung listlessly in the sky like they were tired of being marveled at.

When Vivian answered the door she was listening to an old Joan Baez album. Joan was singing something about diamonds and rust. Vivian let Bridge in without saying hello, or good to see you, or what's up? Bridge two-stepped forward and one backward into the house. He did not say a word for a few moments. Then, looking directly into Vivian's eyes, he said quietly, "I need a hug. I think I am a little short on my ten hugs a day."

Vivian did not grab him in a bear hug. Her blue eyes smiled their childlike smile as she put her big arms around him gently and pulled him into her warmth. Bridge stood with his arms by his sides, rested his head against her shoulder, and silently sighed. He shut his eyes and said to himself, "True art is a hug."

Chapter Twenty-Four

By eleven o'clock in the morning the homeless were lined up from the front door to the Wake Up Or Die to around the corner. It was a great tribute to a depression soup line, but the poor have never truly been out of the depression. The homeless were eerily quiet. Their faces were a mixture of need, anticipation, and disbelief. No customers were allowed in the shop, and all the tables had white paper tablecloths on them, a stack of blue paper napkins, plastic knives and forks, paper bowls and plates, and disposable salt and pepper shakers. Chris was flustered like a gay man should be and was running around like a roadrunner with a lizard stuck in its throat. Vivian was staunch as a drill sergeant and had the servers in the corner with orders not to wander off. All that was wanting was the food. Pill was by her side and had been persuaded to serve the food without wearing his sign. Jackson and The Open Doors were setting up in the corner. "If those people that said they would bring the food don't show up, they'll think pissed off old hippie chick," Vivian said to Pill.

Pill was smart enough to neither reply in a positive or negative way. Impatient old hippie chicks that soon might be angry are good to stay neutral with.

As if on command, the food started arriving. Huge pots of miso soup. Platters of turkey, all cut off the bone. A pot of mashed potatoes that would have made an army cook envious. Brown gravy that was so thick it could almost be spread like jam. Six trays of grilled cheese sandwiches on whole wheat bread. Enough tacos to feed every soccer team in South America. There were cute relish plates with pickles, radishes, celery, cut carrots, and those little pickled beets that nobody eats. There were organic salads already dished into paper bowls. There were sixteen apple pies and enough Folgers coffee no homeless person would sleep for at least three days. Vivian also had take home containers if there was any food left. Take home containers to the homeless are called take to the bench or under the bridge containers.

Vivian pointed at Jackson and The Open Doors, got the servers in place and went outside. She looked at the line of hungry men and women. She was radiant. Her smile was so big her eyes crinkled. Her dress was a swirl of red, blue, green, and orange like it had been in a mixing bowl full of colors. Her blue eyes were bluer than the sky. She had on red lipstick that was so bright people almost had to wear sunglasses. Her hair was braided perfectly. She had polished her silver rings, and they caught the sunlight like diamonds. She was radiant but inside she was sad. Her heart felt like it was lead - all the hungry people, all the mission clothes and unshaved faces. The pleading eyes were trying to be proud, proud of what they did not know, but proud. The lost teeth and taped together glasses were merit badges. The mismatched clothes tattered quilts of hope. The men and women reminded Vivian of mutt stray dogs - dogs with fleas and ticks and sores all over their bodies. Give me some food and a pat and I will be off. I know I am not worthy. How can I beg but still say please? My hunger is stronger than my need for salvation.

"Ladies and gentlemen," Vivian's strong voice cut through the air with no tinge of sadness or mocking, "there will be no pushing or shoving. What you put on your plate you will eat. There is food enough for everybody. After you are done, your dessert will be served. I hope you enjoy."

She wanted to say, "Go with God." But where was God? A lost life and poverty should not be the key to heaven. Sleeping beneath a bridge or bench should not be an altar. Lord have mercy. Christ have mercy. Feed me.

She then curtsied to the first man and the line started to move. As the first man neared the table, Jackson and The Open Doors started to play "Hotel California." The smell of the food wafted through the room and mixed with the odor of unwashed bodies, but it was good - good and simple - odors of earth's dirt. The people did not talk or shout. Some gobbled their food, others ate slowly. Vivian walked through the room pointing for servers to refill coffee cups that were half full and asking people if they wanted more food. When the people were done eating, they sat in a numbed silence - a silence of full stomachs - and as Vivian walked by them they smiled - smiles of gratitude and thanks. Vivian touched shoulders and patted heads and kissed the women on their cheeks. Bridge had come in unnoticed and stood in the corner watching Vivian. She was Cleopatra with no army. She was a saint with no religion. She was a rainbow that would never fade, even in death its memory would shine. Bridge's heart was so full watching her he felt like he wanted to cry. Not sad tears, but tiny splatters of hope and justice and goodwill. Me love you, Vivian, Bridge thought. Me love you very, very much. And Bridge smiled, but then he was sad - sad for all the lost, thinking to himself, each of us in our own way is lost.

Barbara, Jackson's wife, who wrote for the Let's Turn Lost City Into A Political Hotbed or LTLCIAPH, walked up to Bridge. She had a notepad, as she had been assigned to write an article on Vivian's good works. "Hey Bridge," she said. "I understand that the Rock Lady has disappeared into the wilderness."

"She's on a quest to find the true meaning of a conglomerate," Bridge said.

"If she ever comes back, I still want to do an article on her even though I haven't been able to find a talking rock," Barbara said.

"You should talk to the Professor. He had a near death experience with an invisible rock," Bridge said.

"I bet he took the Rock Lady out into the desert to look at the stars when in all truth he was taking her out to the desert to try and fondle her stars," Barbara said.

"Have you been to the desert before?" Bridge smiled.

"Have you told Vivian you love her yet?" Barbara countered.

Bridge shook his head.

"I might need some article space soon. You'd better get off of your snide and sarcastic ass and tell her," Barbara threatened with a sly smile.

"My mouth is snide and sarcastic, but not my ass," Bridge said, trying not to show that her threat was taken seriously.

"Remember what I told you," Barbara said and walked off to

talk to Vivian and some of the homeless people.

The servers were serving the apple pie. Jackson and The Open Doors finished off by playing, "When The Saints Go Marching In," which sounded strange to Bridge - a lead and bass guitar accompanied by a bongo did not really do the song justice.

Vivian went up to the microphone. "And now, ladies and gentlemen," she said, "we have a special treat for you. Bridge McCoy, our resident writer, is going to read one of his poems."

There was a smattering of applause, much like a losing baseball team gets from its ten remaining fans. Bridge two-stepped forward and one backward to the microphone. He scanned the room. Most of the people were intently eating their pie, but several looked at him. Poetry and pie seemed a little weird to Bridge. It should have been poetry and heroin, or poetry and cheap red wine, plus there was no clove cigarette smoke in the air or ladies dressed in black smoking cigars and wishing they did not have breasts. This entertainment thing is a bitch, Bridge thought as he took a folded up sheet of typing paper out of his back pocket.

"How was the food?" Bridge asked - everyone needs an opening line or crowd pleaser. A joke seemed inappropriate.

"Good," echoed through the room like a platoon of new recruits screaming back in unison to their drill sergeant, the recruits knowing if they did not scream at the top of their lungs they would have to drop and do push-ups until the Arabs took Jerusalem again.

"Everyone give Vivian a warm round of applause."

Everyone clapped, and clapped, and clapped. Bridge raised his arms for silence in a lousy impression of Richard Nixon.

Bridge cleared his throat and looked at his poem. He looked at the people. He cleared his throat. He looked at the people. He cleared his throat.

"Read the friggin' poem," Vivian ordered from the back of the room.

The crowd chuckled - homeless people understand 'friggin'.

Bridge cleared his throat one more time and began:

"We are all in our own way homeless
lost in this race against time
judged by people above and below us
like we are only bit players in a nursery rhyme

but who is to say who is right or wrong
or that it all really matters
some people end up being strong
while others only dance for the mad hatters
we are all members of the human race
a fact many can't remember
so please don't embrace disgrace
continue to endeavor."

Bridge folded the typing paper up and put it in his back pocket and added, "The best." He then two-stepped forward and one backward toward the door feeling like he was walking in a large black cloud, tomorrow the homeless would be hungry again, more picked up cigarette butts, and tonight they would be huddled under a bridge or sleeping on a bench and dreaming about miso soup, and turkey, and gravy as thick as jam, and tacos so good the grease ran out of them in rivers. The poor bastards had even eaten all the red pickled beets on the relish trays.

As Bridge neared the door Vivian started to applaud. It was a sad gracious applaud. Not a 'we won' applaud. The people stood and they all applauded. Bridge turned slowly and took a bow. The black cloud grew dimmer but was still gray. He waved, smiled thinly at Vivian, and two-stepped forward and one backward toward his gallery.

Barbara hurried after him. "Bridge, I want a copy of your poem for my article for the Let's Turn Lost City Into A Political Hot Bed."

Bridge did not stop walking and simply said, "No, leave me alone."

He went into the Why Am I Here and locked the door behind him. He two- stepped forward and one backward to his living room, den, and bedroom, sat and stared into the dark computer screen. Memories made manifest appeared on the screen.

The faces of Vietnamese children scraping the creases in garbage cans with their fingers and shoving the grease into their mouths. Young bodies with exposed ribs like wrecked sailing ships and eyes so old they were already beyond death. Fifteen-year-old whores who should have been playing with Barbie dolls but instead played with dicks. Old men and women with no teeth and rickets so bad their knees and elbows looked like broken U-joints. Begging pleading hands covered the screen. Food, not God, should be our salvation, Bridge thought. The host should be a pork chop. All faiths pray for food and not the selfish desire for one's life after death. Hunger is death.

Bridge turned on the computer. The lit screen erased the hands and the U-joints and the whores, sent them back to distant corners of his mind. How do we do no harm that is hateful? Bridge asked himself. Six billion years is a long time to wait for equality.

Bridge scrolled to where he was working on his book, scrolled back several pages and then muttered, "Words, take from me my sorrows. Erase the condition of the earth. Fulfill me with fiction and made-up happy endings. You are my opium, and heroin, and pot, and booze."

But this night it did not work, and tears formed in the corners of his eyes. Tears that were not hungry but could feel hunger. Bridge leaned back in his chair and shut his eyes. Silent tears rolled down his cheeks. "Me love you, Vivian," he whispered. "You are my saint of the rainbows."

Chapter Twenty-Five

Vivian, Chris and Pill were sitting by the window of the Wake Up Or Die drinking coffee. The homeless were gone, clutching their take to the bench or under the bridge containers like bags of gold.

The Wake Up Or Die was once again in business. Philosophy and politics sprouted from the crowded tables like dandelions. "I didn't know Bridge was a poet," Pill said.

"He is deeper than people think he is," Chris said.

"He wears his skin like iron," Vivian said. "Most of the time I have no idea what he is thinking or if he is thinking at all."

"Amoebas have it made," Pill said. "They float around in dirty water and when they want to have sex they just split in two."

"What does that have to do with skin like iron or thinking?" Vivian asked.

"Maybe Bridge wants to be an amoeba?" Chris said.

"We are all amoebas," Vivian said half disgusted, stood and headed for her private room.

"Wonder what got into her?" Chris asked Pill.

"I don't think she likes amoebas," Pill said and was suddenly hit by a paranoid attack. He grabbed his sign, ran from the coffee shop to his truck, and headed for the mountains and the safety of peanut butter and crackers.

Chris cleared the table and went back to the counter. He hated to admit it, but he had liked Bridge's poem. It was not the best poem in the world, and could have been longer, but it was a good poem even though Chris was not into the rhyming stuff. What terrible sins mankind creates, Chris thought as two ladies walked up to the counter who were going to spend enough money on two frothy coffees to feed four hungry people - there for the grace of whatever you believe in go you and I.

Vivian sat in her private room. Light coming through the window made the red, blue, green, yellow, orange, and purple fairies dance. She felt mentally tired. What was life but a mental toilet? Who could make any sense of it? But on the other hand, who would want to? Vivian did not even feel like smoking any pot. What she felt like was going dancing and drinking too much tequila. It was Tuesday, and Tuesday night The Hole had open mike night. Most of the time it was folk singers that were hard to dance to, but one never knew. Vivian took a deep breath, and went back to the real world. Wake Up Or Die, you sons and daughters of man. We have abandoned our poor and our homeless. The earth is smothering in our waste. Bring on another Rolls Royce and a football stadium.

Vivian was headed for the counter when a lady ran into the coffee shop hollering frantically at the top of her lungs, "I have talked to the rock of rocks. The rock of rocks has embraced me."

The lady stopped in the middle of the store. Her hair was jostled like she had been in a wind tunnel for three weeks. Her eyes were bug-eyed and filled with whatever zealots' eyes are filled with - normally stupidity. Her clothes were covered with dirt, and in each hand she held a brown rock the size of a hardball. Vivian hurried over to the lady, put her arm around her shoulders, pulled her over to a corner table and pushed her into a chair. "I think you need a cup of decaf," Vivian said.

"That would be nice," the lady replied calmly, her eyes receding back into her head and losing the zealot's look. "I've been in the desert for two days and have been craving a cup of coffee. But please, real coffee, not decaf."

"You can do me a favor first. Put the rocks down on the table."

The lady set the rocks down gently like they were the last two chicken eggs in the world.

Chris, having heard the conversation, hurried over with a cup of real coffee.

Vivian sat. "I take it you are the Rock Lady that has been going out with the Professor."

The lady was staring at the cup of coffee like it, and not rocks, was the light. She breathed deep the steam rising off of the coffee. She shut her eyes and placed her hands together and muttered, "Thank you, rock, for all that you have given me." She then picked up the cup with both hands and sipped the coffee, looked at Vivian, smiled, and said, "That's the best coffee I have ever tasted in my life."

The Professor ran into the coffee shop looking like he had not slept in two days. He looked around the room frantically, saw Vivian and the Rock Lady, and ran over to the table, at which time the Rock Lady jumped up and they embraced. "I have been so worried," the Professor said.

"I have talked to the rock of rocks," the Rock Lady proclaimed.

Vivian motioned for Chris to bring the Professor a cup of coffee and made her exit unnoticed. Rocks were not really on her agenda, and she had her own love thing to figure out.

Chris delivered the coffee and Vivian headed for the Why Am I Here thinking how at one time in her life she had believed that crystals had healing powers. Now she understood the only healing powers crystals have are the healing powers of money for the people who sell the shiny little things. Rocks, crosses, weird little creatures with sixteen arms, monkeys, cows, feathers - what will mankind believe in next? Astarte, come back, we need you, or Thor or Zeus. Frank, it's your turn if you don't lose the commandments like Moses and Smith.

Vivian beat on the door to the Why Am I Here. Bridge had spent the last hour reading and rereading three chapters of his novel, which was about as exciting as eating dirt. The knocking knocked him out of his funk, and he headed for the door. Seeing Vivian's face peering in the window, he smiled.

"It's hard to sell paintings or your novels if you are not open," was the first thing Vivian said, which, being true, Bridge really had no comment. So instead he said, "You were wonderful during the meal for the homeless."

"I need a hug," Vivian said.

Bridge hugged her for a few moments, receiving more from the hug than Vivian. "Your poem was very heartfelt," Vivian said, feeling refreshed after the hug, but Bridge could tell she really had not liked the poem.

Truth be known, he didn't really like it either, but who was he? He only wrote it. Writers anyway - they always think they know more than most people, but when it all comes down to it they are only copiers of life. Bring on some more toner, my copy machine brain is running out of ink.

Vivian said, "Let's go to The Hole tonight, I feel like dancing."

"They normally only have folk singers on Tuesday," Bridge said, which Vivian had already thought about, but life is redundant most of the time anyway so she didn't make a snide comment.

"I'll smoke some pot and float around like an overweight butterfly," Vivian said, spun around in a slow circle then headed for the door, saying over her shoulder, "I'll pick you up around six."

Pick you up, what a strange statement. Bridge wondered if Vivian was coming to get him with a crane or carry him in her arms all the way to Woodsmoke.

Bridge turned off his quill and inkwell and headed for Bill's Restaurant and Libations. The Professor and the Rock Lady were sitting at a table holding hands with two brown rocks sitting on the table between them. Bridge supposed rocks were a cheaper gift than flowers, plus they didn't need water. The Professor and the Rock Lady were looking into each other's eyes so intently they reminded Bridge of two high school students who had mistaken lust for love. Oh baby, I lust you so much. I want to lust you for the rest of my life. Bridge did think something was really weird as they were drinking iced tea. To Bridge drinking iced tea in a bar was a mortal sin. Have people no respect?

Many of the other tables were full with what seemed to Bridge people from California. Why they seemed to be from California Bridge didn't really know, but one guess is as good as another. Stoops was sitting at the bar drinking a beer and intently reading whiskey bottle labels. Bridge sat next to him. "It's interesting," Stoops said. "There is single malt whiskey, double malt whiskey, bourbon, blended scotch whiskey, and according to their labels they are all smooth, rich, delicious or satisfying. But there is not one whiskey that informs a person, 'Hey drinker; this stuff will knock your socks off.' I think we should bring a class action suit against all the whiskey makers for false advertising."

"How about we blend our own whiskey and call it Pie Faced," Bridge said.

"I bet it would make more money than your books," Stoops said.

Frauline came up behind them. "You're not sitting at a table," she said with a slight frown on her bubbly face. "I can't wait on you."

"Inconsiderate jerk," Bridge said to Stoops.

"I'll go along with that," Frauline said.

Stoops and Bridge went as quickly as they could to a table, not wanting to pop any bubbles. Frauline brought Bridge a Tecate and lime and a glass. "You two are so nice to me," she smiled and left.

"I'd like to nice nice her once," Stoops said.

"Be nice," Bridge said.

Berry walked in like only a man who has had a stroke can. He sat at the table. "Good seeing you, Berry," Stoops said.

"What's good about it?" Berry replied. "I'm old, I'm half crippled, I haven't been laid in four years, and to top it off the doctor put me on four more heart pills."

"I'm glad your life is all screwed up, Berry," Stoops said.

"That's better." Berry smiled his, 'I just gave you an F, you stupid jerk' smile.

Frauline bubbled over. "What would you like, Berry?" she asked.

"I'd like to be thirty years old again, but I'll take a rum and coke," Berry said.

"You can order a rum and coke, but you can't take one," Bridge said.

"I've read your books, so don't give me this proper English bullshit," Berry said.

"I stand corrected," Bridge agreed.

Berry got his rum and coke. "I heard the Rock Lady talked to the big rock," he said, looking at the Professor and the Rock Lady.

"According to the rumors, the Rock Lady more than talked to the big rock, the big rock took her inside of him and filled her with stones of wisdom and told her to go forth and multiply," Stoops said.

"I'd like to multiply her rocks," Berry said.

"I think the Professor is working very hard at it," Stoops said.

"I think you two should take a trip to Mexico and visit a whorehouse," Bridge said.

"I'd fall in love and couldn't be miserable all the time," Berry said.

"I can't afford it," Stoops said, "plus I'm still not over Organic

Muffin dumping me after thinking I was a reincarnated warrior chief."

"Has anyone heard what she is doing?" Bridge asked.

"I heard she moved to El Paso and is working at a topless joint," Berry said.

Stoops nodded his head and couldn't look at Berry or Bridge. Bridge figured Stoops' feelings were hurt because Organic Muffin was now showing her boobs to the world and he had never seen them. Some reincarnated warriors just don't have the right stuff.

"Did you hear about the land deal that is in the works south of town?" Berry said. Bridge's ears perked up like he was Mr. Spock.

"No," Stoops said.

"I guess a group out of California is buying four thousand acres and they are going to build a gated community along with two golf courses," Berry said.

Bridge started to hyperventilate and sounded like a pig giving birth.

Berry and Stoops ignored him, both thinking his impression of a sow needed some work.

"Whe-whe-where are they going to get the water?" Bridge stammered.

"The mine owns all the water rights in that area and they are working out a deal," Berry said.

"I hope it is full of mercury," Bridge said, having completely regained his breath.

"When the development starts we could form a secret society and sabotage the site," Berry said.

"How many members would it take?" Stoops asked.

"At least ten," Berry replied.

"Then it's no secret," Bridge said, adding, "If you want to join a secret society, become a Shriner, then at least you can wear funny little hats and drive go carts."

Sergeant walked over to the table with a smile on his face that was so big it even made his forehead wrinkle.

"Did all of your girlfriends leave you and for the first time in several years you have some money?" Stoops asked.

"No, I sold a painting." Sergeant's grin grew bigger.

A gallery selling a painting in Lost City was so rare it normally put people in shock.

After a few moments of stunned silence, Stoops called to Frauline. "Bring us a round on Sergeant, he sold a painting."

Hearing Stoops, the Rock Lady jumped up, looked at Sergeant, raised her arms to the ceiling and chanted, "Thanks be to the rock of rocks, prosperity will flow to all who believe, bow down ten times and say in thanks, not dust to dust but gravel to gravel."

Sergeant, not really into any ideologies besides naked women, tried his best to smile at the Rock Lady and show his appreciation.

The Professor chanted several times, "gravel to gravel, gravel to gravel."

The Rock Lady sat back down and they held hands again.

Frauline brought the round and a Jamison and Guinness for Sergeant. "To art and money," the men toasted.

"If they do build a gated community, think of all the art the new homeowners will buy," Berry said.

"They might even buy one or two of your books," Stoops said.

Bridge didn't say anything, instead wondering why in life everything had to have two sides. A one-sided life would be so much easier. But then he decided if life was one- sided people would have their face and their ass on the same side. Which would be novel, as people could watch themselves shit and not have to turn around to look in the toilet bowl to see if there was enough fiber in their diet.

Six of Sergeant's beauties came in and Sergeant almost ran from the table. "There goes his profit," Berry said.

"I wish I could waste my money on women," Stoops said.

"You have to have money first," Bridge said.

"Loan me about ten grand," Stoops countered.

Berry finished his beer and without saying goodbye, adios, or you two are boring, headed for the door.

"Have fun taking your pills," Stoops called to him.

"Thanks," Berry replied.

Bridge watched him walk away as only the way a man that has had a stroke can. "I've said this before, but I always feel Berry is going to kill himself," he said to Stoops.

Stoops was silent for a moment, nodded his head in agreement, but then said, "Have you set up an appointment with a hypnotist yet?"

"I forgot," Bridge confessed. "I got lost in my novel."

"I forgot my name for a week once," Stoops said. "I have

forgotten one of my wife's names. I have forgotten what day it is. In fact, I lost a whole year once. I have lost my car keys. I have lost my ass. But when it comes to love, I think you should remember."

Bridge did not really like to be lectured to, but Stoops was right. "I'll call first thing in the morning," Bridge said.

Just then, there was a big commotion. The Rock Lady stood, screamed at the Professor, "You are not a true believer," and slammed him on top of his head with one of the rocks.

The Professor hit the floor like he had been run over by a cement truck. The Rock Lady grabbed the other rock and ran out the door. The gay bartender started jumping up and down like he had to pee. Frauline ran behind the bar to get a wet towel. The other people in the bar, whether they were from California or not, did not want to get involved. Stoops darted over to the stone cold out Professor and knelt down beside him. Since he did not know CPR or any of that other helpful stuff, he just looked at the Professor. Bridge two-stepped forward and one backward as quickly as he could. When he got there, the Professor was moaning something like, "gaag, hoog, ugg," and there was a huge welt on the top of his head that somehow, maybe by intervention from the rock god, was not bleeding.

Frauline handed him a wet towel to hold on his head.

"Love has a funny way of hurting sometimes," Stoops told the Professor as he helped him back into his chair. Bridge two-stepped back to the table and brought Stoops and his beers over to the Professor's table.

"Now you know how Goliath felt," Bridge said, sitting and looking at the two glasses of iced tea in disgust.

"At least she did not cut off my head," the Professor moaned.

The three gay men who owned Bill's Restaurant and Libations glided over to the table. Bobby, normally the spokesman, tapped his foot several times and then said to the Professor, "Your girlfriend can't bring rocks in here anymore. If she wants to slam you with a glass, that's ok, but rocks are definitely out."

Jeremy and Colette nodded their heads solemnly. "I don't think she is my girlfriend," the Professor groaned.

The three men left. The people either from or not from California went back to talking about whatever people on vacation from California normally talk about. They were probably discussing the disgusting lack of crime and wondering why the sky was blue, the air clear and not pea soup green, and why, for some reason, nobody wanted to buy their overpriced houses anymore.

Frauline bubbled over to the table. "Would you take this iced tea away and bring me two Budweisers," the Professor asked in the way only a man who has been slammed on top of the head with a rock can.

"Iced tea is for sissies," Frauline said, picking up the two glasses like they were urine samples and then bubbling away.

"I think the next girl you fall for should think that feathers are the way to truth and eternal life," Stoops said to the Professor.

Bridge thought of a weird question and asked, "Why do people think they have to go to the top of a mountain to see God?"

"Because you can't go to the bottom of the ocean, you'd drown," Stoops said.

"Good answer," Bridge said.

Frauline brought the Professor's beers. The Professor chugged one, sighed, tenderly touched the knot on his head and then started to laugh. It was not a funny laugh, but more of a laugh at the absurdity of life. Fill our insane asylums with laughing screwed-up people. Elect more politicians to laugh at. Global warming, oil, no water, and a shortage of food are really funny, or how about atomic and hydrogen bombs? Now there is a belly roll for you.

With nothing else to do, Bridge started to laugh. Stoops, not wanting to be left out, started to laugh. The Professor laughed harder. Bridge and Stoops laughed harder. Frauline started to giggle. The gay bartender started to giggle. The people from or not from California, even if they didn't want to, started to chuckle. Soon everyone in the place was laughing. Even the owners were laughing, even though they were trying to figure out why straight people were so weird.

Laughter rolled out onto the street, and people passing by looked in and started to laugh. The dogs tied to tables at the Wake Up Or Die started to howl, which in its own way is laughing. The people inside the Wake Up Or Die came outside to see why their dogs were making so much noise, but filled with politics and philosophy, they couldn't laugh - politics and philosophy are never funny.

In the middle of a laugh, Bridge was suddenly filled with a mind full of I, I, I, I, I, Lo, Lo, Lo. He stopped laughing, looked around like he was the piece of the puzzle that no one could find, stood and two-stepped forward and one backward out the door and toward the Why Am I Here.

Chapter Twenty-Six

It was not until Bridge was back at his gallery that he remembered he had not paid his tab at Bill's. Life is credit. Credit cards unite, abolish cash, cash is the root of all evil, credit is the pathway to the truth.

The first thing Bridge did was take the ad for the hypnotist out of his billfold and set it by his quill and inkwell. He then cleaned up and changed his shirt. He was sitting behind the table by the front door when Gertrude came in. "What has the Chamber of Commerce been doing lately to bring wealth and recognition to our fair city?" Bridge asked.

"I was talking to Plastic, and we are going to hire a grant writer to try and raise money so we can dig a mini Panama Canal from L.A. to here," Gertrude said.

"Then we could hire Mexican bandits to rob them as they came through Arizona," Bridge said, "and split the money between the galleries."

"Seriously, in two weeks we are going to have a gallery walk and all the downtown galleries will stay open on Friday, Saturday, and Sunday from three until nine at night. The Chamber is going to advertise all over the state and do radio ads. What we want the galleries to do is chip in one hundred dollars for the advertising."

Without gagging or vibrating, Bridge replied, "That sounds good to me."

Gertrude was so shocked her bottom jaw dropped open and if

she had had false teeth they would have fallen out.

She finally managed to say, "Bridge, are you feeling ok?"

"At my age, my prostate might be starting to enlarge. For sure my arteries are getting hard. My circulation is bad. My memory, although never good, is, on the one to ten list about six. I know after drinking about sixty thousands beers during my lifetime my liver is screaming for relief. I think I need reading glasses, but I am too cheap to go to Walmart and buy three dollar glasses. My back hurts. I have been having nightmares about paving machines and old lampposts that are now living in a commune. And after all my years of writing, I still spell probably, probobly. Besides that, I feel fine. But thanks for asking. It's nice to know you are worried about me."

"Give me the hundred dollars before you wake up," Gertrude said.

Bridge pulled out his wallet and gave Gertrude the money.

"Do you need a receipt?" Gertrude asked.

"Since I have never made a profit on this store, I really don't need a write-off," Bridge said.

Gertrude, feeling about as baffled as a man in a Victoria's Secret store, left.

"Dear Lost City, forgive me," Bridge said.

Vivian's smoke-belching, no-door-opening, flower covered Volvo stopped in front of the store. Bridge locked the door to the Why Am I Here and did his best breaking and entering routine crawling through the Volvo's right front window. The first thing Vivian said after Bridge got settled in was, "Gertrude ran over to the coffee shop and told everybody you gave her a hundred dollars towards advertising for an art walk."

"I did," Bridge said, seeing no reason to lie. Lies have to be saved for either a special occasion or a very dire one.

"Are you ok?" Vivian asked as she drove away from the store.

"I think the tour buses and paving machines are winning," Bridge replied.

"At least it's not those old lampposts that still work," Vivian said.

"They have me a little edgy," Bridge said.

The Hole was its usual self. The mannequin Indian at the end of the bar had still not moved or finished his sixty-year-old beer. The buffalo on the wall seemed bored - years of drunks and worthless conversation can even get a buffalo down. The paintings of the bargirls seemed perplexed, wondering where all the money had gone. A few mountain freaks were sitting at the bar hoping the cops didn't find their pot fields. A few tourists were laughing and joking and taking pictures of each other to go along with the fifty thousand photographs they had back at home.

Bridge and Vivian sat at a table and Terry came over. Terry had dyed her hair bright pumpkin orange and had on orange nail polish. The orange went well with her green pants, mauve blouse, blue eyeliner, and black lipstick. "Do you want me to cut Vivian off at six tequilas so you can take her home and jump her bones?" Terry asked Bridge with a wink.

"Eight," Vivian said. Women are good at answering questions for men - deep down they don't think men have vocal cords.

"I take it you two want the usual," Terry said, which could have been a question or a statement.

"Yes," Vivian answered, "but bring me two tequilas at a time."

When one does not have to talk, life is good, Bridge thought.

Two men came in carrying banjos, which made Vivian happy, as not all the open mike would be folk music. It's hard to get into a groove on folk music. Folk music is for taking mild depression and turning it into a deep and dark depression.

A few seconds later, a man came in wearing tall Spanish boots, high-waisted black pants, a bright red cummerbund, a ruffled white shirt, and a black round brimmed hat. The only thing he didn't have was a pink flamingo on his shoulder.

"He must have taken the wrong turn for Madrid," Bridge commented to Vivian.

"We all took a wrong turn somewhere to end up in Lost City," Vivian said just as Terry set the glass on the table.

We all took the wrong turn when those poor little sperm cells were swimming their little elongated tails off to get to the egg first, Bridge thought. No wonder men were always chasing women - they did it from the beginning. If only once, let the egg chase the sperm. Then Eve would be the hero and not the one who borrowed a rib – sperm spewing Adam anyway trying to pass the blame onto his poor naked wife.

"You look like you are deep in thought," Vivian said, picking up one shot of tequila.

"Nothing that will stop the radical Muslims from hating us," Bridge said.

They clinked beer glass and shot glass together. Vivian's childlike eyes drew Bridge into their depths. I, I, I, I, I, Lo, Lo, gurgled in his gut with the beer. Love went back down with the next swallow - cheap Mexican beer anyway.

The Professor walked into the bar, saw them and came over. He had a bandage wrapped around his head and his eyes were partially black. "I guess the Rock Lady hit you harder than we thought," Bridge said as the Professor sat.

"If you ask me, it helps your looks," Vivian said.

"I didn't ask you," the Professor replied.

"Person who gets hit on head with rock snide and sarcastic," Vivian said.

"Person who gets hit on head with rock has concrete headache," the Professor said.

"I don't know how you could believe in that rock stuff anyway," Bridge said.

"You are the one who helped me make up my mind to chase her," the Professor said.

"That will teach you to take advice," Bridge said.

Terry brought the Professor a Budweiser. "Thanks," the Professor told her.

"No need," Terry replied. "I can always remember who drinks the lousy beers. It's those people who drink beer with all the fancy names that I can't remember."

"Coors is a difficult word," Vivian said.

Terry grinned the 'you are not funny but I have to act like you are funny' grin that all waitresses have to learn and walked away.

Bridge started running through his head names of beers: Fat Tire, Moose Drool, Amber Bach, Grolch, Heineken, Triple Taddy Porter, Monk's Ale, Octoberfest, Pearl, Falstaff, Lone Star, Grain Belt - the list went on and on and Bridge did concede that it would be hard to match a face with a beer the person liked. He then decided people should have a card that they would hold up with what they liked to drink printed on it. It would save barmaids a lot of brain cells from having to think too hard and also cut down on fallen arches. But, there is always a but, it would also set the cushion insole market way back. Dr. Scholl's would have to get a real job.

Roach, the bongo player for Jackson and The Open Doors, came in, and being a bongo player, he waved and did not come over to the table. Drummers are always the loners in life, besides, without blaring music they really can't carry on a conversation.

While the two banjo players warmed up, Vivian finished her second shot and went to the bar and brought back two more. The two banjo players started playing a bluegrass instrumental and Vivian started bouncing around in her chair like a coon dog with fleas. After scratching for thirty seconds or so she got up and she and Roach started dancing. Bridge asked the Professor, "Why did the Rock Lady slam you in the head?"

Everybody in a small town is nosey. They really don't like to admit it, but such is life.

"I don't really know if I want to tell you," the Professor said.

"I'll buy you a beer," Bridge said.

"I'll tell you," the Professor said.

Bribery is a very old crime that has reached its zenith in Washington D.C.

Bridge waved at Terry the old bring us a round wave.

Roach and Vivian bounced by the table like a rabid raccoon was chasing them. Two old hippies dancing bluegrass is really a unique sight.

"People who dance to bluegrass should have to wear bib overalls, a straw hat, and have a few missing teeth," the Professor said.

"I keep telling Stoops he should move to the south if he wants to find a woman," Bridge said.

"His vocabulary is too good," the Professor said.

"Enough is enough. Why did the Rock Lady bean you?" Bridge asked again.

The Professor sipped his beer and took a deep breath. "When she came back from the desert, she told me she had been taken inside the rock of all rocks. The rock of all rocks is hollow inside. So he really isn't a true rock, he is a shell of a rock. The reason he is a shell is that he has worried his guts out over mankind."

Bridge took a sip of beer and wondered if the Professor would ever get to the point. Damn professional students anyway, they think verbosity makes them sound smart. Whatever happened to getting to the point?

"Inside the rock of all rocks," the Professor continued, "the Rock Lady was told there is no way man is going to survive."

"How about women?" Bridge butted in.

"Women will always survive," the Professor said, proving an education is really worth it, and continued. "The rock of all rocks told the Rock Lady she should go out and convert as many people as she could and lead them on a journey to the Petrified Forest in Arizona. There they should build rock circles and walk in them barefoot until their feet are worn down to stumps, at which time the Petrified Forest will become a real forest again, and the rock of all rocks will come down in a spaceship and take them to his home where they will never have to eat, sleep, drink, or be merry. They will only have to spend eternity chanting, 'rock, rock, rock, rock, thank you for our salvation.'"

"You still haven't told me why the Rock Lady beaned you," Bridge said.

"I told her I wanted to sleep with her. She told me I had no faith and that rocks do not believe in sex and then she beaned me for being mortal."

"At least she did not try and crucify you," Bridge said.

"To top it off the Rock Lady called me thirty minutes ago and wants me to drive her and six converts to Arizona," the Professor said.

"What did you say?" Bridge asked with a little concern in his voice.

"I said I would pick them up at seven."

"You'd better buy yourself a football helmet," Bridge advised.

"If you don't see me within a few months I hope you get a best seller," the Professor said.

Terry brought over two more beers. Bridge and the Professor clinked bottles together. "I hope it all works out," Bridge said.

The Professor chugged his beer, stood, and headed for the door. For some reason, he reminded Bridge of a soldier during the war headed out on a mission. Please, dear war god, don't let them kill me. Please, dear rock god, go back to wherever you came from and leave us alone. In six billion years all the earth gods will be homeless.

The banjo music stopped. Vivian sat. "Is there a god of music?" Bridge asked her.

"I don't know," Vivian replied, picking up a shot of tequila.

"Good answer," Bridge smiled.

The Flamenco guitar player was next. Vivian did not dance. Unless a person is into sore feet and looking constipated Flamenco music is hard to dance to. It is definitely not a happy face and life is good type of music. It's more a dead bull type of stuff.

The Hole was now packed with humanity. Young humanity, middle-aged humanity, cowboy humanity, old hippie humanity, artist humanity, mountain man freak humanity, who am I humanity. Bridge suddenly felt like his gallery, the Why Am I Here humanity. He looked at Vivian and said, "Why don't we go for a drive up the mountain? It's a pretty night."

"I'd love to," Vivian replied with a wink.

Bridge could not decipher the wink.

Chapter Twenty-Seven

The night was calm. There were no clouds to diminish the stars. The pine trees were resting, not even fearing the lumber mill. Vivian parked in a turnout where they could see all of Lost City and the dark outline of distant mountains that were on the border with Mexico - Mexico the country that sends its poor scampering across the border chasing the dream of the United States. Mexico, you have succeeded in the power game, there are only those with and those without. Mexico, you will give us our ten dollar a day maids, cooks, gardeners, and cheap tortillas. We will build a wall along the borer so you can dig under it or go over it. Viva la United States.

Vivian got out of the car and Bridge crawled through the window. They leaned back against the hood of the car holding hands. "I'm glad you wanted to leave," Vivian said. "It's nice to take a deep breath once in awhile and get away from all the noise."

Vivian's lavender perfume hung in an invisible cloud around them. Bridge inhaled deeply - the magic of scent, the magic of quiet, the distance of it all, Bridge thought.

He remembered once when his army unit had taken a hill and he was on night guard. The jungle rolled below him like a dark sea, and between the waves rested gray clouds of fog. As if touched by an invisible hand Bridge was suddenly filled with a deep peace - a peace that transcended the killing of the day and the steady hum of the millions of mosquitoes. It was strange. It was eerie. It was wonderful, but it was also scary and dreadful. What a price for inner peace. Unleash the gods of war to bring forth the saints of peace. But peace, are you not also a warrior in your own way?

"How's the Professor?" Vivian asked, not looking at Bridge but looking at the lights of Lost City.

"He is trying to ignore the fact he really likes the Rock Lady," Bridge replied, but wondering if it was the right answer or if there really was an answer. How is anybody?

"I look at the lights and all I can really see are all the homeless people," Vivian said like the homeless people were her fault.

"Only those who care feel the sins of nations," Bridge said.

Vivian squeezed his hand. Bridge kissed her on the cheek. "You are the saint of the rainbows. You warm my heart," he said.

"I don't think you have a heart," Vivian said with a little girl laugh.

"I don't think I had a heart for a long time," Bridge said, "but lately it has been coming back. I feel this pound, pound, pound in my chest and sometimes even in my head."

"In your head the only thing pounding around is all those weird ideas you put into books."

Bridge smiled. "It's probably all the nouns, adjectives, adverbs, and verbs hoping that one day I will get it right."

"You have it right, Bridge. You write what you want to write and most people who read it like it. They just can't understand after meeting you how you can write with such feeling."

"It surprises me," Bridge confessed, feeling I, I, I, I, I, Lo, Lo, Lo churning in his chest.

Vivian and Bridge fell into silence - a comfortable silence that only old friends can enjoy. The light from Lost City headed off into the cosmos.

Oh Bridge, Vivian thought. I have never in my life been so comfortable with a man. I don't have to trust you, but I do. I don't worry about you. I don't fret over you. You are like an old tree, weathered with broken branches, but you survive and each spring you bring out new leaves. You're like an old sofa, or chair, or a pair of slippers that the dog has half chewed up but which are so comfortable it would be a sin to toss them in the garbage. Bridge, don't you know I love you?

"I need a hug," Vivian said, releasing Bridge's hand.

"Me too," Bridge said.

They did not hug, they embraced, and Bridge thought, why can't I tell Vivian I love her?

Lost City went on its way. The mountains in Mexico hid the wetbacks and drug runners. The trees did not see or care.

Bridge stepped away from Vivian. "Did you ever in your life want children?" he asked.

"No. I never wanted to bring people into this world."

"Me either," Bridge said. "Whenever I see kids, I always feel sad, which is double sad, as one shouldn't feel sad for children. They should be sugar and spice and everything nice."

"I guess that is why there are art towns," Vivian said. "A place for dreamers to hide from the world."

"We are all ostriches holding paintbrushes, and clay, and beads, and wood and flopping words on paper. You'd think our butts would be sandblasted and frostbitten from sticking up in the air for so long," Bridge said.

"I think all you artists surf the mighty wave of depression," Vivian said.

Bridge loved the imagery of the statement. "I think most of us crash on the beach," he said, but it did not bother him. Life has to crash. Everyone gets their Waterloo. Napoleon, where are you when we need you? Before you had syphilis, you power hungry midget. That will teach you to be born in France and think you were a Roman. You should have taken a bath and gotten over it.

"You know what I would like to do?" Vivian asked.

"Don't tell me you want to have a heart to heart with the Rock Lady," Bridge said.

"No. I have a blanket in the car and I want to go off into the trees and make love."

Bridge smiled.

The night. The trees. The softness and warmth of skin. The sighs. The release. No cuddling. The hard ground. "I think we are too old for this," Vivian groaned afterwards.

"I think this is why the bed was invented," Bridge also groaned.

They stood in the dark, shadows of nakedness, putting on clothes as quickly as they had come off. "If we ever do this again, you are on the bottom," Vivian said.

They held hands walking back to the car. Bridge crawled through the window. They sat looking at Lost City. "I want to go back to The Hole and I want you to dance with me," Vivian said.

"You know I don't dance," Bridge said.

"Let me rephrase my statement," Vivian said. "We are going back to The Hole and you are going to dance with me. If you don't, I'll slam you upside the head so hard you will wish the Rock Lady would have beaned you with one of her sacred rocks."

"It's about time I danced," Bridge said.

It's a sad thing in life, but violence does solve a lot of problems. Strange, but fear is not always a bad thing.

The Hole was packed. Stoops was standing at the end of the bar talking to the stuffed Indian. Pill, wearing his sign, was standing in the corner trying to decide if he was going to have a paranoid attack or not. Damn life is always full of decisions. A fiddle player was playing a jig, but he was so bad he had to have been kicked out of Ireland, or at least Tennessee. Roach was accompanying him on an Irish drum. The people that were dancing were bouncing around like drunken pogo sticks on a bumpy road and whooping like Indians having an after battle scalp party. Primitive is what primitive does. Who cares if the music is lousy, dance.

The song stopped and the fiddle player went immediately into another jig. Vivian pulled Bridge into a small space and started dancing. She made her right hand into a fist, shook it at Bridge, and Bridge, without moving his feet, started moving up and down like a little boy who had to pee. Vivian shook her fist at Bridge again. Bridge's feet started to move up and down in place. One, two, one. One, two, one. Vivian danced around Bridge like he was a maypole with no ribbons. One, two, one. One, two, one. Faster, one, two, one. One, two, one. Bridge's arms started to move up and down. He started to clap. Faster, one, two, one. One, two, one. He hooked his arm with Vivian's. Circle, one, two, one. Circle the other way, one, two, one. Bridge leaned his head back and closed his eyes. The fiddle player played faster. One, two, one. One, two, one.

Vivian laughed. Her childlike eyes sparkled. Her 185 pounds rolled and bounced. Faster, one, two, one. Faster yet, one, two, one. Pill, seeing Bridge dancing, was so shocked that he started bouncing up and down. Six billion years and who really gives a dime. Dance and be merry, the world will do what it's going to do. Democrats and Republicans unite. Liberals get over it. Stoops was so freaked out at the sight of Bridge dancing he stopped talking to the stuffed Indian. The buffalo on the wall was in shock. The paintings of the bargirls rubbed rouge on their nipples and smiled enticingly. The music stopped. Vivian stopped. Pill ran from the bar. The fear of six billion years cannot be danced away. Bridge kept dancing. One, two, one. One, two, one. One, two, one. The people in The Hole clapped their hands.

Bridge stopped. He opened his eyes. He took a deep breath. Not a sound crept through The Hole. The people froze in place. Bridge looked at the buffalo. He looked at the smiling painted bargirls with fresh rouge on their nipples. He looked at the stuffed Indian. He looked at Vivian. Dear lovely Vivian. Dear lovely Vivian with the childlike eyes. Dear lovely Vivian, who, if she could, would feed the world. "I, I, I, I, Lo, Lo, Lo," Bridge mumbled to Vivian and then started to choke on that pesky meatball.

Love did not move from his heart.

Vivian smiled, leaned close to him and whispered in his ear. "I know, Bridge. It's ok. I know."

But Bridge, in the middle of choking, did not completely hear what she said.

He leaned back his head and raised his hands toward the ceiling and hollered, "Bring on the paving machines. Bring on the tour buses. Toss the homeless a turkey leg. Ambition is not virtue. The rock of rocks is hollow and lonely. Six billion years and counting. But please, please, do no harm that is hateful."

He then lowered his arms, looked at Vivian, and said in a faraway voice, "Can you believe, Vivian, that I donated a hundred bucks for an art walk."

Vivian led him to the car like he was a lost vagabond. Bridge crawled through the window. All the way back to town they did not talk.

The silence of old friends - bless the silence of old friends. Love is more than a spoken word.

Chapter Twenty-Eight

It was ten in the morning on Friday and Stoops and Plastic were sitting at the This Isn't Heaven Bar drinking Bloody Marys. Stoops had gone by the Why Am I Here, but Bridge was not there. Berry was sitting by himself at a table scowling at the wall. Stoops looked at him and felt worried, but he could think of nothing he could do. Both Gloria and Plastic were almost speechless after Stoops had told them Bridge had danced. It was a bigger surprise than if the Palestinians and Jews got together and formed a soccer team.

Gloria was in a great mood, having informed Plastic and Stoops she had gone back to women. She did not have large dark circles under her eyes and she was wearing clean Levi's and a T-shirt with no slogan on it. Plastic thought it was an improvement, as there was nothing to distract from her nipple rings.

Bridge two-stepped forward and one backward into the bar and sat by Stoops. He called to Berry. "Good morning."

"Fuck you," Berry said.

"No thanks," Bridge said.

"If it isn't the reincarnated Fred Astaire," Stoops said.

"Twinkle toes," Plastic said.

"If you two would ever dance, you might get a girlfriend," Gloria said to Stoops and Plastic.

"Hey Bridge, give us dancing lessons," Plastic said.

"Where were you when I came by the store this morning?"

Stoops asked Bridge.

"What are you, my mother?" Bridge said, not going to tell Stoops he had gone to the pay phone at the bus station and set up an appointment to see a hypnotist.

Stoops could not think of a funny snide comeback, so he took a sip of his breakfast.

"I heard you donated for an upcoming art walk," Plastic said.

"There are times in life when common sense wants to go slumming," Bridge replied as Gloria set a Bloody Mary in front of him. "You look nice," Bridge complimented Gloria.

"So do you," Gloria smiled.

"If Bridge looks nice, a donkey's ass looks nice," Berry called across the room.

"A donkey is an ass, so in truth a donkey is two asses," Plastic said.

"I wonder when a donkey is called an ass whether it's two asses or not?" Stoops pondered.

Plastic, Stoops, Bridge, and Gloria were silent for a few moments trying to think of an answer. There was not one. They all shrugged at the same time. Some things in life are not worth knowing the answer. Some things in life are not worth asking a stupid question.

Berry, without saying goodbye, walked out of the This Isn't Heaven Bar in only the way a man who has had a stroke can. Bridge did not watch him leave - he did not want to feel worried. "One thing about Berry, he is never in a good mood," Plastic said.

"It's his birthday tomorrow," Stoops said.

"He wouldn't like a party," Plastic stated.

Bridge wondered to himself if maybe the grump would like a party. Many times in life grumpy people need parties more than happy ones.

"I still can't believe you donated for an art walk," Plastic said to Bridge.

"I had a nightmare about it last night," Bridge said. "I dreamed Lost City sprouted arms and legs and the town was chasing me around the desert screaming, 'Traitor, traitor,' and trying to stomp me into oblivion."

"They say if you have a dream and in the dream you get killed then you are really dead," Stoops said.

"Who are they?" Plastic asked.

Stoops didn't know who they were, so he didn't answer.

"I don't think dreaming about getting killed and then dying before you wake up can be proven," Bridge said.

"Why not?" Plastic asked. He was a regular question guy this morning.

"Dead people don't talk," Bridge said.

"Yeah, stupid," Gloria said. "Haven't you watched any pirate movies?"

"Thank you," Bridge said to Gloria, tired of all the questions.

"Did you hear there is going to be another coffee shop in town?" Stoops said.

New coffee shops no longer made Bridge go into convulsions. Caffeine is a given in life, and there can never be enough of it.

Bridge, Stoops, and Gloria did not comment, so Stoops answered his own question. "It's going to be at the end of Bullard and they are gong to serve only organic coffee."

Bridge stood, paid for his drink, said goodbye to the breakfast crowd and two- stepped forward and one backward toward the door. The aftermath of donating a hundred bucks toward an art walk was finally catching up to him. He felt weak and wobbly, but that could have been from dancing and thinking he was young and doing it on the ground.

"I think Bridge is changing," Plastic commented.

"I hope he gets over it," Stoops said.

Outside, Bridge remembered again he had not paid his tab at Bill's, but he decided he could pay it at four. Debts are easy to put off.

There was the usual array of dogs in front of the Wake Up Or Die sniffing and slobbering and hoping that in another life they would not be cursed and come back as people. There were also quite a few tourists walking around town. Bridge, feeling like a capitalist, figured he would get a cup of coffee to go and open the store until it was time to see the hypnotist.

Vivian was watering plants that were probably going into shock since they had not been watered in at least a month. She waved at Bridge and Bridge waved back. Sometimes lovers should not make things so complicated - a wave is simple and to the point.

Chris was having one of those moments. Women have moments, but gay men have moment moments. He was exasperated about something and darting around behind the counter like a sparrow that had flown into a living room and was too dumb to fly back out the open window. Watching him, Bridge wished he had a tennis racquet and could swat him a good one. Chris, seeing Bridge, stopped darting around and started ranting. "I just can't get anything right today. My froth is flat. My lattés are too sweet. The steamer is either too hot or too cold and I have dropped three cups and broken them. What am I going to do, Bridge? I just, I just, I just feel that I can't go on."

"I think you need a hug," Bridge said.

"Oh Bridge, you are so wonderful," Chris said and pranced around the counter before Bridge could say he was only joking. Being nice sometimes is a real pain.

Bridge timidly hugged Chris. "Oh give me a good squeeze. I'm not going to kiss you," Chris said.

Bridge gave him a good squeeze and let go. Chris pranced back behind the counter as happy as a little girl with a Christmas puppy.

Vivian, seeing Bridge hug Chris, could not believe her eyes and commented to herself, "Bridge, this art walk thing has you all messed up. Either that, or you are going into male menopause."

"I'd like a medium coffee to go," Bridge told Chris.

Beaming like a lighthouse, Chris gave him a large coffee. "On me, for the hug," he said.

Bridge wanted to tell him he wanted a medium coffee. If he had wanted a large, he would have ordered a large. Jesus Christ. But, Chris looked so happy, Bridge kept his mouth shut.

Two-stepping forward and one backward toward the door, Bridge figured a gay man hugging a straight man must be as exciting to the gay man as a straight man hugging someone else's good-looking wife with big tits. Sometimes the pleasures in life are simple and have no complications.

Bridge put out his open sign, turned on all the lights in the store, and sat behind his table. He took the lid off his coffee cup, smelled the deep aroma, took a sip and whispered to himself, "Come to me, people of the world, come look at my wares, words, paintings, beadwork, and art. My price tag is cheap for the pleasures you will receive."

Bridge suddenly had a strange feeling - a feeling that left him puzzled and perplexed. After he had stopped dancing at The Hole

Vivian had whispered something in his ear. What did she whisper? He did not know, but he knew it was important.

A cowboy couple came into the store. It is easy to tell a cowboy couple - something about boots, cowboy hats, tight Levi's, and big belt buckles takes the mystery out of what a person is. A person does not see a cowboy and say, "Hey, look at the hippie." A real cowboy as opposed to a dime store cowboy is always easy to spot, as the real cowboy's hands will be big and covered with calluses. Get along little doggie and building fence does a number on fingers. Their back pocket will also normally have an imprint of a large circle in it from a can of dipping tobacco, which also means they have holes in their gums about the size of dimes.

The couple was in their early thirties and by the size of her diamond rings and the man's gold belt buckle, whatever cowboy business they were in was doing well. Probably stealing cattle, as the only people making money in the legitimate cattle business are the distributors, which seems to be the rule for modern business - the good old middleman - the one with the suit and tie and no crap on his shoes.

"Good morning," Bridge said. One can't be a Berry and run a store and bring in customers by telling them to fuck off.

"Good morning," the lady beamed.

The cowboy gave Bridge the old traditional cowboy nod. Bridge nodded back letting the cowboy know he had been a cowboy also. Only old cowboys know how to give a real cowboy nod. You don't nod down, you nod up, leading with your chin. Body language is a strange thing. Bridge had a weird thought. If he could write a book using only body language he could cut out all the useless words.

The couple started walking around the store and whispering to themselves in front of each painting. Bridge looked out the window. When people were in the store, he always felt like a spy, and not a very good spy at that. When they had toured the complete store they stopped in front of the table where Bridge displayed his books. "I read your book *The Land*," the man said. "I checked it out of the library in Abilene. You're one hell of a good writer. I could tell you really have worked on ranches."

"Thanks," Bridge said, soaking in the praise like a dry sponge.

"I want to buy a copy of each of your books," the man said.

Bridge headed for the storeroom trying not to show his

excitement. Seven books, I am a writer. They even know me in Abilene. Bringing the books back to the table, the lady was standing in front of the painting of the buffalo, the most expensive painting in the store, and also Bridge's favorite.

"Make all the books out to Billy Bob," the man said.

Bridge signed each book with a different salutation - Billy Bob, thank you, the best, good luck, time flies, ambition is not virtue, take care and, do no harm that is hateful, Bridge McCoy.

The man pulled a wad of cash out of his pocket that would have made a dope dealer envious and paid.

Bridge put a card in each book and a copy of his bio. What self-centered creatures we all are.

"Honey," the lady said in a slow Texas drawl that would make even a born again get horny. "Honey, would you buy me this here painting of a buffalo? It would look so good over the fireplace in our bedroom."

Bridge tried not to gulp. A $5,900 painting, 40% for him - praise the middleman. Who cares if I don't have any crap on my shoes?

The man walked over and stood by his wife, girlfriend, mistress, whatever the case may be, and looked at the painting. "It is kind of pretty," he said.

Bridge knew the man could care less about the painting. He was thinking about the fantastic sex he would get if he bought it. The lady took the man's hand. Good old body language - to hell with words.

"I'll buy it for you, sugar," the man said.

The lady turned toward Bridge. "He is such a darling," she said.

"I don't take credit cards," Bridge said, hoping his voice did not crack.

"If I couldn't pay cash I wouldn't buy it," the man said, pulled up his pant leg and took a wad of hundreds out of his boot. Good old Texas bank, the best in the world. Credit cards, eat your cold-blooded hearts out - mob interest rate blood suckers that you are.

Fifteen minutes later the couple was gone. They were going to lunch and would pick up the painting afterwards.

Bridge hid the money in the storeroom and then lovingly wrapped the painting in bubble wrap. I hope you like your new home. It was strange, but when he sold a painting it made him sad. Goodbye, dear friend, goodbye. We have had many good and silent times together. He went to Gertrude's and phoned the artist. I am the bearer of good news. Your life has merit. The fact Bridge had sold a painting for $5,900 gave Gertrude a dizzy spell.

Back in his store, he sat behind the table, drank the now lukewarm coffee, wondered how he had merited such good luck, and wondered once again what Vivian had whispered in his ear.

Chapter Twenty-Nine

The painting was on its way to Texas. A home, everything and everyone needs a home - even if home is a wall. The artist after receiving her money was so shocked she could not speak and was in tears as she headed to the bank - recognition is a wonderful thing. Bridge was two-stepping forward and one backward toward the hypnotist. He really did not know how he felt. He was in between, out between, or between. He did know he was richer than he had been in the morning. Across the street, Sergeant was walking with all sixteen of his girlfriends, one on each side of him and the others following in twos. Bridge waved at him, but Sergeant did not wave back - having to listen to sixteen women all at the same time takes a lot of attention.

Several blocks from the art district Bridge knew he had found where the hypnotist lived. The house was an old red brick that leaned to the left like a sinking ship. Hanging from the front porch were over a hundred crystals of varying sizes and at least fifty wind chimes. There were twenty birdbaths in the front yard and a very contented black cat was sunning on the railing of the porch. There was a hand painted sign - **HYPNOTIST.** Bridge appreciated the sign, it did not say the best hypnotist in the world, it did not have balloons tied to it - it just said hypnotist - straight and to the point. The house had a disheveled look, but Bridge figured anyone who was messing with people's minds most of the time had to be somewhat disheveled. The front door and window jambs were all painted a deep blue. The

Mexicans years ago believed blue around doors and windows kept evil spirits out of the house. The windows were so dirty they looked tinted. But Bridge figured the hypnotist probably believed in the third eye and really didn't need windows. Bridge knocked on the door, thinking - What am I doing? But he thought that at least ten times a day, so it was really no big deal. What are we all doing? Please, Rock God, tell us before you sail away in your spaceship.

The door swung open. If Bridge would have been in his twenties, he might have fainted or at least drooled all over his shirt. The lady was over six feet tall and had honey blond hair that hit her at the shoulders. She could have been the highest paid stripper at a gentlemen's club in Phoenix that only catered to politicians. She was wearing a pale blue belly dancer's outfit that was so transparent she might as well have been naked. She was also barefoot. Her toenail and fingernail polish was bright red. She had silver sparkles on her face, earrings that were small Tibetan bells and eyes that were so black and bottomless a black hole could have fallen into them. In her bellybutton was a shiny stone that, if it was a real diamond, she could have used it to buy New Mexico. "You must be Bridge," the lady smiled.

"I think so," Bridge managed to say, trying his best to be a gentleman and look only at her eyes, which was as hard to do as a man telling their wife or girlfriend he only bought *Playboy* to read the articles.

Bridge two-stepped forward and one backward into the house. He had never been into a gypsy's house, but he figured he was in one now. The furniture was red. The curtains were red. The carpet was some obscure color that was looking for an identity. The single light in the middle of the ceiling had a red shade. In every corner of the room were tables covered with lit candles. There were also incense burners that were burning some sweet scent that should have been in a motel room in Kansas that a Chinaman owned. From another room, music was playing that made Bridge want to go buy a Persian carpet, teach it how to fly, and then fly over and tell the Arabian Knights he knew that they were really all just a bunch of whoring, drinking thieves. There were no paintings or decorations of any kind on the purple walls.

"Sit down, please," the lady said, pointing at a red sofa. "I am Melinda."

Bridge sat quickly. His legs were weak.

"And what seems to be your problem?" Melinda asked as she sat on the floor not more than two feet in front of Bridge.

Bridge wanted to say, "My problem is I gave all of my money for an art walk so I don't have a hundred bucks to give you for a table dance," but instead he said, "I am in love, but I can't tell the women I am in love with that I love her."

"All men have that problem," Melinda said simply. "I can cure you for fifty bucks."

"Where are you from?" Bridge asked.

"Malibu," Melinda answered.

"How old are you?"

"Twenty-seven."

"Fifty bucks?"

"Fifty bucks."

"Are you a virgin?"

Laughter.

California girls. Go figure.

"Fifty bucks in advance," Melinda said.

Not all California blonds are dumb.

"For another hundred I can get you to walk normal," Melinda said with a crooked little car salesman grin.

"One thing at a time," Bridge said.

Bridge handed Melinda the money. Wearing a belly dancer's outfit, she did not have any pockets, even though she had enough cleavage to stash about a million dollars. She took the money to another room. While she was gone she turned off the music. Back in the room she adjusted the overhead red light until it was a pale red light. For some reason, the light reminded Bridge of whorehouses in Thailand while he was on R and R. Dear Mom. I am going to Thailand for my R and R from Vietnam. I plan on going to all the Museums and find out more about the culture. I am also going to spend some time at the library. I am also going to try and get over my mistrust of little yellow people and not shoot as many of them when I get back to Nam. All is well. Love, your son.

Melinda stood in the middle of the room with her legs slightly apart and her hands on her hips. She shut her eyes and started to turn her head from left to right. Her bell earrings tinkled. Bridge hoped her head did not do a couple revolutions on her shoulders and her feet come off the ground. It's hard for a guy who takes two steps forward and one backward to run - besides, he had already paid.

Melinda started to hum. It was not a tune that made Bridge want to dance, but it was peaceful. Bridge's eyelids started to grow heavy. Maybe there is opium in the incense, Bridge thought.

Melinda walked toward Bridge and stopped about six inches away. "Watch my bellybutton," she hummed and started to move her stomach in rhythmic circles.

This is tough, Bridge thought.

Eyelids growing heavy, heavier. Eyes closed.

"Say to me, I love you....what is your love's name?"

"Viv.....i......annnnnnnnn."

"Say I love you Vivian. I love you."

"I.....I.....I.....I.....I."

"You can do it."

"Lo....Lo.....Lo....Lo....."

"Let your heart be your guide. Free yourself to the spirit of love."

"Lov....lov....lov....lov...."

"Come on, big boy. Release yourself."

Eyes open slightly.

"Come on Bridge. Say I love you Vivian." Stomach moving in circles.

"Lov, Lov, Lov, Lov."

Stomach moving faster.

"I, I, I, I."

Stomach moving slower. Stomach moving in and out.

Bridge noticed she had an outie bellybutton.

He suddenly jumped up, looked madly around the room, looked at Melinda's one million-dollar cleavage, looked at her bellybutton with the shiny rock that, if it was real, she could have use it to buy New Mexico. He was suddenly afraid, afraid of what, he did not know, but he two-stepped forward and one backward out of the house as fast as he could.

He did not slow down until he got back to the Why Am I Here. He felt tired. He felt old. My God, I've danced. I've hugged a gay man. He shut his eyes. "Paving machines, stop tormenting me," he begged. "I, I, I, I, I, I, Lo, Lo, Lo. A hundred bucks for an art walk. Rock God, save me. MeJoe, you are full of shit. Hypnotist my ass. Oh dear Vivian, I, I, I, I, Lo, Lo, Lo."

Bridge two-stepped forward and one backward to his quill and inkwell. The screen came to life. Bridge hit the file button. The new book popped on the screen. He always wondered what the words of a book being written did while the computer was off. He figured they sat around talking and drinking and wondering what their fate was. Let me have the sex scene. Let me kill the bad guy. Let me fall in love. Let me be beautiful and wise and kind. Why do you keep misspelling me?

Bridge typed in all caps, WE ARE ALL HYPNOTIZED BY OURSELVES.

Somewhere in Abilene, Texas, a painting of a buffalo was being hung on a bedroom wall. Somewhere in Abilene, Texas, a pretty Texas lady was taking her clothes off. Somewhere in Abilene, Texas, a cowboy was saying, "Now those are some nice buffalos."

Please, please, what did Vivian whisper in my ear?

Bridge got up and two-stepped forward and one backward toward Bill's Restaurant and Libations. Thank the powers that be, or are, or will be, for beer - the communion host for the masses.

Chapter Thirty

It was late afternoon and Vivian was sitting in her private room. She had not turned on the light so the fairies were not dancing around the room. Vivian was perplexed and was mumbling to herself, "Bridge danced."

"I hope he is not changing."

"Why do people change?"

"Is he changing for me?"

"Be yourself, Bridge, please be yourself."

"Besides, you are a terrible dancer."

Tired of her mumbling, Vivian went back into the Wake Up Or Die.

The Professor was sitting at a table by himself. He looked like he had spent the night in jail and instead of one bandage on his head he now had two. Vivian got a cup of coffee and went and sat with him. "You look like you need this," she said, setting the coffee in front of the Professor.

The Professor stared blankly at the coffee like it was something alien. "I take it the Rock Lady beaned you again?" Vivian said.

The Professor nodded his head.

"You must like pain," Vivian said.

The Professor nodded his head twice.

"Is there anything I can do?"

The Professor shook his head.

"I take it the rock of rocks is not the key to salvation?"

The Professor shook his head again.

Vivian was not really into making conversation with nods or shakes so she got up. She had to do inventory, which was about as exciting as doing dishes, but it had to be done. Capitalism comes with reams and reams of paperwork - not counting the double books for cash.

The Professor put both hands around the coffee cup and with trembling hands picked it up and slurped loudly. He slurped again and took several deep breaths. He finished the coffee, stood and hollered at the top of his lungs, "Jesus walked on water, but rocks only sink."

Nobody paid any attention to him. His spontaneous poetry was not even close to Bridge's and his delivery needed some work. It is a fine line between genius and insanity. The Professor then staggered out of the Wake Up Or Die and headed for Bill's. He had to talk to Bridge. If he couldn't find Bridge he'd go up to The Hole and talk to the stuffed Indian. The Indian was always a good listener and was not into preaching or telling people I told you so.

Bridge was drinking a beer. Stoops had not yet arrived. Seeing the Professor, Bridge wished he was invisible or at least transparent.

The Professor flopped down at the table like he weighed about ten tons.

"I see the Rock Lady is still not into sex," Bridge said, eyeing the other bandage.

"She stole my car and took all my money," the Professor lamented.

"Did you make it to the Petrified Forest?" Bridge asked - a woman getting away with all of a man's money was nothing unusual, and since he did not own a car or like them he really didn't give a damn - everybody should have their car stolen.

"I picked up her and her five followers this morning like I said I would," the Professor said. "Outside of town the Rock Lady said she had to go to the bathroom, so I stopped at the rest area. When she came out, I was talking to one of her followers and she beaned me with a rock. When I woke up, the car was gone and so was my wallet. I had to hitchhike back to town."

"Did you call the police?"

"No."

"Why not?"

The Professor took a rumpled piece of paper out of his pocket and handed it to Bridge. Bridge read. "Dear Professor: I know you do not believe in the rock of all rocks. I cannot take you with us and sacrilege our god. So I am going to steal all your money. When the rock of all rocks picks us up in his spaceship and takes us to his planet the exchange rate on American money might be good. You will find your car in the Petrified Forest. Wish me luck. You know I love you, but true faith can have nothing to do with the flesh. May one day you see the rock. The Rock Lady."

"Very romantic," Bridge said, "But what happened to go out and multiply and all that good stuff?"

"Why couldn't I fall for a Mormon girl?" the Professor asked, holding his head in anguish.

"I think you need a double shot of cheap whiskey," Bridge said.

"What will that do?" the Professor pleaded.

"Nothing, but people fall for that line all the time in the movies."

Frauline bubbled over. "You look like you need a double shot of cheap whiskey," she said to the Professor.

"What will that do?" the Professor asked. People who have been beaned in the head twice by a religious rock have a shorter memory than fifty-year-old potheads.

"Nothing," Frauline said, "but I saw it in a movie."

Bridge grinned.

"I'll take one," the Professor said.

"You mean one, or a double?"

"I'll take one double."

"I'll bring you another beer," Frauline said to Bridge and bubbled away. People who are always bubbly don't let other people's bummers get them down. It's kind of a selfish deal, but it works.

Stoops joined them at the table. "Organic Muffin wanted to tie me up and whip me, but at least she was not into rocks," he said to the Professor.

"You still miss her, don't you?" Bridge asked Stoops.

"Yes I do."

Bridge felt a pang of sadness for Stoops. Missing is not a good thing in life.

"Do you know where there are any single Mormon women around here?" the Professor asked Stoops.

"There is no such thing," Stoops answered.

Frauline brought the double shot of cheap whiskey, Bridge's beer, and one for Stoops. "To the pain of love," Stoops toasted.

They clinked glasses together. The Professor shot the double down. He groaned, he moaned, he clutched his throat, his eyes watered, he gagged. "Tha-tha-that tastes terrible," he stammered.

"Bring him another one on me before he recovers," Bridge ordered.

Frauline quickly brought another double shot. The Professor gulped it down. He choked, he gagged harder, his eyes watered more.

The Professor touched both knots on his head. "I think I will go back to being a student for awhile," he said to Stoops.

"You can't force love or look for it, it finds you," Stoops said, which was one hell of a statement for a guy whose only girlfriend in years dumped him for the runway lights of a topless bar.

"I'll never take advice from you again," the Professor said to Bridge.

"Smart man," Bridge said, not saying out loud what he really thought - you want advice, talk to yourself.

"I feel ten times better," the Professor said and then stood and walked out the door a two shots of a double, double shot of cheap whiskey recovered man. At times, some things people see in the movies work - very few times, so don't get overconfident.

"How was the hypnotist?" Stoops asked Bridge after the Professor had gone.

"How'd you know I went to see a hypnotist?" Bridge answered the question with a question, which in normal life is only done by lawyers and other people who are trying to swindle you.

"I saw you go into the house."

"If you have fifty bucks, it's worth the show," Bridge said. "She has million dollar cleavage and an outie belly button to die for."

"And she shows it all for fifty bucks?"

"This is Lost City."

"You had better not tell Vivian."

"I ran out of there as fast as my two steps forward and one backward would carry me," Bridge said.

"Loan me fifty bucks," Stoops said.

Bridge and Stoops clinked glass and bottle together.

Vivian came in. Frauline bubbled over. "It's nice when you come over," Frauline said to Vivian.

"I would like a Tecate, a lime and a glass," Vivian ordered, not really understanding why it was nice when she came over, but it made her feel good - compliments go a long way in life.

Frauline bubbled away. "The big empty building on the edge of Bullard sold today," Vivian said like she really did not want to say it, but she knew Bridge would find out anyway. "They are going to make a co-op gallery out of it."

Stoops looked at Bridge. Vivian looked at Bridge. Bridge did not choke, gag, or turn purple. "It will probably do well," he said. "It will give a lot of artists who can't get into galleries an inexpensive place to show their stuff."

Stoops was shocked. Vivian was shocked. Bridge smiled. "I sold my most expensive painting today and seven books," he said, feeling like a mini Mark Twain with a whole box of expensive cigars and no debt.

Vivian jumped up and hugged him. "You can loan me fifty," Stoops grinned.

"Which one was it?" Vivian asked.

"The big one of the buffalo," Bridge said, but in truth, selling the seven books meant more to him, even though people who buy books normally throw them in the trash, or give them to the library, which then throws them in the trash.

Frauline bubbled back with Vivian's beer. Bridge, Vivian, and Stoops all clinked glasses and bottles together and drank. They clinked and drank again. Clinking and drinking are always happy times. There should be more clinking in the world, even if there is no drinking.

Barbara came into Bill's. Being a reporter for the Let's Turn Lost City Into A Political Hotbed, or the LTLCIAPH for short, she should drink more than she did. Bridge had told her before. "If you really want to know what people think, go to a bar and get smashed with them."

Barbara had explained that thinking and the truth are two different animals.

Barbara joined the clinking musketeers at the table. "Bridge sold a painting," Stoops informed Barbara.

"Bridge sold seven of his books," Vivian informed Barbara.

"I don't think I can write an article about that," Barbara said - journalists are always serious and looking for a tag line that will make them famous.

"How about Bridge McCoy," Bridge said, "Lost City's not so well known author blew up two buildings last night that had recently been purchased by Eskimos. The Eskimos informed the Let's Make Lost City Into A Political Hotbed that igloos had fallen so much in value in the last year, they let the bank repo their igloos to cut their losses and decided to move to an art town and sell fake walrus ivory from China. When asked why they chose Lost City, the distraught Eskimos said they had learned that there was not an artist alive who had good credit, and since their credit was also now shot, it seemed like a logical choice. Plus, stupid Americans don't know the difference between real ivory and fake. According to this reporter, the only thing that would know the difference between real ivory and fake is the poor walrus with no tusks. And personally, as a side note, I think we should applaud Bridge for driving away new gallery owners and doing his best to ruin tourism. Elect Bridge McCoy for mayor. What do you think?"

"I think you have had too many beers," Barbara said, but added with a smile, "I heard you gave a hundred bucks to help finance an art walk in town."

"Damn Bridge, just when I thought you were getting back to normal," Stoops said.

Frauline bubbled up. "Buy a round on me," Barbara said, "and bring me a glass of the house red wine."

Barbara never bought a round, so Bridge asked, "Did you find some money on the street?"

"No, Jackson and The Open Door just cut their new CD and they are going to get some radio time in Tucson."

"What is the album called?" Vivian asked, dating herself by not saying CD.

"It's called, 'We are sick and tired about hearing about Paul McCartney. At sixty-five years old his sex life couldn't be that good,'" Barbara said.

"At sixty, mine isn't exactly stellar," Stoops said.

Vivian gave Bridge a wink that meant, 'if you say anything your sex life is going to be nil.'

Bridge understood exactly and kept his mouth shut. Then he wondered if he could add winks to his book of body language and no words. Genius is a hard game to follow.

"Where's Jackson now?" Bridge asked Barbara.

"He's over at the coffee shop sitting at a table with four married women who are telling him he is the best thing to music since guitar strings."

"That's one thing about going with a writer," Vivian said. "You don't have to bolster their ego. They need rejection so they can be deep and dark."

Bridge wanted to tell Vivian that wasn't exactly true, but if he wanted to get into a philosophical debate he'd go over to the Wake Up Or Die and talk to a couple of college dropouts that had majored in art, so instead he said, "No, authors need an excuse to drink."

"What's the excuse for the Scots and Irish?" Stoops asked.

"The weather," Bridge replied.

"They've had a lot of good writers," Barbara said.

"Good editors," Bridge said.

Frauline bubbled over with the drinks. She could have had a great job with Lawrence Welk, Bridge thought.

They all clinked glasses and bottles together.

"I got my story on the Rock Lady," Barbara said. "Did you know she is at the Petrified Forest with five other people waiting for the rock of rocks to come back and take them away in a spaceship?"

Bridge did not want to tell her he knew all the gory details. Busting a reporter's story is not good for karma whether you believe in karma or not. Karma, not being a god, is doubly hard to try and figure out.

"Don't tell me you found a rock to interview?" Bridge asked.

"No, I told the Rock Lady if she isn't on a spaceship in three weeks to not come back and to give the Professor a break."

"He's had several breaks," Stoops said.

"Nice gesture, looking out for the Professor," Vivian said to Barbara.

Barbara shrugged her shoulders like she had had a weak moment.

Jackson walked in. After having his ego stroked by four married women he was puffed up like a puffer fish.

"Oh Jackson, your music just makes me want me to jump up and rip my clothes off," Barbara taunted in jest. Married couples have their own means of communication that to most other people is just gibberish. But what she was really saying was, "If you sleep with any of those dizzy broads it will be hard to play the guitar with broken fingers."

Jackson smiled. What else could he do? Men have such a strange existence.

"Barbara tells us you just cut your first CD," Stoops said as Jackson pulled up a chair and sat.

"It feels great," Jackson said.

When I finish a book, I want to puke, Bridge thought, wondering why it did not make him feel great.

Frauline bubbled over with a house red wine for Jackson. Smooth and sexy singers drink red wine. Beer is more for the blues and punk rock boys and whiskey is for the true country singers - speed having gone out of vogue when Hank Williams found out that not sleeping or eating for a couple of years will kill you.

"I hope you get rich and famous," Vivian said to Jackson.

"That's all I need is twenty-five thousand married women tossing their underwear at him," Barbara smiled, knowing the rules of the game.

"If Bridge gets famous the women will toss erasers at him and tell him to clean up his punctuation," Vivian said.

They all clinked their glasses and bottles together. Clinking is a contagious thing, and one doesn't have to worry about penicillin shots.

Sergeant walked in with none of his sixteen girlfriends.

"This is turning into a party," Stoops said.

Sergeant pulled up a chair. He looked tired, but someone with sixteen girlfriends is always tired. "Are you going to serve hors d'oeuvres during the art walk?" Sergeant asked Bridge.

"I haven't thought about it," Bridge said.

"You should. It's the proper thing to do," Sergeant said.

"Proper is a terrible word," Bridge said. "It's so British."

"Being an old cowboy you could serve Vienna sausages and sardines," Stoops said. "And Vivian could make you some real cowboy coffee with the grounds still in it."

Bridge liked the idea of his patrons having to pick coffee grounds out of their teeth. But Vienna sausages and sardines can cause terrible gas. Gas at a gallery opening would be worse than having gas on a long airplane ride.

Four of Sergeant's women came in and Sergeant got up from the table quicker than Michael Jackson can no longer say, "I only sleep with little boys to keep them warm."

Watching Sergeant walk away, Bridge was slightly angry. Sergeant had started the whole hors d'oeuvres conversation. Do people go to a gallery to eat or buy art?

Bridge suddenly couldn't take it anymore. Sadness did not sweep over him. Visions of million-dollar cleavage didn't sweep over him, or an outie bellybutton, but he felt like being alone. He waved at Frauline, who bubbled over. "I'd like my bill, and I owe for yesterday."

Stoops and Vivian, and Jackson and Barbara, were deep into a conversation about how the coffee farmers in South America had to grow coca because the price of coffee was so low. They did not see Bridge leave. Cocaine and coffee are very important topics. Six billion years won't seem like such a long time with everyone jacked up.

The sun was going down as Bridge two-stepped forward and one backward toward the Why Am I Here. Music blared from the This Isn't Heaven Bar and a group of bikers were outside smoking and wondering if there was any other place on their bodies they could add another tattoo. Young people with green and blue and orange hair, pierced body parts, and clothes that could have been on a scarecrow were skateboarding down the middle of the road. Our salvation, Bridge thought. All the galleries were closed. MeJoe was standing in front of his gallery. He was not talking, but he was peering up at the sky. Bridge wondered if a blind person really peered. But if they didn't peer, what did they do? Did they blank? I blanked at the sky. At times language is very inadequate. A wordless book made up of body language makes a lot of sense.

Bridge, for one instant, felt like going over to MeJoe and telling him his hypnotist idea was a bunch of bunk but decided against it. He did not want to start a fight between Me and Joe. He went inside, locked the door behind him, and two-stepped forward and one backward to his living room, den, and bedroom. He turned on his quill and inkwell, sat, took a deep breath, and sighed. He brought up his novel, went to the last page and read - WE ARE ALL HYPNOTIZED BY OURSELVES. He deleted the line. He typed the line again once more - WE ARE ALL HYPNOTIZED BY OURSELVES.

He sat back and read the line several times. "What is happening to you, Bridge?" he asked himself.

You came here not liking anything.

You came here for a refuge.

You came here to hide.

From what?

You came here and wanted nothing to change, but you know everything changes.

What the hell?

You don't like cars, but you ride in one.

Hypocrite.

You don't like tour buses. New galleries. Advertising. Hors d'oeuvres.

You fell in love.

You fell in love, but you can't say I love you.

And now.

And now.

You donated money for an art walk.

You didn't freak out when a building sold.

The old lampposts are disappointed in me.

The paving machines are winning.

I think I will serve Vienna sausages and sardines with cowboy coffee.

I would like to not give a damn if people get gas.

What did Vivian whisper in my ear?

Then Bridge remembered something - something very important. He two-stepped forward and one backward quickly out the door, leaving the back light on. MeJoe was still blanking at the night sky. Maybe there are shooting stars in his head, Bridge thought, adding, I hope there are shooting stars in his head.

Bridge two-stepped forward and one backward through the art district. He stopped at a corner convenience store. The cashier did not smile - minimum wage is not a happy thing. Bridge then headed toward a residential area. Most of the houses had inside lights on and the curtains were drawn shut. The sky was alive with stars, but the curtains shut them out. Two cats screeched in the distance and several cars drove by, the drivers merely shadows.

Chapter Thirty-One

It was Berry's birthday. He was sitting in the living room. He had all the lights out except one. The TV was off. The room was a no man's tone of gray. There was no order to the house. It was not dirty, but it was unkempt. Still, after four years in Lost City, he had not hung on the walls the photographs of plants he had taken all over the world. They leaned against the wall like flowers trying to bloom. Many of his clothes were still in boxes. The kitchen was a collection of dirty plates and take out containers. His old backpack was in the closet still packed with his first aid kit, flashlight and binoculars. His hiking shoes were dried out. His camera lay on a shelf unused. Berry was drinking Scotch - already half of a bottle. He was not drinking it out of the bottle but in a glass with two ice cubes. If nothing else, man has to be civilized. He was celebrating his birthday and also thinking about his wife, who had been dead for five years. No one in town knew about his wife. He had told them he was divorced when he moved to Lost City. He had told them he had been married twelve times. He had only been married once. Who wants pity? Who needs pity? The hell with pity and caring and softness - life is a stroke, a crinkled left arm, a foot that drags, and words that hang in the spittle on the edge of one's mouth. Life is a dead wife and another useless year.

Berry remembered all the hikes he went on doing research on plants - hikes in Japan, China, Europe, Utah, Washington, and Mexico. Now, please, one block without stumbling - one block. He remembered his wife's smile. Her auburn hair and the funny little mole she had on her left shoulder - the mole that looked like a butt - a funny little cute butt. He remembered. Fuck memories and warmth and funny little moles. Remember cancer. Fuck cancer. Remember dancing and making love and smiling. Remember the time we made love above Lake Shasta. Fuck Lake Shasta. Fuck trees and birds and flowers and a blue sky so blue there is no blue to describe it. Berry had always been a grump. But she had been his anti-grump. With her, he was not a grump. She was somehow above the shit of life. She was an angel - an angel of mercy. They met in high school, married, could not have kids, and he got his PHD in botany. Plants and grasses are the salvation of man - the food source of the ages. Berry poured himself another Scotch. He toasted the ceiling. "You would not like to see me like this, my love, crippled, my dignity only in my crassness. The good always goes - the bad remains - but not for you, my love. For you the bad always went and the good remained."

Berry felt that life was a TV program that was mostly commercials. People forget the show and remember the commercials. I am a car. I am a new dress. I am a clean floor. I am spotless windows and matching plates. I am red wine and beer and fifty-year-old Scotch. I am a lawn mower and a happy dog. I am forever young. I am Christmas with thousands of presents for every child in the world. I am what I am told I am. What am I?

Berry drained his drink and poured another one. In the corner of the living room was a shotgun. A twelve-gauge pump loaded with five number eight high-brass birdshot shotgun shells, one of which was in the chamber - shot that would send a dove or quail to either heaven or hell - shot that would stop a burglar in his tracks and before he died wonder why he had taken up a life of crime. Shot that, if one put their mouth on the barrel, with a little squeeze on the trigger, would blow off the back of their skull. No pain, no thought, no remembering the blast, no twisted arm and dragging leg, no cute little moles that look like a butt, no useless hiking boots or unused cameras.

Berry looked at the shotgun. His father had given it to him, but Berry had never liked to hunt. Botanists do not kill, they grow. They grow green living things. Things that nurture and sway in the wind. But even plants made no real sense. Some were poison. Some had thorns. Are thorns necessary in life? "I am nothing but a thorn,"

Berry said to the shotgun.

The shotgun did not really give a damn one way or the other.

Berry stood and walked over to the shotgun like only a man who has had a stroke can. He picked up the shotgun and took it back to his chair. "You are deadly but also serene in your simplicity," he said to the shotgun.

He slipped off the safety.

He finished his drink.

No goodbye letter.

The cancer foundation gets everything. Cancer, at least you are not prejudiced. Fuck cancer, you gutless mother fucker - killer of men, women, kids, gays, blacks, chinks, dagoes and gooks - killer of dogs, cats, birds, and fish.

Berry put his mouth around the barrel of the shotgun. He placed his finger on the trigger.

He shut his eyes - one more vision of her smile.

The doorbell rang.

"What the fuck?" Berry swore.

The doorbell rang once again.

Berry opened his eyes but did not remove his mouth from the barrel or his finger from the trigger.

The doorbell rang again.

Berry leaned the shotgun up against the wall and walked to the door the way only a man who has had a stroke can. He opened the door.

Bridge was standing there holding a brown paper bag. "What the fuck do you want?" Berry grumped.

"I brought some beer to celebrate your birthday," Bridge said, holding out the bag.

Berry seemed to sag for a moment and then stepped outside. He looked up at the night sky. Bridge looked up at the night sky. "It's a nice night, isn't it?" Berry said more than asked.

"Yes it is," Bridge replied.

"Come on in and let's drink a few beers," Berry said.

They drank beer. They talked about flowers and plants and hikes. Berry talked about when he was young. He talked about some of his boyhood girlfriends, but he never mentioned his wife. He did not laugh, but he did not grieve.

Bridge talked little. He only listened. He never said a word about the shotgun leaning up against the wall with the safety off.

Chapter Thirty-Two

In the morning, to Vivian's surprise, MeJoe was drinking coffee at the Wake Up Or Die. He had never been to the coffeehouse. Vivian had never really talked to MeJoe. When she did see him, he always made her feel uneasy, and it was hard to wave to a blind man. There was something about a blind man who was pink and dressed all in white that unnerved her. Why it unnerved her when most of the people in town dressed like discarded circus people she did not know. It was one of those strange things in life. For some reason today Vivian wanted to talk to MeJoe, and she walked over to the table. Before she could open her mouth, MeJoe said politely, "Vivian, why don't you sit with me and have a cup of coffee?"

"How did you know it was me?" Vivian asked, noticing MeJoe was drinking black coffee.

"Your perfume," MeJoe said.

"Scent of a Woman," Vivian said, sitting.

"I didn't see the movie, I heard it," MeJoe said.

Vivian laughed, and then because she had laughed, she felt guilty.

"I'd rather be blind than be like the rest of you," MeJoe said, not offended at all. "With sight, everything is cut and dry. There is night and day, sunshine and clouds, fall colors. With no sight, there is every color that cannot be seen, all the in-between hues that people ignore. There is true imagination. My mind is a kaleidoscope. I see color from the inside of a rainbow, not from miles away."

"I never thought about it," Vivian said. "It must be beautiful."

"It is," MeJoe replied, adding, "You have good coffee here."

"You sound surprised."

"I am. I thought you would only have all the fru fru crap with milk and sugar that is steamed until it tastes like a milkshake."

"You sound like Bridge."

"I like him," MeJoe said. "Why, I don't know. Anyone who spends hours and hours typing novels has to be dumber than a painter."

"You think painters are dumb?"

MeJoe laughed. "All artists are dumb. It's the prerequisite of the trade."

"So you are dumb too," Vivian smiled.

"One has to be what they are," MeJoe said. "Besides, dumb isn't the worse thing to be in life. I could a politician, or a thief, or own a car lot. Need I go on?"

"How about owning a coffee shop?"

"You love your job. I can tell."

"I do. I really do."

"Love is a nice thing," MeJoe said.

"Would you like another cup of coffee?" Vivian asked.

"No. The reason I came over here was to talk to you."

"Me?"

"Yes."

"About what?"

"Me and Joe want to give you some advice."

"Yes."

MeJoe stood. "If a man will not tell a woman he loves her, then maybe the woman should play hard to get."

"That's hard for an old hippie chick. We were always easy to get, too easy most of the time," Vivian said truthfully.

Without another word MeJoe stood and tapped away.

Vivian watched MeJoe until he was out of the store. How does he know Bridge loves me? How does he know I love Bridge? she wondered and headed for the counter. Hell, she thought, I am as easy to get as a fifty-dollar whore trying to play hard to get with a man with two one-hundred-dollar bills in his hand.

Chris was not a happy gay man. The supposed love of his life had been seen at the movies with another man. To make it more troubling, the other man was younger. Chris had been crying all night and his eyes were puffy and red. He would have made a great advertisement for a gay man hay fever commercial. "Is my butt getting big?" he almost begged Vivian.

"No, it looks fine to me," she said, although his butt did not even come close to a good cowboy butt.

"Do you think I look old?" Chris lamented.

"How old are you?"

"Twenty-eight."

"Give me a break, Chris. If I had had kids, you would be the youngest."

"My boyfriend is cheating on me," Chris said, and his lower lip started to tremble.

"I have some advice for you," Vivian said.

"Yes."

"Play hard to get," she said and headed for the door, figuring she could have a better conversation with the dogs that were tied outside.

With three dogs wagging their tails at her like she was the best thing since dried pig's ears she had an idea. Why not write the Let's Make Lost City Into A Political Hotbed and see if I can have my own advice column for gays only. It would be unique, as it would be answered from the straight perspective. Sometimes one has to live outside the bubble to really know what is going on inside the bubble.

Vivian saw Bridge and Stoops going into the This Isn't Heaven Bar. For some reason she felt like going over and whacking both of them upside the head. It wouldn't be out of anger but just for the hell of it - a just for the hell of it good whack upside the head. There is a time in everyone's life when they need a good unprovoked, just for the hell of it, whack upside the head. Most people didn't have the advantage of MeJoe and could hit themselves every so often.

Vivian quelled her whacking idea. She bent down and patted the three dogs. As she started to go back into the store the dogs looked like their little doggie hearts had been broken. Dogs have it down. They can look sad or happy and still get patted. No one tells a dog, "Hey, get over it, you stupid jerk, don't you know how life is? Don't give me that tail wagging shit. Pat your own self you dumb fuck."

Vivian did not see Pill or the Professor go in the Wake Up Or Die, but they were sitting by the window.

The Professor was a reborn man. He was clean and the bandages were off his head. Pill still looked like a longhaired hippie from Texas who had to learn how to talk all over again - y'all, whoopee shit, and do you have a dip not being phrases that are readily used anywhere else in the United States. The only thing that made him look different was the sign hanging on his chest - THERE ARE ONLY SIX BILLION YEARS LEFT FOR THE WORLD. Vivian, after talking to MeJoe and Chris, and patting three dogs, was emotionally drained, and besides, she had to take a pee, so she headed for the bathroom. It is a strange thing in life, but for most people the only time they get solitude is when they have to go to the bathroom. I found my true self in the bathroom. My life has never been the same since. Lock the door, pass the toilet paper, and give me a good book.

"I found out something that might disturb you," the Professor said to Pill.

"Don't tell me the price of peanut butter is going up," Pill said, looking worried.

"No. I read in an article that it is not six billion years before the sun explodes and becomes a black hole that will suck the entire universe into its bottomless stomach but ten billion years."

Pill's eyes grew large like he had just eaten ten peyote buttons and was about to puke for three days. He started to vibrate. "Wha, wha, wha, what?" he vibrated.

The Professor knew he had screwed up. Most of the time illusions are far better than the truth. One can always make up another illusion to get by, but the truth is the truth, unless you are one of those with weird ideas like everyone has their own truths or the truth of the matter is there really is no truth.

"Wha, wha, wha, what?" Pill vibrated again since the Professor had not answered him quick enough.

"Ten billion years instead of six billion years," the Professor said.

"You, you, you, you're lying," Pill vibrated.

The Professor shook his head.

Instantly, like someone had turned off a switch, Pill stopped vibrating. His eyes went back to normal. He smiled. "What's four billion years?" he asked, shrugging his shoulders.

"Not much more than six billion," the Professor said.

Pill smiled. "At least peanut butter has not gone up."

In the morning Berry, Bridge, and Stoops were sitting at the This

Isn't Heaven Bar. Four men who didn't know if they were hippies or just bums were playing pool. Berry had come in first and had unplugged the jukebox. The pool players had tried to play it, and when it wouldn't play, they had complained to Gloria. Gloria had beat on it, kicked it, but it still didn't work. She had never thought of checking the plug, and Berry wasn't going to tell her.

The first thing Berry had said to Bridge was, "Thanks for last night."

They shook hands.

"Buy these two assholes a drink," Berry told Gloria.

It's good to see a man get back to his normal self.

"I heard you gave money for an art walk," Berry said to Bridge.

"I don't want to talk about it," Bridge said.

Stoops was not talking. A late night at The Hole had left him speechless. He looked at his Bloody Mary, which to him looked like two Bloody Marys. If he tried to pick up the wrong one, he got nothing, but on the other hand if he tried to pick up the right one, his hand was shaking so bad he might spill it. He finally got lucky and picked up the right one with both hands and slurped it, sounding like a cow at a water trough that had not had a drink in three days.

Bridge looked at him disapprovingly. One of his pet peeves in life was people who made noise when they ate or drank - inconsiderate slobs - smack, smack, smack, slurp, slurp. Go live with the pigs or go to India and eat with your fingers.

"A new gallery is opening," Berry said. "An impressionist from New York is going to show his own work."

Stoops looked at Bridge. Berry looked at Bridge.

Bridge calmly and quietly took a swallow from his drink.

"I said a new gallery is opening," Berry said again.

Bridge drained his glass. Gloria came over. "Your nipple rings are outdoing themselves this morning," Bridge said. "I'd like another order of toast."

Gloria smiled and went to make another Bloody Mary.

"Is there any place in the world I could move to and not have to talk to someone from New York or California?" Bridge asked either Stoops or Berry.

"I don't think so," Stoops said.

Berry shook his head.

"Is there any place in the world where little kids don't dream about riding horses and being either an Indian or a cowboy?" Bridge asked.

Stoops and Berry both shook their heads.

"Is there any place in the world I could walk two steps forward and one backward and people would not think I was a freak?" Bridge asked.

Stoops and Berry shook their heads.

They were starting to remind Bridge of those weird little things people buy in gas stations and stick to their dashboards that shake and wiggle.

"I can no longer hide. I can't stop anything," Bridge said almost sadly.

Gloria brought Bridge his other order of toast. The three men did not talk. Inwardly, Bridge's guts were spinning about ninety-seven thousand miles an hour. He wanted to scream. He wanted to jump up and down. He wanted to toss impressionist paintings in front of a paving machine. He wanted Lost City to build a fence around itself and put guard towers every fifty yards manned by men with fifty-caliber machine guns. He wanted the old lampposts that still worked, and were living on a commune, to go on a rampage and run down the streets naked. He wanted all the tour buses in the world to suddenly wake up with all their tires flat.

"You know," Bridge said, his voice distant like it was coming from the moon, "I think I should write a book about this little town before we are like all the other art towns."

"What would you say in it?" Berry asked.

"Who would know?" Bridge said.

"That would be a great title," Stoops said.

"It's funny when you think you are at the end of a rainbow," Berry said.

"I don't understand," Bridge said.

"Maybe the end of one rainbow is the beginning of another rainbow," Berry said.

"Thanks," Bridge said, put some money on the bar, stood and started two-stepping forward and one backward out of the bar.

"Hey Bridge," Berry called as Bridge got to the door.

Bridge stopped and turned.

"Next time you come over, bring some better beer." Berry smiled his, 'I just gave you an F' smile.

Bridge gave Berry the old cowboy nod.

"What was that all about?" Stoops asked Berry.

"Strokes, love, photographs, shotguns that don't care one way or the other, and friends who don't forget," Berry said. "Is there anything else you want to know, you nosy son of a bitch?"

"For a matter of fact, there is. I want to know how space cannot have an edge."

"It's easy," Berry said. "It doesn't have a center."

"Is that why we are all stuck up somewhere in between?"

"It's as good of an excuse as any."

Chapter Thirty-Three

Pill was in the mountains sitting in his truck and clutching a jar of peanut butter so hard that if the jar had not been made out of plastic it might have broken. The fact there were ten billion years left for the world and not six billion, which he at first had accepted when the Professor told him, had come back with a four-billion-year paranoid vengeance. He had eaten half the jar of peanut butter, which had calmed him down considerably, and now he was trying to assess his life.

What does one do when all that they felt was true is suddenly found out to be false?

Pill screwed the lid back on the peanut butter jar and took several deep breaths. "I don't have to believe what others believe," he said defiantly.

"There are people who believe that the earth is flat."

"There are people who believe the earth is hollow."

"There are people who believe that Elvis is still alive."

"There are people who believe male aliens come down and sleep with our women."

"There are people who believe in Bigfoot."

"There are people who believe that art will save the world."

"There are people who believe God is a woman."

"There are people who believe man can live in peace."

"There are people who believe there is a rock of rocks."

"There are people who believe that the government really gives a damn."

"There are people who believe that history does not repeat itself."

"There are people who believe man has only been on the planet for six thousand years."

"There are people who believe drugs bring you enlightenment."

"There are people who believe that cows and monkeys are sacred."

"There are people who believe if a person drinks ten gallons of carrot juice a day they will not get cancer."

Pill ran out of, there are people who, although he knew there were at least ten million more - beliefs being more numerous than grains of sand on a beach and cheaper than popcorn.

Pill got out of his truck and held up his arms toward the sky like either he was beseeching the sky or he wanted to get hit by a lightning bolt. He hollered at the sky, "I believe there is only six billion years left for the world."

Pill got back in his truck and headed back to town. People had to know the truth. Six billion years and counting. He had a strange idea. In six billion years, when the sun does ingest the entire universe, would it get indigestion from having to eat so much shit? You are what you eat.

****

Rudolph and Rebecca were sitting in their restaurant, Sally's. Lunch was over and nobody except the hostess was in the restaurant. The hostess was cleaning tables and chanting her mantra - her mantra being, I need more tips, Jew bastards. She, being Jewish, was not offended. She had never recovered from the lousy allowance her father used to give her and had sworn she would never marry a Jewish man, date a Jewish man, or, for that matter, date a Jewish woman - she couldn't stand to hear one more time in her life a Jewish woman whine through her nose, "You schmuck, I want a house in Florida."

Luckily for her the only Jewish people living in Lost City were stoners who couldn't remember how many candle holders were in that funny candle thing that they were supposed to light around Christmas.

Rudolph seemed depressed, which most people from California

are. It takes many years for people who have moved away from California to get over the shock of living somewhere where people are civil and women have not had nose and boob jobs. "I think I want to close the restaurant and open an art gallery," Rudolph said.

The statement was so absurd Rebecca did not bother to make a reply.

"I have always wanted to be an artist and have never followed my true desires in life," Rudolph continued.

"What did you say?" Rebecca asked.

Rudolph was not offended. Most men learn to be their own listeners anyway. It is only women who get offended when they are not listened to - also the woman side of a gay relationship. Trying to be politically correct at times is ridiculous.

"I said I have never followed my desire to be an artist," Rudolph said.

"You have never painted, drawn, written, carved, doodled, or done anything artistic your whole life," Rebecca said. "I think you should go have a few drinks with the boys this afternoon and get over your self-pity. You haven't gone to Bill's Restaurant and Libations in weeks."

"Thanks honey," Rudolph said.

His ploy had worked. He could go and get pie-eyed without getting in trouble. There was no way he would ever be an artist - poverty did not appeal to him. Besides, he smoked too much dope to ever really be dedicated to anything.

Life is good when one pulls off a small larceny.

****

Bridge had spent the afternoon in the store doing what most gallery owners do in Lost City - stood and looked out the window waiting for a customer. He had not worked on his novel, but he had made a brief outline for a novel about Lost City. Like most of his novels he had no idea where it would start, what it would be about, or where it would end, but he liked the idea. He didn't really give a hoot about all the tiny details.

Stoops had spent the afternoon in a funk. He had sat by a table in front of the Wake Up Or Die watching humanity walk by and wondering if he was really a member of humanity or if humanity had somehow left him in the dirt. What was really bothering him, but he would not admit it, was he missed Organic Muffin terribly.

Berry had gone home and started cleaning up his house. He began by hanging a few of his photographs on the wall. He unloaded the shotgun and put it under his bed.

The Professor, telling everyone he was over the Rock Lady, was studying and trying to put the moves on a nineteen-year-old girl from Minnesota whose only belief was she didn't like mosquitoes.

Sergeant had stomach cramps, a migraine, and hot flashes - he had absorbed them from one of his sixteen girlfriends.

In the late afternoon, Bridge, Stoops, Berry, the Professor, Rudolph, and Sergeant were at Bill's Restaurant and Libations. Everyone was in a good mood except Sergeant, who was holding his head and still having hot flashes. They each had their own choice of drinks. There has to be some freedom left in life. Rudolph was so happy to be out with the boys he was one big smile. Stoops had gotten over his funk, deciding he really didn't care if humanity had past him by or not. If it really had, he could always go live with monkeys, although he was not really a big fan of bananas. Berry was so friendly everyone thought he had taken at least a dozen Valium and were wondering when he would explode and tell everybody to enjoy their failing grade. The Professor was content, deciding there had to be some form of meaning in chasing younger women - preferably dumb naive ones, which the mid-west seems to have a lock on. California, East Coast, and Southern women might be dumb, but they aren't naive - they wear too much jewelry, which, as everyone should know, they do not buy themselves. "Oh Gloria, look at this twenty-two-carat diamond I just bought myself. My boyfriend will be so jealous he will run out and buy me a Porsche."

"I saw Pill carrying a new sign that reads, 'There is only six billion years left for the world. Whoever wrote there are only ten billion years lefts is a liar,'" Berry said.

"Wouldn't it be ironic if all of mankind died and Pill was the only one left?" the Professor said.

"Why?" Berry asked.

"Can a person be paranoid without other people?" the Professor asked.

"That's a good one," Sergeant said, fighting through his migraine and hot flashes.

"I heard Vivian is having another fundraiser in two days," Rudolph said.

"I'm not going to read poetry for this one," Bridge announced sternly.

"It's her annual fundraiser for vitamin-enriched winter birdseed," Rudolph said.

"Tweet, tweet, tweet, depression, bad cat, bad cat, why can't we all just get along," Berry smiled.

The group still wasn't used to Berry smiling and they all gave him a, 'what is wrong with you' glance.

"If you are going to remain true to yourself, you have to remain grumpy," Bridge said to Berry.

"I think that I am now a happy grump," Berry said.

"Happy Grump could have been the eighth dwarf in Snow White," Sergeant said.

"Happy Grump could have been the adopted child of Happy and Grumpy's gay relationship," Rudolph said.

Being from San Francisco, Rudolph was an authority on gay relationships.

"There's a slot market for a young adult book for you, Bridge," Stoops said.

"You write it," Bridge said.

"You know I can't write."

"Neither can Bridge," Berry said.

"I'm the first one to admit it," Bridge replied.

Frauline bubbled over. "I want all of you to buy vitamin-enriched birdseed for Vivian's fundraiser," she said, which was a lot more words than, "Would you guys like another round?"

"Bring everyone a drink on their own tab," Berry said.

"I didn't want one," Sergeant said after Frauline left.

"I'll drink yours," Rudolph said - gay authorities from San Francisco who have not been out with the boys in a long time have a big thirst.

Three gay couples came into the bar. It was easy to tell they were gay, as three of the men had dresses on and had not shaved their legs, which was not a pretty sight.

The group said hello as the couples headed for another room. The gay men glared at them while the gay men women smiled.

Frauline brought the drinks. Sergeant paid his tab and started to leave. "You should take two Midol," Stoops told him.

Sergeant ignored him, waved, and was off to one, or two, or twelve, or maybe all of his sixteen girlfriends.

The guys were all talking and Bridge went into one of his things where he could see their lips move but could not understand anything they were saying. He went off to the ozone land, which many times in life is not a bad place to be.

Where did you spend your life?

I spent it in the ozone.

I went there once. The beach was great and the food was inexpensive. I wish I could go there more often, but reality always seems to get in the way.

I've been in reality most of my life. It sucks.

Yeah, I know. Reality really isn't what it is made up to be.

Bridge's mind was suddenly pulled into a time warp where instead of going back in time he went forward. He was no longer at Bill's. Bridge was wearing a nice pair of brown slacks, a tan silk shirt, ribbed socks and expensive Italian slip-on shoes. He had a gold chain around his neck, a diamond pinky ring, and a gold bracelet that was so thick it was a week's take at the biggest gold mine in Alaska. He was standing in his gallery surrounded by men and women dressed to the nines. A pretty college girl wearing black slacks and a starched white shirt was serving hors d'oeuvres. There was smoked salmon, caviar and mushroom caps and other things so fancy Bridge could not pronounce their names. Everything was being served on delicate china with solid silver utensils. Two ladies circulated through the room refilling wineglasses. The wineglasses were hand etched. There was a man dressed in a tuxedo by the door with a silver tray in his hand where patrons coming into the gallery placed their gold-plated private invitations. Outside, the entire block was bumper to bumper with limousines.

The artists stood by their art and expounded on their creativity and their sources of inspiration. Bridge walked around the room smiling, nodding his head, and enjoying his aura of gallery owner. Already he had sold five paintings for a gross of over two hundred thousand.

A lady came up to Bridge who was so pretty and rich she had already been through ten husbands and twenty-five lovers. "Oh Bridge," she said, "you must dump that frumpy girlfriend of yours.

It is so below you to be going with some old hippie chick who owns a coffee shop."

"I already have," Bridge answered. "I don't know what I was thinking or what got into me to spend my time with somebody so common."

The lady winked at him and said, "Come over after the opening. I want to show you some of my etchings."

Bridge kissed her hand.

Vivian was standing outside the gallery peering in the window. She had not received an invitation. Tears were streaming down her face. She kept tapping on the glass, but nobody paid any attention to her. She kept muttering, "Bridge, Bridge, I love you. I love you."

Bridge glanced over and saw her but ignored her. Vivian stepped away from the window and ran down the street. As soon as she started running Bridge had a sinking feeling in his heart. He felt alone. He felt the deepest sense of sadness he had ever felt. He glanced quickly around the room. The people were patrons, but they were not friends. He ran from the gallery and saw Vivian running around a corner. Tears were streaming behind her so thick they looked like a comet's tail. "Vivian, Vivian," Bridge called and started chasing after her.

He rounded the corner and Vivian stopped. Bridge stopped. Vivian looked at him so forlornly he cried out, "I am so sorry. Please, please forgive me?"

Bridge tried to walk toward Vivian, but he could not move. It was like he was stuck in tar but he had no tusks. Vivian started to back away from him. She was shaking her head. She was crying. Bridge tried to follow her, but he was immobile. He reached for her. She continued to back up. Bridge was frozen in place. "Vivian, Vivian, I, I, I, I, Lo, Lo, Lo, Lo," he cried then choked on a meatball.

Vivian grew smaller and smaller as she backed up until she was only a pinpoint, and then she vanished. "No, no, no," Bridge pleaded. "What have I done?"

Everyone at Bill's Restaurant and Libations jumped when Bridge shouted, "No! No! No!"

Bridge, with terrified eyes, looked at Berry, Stoops, Rudolph, and the Professor. "Vivian vanished," he muttered and then two-stepped forward and one backward out of Bill's Restaurant and Libations as fast as he could.

No one at the table said anything for a few moments. Then Berry said, "That is one creative way to get out of paying your bill."

Chapter Thirty-Four

Bridge quickly two-stepped forward and one backward to the Wake Up Or Die. His heart was going at least three thousand miles an hour. Had Vivian disappeared? He huffed up to the counter. Chris and his boyfriend had made up, so Chris was in a merry mood. "Where's Vivian?" Bridge wheezed, almost out of breath.

"She gave me the coffee shop and eloped with a gay hairdresser," Chris said.

"No, she can't be gone," Bridge moaned and clutched his head.

"Bridge, get a hold of yourself, she is in her private room."

Bridge took a deep breath. "Please tell her I am here," he almost begged.

"I can't," Chris said. "She will come out when she is ready."

Bridge sat at a table by the window. Six mutt dogs, ranging in size from a foot to several feet tall, and colored varying shades of dirty dishwater, peered through the window at him. He felt like he was a TV and wondered if the dogs wanted him to change the channel.

Vivian came over and sat with him. "If those dogs were people, I bet you could sell them a book of yours," she said.

"I am so glad you are here," Bridge said like a little boy who had missed his mommy.

Vivian did not know what to say, but she smiled. "I need a hug," Bridge said.

"Go hug Chris."

"Vivian."

Vivian gave Bridge one of her I'll squeeze you till you fart hugs.

They sat back down. "Have you ever thought about leaving this town?" Bridge asked, feeling much better after the hug and holding back some gas.

"Not really."

"Have you ever thought your old boyfriend might hire someone to collect the money you stole from him?" Bridge asked.

Vivian laughed, which seemed strange to him - being hunted by a collection guy for a dope dealer didn't seem funny at all. "He can't hire anyone. I have all his money. Those kinds of people don't do favors," Vivian said and shrugged her shoulders like that was that and there was no more to it.

"You're something," Bridge said with a warm smile.

"You have me worried," Vivian said seriously. "You don't gag or gog or goggle anymore when someone comes into town and buys a new building. You don't scream when a road gets paved. You seem to have accepted the fact one day tour buses will be coming to town. And you have chipped in for an art walk. Are you depressed?"

Bridge looked at the dogs. They wagged their tails at him. "We are all like those dogs," Bridge said. "When it all comes down to it, we all want attention, a pat on the head, a scratch behind the ear, and a smile. Someone to tell us we are doing well and at times to tell us we've been bad. No, I'm not depressed. I think I am finally learning to accept life."

"If you weren't sleeping with me I'd tell you I think you need to get laid," Vivian said.

"Really?"

"Really."

"How about let's go back to your house for a quickie?"

"Now?"

"Now."

"Ok."

They headed for Vivian's house. Vivian was walking in front because at times she couldn't stand walking beside Bridge. When Bridge got to the house, Vivian was already naked and in bed. Bridge took his clothes off. As he was getting into bed, Vivian said with a smile, "Bridge, don't let this go to your head, but you have always been quick, so, I hope this isn't a quicker than normal quickie."

For some reason the phrase, rolling in my sweet baby's arms, flashed through Bridge's head.

As Bridge put his arm around Vivian he asked timidly, "Do you think you would ever leave me?"

Vivian did not answer for a few moments. Then she replied, "There are no guarantees in life, Bridge."

"I, I, I, I, I Lo, Lo," choke on a meatball.

"Yes, Bridge."

"I, I, I, I, I, Lo, Lo," choke on a bigger meatball.

"Shut up and let's play."

Rolling in my sweet baby's arms. Dear Jesus, don't take me now.

By the time the quickie was done, the sun was beginning to go down. Bridge asked Vivian if she wanted to go eat. "McDonalds, you sexy stud you," Vivian chided.

"No, let's go get some Mexican food."

There was a nice Mexican restaurant only two blocks from the coffeehouse.

Vivian did not walk in front of Bridge but mimicked his walk as they walked. They held hands. Bridge did not try to tell Vivian he loved her. Quickies have a way of taking words right out of a person's mouth or stuffing other things in it.

Bridge was hoping for a nice quiet dinner. But as many things in life never go as planned the restaurant was packed with couples with young children and was about as intimate as a chicken coop with a fox in it. Vivian did not mind the noise. Living most of her life in a coffeehouse filled with the noise of politics, philosophy, and bad poetry, the sound of children was refreshing and in a lot of ways more intelligent and stimulating. Bridge was famished and had the super combo Mexican plate that, in keeping with the American tradition of serving too much food, was large enough to feed four people and two dogs. That is if the dogs liked hot green chili and lard.

Vivian had one enchilada and one taco. Watching Bridge eat, she was amazed. "How long has it been since you have eaten?" she asked as he shoveled in another mouthful of food.

"I don't know. I don't really think about food," Bridge chomped.

"I know you don't burn many brain cells while you write your dribble, so what in the world could you be thinking about?" Vivian asked.

"You," Bridge chomped.

"You're so sexy with a taco in your hand and beans dripping off your chin."

"Oh Vivian, I, I, I, I, I, I."

"I know you don't know what to say."

Bridge reached across the table and lightly stroked her cheek. "I had a dream you had vanished and it made me feel sadder than I have ever felt in my life."

"Bridge, a woman who weighs 185 pounds would have a hard time vanishing."

"What did you whisper in my ear the other night at The Hole?"

Vivian knew what she had said, 'I know,' but she replied, "I don't remember."

Bridge could see a momentary flash of sadness in her eyes. But then her eyes sparkled again - the childlike eyes that captivated him. She smiled. A halo seemed to materialize around her head. A golden glow circled her body. Her large hands with their rings were blessings. "Do birds really need vitamin-enriched birdseed?" Bridge asked.

"No, but they know it is special and they are very thankful."

"They are just birds."

"They are not just birds. They are gifts. They are gifts like red, blue, green, yellow, orange, and purple fairies. They are song and flight. They are a reminder that there is always hope."

"Is there always hope?"

"Bridge, if you didn't believe in hope, you wouldn't write books."

"Vivian, you are the best friend I have ever had in my life."

"Bridge?"

"Yes."

"Wipe the beans off of your chin and take me home for another quickie."

They walked as quickly as they could to Vivian's house. These quick things have to be taken very seriously and acted on quickly or at times they can quickly go away.

How quickly time flies.

Chapter Thirty-Five

The next morning the Professor was at the Wake Up Or Die. It was a glorious day. Not too hot. Not too cold. Just enough wind. There were a few clouds in the sky that seemed to be happy children playing on a swing set. All the dogs outside were lying down snoozing. There were no huge political or philosophical debates going on. Everyone was looking out the window and silently thinking some tranquil thoughts. It was one of those days when the earth seems to sigh and enjoy itself - enough of thunder, lightning, floods, earthquakes, and volcanoes.

The Professor was lost in thoughts of the girl from Minnesota and was wondering why people from Minnesota say toe for ta? And then, like a sudden sand storm, the Rock Lady blew into the Wake Up Or Die. The Professor gasped. The Rock Lady saw him and ran toward his table. She looked like she had spent two lifetimes in the desert trying to figure out what Moses was trying to say. She was covered with so much dust she could have been a female Linus. Her hair went off in every direction like she had stuck her finger into a light socket, unfortunately for the Professor it had not killed her, but fortunately she did not have any sacred rocks in her grimy hands.

At times like this, the Professor thought, it should not be against the law to shoot women.

The Rock Lady sat. Her eyes were empty like a cheap Chinese copy of a expensive German porcelain doll. The first thing the Professor said was, "Where is my car?"

The Rock Lady looked at him like she could not understand a word he said.

"Where....is....car?" the Professor said slowly.

The Rock Lady started crying. The tears left little dirt trails down her face. The Professor did not feel sorry for the Rock Lady, his first wife's crying had cost him over a hundred big ones, and he had no doubt his car had gone to car heaven, or at the very least a chop shop in Tucson.

"It's ok. I have insurance," the Professor said - retired attorneys know how to cover their tracks. Old hippies and artists don't know how to spell insurance. To most of them insurance is a couple of ounces of pot stashed away behind a switch plate.

Vivian came into the store, saw the Rock Lady, and went and stood behind the counter with Chris. She kept a Louisville Slugger behind the counter which she had never had to use, but one never knew when political discussions could turn into a brawl, or a religious fanatic figured they had to kill a few coffee drinkers to make the rest of the world see the light. "You wouldn't hit the Rock Lady with a ball bat, would you?" Chris asked Vivian.

Vivian nodded her head.

Chris started washing cups that had already been washed. During dangerous times it is better to stay busy and put out neutral vibes.

"The rock of all rocks abandoned me," the Rock Lady choked.

The Professor told himself he didn't really give a hoot but said nothing.

"We picked up rocks for days," the Rock Lady continued. "We chanted. We danced naked. But the spaceship never came. And then five men showed up who were stealing pieces of petrified wood to take back to California and sell as doorstops. They stole your car. They stole the money I had stolen from you, and to top it off, all of my followers went off with them. They told me money has a way a destroying faith."

"I bet you can find them at the Crystal Palace," the Professor said about as heart-broken as a mouse trapped in a peanut factory.

"Oh what can I do?" the Rock Lady beseeched, putting her dirty hands over her dirty tear-streaked face. "My god has forsaken me. I am broke. I have nowhere to go. Oh what can I do?"

The Professor thought. The Rock Lady has beaned me twice

with a rock. Even if it was a sacred rock, it was still a rock. She has stolen my car. She has taken my money. This is a hard decision. "Rock Lady, you should go to Sedona," the Professor said, which was a lot nicer than saying, "I think you should just get the hell out of here and leave me alone."

The Rock Lady stopped crying. She dropped her hands to her sides. Her eyes held a tiny portion of hope. "Why?" she asked breathlessly.

"In Sedona most of the people are old hippies, even though they now drive Porsches and Jaguars. They believe that they live in the vortex of the earth. Patchouli oil hangs in clouds around the town waiting to be transformed into something that smells good. They welcome all believers, and there is no way in hell you can't get a job at an alternative bookstore that specializes in crystals and carries a large line of organic cook books."

"Why haven't I ever been there?" the Rock Lady asked dumbfounded, which, since she was already dumbfounded, was not that hard to do.

"Sometimes the light is hard to see," the Professor said, wondering what the hell he had just said.

"How will I get there?"

"I'll buy you a bus ticket."

"You will?"

"It will be my pleasure."

"But I am dirty."

"Every disciple in history has been dirty." No way was the Professor going to let the Rock Lady take a shower at his house.

"When can I go?"

The Professor stood, took the Rock Lady by the hand, and led her out the door.

Two hours later the Professor was back in the Wake Up Or Die sitting with the girl from Minnesota. She was smiling at him like he was the best thing since spray-on oven cleaner. Vivian, seeing her, thought to herself, my god, that poor dumb little thing, and deep down she hoped that the girl carried a fist-sized rock in her purse.

The Rock Lady was on the bus toward Sedona. There would be a stop in Tucson and Phoenix. The Professor had bought her a one-way bus ticket and given her twenty bucks. She was sitting on the long bench in the back of the bus with a Born Again Christian, a

Jehovah's Witness, a Mormon, a Hari Krishna, and two wetbacks who could not speak English. They were having a grand old time.

****

Berry finished straightening his house. He had even done the dishes. It looked nice. I should give Bridge something for coming over the other night, he thought to himself. But the more he thought, he couldn't think of anything that Bridge really needed. It is nice when people don't need. It's the wanting that can really mess up a good thing.

Vivian spent most of the morning getting ready for her multiple-vitamin birdseed fundraiser. Whoever gave a donation or brought a bag of birdseed would get a free cup of coffee and a hard breadstick that still wasn't selling. Once again the faithful had gone around town putting up flyers. The flyers made the homeless a little bummed out because birds don't eat turkey or mashed potatoes and dried breadsticks really aren't that good. But a few of them did get together and devise a plan. They would tell Vivian they would feed the breadsticks to the birds. They would then sell the breadsticks on the corner and maybe get enough to buy a bottle of wine - even the homeless know the way capitalism works - steal from Peter to pay Paul, pay Paul, steal from Bill to pay Peter, pay Peter, steal from Peter to pay Bill, pay Bill, steal from Peter, Paul, and Bill, declare bankruptcy and keep the million dollar home in Florida and the island in the Caribbean and find another Peter, Paul, and Bill who think they are your friends and don't believe you would steal from them. It is really such an easy system based on the undeniable truth that deep down we are all thieves. Communists, dictators, socialists, eat your hearts out, in your systems there is only one thief. How dumb can some people be - only one thief - it's a strange world.

Pill was walking around town carrying his original - **THERE IS ONLY SIX BILLION YEARS LEFT FOR THE WORLD** sign, but nobody could read it because it was covered up with birdseed donation flyers.

MeJoe was sitting in front of his gallery, All Art Is The Same In The Dark. Me and Joe were not talking. They had had a huge argument over a color to use in a painting and gotten so angry they were now ignoring each other. Lotus Blossom, from, Love Is Only

A Painting Away, noticed MeJoe not talking and grew worried. She went outside and stood by MeJoe, waiting for him to tell her to fuck off. Strangely he smiled at her and said, "Me and Joe are not talking, but MeJoe says good morning."

"Good morning to you also, and to Me and Joe," Lotus Blossom said.

"I feel like something terrible is about to happen," MeJoe said very seriously, so seriously that Lotus Blossom shivered. Most artists are into premonitions and signs - not so much chicken guts and tea leaves, but premonitions cannot be ignored.

"What do you think terrible is going to happen?" Lotus Blossom asked in a haunted house tone.

"I think someone very nice is going to die," MeJoe said.

"I have to go," Lotus Blossom said and rushed off to tell Rainy Day at the Sunbonnet gallery. Rainy Day in turn told Gertrude. Gertrude in turn told Sergeant at The Beginning of a Rainbow gallery. Sergeant in turn told the owners of The End Of War and Art Beyond Words. Nobody told Bridge, who was working on his book and wouldn't answer the door. It was the buzz of the Wake Up Or Die. Soon everyone in town had heard the rumor, but since the people who had heard the rumor knew they were not nice, they weren't really worried. The question became, who is the nice person? The one thing everyone knew for sure was that since it was August, and Christmas was four months away, it wasn't Santa Clause, which was a big relief whether they believed in him or not.

Stoops and Plastic started the day as usual in the This Isn't Heaven Bar. Bridge had not shown up, which was highly unusual. Bridge was really into breakfast - breakfast being the most important meal of the day. Gloria was not talking to anyone and was playing gloomy songs on the jukebox. Plastic figured it was one of those woman woman type things. "You know, I never thought about it," Plastic said, "but a male gay couple has doubled the threat of prostate problems."

"Too much information," Stoops said.

Berry walked in as only the way a man who has had a stroke can. Berry was beginning to be a regular, or he was becoming an alcoholic, which in all truth is not a bad thing to be in life - for one, it is cheaper than drugs, and nobody who is a drunk really thinks they can fly or that one more drink will bring them closer to the truth.

Berry sat. He looked concerned. "The rumor is going around that MeJoe thinks something terrible is going to happen to a very nice person in town," he said.

Gloria brought him a beer. "Piss off, Berry," she said.

"No, you piss off," Berry said.

"Thanks," Gloria said.

"You're welcome," Berry said.

"I wonder who the nice person is," Berry asked, since his statement had been interrupted, and nobody likes to be interrupted.

"There is only one nice person in town," Stoops said, who he could have named if he had been polite and not trying to dramatize his statement.

"Who?" Berry was forced to ask.

"Vivian," Stoops replied, but as soon as he said it he felt a pang of fear shoot through his body.

"That would be terrible," Plastic said.

"Terrible," Berry said.

"Shit," Stoops said.

"We should go warn her," Plastic said.

"I went by her coffee shop the way here. Even though the fundraiser for multi-vitamin birdseed is not until tomorrow, there is already so much birdseed stacked up in the store its hard to go inside without one of the five thousand birds that are fluttering around outside pooping on you," Berry said.

"You could really mess with the birds and go get a bunch of cats," Plastic said.

"Be nice," Stoops said.

"Not with this rumor going around," Plastic said.

"I wonder where Bridge is?" Stoops asked.

"He is not answering his door. Every so often he gets on a roll on his novel and will spend all day typing," Berry said.

"Is that a roll like a jellyroll, or a belly roll, or a roll of quarters, or to roll on the ground, or roll a snowball, or he ate a roll?" Plastic asked.

"Are all those rolls spelled the same?" Berry asked.

"People don't spell when they talk," Plastic said defensively, remembering the time in the fifth grade when he was kicked out of a spelling bee for spelling roll, something one eats, as role as in role model - picky teacher anyway.

Six bikers came into the bar. On their leather coats they had an emblem that stated in large gold letters, 'Bikers for Jesus,' and underneath it in smaller gold letters, 'I am only responsible to God.'

They started playing pool and drinking boilermakers. Jesus might have been into watered down wine, but he sure as hell wasn't into boilermakers. But, times do change, and who knows, in these modern times He might be into boilermakers. The Church Of The Boilermakers. Take this boilermaker and go in peace. Drink ten boilermakers and everything will be forgiven.

Stoops, Berry, and Plastic were so worried over Vivian they decided they would all go sit in front of the Wake Up Or Die and keep vigil. What's a little bird poop in life anyway?

Bridge was typing away. It is a wonder what two quickies in one afternoon can do for the creative process. Three times people knocking at the door had interrupted him, but he had ignored them. Who were they to interrupt such creativity? About noon Bridge realized he had missed breakfast. What? No invigorating conversation about life and death. No discussion on why he could not make the *New York Times Book Review*. No deep study of Gloria's nipple rings. No study of bikers and leather and the reason why loud mufflers have led to better organizational skills in the multicultural business conglomerates of today.

Bridge stood and stretched. He had done enough damage to the English language for the day. He knew he had at least fifty commas moaning. At a minimum twelve adjectives were wondering what the hell they were doing. There were at least fifteen run-on sentences that were happy at being what they were - who wants to be complete anyway? Low-life conforming complete sentences anyway. Where is your diversity? Where is your challenge to life? Conformity has ruined it all. There were pronouns that with a little work could have been nouns. Some of the pronouns were forming a secret cult to kill a few nouns and take over.

Bridge turned off his quill and inkwell. For some reason he felt strange. Then he felt fear. He feared for Vivian. He two-stepped forward and one backward toward the Wake Up Or Die. Dipping and turning over the coffee shop were thousands and thousands of birds. Never really being a bird man, Bridge could only recognize the robins and sparrows, but there were blue birds, red birds, spotted birds, black birds, little birds and fat birds.

Plastic and Stoops were sitting outside the Wake Up Or Die holding a spread out copy of Let's Make Lost City Into A Political Hotbed over their heads. The hundred dogs outside were covered with bird poop, but being dogs, they went with the flow and were wagging their tales and thinking, 'Isn't this an invigorating experience.'

Stoops handed Bridge a copy of Let's Make Lost City Into A Political Hotbed. Even being a writer, Bridge was smart enough to spread the copy out over his head as he sat. "What are you guys doing sitting out here getting pooped on?" he asked.

"MeJoe had a bad feeling that someone nice in town is going to get terribly hurt, and the only person we could think of who was nice was Vivian," Stoops said.

"I had the same feeling without the rumor," Bridge said. "Where is Vivian?"

"Vivian's fine," Plastic said. "She's inside."

Bridge went inside. No one was talking politics or philosophy. They all had bird books and were naming all the birds that were flying around outside. "Oh look, that is a blue-breasted bee sucker," and on and on and on.

Bridge figured young children had it down better. They only pointed and said, "Bird."

Vivian was standing with Chris by the window. Chris looked distraught. He knew who was going to have to go out and clean up the bird poop after the fundraiser. "I'd like to be king once in my life," Chris lamented to Vivian.

"You can't."

"Why not?"

"You are and forever will be a queen," Vivian said.

"We women always get the short end of the stick," Chris said.

Bridge two-stepped forward and one backward up to Vivian. "Have you heard the rumor going around town?"

"Which one?" Vivian grinned. "Right now there are about three thousand."

"The one where MeJoe thinks someone nice in town is going to get terribly hurt."

"I heard it, and I also heard that a lot of people think it is going to be me."

"I'm worried," Bridge said.

"Don't be," Vivian replied without a care in the world. "I am not a Catholic and my past sins are many."

"I'm glad," Bridge said, thinking how strange that sin can have a good place in life.

Chapter Thirty-Six

When the sun went down the five thousand birds flying around the Wake Up Or Die all flew to trees and telephone wires to have nightmares about cats and kids with B.B. guns. Vivian and Chris were scraping bird poop off of the sidewalk. Vivian was helping because she had given herself a guilt trip by telling Chris he would always be a queen, and a depressed queen is not fun to be around.

The complete community of gallery owners were all at Bill's Restaurant and Libations. Sergeant and Berry were debating the pros and cons of the United States disbanding its entire military, giving up all its overseas bases, and telling the world it wanted to live in peace. They decided if it did happen they would move to China, as there was no Arab nation that would ever invade China. China had enough soldiers to circle the globe twenty times with a few battalions left in reserve and was not into religious tolerance.

Lotus Blossom, Rudolph and Rebecca, were discussing the color cadmium red, which for many artists can lead to arguments that make the presidential candidate debates seem like kindergarten kids arguing over why there really has to be a nap time. But since Rudolph and Rebecca were not artists, it made for a good one-sided conversation, which is what most conversations are anyway.

Rainy Day and Gertrude were drinking white wine and planning activities for the upcoming art walk. They wanted musicians on every corner. They wanted every gallery to have balloons in front of it - for some reason, they felt that gallery walks should copy car lots. And they wanted the high school marching band to parade through town playing Beethoven. The truth be known, Beethoven didn't really give a hoot about art. He was the rock star of his day and was more into collecting women.

Stoops and Plastic were half pie-eyed and really didn't know what they were talking about, but whatever it was it sounded good, and made a lot of sense.

MeJoe and Bridge were sitting at a corner table and having a four-way conversation, as Me and Joe had made up and were once again communicating with each other. "How did the hypnotist work out?" Me asked Bridge.

"It was a total disaster," Bridge answered, not really telling the complete story, as cleavage and bellybuttons can never be a total disaster.

"I told you so," Joe told Me.

"You are always right," Me told Joe.

"Don't be condescending," Joe told Me.

MeJoe butted in saying to Bridge, "I take it you have not been able to tell Vivian you love her."

Bridge nodded his head gravely, which MeJoe could not see but somehow felt.

"You must have a very deep and hidden part of your personality that is afraid to make any form of commitment with a woman," Me said to Bridge.

"I don't want to get hurt and I don't want to hurt anyone else," Bridge said.

Me and Joe and MeJoe muttered to themselves for a few moments. "Interesting," Me finally said in a very bad impression of Jung.

"How is your sex life?" Joe asked.

A lot of shrinks think this is a very important question, when in truth they are just kinky bastards who live out their fantasies through other people.

"None of your business," Bridge replied.

The Professor came into Bill's. Since his new love from Minnesota was not yet twenty-one, he could not bring her in the bar, which was a great excuse for going to have a few drinks with the boys. He looked at the scattered artists and gallery owners and decided he would rather have a meaningless conversation with Stoops and Plastic. Besides, he had to learn a few meaningless conversations to have a good conversation with a girl from Minnesota who was only nineteen.

Is digression really the only answer for mankind? We seem to think so. Once we digress enough to only talk in baby talk, mankind might have a chance.

Me, Joe, and MeJoe, unable to get Bridge to talk about his sex life tapped their way out of Bill's Restaurant and Libations and headed for the Art Is All The Same In The Dark. Any conversation without sex involved is normally boring and not worth a thinking man or woman's time.

Bridge went and sat with Stoops, Plastic, and the Professor. Frauline bubbled over. She had been having a hard time waiting on all the different tables, but it had not even slightly diminished her bubbling. "I heard that Vivian might be in a terrible accident," she bubbled.

"Vivian told me there is no way in the universes she is nice," Bridge said, avoiding any mention of past sins, as he did not want to get into a religious discussion with Stoops and Plastic and a cradle robber.

"Oh good, I am so happy she is not nice," Frauline bubbled.

The absurdity of life only grows bigger.

"Buy us a round, Bridge," Stoops said, lowering his eyes in a submissive gesture that was almost begging.

"How have you been able to afford drinking when you have not worked in over a week?" Bridge asked Stoops.

"I've been picking up cans and bottles during the day."

"That's good honest work," the Professor said.

"Why haven't the homeless been doing it?" Plastic asked.

Stoops grinned. "I get up before they do and beat them to the punch."

"Get them a round on me," Bridge told Frauline - hard work and creative planning should be rewarded.

"Stoops, you are going to have to get a job and make some steady money," the Professor said.

"What can I do? I am an ex-felon."

"You are only looking for an excuse," Plastic said. "Most of the people in town are ex-felons."

"Is there such a thing as a non ex-felon?" Bridge asked.

"Anyone who has never been caught is a non ex-felon," Plastic said.

"Next week I start cutting firewood," Stoops said.

Every old hippie in Lost City has spent time cutting firewood. Most of them learn it is really a lot of work and does not pay well, so they only do it for one season and go back to their old job of selling pot. Selling pot is not hard on the body, nor is there a chance of cutting off a finger or toe or getting crushed by a falling tree.

Frauline bubbled back with the round of drinks and hurried over to another table. "And how are you making money?" Stoops asked Bridge.

"I still get a few bucks from the publishers on my novels and the store has been making me a little."

"I bet during the art walk you sell a few paintings," Plastic said.

Gertrude came over to the table. "Grandma," Bridge smiled, "what kind of Chamber of Commerce mumbo jumbo have you gotten me into now?"

"We are having a meeting at four tomorrow at my gallery to discuss the art walk," Gertrude informed Bridge. By the authoritative tone in her voice, he knew he was expected to be there.

"Bridge hates meetings," Stoops told Gertrude.

"Meetings are for politicians and city planners and for members of the PTA," the Professor said.

"I'm not talking to you two," Gertrude said crossly.

Stoops and the Professor looked around like two little boys who had just been caught with their hands in the cookie jar.

"I'll be there," Bridge said.

Gertrude gave Stoops and the Professor a disgusted look and left.

"You don't mess with grandma when it comes to the Chamber of Commerce," Bridge told them.

Berry came up to the table like only a person who has had a stroke can.

"I hear you bought a bus ticket for the Rock Lady to get to Sedona," Plastic said to the Professor.

"How did you find out about that?"

"While Stoops and I were being pooped on by the 5,000 birds outside of the Wake Up Or Die the dogs caught us up on all the local gossip."

"There's one black and gray mutt with one blue eye and one brown eye that knows about everything there is to know," Stoops said.

"I'll give you a brown eye," the Professor said.

Since the day's conversation wasn't really going anywhere, Bridge decided to go to the bathroom. Bathroom runs, many times in life, are really nothing but an excuse to break up the boredom of conversation. If Bridge would have been gay, he could have told the guys he needed to touch up his eyeliner, but since he wasn't, he didn't tell them anything.

The door had just swung shut behind Bridge when a scream cut through the air. There are all kinds of screams in life. There are baby screams when they are spoiled brats. There are Halloween screams. There are exasperated screams. There are angry screams. But then there are screams when a person immediately knows something terrible has happened. Bridge raced back into the bar. Stoops shouted, "Call 911."

There was a crowd of people standing around a person lying on the floor. Bridge pushed his way through - war has a way of teaching people how to help those who are hurt. The Professor had straightened Frauline's body out and was pushing on her chest. Bridge knelt down and held her left hand. He knew Frauline was dead. There is an emptiness with death. Either the soul, or the will, or the heart, or whatever one wants to call it leaves the body. Instantly the body is empty. It is now only a shell, or as Bridge believed, a doll that has found rest. The Professor feverishly continued to push. The room was silent. A few ladies sobbed. A few gay men cried. Humanity is not bound together by laughter, we are glued together by tears.

The Professor stopped. Sweat was pouring down his face. Bridge continued to hold Frauline's hand. He closed his eyes and whispered, "If you had beliefs about life after death, Frauline, I hope they are true."

Bridge opened his eyes and rested Frauline's still warm hand over her heart and noticed that even in death she was smiling.

Sirens cried in the distance. Soon the medics arrived. Death by sudden heart attack cannot be cured. The old ticker is a time bomb.

Chapter Thirty-Seven

Death in a small town is not like death in a large city. In a large city, death is only a family affair, if one is lucky enough to have a family. If not, it is just another hole in the ground or a body sent off to a university to be cut up and studied like a frog or snake. Salvation is emersion in formaldehyde. That is, unless you are rich or famous, then many people come to the funeral, if for no other reason than to show off their nice clothes and jewelry.

In a small town, when someone dies everyone is affected. Even if the person who dies was disliked by most people, there is still a hole in the fabric of the community. Who can we dislike now? Sad to say, but liking and not liking both seem to have a function. A lot of times the ones who are not liked are the true individuals and thinkers - most people who need crowds more often than not get lost in the mass. I am the individual of the herd - all a herd ever really does in life is trample everything around it.

After Frauline was taken away most of the people at Bills Restaurant and Libations went to the Wake Up Or Die to debate death. Who? What? Why? Where?

Stoops, Berry, the Professor, and Bridge did not leave Bill's. The bartender brought them each a beer, saying sadly, "It's on me."

Is death a thank you?

The four looked at the beers vacantly and then Bridge held up his beer. They clinked glasses and bottles together in a silent tribute and drank. After a few more minutes of silence, Stoops said, "We should have known she was the only nice person in town."

"I'll miss her bubbles," Berry said.

"There is nothing we could have done," the Professor said.

"We could have tipped her better," Stoops said.

"You never had enough money to tip her," Berry said.

"If I could have I would have," Stoops said.

"Some people say intentions mean nothing," Bridge said.

"They are wrong," the Professor said.

"To bubbles," Berry said, and they clinked their glasses and bottles again.

After the beer, they each went their separate ways. Stoops went to the This Isn't Heaven Bar. What is death but loud music and conversation that cannot be heard? The Professor went to see the young girl from Minnesota, who, being nineteen, hadn't thought much about death. Berry went home and thought about his wife - dead now for five years. But he did not think about the shotgun. Bridge went over to the Wake Up Or Die. Vivian and he did not say a word to each other. They hugged, not a fart holding hug but a soft quiet hug. After the hug, they still did not speak, but they smiled a sad little smile at each other. Then Bridge two-stepped forward and one backward to his gallery.

He left all the lights off in the Why Am I Here and turned on his quill and ink- well. "Is life nothing but a coffin?" he asked himself.

He sat and hit the key that brought his book to life. What is fiction? Is death fiction? Is war fiction? Is injustice fiction? Is hunger fiction? Fiction - be my redeemer in the truth of your absurdities. Fiction - let me make love real. Let me make death painless and worthwhile. Tears that are only words do not have to be wiped away or sniffled away - the cover can be shut and they never were. What happens to the hole that is left in the fabric of the world when a person dies? Does it forever stay empty? There are millions and millions and billions of empty little holes. Six billion years and it will all be one big hole.

Bridge scrolled to the last entry in his book. He read a few lines. He sat back in his chair. He remembered a poem his grandmother used to read to him when he was a little boy that he had never forgotten.

count your garden by the flowers
never by the leaves that fall
count your days by golden hours
don't remember clouds at all
count your nights by stars not tears
count your age by friends, not years.

Bridge remembered his grandmother. She was a poor farmer's wife and a survivor of the depression, but her eyes never showed any defeat. She was buried in Iowa on a day when the snow was over a foot deep and the sky the color of spoiled milk. The mourners were bundled up like newborn children. Their tears were frozen on their faces like sparkling jewels that only the rich could afford. And for the first time in his life, Bridge saw his parents as people, people who, if they were lucky one day would also have mourners. And it was then, for the first time in many years, he had cried with no shame.

Bridge remembered the meal at the Presbyterian Church - hot roast beef smothered with rich brown gravy with piles of mashed potatoes so big children could have made castles out of them. The warm bread smelled of life and rebirth and the warm apple and cherry pies smelled of love. After the funeral he went back to New Mexico and being a cowboy getting lost in the vastness of the land. Love, have I forsaken you, or have you forsaken me?

Bridge shut his eyes and whispered, "'In the beginning God created the heaven and the earth. And the earth was without form, and void, and darkness was upon the face of the deep. And the spirit of God moved upon the face of the waters. And then God said let there be light and there was light.'"

He opened his eyes. "Go with the bubbles, Frauline. If there is a God I know He needs someone to bring Him a drink."

Bridge turned off his quill and inkwell. He turned off the light and lay down on his cot. Staring into the darkness he was filled with a deep fear. What if Vivian died and he had never told her he loved her?

Chapter Thirty-Eight

Being from Germany Frauline had no family in the states. A lawyer was trying to contact any living relative in Germany and find out what they wanted done with the body. Moving bodies around the world is a very difficult situation and takes a lot of paper- work. That is, unless one is killed in a military action. Then they fill the body full of embalming fluid, if there is a body left, put a tag on a toe, if there is a toe left, stuff what ever is left in a black plastic bag, put the bag on a transport plane, fly it to the States, play a few songs over the casket as they put it in the ground, and go back for the next load. It is very neat and efficient with a minimum of paperwork and, by modern funeral standards, very cheap.

Life for the living does not stop with the death of another person. Frauline was in the back of everyone's mind, but the subject was not brought up. The birdseed fundraiser was so successful there was two tons of multi-vitamin birdseed stacked up outside of the Wake Up Or Die by one in the afternoon. By two Vivian had given away as much birdseed as she could and was now wondering what she could do with the rest. Stoops and Bridge had missed breakfast because Vivian needed help unloading the birdseed and stacking it. Berry had supervised the stacking. Vivian had given the homeless people all of the breadsticks, and they were peddling them on the next corner and really doing quite well - it was a four gallon of cheap wine day - life is good, who needs a home? Bridge wondered why

Vivian needed a birdseed fundraiser when all the people who had brought the birdseed could have fed the birds. Why do simple things get complicated?

Unlike the day before there were now at least six thousand birds flying around downtown. People were walking around with open umbrellas, and every copy of Let's Make Lost City Into A Political Hotbed was being used for protection. It was the first time in the history of the newspaper a complete print run had been sold out. Vivian had let all the dog owners bring their dogs inside, but out of their routine they were sitting by the windows looking out like they were prisoners in jail. Looking out on life does not have the same clout as looking in.

In desperation as to what to do with the overabundance of birdseed, Vivian called a bird watching nature group that had swindled the government out of a parcel of land not far from Lost City - besides watching birds they were building a hotel and condominiums. She told them they could have all the birdseed if they would come and get it immediately. Within two hours, sixteen Volkswagens, three Subaru's, and two jeeps showed up to take all the birdseed. The vehicles were plastered with stickers - Peace, Birds Are God's Voice, Fly Away With Me, but the most common one stated simply, Fly, Fly, Fly - whatever the hell that means. All the drivers, both men and women, had binoculars around their necks, were wearing khaki short pants, shirts with numerous pockets, hiking boots with gray socks up to their knees and looked like retired English professors. They were followed out of town by a swirling cloud of birds that knew it was going to be a good winter. Only a few sparrows stayed behind. They were the ones who liked muffin crumbs and picking at cigarette butts better than multi-vitamin-enriched birdseed - some things just can't get into multi-vitamins. Take this multi-vitamin and you will live to be one hundred and sixty-four years old and have the complexion of a twenty-year-old. Of course, you will not be able to walk, see, or hear, and you will have to pee and crap in a plastic bag that is sewn into your gut, but what the hay? Isn't a long life grand?

Stoops, Berry, and Bridge were standing in front of the Wake Up Or Die. After moving two tons of multi-vitamin-enriched birdseed, Stoops and Bridge didn't really care if every bird in the state died from starvation. The birds had been taking care of themselves for millions of years why did they need help now?

Bobby, from Bill's Restaurant and Libations, came over. "In memory of Frauline, every beer from four on will be one dollar," he announced.

For some reason, Bobby reminded Bridge of a gay Julius Caesar. He also wondered why only beer was being discounted. But decided the biggest profit margin was on mixed drinks, and more people than the undertaker had to make money on death.

It took about five minutes for the complete downtown to know there was one-dollar beer at Bill's. For a buck, even wine drinkers will lower their standards and suck down a dozen or so beers.

Berry, Bridge, and Stoops went home to clean up.

Vivian was drinking a cup of coffee. If she ever saw another bag of birdseed it would be too soon. Vivian felt a deep sadness over Frauline's death. She had not really known Frauline, but she had seen her many times, and now she wished she had bothered to talk to her more. But even with her sadness, Frauline dying was like reading the obit of a stranger. Vivian got up and headed for the sink to wash her cup. Is death nothing but washing a cup?

Bridge had cleaned up and was headed for Bill's Restaurant and Libations when he remembered Gertrude was having a meeting about the art walk. Bridge debated his options, one-dollar beer or a meeting? This is a tough call. Let me think one more time, one-dollar beer or a meeting?

Sorry Gertrude.

Down with art walks.

Down with paving machines.

Down with new galleries.

Down with balloons.

Let the old lampposts that still worked and are now living on a commune dance and rejoice.

If someone else comes in from California or New Jersey and wants to open a gallery I will paintball it.

Western art is also art, you snob bastards.

Let's get drunk and rejoice Frauline.

Stoops and Berry and Bridge were sitting at Bill's and staring at the clock. It was 3:45 and they had fifteen minutes to wait for the dollar beer. None of them had ordered a beer at the regular price, and Bobby, since they were not gay, wasn't going to cut them any slack.

All the employees were wearing black armbands. For some strange reason that even Bridge could not figure out, they reminded Bridge of Black Panther sympathizers.

Bridge pulled some extra chairs over to the table. A waitress came over to the table that made Stoops' jaw drop, which is not a pretty sight for a man with no teeth. Bridge coughed and Berry did nothing, as he didn't know her.

"Organic Muffin," Stoops finally managed to slobber.

"My reincarnated Indian warrior," Organic Muffin smiled.

"I thought you were dancing at a topless bar in El Paso," Stoops said.

"I was. But I decided it was not a good career choice. The college girls have the boob market cornered and all I could do was think about you."

Now that's an original if I have ever heard one, Bridge thought, but then looking at Stoops, he could see Stoops' eyes fill with that certain glint that everyone knows is the 'I like her and no matter what she does or has done I will always like her, even if ten thousand men have seen her boobs and stuffed dollar bills in her thong.' In other words, Stoops was smitten - smitten being much harder on a person than hunger or thirst.

"Are you still into smacking reincarnated Indian warriors with black whips?" Stoops cautiously asked Organic Muffin.

"I was just teasing," she smiled.

If you fall for that one, you really are smitten, Bridge thought. Whips don't tease, they hurt.

"Would you have a drink with me when your shift is over?" Stoops asked.

"I'd love to," Organic Muffin said and looked at the clock, which was at straight up four. "I'll even buy you guys your first round."

They ordered, and Organic Muffin went to get the beers. Stoops' smile was so big he reminded Bridge of one of those yellow smiling faces that made a lot of people huge amounts of money, but the guy who had thought of the idea had forgotten to patent it. So sorry non-intelligent one, but I will name my yacht after you.

"I have never gotten over Organic Muffin," Stoops said like some cheap dime store romance.

Bridge did not know what to say, but he imagined butterflies dancing all around Stoops' head.

"She's cheap," Berry said. "Dollar beers, she could have bought us each two."

As if by magic, the bar was suddenly overflowing with people. Death and cheap beer can make for one hell of a party. Ask the Irish. Of course, the Irish have parties for rain, sleet, sheep, war, peace, poetry, a good crop of potatoes, a bad crop of potatoes, and about anything else that comes up.

Jackson came in minus the rest of the Open Doors and set up an amplifier in the corner. He twanged his guitar a few times and started playing. The bar was so noisy no one could hear him, but Bridge thought it was a nice gesture.

Barbara came in, weaved her way through the crowd and sat at the table. The first thing she said to Stoops was, "I heard Organic Muffin is back and she is looking for you."

Organic Muffin delivered the beers.

"She found you," Barbara said.

Barbara and Organic Muffin winked at each other in some primeval woman wink of which the meaning has never been discovered by a man. The only thing men really know about the wink is that there is some connotation of stupid in it.

Vivian bowled her way through the crowd. Being 185 pounds, she did not have to weave through any crowd. The first thing she said to Organic Muffin was, "I told you your boobs weren't big enough to make a go at a topless bar," and then ordered a beer.

Barbara ordered a house wine. There is always one in the crowd even when there is dollar beer.

"Wine is not what one should drink at a wake," Berry said, making a sour face.

"Up yours, Berry," Barbara said.

"Thanks," Berry replied.

The Professor came in and mediated his way to the table. Old lawyers can never really get away from their trade.

"I got a phone call from the Rock Lady," Barbara told the Professor. "She told me to tell you thank you for everything you did for her. She already has a job at a bookstore and she has joined a group that worships crystals. They told her the rock of rocks was only an impostor. There is only one god and he or she is the crystal of crystals."

"She could have called me," the Professor said, sounding like his feelings were hurt.

"How is your young thing from Minnesota working out?" Barbara asked the Professor.

The Professor made a face. It was a 'my pride has been hurt' face. "She met a guy from Wisconsin. They have cheese in common."

"You were too young for her anyway," Barbara said.

Organic Muffin came back with the beer and wine. "Bring me two Budweisers," the Professor ordered.

"If you all came in at the same time I would only have to make one trip," Organic Muffin said under her breath but still slightly perturbed.

"Are you related to Gloria from the This Isn't Heaven Bar?" Berry asked Organic Muffin.

"Cousins."

"Don't get any nipple rings," Berry said.

Stoops gave Berry a dirty look. Boyfriends of topless dancers can be very protective of their girlfriend's knockers.

Pill came in. He must have been going through a stressful time, as he had peanut butter dripping from his chin, but at least he did not have his **THERE IS ONLY SIX BILLION YEARS LEFT FOR THE WORLD** sign on.

The crowd parted for him to get to the table, as no one wanted any peanut butter on them. When he got to the table, Vivian picked up a napkin, grabbed Pill by the top of the head, and wiped the peanut butter off his face. He squirmed around like a little kid but was smart enough not to protest too much because Vivian might bonk him upside the head.

Organic Muffin came back with the drink order, saw Pill, and shook her head.

"He can drink one of my beers," the Professor told her.

She smiled. Pill smiled.

Some people are easy to please.

"I need a glass for my beer," Bridge told Organic Muffin.

Organic Muffin gave him a puzzled look.

"Beer, like wine, must breathe," Bridge said, feeling a little snobbish.

When Organic Muffin brought the glass back, she almost tossed it at Bridge.

Bridge poured his beer. He was not man enough right at the moment to tell Organic Muffin he also wanted a lime. It takes time to break in a new barmaid.

"To Frauline," Bridge said, raising his glass.

"Rest in peace," Barbara said.

"No money, no litigation," the Professor said.

"I'll miss you," Stoops said.

Berry said nothing.

Vivian said nothing.

Pill said nothing.

"May bubbles follow us all," Bridge said.

They drank and the party was on.

Somewhere in heaven, or the sky, or infinity, or wherever Arabs go with all those virgins, Frauline smiled - bubble, bubble, bubble.

Chapter Thirty-Nine

Too many one-dollar beers does not make for a good night of rolling in my sweet baby's arms. Bridge slept on the sofa, if it could be called sleeping. Vivian, from her own bed, snored so loud during the night she sounded like a hibernating black bear that was allergic to snow.

It was still dark when Bridge got up, tiptoed to Vivian's room and looked at the pile of blankets that was Vivian. He smiled, patted the pile, and whispered, "I, I, I, I, Lo, Lo, Lo," felt the meatball, and two-stepped forward and one backward out the door. For the first time in several days he wondered once again what Vivian had whispered to him the night he danced at The Hole. Thinking about it made him feel hollow.

Bridge turned the corner on Texas and Yankee Streets as the sun popped over the horizon. All the stores seemed to be confused. The art inside of them was having a mini-rebellion. The art did not know if they wanted to get up or not. There are some days when pottery, jewelry, and paintings are like people and they would just as soon be left alone. Said by a piece of art, "Please, gallery, I don't want anyone looking at me today. I don't want anyone saying if they would have created me they would have used a different color. And for sure I don't want anyone saying I can do that. I just want to hang here and for one day be left alone to be what I am. In my mind, opinions really aren't worth the time and effort that goes into them. There are sixty billion people in the world and they all have an opinion. Tell me please, how can opinions have any merit? And in my opinion, all you people with all your opinions are all screwed up. Why don't you take your opinions and get back to living - living being let one another be what they need to be and keep your opinions to yourselves. This being a piece of art is tougher than you think."

Bridge did not go into the Why Am I Here but continued two-stepping forward and one backward onto Bullard Street. A street sweeper inched its way along, sweeping the trash from one side of the street to the other. Two homeless people sat on a corner polishing off a gallon of wine and wishing they would have saved a few breadsticks for breakfast.

Chris had already opened the Wake Up Or Die and a hundred dogs were at their normal occupation of looking through the window. A few pigeons bobbed down the sidewalk like drunks coming home from the bar trying to figure out an excuse to tell their wives. A window washer was busy washing windows. Four people jogged by. Just watching them made Bridge feel tired. Three stray dogs raided a garbage can by the organic co-op. Bridge figured they had belonged to old hippies and still hadn't gotten over their addiction to alfalfa sprouts. He walked by the building that would soon be a consortium of businesses. There was a sign where the organic bakery would be, a sign for a used bookstore, a sign for gallery space openings, a sign for another coffee shop, and a sign for a lost dog. Bridge turned around and went to the other side of the street. He looked in the windows of all the stores that were under renovation. There were no stores left for sale in the art district. Progress had won. The Chamber of Commerce runs supreme and realtors get rich. Bow down to promotion and expansion. But, although it did make Bridge feel queasy, he did not hyperventilate.

A man and woman walked toward him. The lady had a gallery guide in her hand. "May I ask you a question?" the man asked Bridge as they met. He had an East Coast accent but not New York - maybe Jersey or New Hampshire or another one of those foreign countries.

"Sure. But I might not have an answer," Bridge replied.

The lady smiled at him. She seemed shy and nice, slightly out of her element.

Bridge returned the smile.

"Have you lived here long?" the man asked Bridge.

"About two lifetimes," Bridge said.

"What do you think of the town?" the man asked.

Bridge looked at the new lampposts. He looked at the buildings, now redone or being redone. The street sweeper turned the corner. A few more cars came down the street. The homeless men, done with their wine, wandered off to find a bench. A few people went into the cafe. A lady went into a vacant lot and tossed out birdseed, and fifty pigeons flew in. Down on the corner, Vivian stopped in front of the Wake Up Or Die and patted several dogs, whose tails wagged so much Bridge thought they might fly into the air like a bunch of hairy, drooling helicopters.

Bridge looked back at the man. “It’s a great little town,” he said. “It lets you be what you want to be. And if you want to you can chase your demons away.”

The lady smiled again.

“Come by my gallery. I have a gallery on Texas Street called the Why Am I Here. I sell western art and seven of my novels that are still in print,” Bridge said and shook hands with the man and woman.

“We will,” the man answered.

The couple continued on their way. For some reason Bridge remembered some of the MEN in his squad in Vietnam. Spike, black man from Newark, New Jersey - dead. Lazun, wop from New York - dead. Broom, Georgia redneck - dead. Honaker, Alaskan - no legs. Chang, oriental from California - no left arm. And a few more, no names now, just faces, body bags and body parts.

Fiction. Fiction is life. There is no fact. Fact is fiction. Fiction is fact. And then love. Fiction is love. Love is fiction. What is love?

And now a new war. A new crop of boys off to lose dreams.

A history circle jerk.

Fuck.

Fuck me.

Fuck you.

Fuck it.

Would the boys who did not make it back give a rat’s ass about change?

The street was coming alive. People said hello as they walked by. Old hippies, and cowboys, and gays, and lesbians, and New Yorkers, and Californians, chasing what ever dream they were chasing or running from a dream they now understood they could no longer catch. Dreams are like that - little slippery bastards.

Bridge headed for his gallery. Rounding the corner he saw

Gertrude standing in front of the Why Am I Here. The first thing she said was, "Why weren't you at the Chamber of Commerce meeting?"

Bridge could not lie. "Bill's Restaurant and Libations had dollar beer."

"That is a good reason," Gertrude said, smiled, and went into her own gallery.

I could have been using that excuse my complete life, Bridge thought as he unlocked the door. He put up his open sign, turned on all the lights and turned on his quill and inkwell. He got out his feather duster and started dusting the paintings. They laughed and giggled. They were over their, I want to be left alone kick. I am what I am and that is all I am.

Finished dusting, Bridge borrowed Gertrude's mop and mop bucket and mopped out the store. When he was done, the Why Am I Here might not have passed a drill sergeant's inspection, but it was clean and orderly - but Bridge was always clean and orderly.

Bridge was about to sit and type some more of his gibberish when the couple he had talked with earlier came into the store. The paintings slicked back their hair. His novels on display sucked in their beer bellies.

Bridge two-stepped forward and one backward out of his living room, den, and bedroom and stood behind the table by the front door. The couple did not look at the paintings but went directly to the table where Bridge's novels were. "I always wanted to be a writer," the lady said.

Bridge had heard this about four thousand two hundred and sixty times.

"All it takes is to put your rear end down in a chair and start writing. The only rule that there is to being a writer is to write," he said.

"But it frightens me," the lady said.

"I think we are all in some way afraid of ourselves," Bridge said. But then he added with a grin, "The thing about being afraid of yourself is that if you don't tell anyone, no one knows."

The couple bought four books. They were thinking of moving to Lost City. Bridge knew they wanted a new start.

Bridge headed back to his quill and inkwell. He had not gone three two steps forward and one backward before another couple came into the store. They also bought four books. They did not like Lost City. Lost City was too small, but it was fun, and they had heard about Bridge from a man in Tucson.

Bridge almost skipped back to his quill and inkwell. Fame might be fickle, and according to Bob Dylan not what it claims, but a taste of it was a kick.

Bridge read a few paragraphs of his novel. A woman came in the store. Bridge took his storekeeper position behind the table by the door. The lady did not say hello, but she looked at the paintings and then looked at his books. She bought three books. She had run into a couple from the East Coast who were thinking about moving here and had told her the guy who owned the Why Am I Here was a great guy and she should buy some of his books.

Smear me in honey, Bridge thought.

Eleven books in one morning. It beat the hell out of loading and unloading birdseed, but it was not the kick of one-dollar beer.

Bridge was about to go to the This Isn't Heaven Bar for breakfast when three ladies came in the store. They bought two books each, six books, which made seventeen sold books all before breakfast. It was almost reaching a point Bridge couldn't count that high. Call the *New York Times Review of Books.* Call *Publishers Weekly.* Call the big-shot publishers - I told you so, you only publish format stuff, cowards.

Organic Muffin came into the store. Every party has an ending, Bridge thought. "I want to buy one of your books," Organic Muffin said.

"Do you really like Stoops or are you just playing with him?" Bridge asked.

Friends are more important than book sales.

"I do, Bridge. I can't tell you why, but I do."

"I know he likes you."

"I figure an old busted-out pot smuggler and an over the hill topless dancer might have a chance," Organic Muffin smiled, but with a trace of too much of life's wrong side and a little sadness in the smile.

"I hope so," Bridge said.

"Me too," Organic Muffin said.

Organic Muffin bought three books. Twenty books, but it was too late for breakfast.

Stoops came in only a few minutes after Organic Muffin left. Bridge knew Stoops would not buy a book - there are a few things in life that are a given. They are not all good givens, but at least they are given.

"Organic Muffin is going to move in with me," Stoops said.

"You only had a drink with her yesterday," Bridge said, feeling somehow like Stoops' father.

"She came up to the house," Stoops grinned.

By Stoops' grin, Bridge knew Organic Muffin had not gone up to the house to do the dishes or laundry or wash the windows.

"We are destined," Stoops said. "She and I have always been together even though we have been separated. We are two hearts that beat as one. We are two souls that together make one. Without each other we are nothing but an empty shell, an unhatched egg, a fish without a worm."

"No need to go on," Bridge interrupted. He remembered some of his old love poetry. It was almost as bad.

"Is she on the pill?" Bridge asked - his father thing was in high gear.

"I was tied years ago," Stoops said.

"I didn't know that."

"Women libbers love me."

"I guess this means no more breakfast at the This Isn't Heaven Bar," Bridge said.

Stoops nodded his head. "I have to get serious and get a steady job."

"It won't hurt you," Bridge said, adding, "She even has teeth."

"I want to buy a few books for Organic Muffin," Stoops said.

Bridge was about to say, Organic Muffin just bought three, but then he remembered when Stoops had told him Vivian was pregnant.

Stoops picked out a book that Organic Muffin had bought, and then he picked out another book Organic Muffin had bought, and then, surprise of surprises, he bought them. Some givens are not givens. There goes another philosophy of life shot to hell.

Twenty-two books and a payback - paybacks might not be nice, but there are times they are better than blueberry pie with a scoop of vanilla ice cream on top.

Bridge put up his Running An Errand sign and two-stepped forward and one backward to the Wake Up Or Die.

Vivian was cleaning the last of the bird poop off of the sidewalk. The dogs were looking the other way in fear she might make them help. "Would you like to go out to dinner tonight?" Bridge asked her. "I'll take you to the Adobe Deli."

"Bridge, that is expensive," Vivian protested.

"I sold twenty-two books," Bridge said.

"I didn't know you had that many relatives," Vivian smiled.

"Pick me up around seven," Bridge said.

"You clean up and look nice," Vivian ordered.

Bridge hurried back to his store. Capitalism is contagious. He might sell a few more books.

Vivian watched him hurry away. He reminded her of a little boy. So serious at times, but she knew he had a soft heart. But she was glad his heart was not as soft as a soft-boiled egg - men were not supposed to be runny and gooey.

Vivian went home early. The Adobe Deli was a wonderful place and she wanted to dress for the occasion.

Vivian was taking a long hot bath and was listening to a new folk singer. Now that the United States was back in a war, folk music was coming back. Vivian hoped hippies weren't coming back. She didn't wish that fate on anyone. Vivian had put so much lavender bath soap in the water, she felt like she was in the middle of a strange-smelling banana split. She was so relaxed, she did not know if she could ever get her muscles to move again. At times a state of putty is a very good thing. Even though the bath was wonderful, Vivian felt sad. It was a strange sadness. She felt like she was standing on the end of the high-diving board at the deep end of the pool, and although she could not dive or swim, she knew she was going to jump. Who would save her?

Vivian lathered up a loofah sponge and started washing. The folk singer ran out of disc. The house was quiet. Vivian lay back in the tub and closed her eyes. Her mind ran through a gauntlet of questions. Why is it you love someone and yet you don't really know them? Why is it holding hands does not make two people one? Is love only a chemical reaction? Why is it when you get older and you know you love someone when you are not with them you really don't miss them? Bridge, I think you and I are just a couple of old mutt dogs.

With the thought, Vivian was no longer standing on the end of a high-diving board at the deep end of the pool. She was not sad. She still couldn't swim. But so what? She could dog paddle. If she started to drown, somebody would pull her out. No matter how bad life gets there are always a few lifeguards. God, Allah, Confucius, Frank, whoever or whatever, bless the lifeguards.

Vivian drained the tub and toweled dry. She wrapped the towel around herself and put on another album. Only this time it was not a folk singer wondering why the water was polluted, the poor still poor, and war still war. Vivian put on an Irish quartet. The fiddles fiddled and the drums pounded and the flute fluted. The Irish know why everything is all screwed up. It's all screwed up because it has always been screwed up and will always be screwed up. The only way to go through life is to drink and dance. "Bring on the love," Vivian shouted. "Bring on dancing."

She danced around the room. The towel fell to the floor. She jiggled and rolled. The house smiled. There is always a lifeguard.

Vivian painted her fingernails and toes bright orange - so orange they would have made a pumpkin jealous. She shined her finger rings and toe rings. She put on a floor length red dress covered with yellow daisies that if she was not careful would cause ten thousand hummingbirds to swoop down and carry her away. She braided her hair. To top it all off she wore a pair of silver shoes. Standing in front of a mirror, she had to smile. "Vivian," she said, "about the only thing that has gone wrong in your life is you weren't born black. Then you could get away with dressing like this."

Vivian did not pour on the lavender perfume. She dabbed a few drops on her neck. If Bridge was going to shell out fifty to sixty bucks a plate, she wanted to smell the food.

As good days go, Bridge sold two more books. Twenty-four books in one day. At five he put up the closed sign and apologized to the paintings that they had not found a home. Bridge washed himself the best he could and put on his best pants, shirt, and shoes. Most art types don't wear ties. Ties are a mark of conformity and respectability and no artists would ever want to be a conformist or respectable. But due to the occasion, Bridge wanted to wear a tie. He hurried over to MeJoe's. If anyone had a tie, it would be MeJoe.

MeJoe was sitting in his gallery and started to speak, but Bridge cut him off. "I need a tie. I'm taking Vivian to the Adobe Deli tonight."

Without a fuck you or fuck off MeJoe tapped to his back room and tapped back with a tie. "All I have are white ties," MeJoe said, which, since he only wore all white outfits, wasn't that weird of a thing.

"Can I borrow one?"

"No, I only brought it out here so you could look at it," MeJoe said.

Feeling stupid, Bridge took the tie. "Don't ask me to tie it for you either," MeJoe said, "I could never tie a Windsor knot."

"Thanks," Bridge said and headed for the door.

"One more thing," MeJoe said. "Me wants me to tell you if you don't tell Vivian you love her tonight he is going to strangle you with that tie."

"Me wouldn't do that," Bridge said.

"You bet I will," Me said.

On the way back to the store, Bridge wished he would have gone to the store and bought his own tie - at times borrowing can get out of hand, especially if it leads to murder.

It took Bridge four tries to tie the tie without the small end being longer than the wide end. Damn short ends in life anyway. Looking at himself in the mirror, he felt like a little kid who was going to get his sixth grade class photograph taken. All he needed was his hair slicked back with Butch Wax and a pimple on his forehead.

At a few minutes before seven, the Volvo belched around the corner. Bridge did his breaking-and-entering routine through the window. Once he was settled, Vivian said, "Bridge, you are as handsome as a sixth grade boy who is about to get his class photograph taken."

"Thank you," Bridge said, swelling up like a bullfrog.

"All you need is short hair, some Butch Wax, and a pimple on your forehead."

Bridge laughed.

"What are you laughing at?"

"The irony of it all."

Vivian looked confused.

"Vivian, you look grand," Bridge said, leaned over and kissed her on the cheek.

The Volvo took off in a cloud of black smoke.

Can I really get strangled with a borrowed tie? Bridge pondered.

Chapter Forty

The Adobe Deli Restaurant was on a hillside overlooking Lost City. It was a large adobe hacienda that a wealthy land swindler had built in the 1890's. Land swindling in the old west paid more than cattle rustling and was normally done by the politicians, so they never got caught, or, if they did, they only paid a small fine. When swindling was no longer lucrative the house fell into ruin for many years. In 2001 it was bought by a Jewish couple from New York who completely remodeled it and turned it into a high end restaurant where they even served pork. There is only so much Jewish food a person can eat, and being kosher isn't at all what it is made out to be.

Vivian and Bridge were seated at table for two by a huge picture window. There was no one else in the room. The lights of Lost City sparkled below them like thousands of tiny Christmas trees. Vivian's childlike eyes were glowing. Her dress was a bright ornament. Her smile was the angel on top of the Christmas tree.

The lights in the room were dim and there was a candle in the middle of the table. The shadows danced in time with the low orchestra background music. The table was set with white linen and the utensils were silver. The wine and water glasses reflected the candle light into tiny rainbows.

The waiter wore black slacks, a starched white shirt, and shoes that were so shiny a four star general would have been jealous. His name was Heinz and he was very proud to be their server for the evening. "Would you two like a glass of wine before dinner?" Heinz asked in a European accent. Being smart, he had left Europe - all those accents can get confusing.

To Bridge there were only two types of wine - red and white - and only a few brand names - Boones Berry Farm and Gallo.

But he, for some reason in the mood to drink wine, asked, "What would you recommend that is not so expensive I can't afford to eat a salad?"

Heinz smiled. It is always good to trust those that are in the know. "We have a very nice California Merlot for only twenty dollars a bottle," he said.

"Can we trust you?" Vivian asked.

"My lady," Heinz replied with a sly European smile, "when it comes to wine you can."

Vivian returned the smile - all women like to be flirted with, and, whether they will fess up to it or not, all men like to be flirted with also. Flirting is a nice thing.

Heinz went to get the wine.

Vivian looked out the window. "It is so beautiful," she said.

"Not as beautiful as you are," Bridge said.

"Bridge, you don't have to lie to me," Vivian said. "I have never been pretty."

"I'm not exactly Prince Valliant," Bridge said.

"No, you are my knight in tarnished armor."

"Will I ever shine?" Bridge asked, looking at the city lights.

"We all shine in our own way, some dimly, others brightly, and still others only with a flicker. But somewhere in all of us is a glow."

"You always see the good side," Bridge said. "I dwell on the dark."

"You're a writer, Bridge, to you the dark is the glow."

Heinz came back holding the bottle of wine like it was a newborn baby. He uncorked the bottle and handed Bridge the cork. Bridge wondered if he was supposed to stick it in his ear or put it in his pocket. Heinz smiled and poured Bridge a taste of wine. Bridge had seen Barbara do the wine routine. He spun the wine in the glass. He sniffed the wine. He sipped. "My God, Heinz, this is some good stuff," he beamed.

"You two are fun," Heinz smiled and filled their glasses and left.

"To selling twenty-four books in one day," Vivian toasted.

"To my lady of the Christmas trees," Bridge toasted.

I, I, I, I, I, Lo, Lo, Lo, sloshed around with the wine.

There are little red, blue, green, yellow, orange, and purple fairies in life that do not live in lampshades and do not need light to exist. They fly unseen through the air at certain times and they pray to all gods that all will end well, and that each life will be a good life. Some people they touch more than others. The ones that are touched the most can smile through their tears.

The fairies danced around the room. They danced with another glass of wine. They danced over the mixed lettuce salad with croutons and English walnuts topped with a raspberry vinaigrette dressing. They danced over the fresh baked rolls with real butter. And they danced over the two medium-rare filet mignons wrapped in thick bacon with four spears of asparagus for company.

Vivian and Bridge ate slowly and did not talk. Each delicious bite of food was a bite of each other. Each sound of silence a sigh, a song, an old dream relived.

Dessert was a wineglass filled with raspberries covered with cream so rich it made the Queen of England's jewels seem like costume jewelry, and coffee that made Vivian's best coffee seem like Sanka.

Finished, they looked at each other. They toasted their last sip of wine silently. And what will you give me, my love? Will you give me silence when I need it? Will you give me warmth? Will you give me my own space to pursue my own selfish goals of self? Will you give me what I am not able to give to you? Will you hold my hand when I fail? Will you give me a pillow when I am so drunk I cannot walk and am sleeping in the bathroom? Will you laugh with me and never at me? Will you always be a friend even when you do not like what I am doing? Will you give me no standards to bear? No flags to pursue? No glory that takes battle? No loses that only kill the heart? I do not want to possess you. I do not want to own you.

Heinz came back to the table with another bottle of wine. Bridge was about to say, "I didn't order another bottle," but he did not have time. Heinz said, "From me, for the two in love."

Heinz opened the bottle and poured two glasses. Vivian stood and gave Heinz one of her hug you till you fart hugs. Heinz was taken back at first, but when a woman who weighs 185 pounds wants to hug you, you get hugged or else.

Heinz walked away with a little bounce in his step. Hopefully at home he had a rolling in his sweet baby's arms.

The soft background orchestra music played. The invisible fairies flew.

"Dance with me, Bridge," Vivian said.

Bridge, without hesitation, and to Vivian's surprise, stood.

They held each other and danced. Slowly two steps forward and one backward. Circle two steps forward and one backward. Around the room two steps forward and one backward. "I, I, I, I, I, Lo, Lo, Lo," Bridge whispered in Vivian's ear without feeling a meatball in his throat.

"Yes," Vivian said.

Love moved up his throat. "I, I, I, I, I, Lo, Lo, Lo, Lo, Lo."

Love stuck in his throat.

Circle two steps forward and one backward.

"I, I, I, Lo, Lo," Bridge said.

"Yes," Vivian said.

She was like a warm apple pie in Bridge's arms. She was a hot cup of coffee on a cold morning. He remembered after the war wondering if he would ever be warm again. His wife had not brought him warmth. Is love only a thought? Is it true? Please, please, be true. Be warm.

"I, Lo, you," Bridge whispered.

"I know," Vivian said.

Vivian's whisper at The Hole. I know.

"Oh Vivian, why can't I tell you I love you?" Bridge whispered like a plea.

"You have," Vivian replied as they two-stepped forward and one backward by the window. The tiny Christmas trees glowed. The fairies stopped flying around and embraced.

Bridge stopped dancing. He stepped away from Vivian. He held his hands up to the heavens. "I have, I have," he shouted.

"I have, I have," he shouted again.

He danced a two steps in place and one step in place jig. He grabbed Vivian, and even though it was an effort, he picked her up and spun her around, around, and around like a big red and yellow top. He set her down. He was dizzy and out of breath. "I, I, I, pant, pant, love, pant, pant, you. I love you. I love you." The words echoed around the room.

Bridge started two-stepping forward and one backward quickly around the room. He reminded Vivian of a gimp grasshopper. “I love you, I love you, I love you,” he hollered over and over.

Heinz came into the room. The chef came into the room. A waiter from another room came into the room. They started shouting, “He loves you. He loves you.”

Bridge stopped on the other side of the room from Vivian. In the dim light and the candlelight she seemed to glow. She was smiling. Her childlike eyes were filled with tears - those happy little tears that no one can explain. The happy little tears that let passion know it is only a child and even when it grows up it will never be the equal of a happy little tear.

To Bridge, everything around Vivian disappeared. There was only her. 185 pound Vivian wearing a bright red dress with yellow flowers. Vivian with orange toe and nail polish and silver shoes. Vivian with sparkling rings. Vivian smelling like lavender. Vivian with those childlike eyes.

Bridge walked toward her, one step at a time, not two steps forward and one backward, but one step at a time.

He stopped in front of her, took her face in his hands, looked directly into her childlike eyes and said in a hush, “I love you, Vivian.”

Vivian took Bridge in her arms. She did not hug him until he had to fart. She hugged him with the softness of spring, the touch of feathers, and the warmth of a just out of the oven apple pie. She whispered, “I love you too.”

There are fairies in the world, little red, blue, green, yellow, orange, red, and purple fairies that don’t live in lampshades and don’t need light to glow. Just look, they need you.

Chapter Forty-One

It was midnight when Bridge and Vivian left the Adobe Deli. Vivian did not say a word about the fact Bridge was walking normal. She figured that when he woke up in the morning he would probably start walking two steps forward and one backward and speak with his words in reverse. Done I have hell the what?

Bridge and Vivian did not spend the night together. Bridge was so emotionally drained he felt like a soggy cigarette filter. They kissed and hugged at her front door and thankfully to each of them there was no more I love you. Saying I love you too many times can make people feel like they are fourteen again. Bridge one-stepped toward the Why Am I Here.

He was halfway back to the Why Am I Here before he realized he was walking normally. He stopped. He started to walk again. Once again he walked normally. He stopped again. He walked normal. He walked in a circle. He walked backwards. He skipped. He hopped. He walked. Bridge walked to his store feeling like a new man - not reborn, but new. And what was the war? Does it matter? And who was that first woman who dumped you? Don't know. And who was that second woman who dumped you? That is a tough one. And now let's talk about change, ok? Ok. You can't run from change. I know. Let people be people. Ok. Tell the paving machines they have their place. Ok. Tell the old lampposts that still work that a commune is not the worst place to be. Ok. People who think western art is not art are entitled to their opinion. Screw them. Tour buses are filled with people who want to see more of the world. Damn, I guess so. Realtors have the right to make a living. Let the jerks move to California and make a living. Now, now, Bridge. New galleries only give other people a chance to see different forms of art. No comment. Art walks benefit the neighborhood. Do I have to serve cheese and wine? Yes, it is what they expect.

Bridge went into the Why Am I Here. He tiptoed past the paintings. Let them sleep. He lay down on his cot.

****

After Bridge left, Vivian sat on the sofa for about fifteen minutes. She felt like she was in the middle of a bubble. The bubble was a dream and she did not want to move and break the bubble. She wanted to put the bubble inside a container and screw the lid on tight so it could never escape. She got up and headed to the Wake Up Or Die.

The street was deserted. The coffee shop was sleeping. Vivian unlocked the door and went in. She turned on a few lights. The dim light did not disturb the snoozing games, magazines, or plants. The chairs were enjoying not being sat in. The espresso machine was snoring - even with caffeine running through its veins all day long it slept like a rock. Vivian locked the door behind her. She spun around in a slow circle, her dress barely billowing away from her legs. If her shoes had been red, she could have clicked her heels and started to fly.

Vivian sat at a table by the window. A cop car drove slowly by. Vivian waved. The cop waved back. Wave at a cop in New York or L.A. and they might shoot you. She stood and walked around her store. What was her life? Hippies, free love, protests, men, Lost City, and then Bridge. Bridge wasn't men - he was a man. Bridge was one man, an old soldier that very seldom talked about it. Many times Vivian wanted to ask him about the war. But she never did. Bridge didn't really talk that much about anything. Vivian smiled. She had never told him she really enjoyed his books. For some reason, she had always cracked jokes about his books. She should tell him, but she figured Bridge would say something like, "If everyone liked my books, it would give me an excuse to have six ex-wives, an alcohol problem, and wreck a lot of cars."

Vivian went to her private room. She locked the door behind her. She turned on the light. The red, blue, green, yellow, orange, and purple fairies rubbed the sleep out of their eyes and fluttered around the room. Fairies are always on call, but unlike doctors, they never bitch about having to go to work and deal with the ungrateful public. Vivian sat on the sofa. She pulled her little carved box filled with pot from underneath the sofa. She opened the box and looked at the pipe and pot. "Why?" she asked herself.

She put the box back.

The hummingbird hanging by the window buzzed its wings. The lace curtains did not let the dark into the room. She lay down on the sofa and watched the fairies on the ceiling. She said, "To Bridge, I am young and thin. My fingers are long and graceful. To Bridge my voice is not harsh and grating, it is like a soft wind moving peacefully through a mountain canyon. To Bridge, I am a child."

She shut her eyes. "Please let me forever be a child."

She slept.

Don't be afraid of the deep end of the pool. There is always a lifeguard.

Chapter Forty-Two

In the morning, Stoops, as Bridge expected, was not at the This Isn't Heaven Bar. Gloria, Berry, and Plastic, seeing Bridge walking normally had only one thing to say, which they said in unison. "What the hell?"

"It's a miracle," Bridge said, sitting. "Last night the ghost of Billy Graham came to me in a dream. He touched me on the forehead and said, 'In the morning, you will rise with God's dawn and walk normal like every other biped. Amen.'"

"Normal is a broad term," Berry said. "Since I have had a stroke, I walk as normal as only people who have had strokes walk."

"That's interesting," Plastic said.

"You want to talk that kind of garbage, go to the coffee shop," Gloria said.

"Really," Bridge said. "This is a bar. In a bar, we are only supposed to talk about women, cars, hunting, football, baseball, venereal diseases, lost love, and why we are broke."

"Where's Stoops?" Plastic asked, not hitting any of the categories.

"Organic Muffin has moved in with him," Bridge said as Gloria gave him his Bloody Mary.

"No?" Plastic said.

"Yes," Bridge said.

"No?" Berry said.

"Yes," Bridge said.

"No?" Gloria smiled. It was an I feel good day for Gloria, which was a good thing, bartending lesbians don't have that many good days - having to work in a straight bar starts every day off wrong.

"You are walking normal and Stoops has moved in with Organic Muffin," Plastic said. "What is the world coming to?"

"According to Pill, in about six billion years, the end," Berry said.

Rudolph, from Sally's restaurant, came in, which was highly unusual, as he normally spent his mornings prepping for the restaurant. The only reason most people thought he did his own prepping was because he was too cheap to hire some poor slob who needed a minimum wage job to take care of his ex-wife with two kids and his new wife with four kids. Rudolph looked like he had taken the wrong turn at the meat grinder.

"Bad cheese day," Berry said to Rudolph.

"Screw you Berry, you grumpy bastard," Rudolph replied.

"Thanks, it's about time somebody said something nice to me today," Berry grinned, "Plus, hearing that Organic Muffin has moved in with Stoops makes me want to throw up."

"Old pot smugglers can't fall in love," Rudolph said. "There's no buzz in it."

"No top or bottom line," Plastic said.

"Hopefully he doesn't get ripped off," Gloria said.

The way the conversation was going, Bridge for sure was not going to fess up that he had told Vivian he loved her.

"I came in here to talk about my problems and not discuss people falling in love," Rudolph said.

"Give Rudolph a drink," Berry said. "Booze always goes good with a good cry."

"I didn't say I wanted to cry, but I'd like a brandy and water," Rudolph said.

Gloria went off to do her bartender thing, which, with a brandy and water, is not that difficult. She brought back the drink.

"Ok," Berry said, "tell us your sob story."

"Rebecca told me this morning she is going to leave me," Rudolph said, although he didn't sound as depressed as he looked.

"That's too bad," Bridge said, thinking at the same time how ironic it was that Stoops was moving in with Organic Muffin, he had told Vivian he loved her, and now Rudolph and Rebecca were breaking up. It's an endless man and woman thing. Not true, it's an endless man and woman, man and man, and woman and woman thing. All and all, it's just an endless thing.

"The only thing that really bothers me is that she is leaving me for a woman," Rudolph said - this modern world has its own unique ups and downs.

"No?" Berry said.

"Is that a question or a statement," Rudolph asked.

"Both."

"Well then both of your no's are yeses," Rudolph said.

Berry, Bridge, and Plastic did not know what to say after the two yeses.

"I can understand that," Gloria said.

"What is it women have over men?" Rudolph moaned.

"That's a stupid question," Gloria said.

"It is a stupid question," Berry said. "Women have everything over men. That is why they rule the world. They just let men think they do."

To Bridge's surprise Stoops came into the This Isn't Heaven Bar. His smile was so big the tips of his moustache were hitting him on the nose. "It's an 'I've made love more times in one night than I have in two years' smile," Berry commented.

"What am I going to do?" Rudolph asked, ignoring Stoops.

The three men and Gloria pretended to be thinking, which for them really wasn't that hard - the pretending part. Stoops, not wanting to be left out, pretended to be thinking, but at least he did not know what he was supposed to be thinking about.

After about thirty seconds all five of them shrugged their shoulders. Stoops shrugged his shoulders just because it seemed like the right thing to do.

"What can I do?" Rudolph moaned again.

None of the five bothered to even try and think this time. Too much thinking in life is the source of many problems. Berry said, "Get a dog."

"I have six dogs," Rudolph said.

"Get a cat," Berry said.

"I have a cat."

"You're done."

"I'm done."

"Have another drink."

"Thanks."

Stoops sat.

"One day living with a woman and you look like a changed man," Bridge said to Stoops.

"I am," Stoops said. "I have already been told how to comb my hair, what to eat for breakfast, I had better have a job within five days, and we are going to save to get me some teeth." Stoops then looked at Bridge seriously. "She also told me if I am ever going to buy books from you again to check with her first."

Bridge smiled.

"But the funny thing is I like being told what to do," Stoops said.

"Does she know you are here?" Rudolph asked, apparently over the fact he was done.

"Yes, but I am not going to have a Bloody Mary."

"What's the purpose of going to a bar if you are not going to have a drink?" Berry asked.

"I just wanted to say hi to you guys," Stoops said.

"Hi," Berry said.

"Hi," Plastic said.

"Hi," Rudolph said.

"Hi," Gloria said.

Bridge and Stoops shook hands.

Stoops left with a little bounce in his step.

Rudolph finished his drink and left with no bounce in his step. Breaking up is a no bounce situation.

"Too bad about Rebecca and Rudolph," Plastic said.

"Maybe she is only going through a phase," Berry said.

"Once a woman goes with another woman there is no going back," Gloria said.

What can three men say to that? Nothing. Which is exactly what Bridge, Berry, and Plastic said.

In fact, it was such a knock down men statement, they all paid their bill and left. Women really know how to put men in their place. But where do you put men who really don't know where their place is? Is there such a thing as being put out of their place?

Bridge headed for the Wake Up Or Die. After being put in his place, even though he did not know where his place was, he had the urge to kick a few dogs. But when he got there, all the dogs were wagging their tails and so happy to see him he felt like a dog's Mickey

Mouse. Damn dogs, why do they have to be so nice all the time? Don't they know the world is all screwed up, and all that tail wagging makes it hard for a person to stay depressed, or stay in a place they have been put in even if they don't know where that place is?

Vivian was sitting at a table talking to Barbara. Not another fundraiser, Bridge thought, hoping if it was it was not alfalfa for horses. His days of tossing hay bales went out the window when he turned fifty.

Chris was doing his normal Chris thing - making coffee. Chris smiled at Bridge. "Vivian told me, but I wouldn't believe it, but now I know it is true. You are walking normal."

Bridge walked in a circle. He took several steps backward. He stepped forward. He smiled at Chris and said, "Do you think I can get a job for an evangelist? Rise and walk, all you who have been afflicted. Come to the light and as you pass the donation basket empty your pockets of all that evil money."

"I don't think so," Chris said. "I think you should do what you do."

"What is that?"

"Stay a writer that most people don't read. It suits you."

Bridge didn't know if Chris had complimented him or ridiculed him. He thought about it for a moment and then shrugged his shoulders. There really wasn't that much difference between the two.

Chris gave Bridge a cup of black coffee. "This is our new dark blend," he said. "We have named it Roast In Hell."

Bridge peered into the cup. The coffee was darker than engine oil that had not been changed in three years. It smelled like it had been reheated six or seven times and each time a little water was added and a handful of coffee. Bridge breathed deep the odor. He took a sip. It was strong and bitter and would have made any cowboy standing around a fire want to start singing "Come Along Little Doggie."

"This is great," Bridge hollered so loud everyone in the Wake Up Or Die looked at him. "This is how coffee is supposed to taste, terrible."

Bridge sat at a table by the window with a grin on his face so big it could have ruined his reputation for being a serious writer that is if anyone was looking. Writers are never supposed to smile. Not smiling is the first thing that is taught in Writing 101. The second thing that is taught is drug use and alcohol. Punctuation and spelling aren't even messed with until the senior year, but by then most of the people who wanted to be writers have copped out and changed their degree to English - deciding teaching or being an editor will make them a living even though they will be miserable their complete lives because they really didn't do what they wanted to do. God, twenty-five years of diagramming sentences and reading old books has to be depressing. In twenty-five years they could have accumulated at least fifteen thousand rejection slips, worked sixty odd jobs and never lived in one place longer than four months - four months being how long the law lets a person string out the rent before they can be evicted.

Bridge took another sip of the Roast in Hell coffee. He felt like running out and jumping on a horse and roping a few steers.

To Bridge's surprise, Stoops came into the Wake Up Or Die. He waved at Bridge, got a cup of coffee, and came over. Stoops sipped his coffee. "It's about time they made a cup of coffee that tastes terrible," he said. "This tastes like the stuff I got in prison."

Bridge pondered the sameness of being a cowboy and being in prison but couldn't see where they compared at all. And then his mind went on a tangent, and he wondered, is everything on Earth in prison because the bars of space and infinity surround us? He decided if he ran into a person on mescaline he would ask them, or he could write a letter to the Neo-American Church. If not, the Dalai Lama could answer his question with another riddle.

"I got a job," Stoops said.

"I just saw you at the This Isn't Heaven Bar fifteen minutes ago and you were looking for a job," Bridge said.

"Organic Muffin got me a job at Bill's Restaurant and Libations as an assistant cook. I start tomorrow."

"I didn't know you could cook," Bridge replied in surprise.

"I've cooked in three prisons," Stoops said.

"An education is everything," Bridge said.

"Funny how bad luck can turn into good luck," Stoops said.

"I'm really happy for you, Stoops," Bridge said, meaning every word.

They clinked their coffee cups together, which in the realm of clinks is not as powerful as two beers together clinking, but it is still a clink.

"You told Vivian you love her, didn't you?" Stoops said and asked.

"How did you know?" Bridge replied, slightly surprised.

"I can see it in your face."

"Did I get a tattoo on my face and don't know it?" Bridge asked.

"What a life, huh Bridge?"

"What a life."

Stoops finished his coffee and left. Eight dogs looked at Bridge through the window. "You mutts are as ugly as I am," Bridge said.

Even though they could not hear him, the ugly mutts wagged their tails. Who gives a rat about ugly? Why are dogs smarter than humans?

Barbara came over, but she did not sit. Reporters out to make a scoop are always on the go. Of course, Lost City is not New York City or Chicago, but a scoop is still a scoop - it's the big fish in a little fish bowl syndrome. "You have to read the headlines tomorrow," Barbara said with a suspicious look on her face.

"Do I have to?" Bridge asked.

"Yes," Barbara said and hurried off to find that scoop.

Vivian was sitting at a table with four other people. Bridge did not know what they were talking about, but they were all waving their arms around so much it looked like five people who were being attacked by killer bees. Bridge for sure did not want to go over and get involved with whatever the conversation was. He headed for the Why Am I Here. All the locals he walked by said hello and good morning, but they gave him a funny look. Now that he was walking normal Bridge felt like a freak.

Bridge did his good gallery owner thing and put out the open sign and turned on all the lights. He didn't really feel like writing, but after all the years, he knew writing was never really inspiration - it was constipation from sitting so much. He turned on his quill and inkwell and went around the store straightening paintings and all those little things one does in a store. He went back to his quill and inkwell and brought up his novel. He was about to start typing when MeJoe tapped into the store. "Bridge, you bastard, where is my tie?" MeJoe hollered.

Bridge quickly got MeJoe's tie and took it to him. MeJoe held the tie between his outstretched hands like it was a garrote. "I told Vivian I loved her," Bridge said, taking two steps away from MeJoe even though he was blind.

Blind guys can be sneaky at times.

MeJoe started to laugh, which surprised Bridge, as no one in town had ever heard him laugh. People who tell people to fuck off all the time really are not known for being jolly.

"I can't believe you told Vivian you love her," MeJoe laughed.

"Why?"

"You being a writer, I figured you were so selfish you would not give up your time for anything that was enjoyable."

"Am I going to start writing format romances?" Bridge asked, suddenly filled with a deep dread and picturing in his mind a housewife having an affair with her dog groomer even though she was really in love with the grocery store clerk, but, little did she know, her husband was sleeping with the wives of both the dog groomer and the grocery store clerk even though down deep he was truly in love with his wife.

"No, Vivian will start telling you what to write," MeJoe said.

"No she won't," Bridge said. "She is different. She wants to be herself and she wants me to be myself."

"That's always true until you tell them you love them," MeJoe said.

"Not with Vivian."

"I'm glad you told Vivian you love her," MeJoe said.

"I have even started to walk normal," Bridge said.

"Bridge, your life will go to hell if you become normal," MeJoe said and left.

Bridge headed for his computer, once again trying to figure out how to write a book with only body language in it.

Just as Bridge sat Rudolph ran into the store hollering, "She is not going to leave me. My wife still loves me."

"If you get this excited, you should break up every day," Bridge said. "It's good for your heart."

Rudolph ran out of the Why Am I Here.

After a case of MeJoe and Rudolph, whatever writing he was going to do went wherever words go when they are not going to be used. Bridge looked out the window. He suddenly felt sad. His mind filled with questions. Will you try and change me, Vivian? Will you try and control me, Vivian? Will you tell me that books are useless when down deep I know they are? Will you tell me life passes us by so quickly that most of the time we only catch glimpses of it? Will you tell me that love is useless even when we embrace? What if we were living five billion and ninety-nine million and ninety-nine thousand and nine hundred ninety-nine years and ninety-nine days from now and we only had one day to go until poof, no more, no nothing. Would the last day be a great day? Come on, baby, let's party. All you Jews, Christians, Arabs, blacks, whites, yellows, browns, and every shade of people, Liberals, Democrats, Republicans, communists, socialists, dictators, and kings and queens, you don't have to fight anymore. It's over baby, hug and make up, time has finally won.

Bridge stepped outside and gazed at the sky. A few clouds hung motionless. The sun was bright and warm. A dozen or so pigeons circled. Sergeant came out of his gallery and stretched. He waved at Bridge. Bridge waved back. Gertrude came out of her gallery. She smiled. Bridge smiled back. Across the street on Yankee Street the other gallery owners were talking.

Sergeant and Gertrude went back inside. Bridge took several deep breaths. A lady in her mid to late sixties walked up to Bridge. She reminded him of an aunt everyone would love. "You're the writer," the lady said.

"That's what I call myself, but at times I wonder," Bridge said.

"Can I come in your shop?"

"Of course." Bridge held the door open for her.

The lady went to where Bridge's books were displayed. "I by chance ran into a man at the airport in Kansas City who bought one of your books when he was in town," the lady said.

"Did he like it?" Bridge asked.

The lady smiled her good aunt smile and replied, "He didn't say, but he told me I should stop in on my visit to Lost City and buy one of your novels. He told me anyone who is stupid enough to try and sell their own books needs support."

"It is a futile undertaking," Bridge agreed.

"Everything is futile, but if you do what you love, futility takes a back seat," the lady said.

"A back seat to what?" Bridge asked.

"Does it matter?" the lady smiled.

"No, I suppose it does not matter," Bridge said.

The lady bought four books. Life is good. Go away, sadness.

After signing the four books, Bridge handed the lady another of his books. "This is for you in thanks," he said.

"For buying the books?" the lady questioned.

"No."

"Then for what?"

"For the back seat," Bridge replied with a smile.

Chapter Forty-Three

Bridge woke up in Vivian's bed. He felt like a John Deere tractor was gunning its engine in his head - not a small tractor but one of those monsters with huge double wheels and an engine big enough to power a submarine. Vivian was gone. Bridge and Vivian had not talked much the night before at Bill's Restaurant and Libations. They had basically sloshed down drinks, then sloshed to Vivian's, and then sloshed in bed until they fell asleep. Bridge decided that one sloshing a day was enough, two was pushing it, and three was way out of bounds. "Now that Vivian knows I love her, I might be dead in two weeks," Bridge told himself as he got out of bed.

Bridge went to the Wake Up Or Die. Chris, seeing him, quickly poured Bridge a cup of Roast In Hell coffee and hurried over to him. "You look like you would do a lot better if you crawled," Chris said, putting the coffee down on a table and pulling out the chair for Bridge.

"Ugh," is all Bridge could say.

Vivian was running around the store like nothing had happened, which for a few seconds made Bridge wonder if last night was only a dream. But if it was a dream, he had had worse.

"You'd better drink some of that Roast In Hell quick," Chris said with concern. Gay men have a lot of concern over their straight friends.

Bridge took a sip. "All of those sweet frothy coffee drinkers should be drinking some of this," he told Chris.

Stoops came in. Bridge almost fell out of his chair. Stoops' pants and shirt were pressed. Although his hair was still long his hair had been trimmed along with his beard and moustache. To top it off, his boots were shined.

Chris, out of the kindness of his heart, brought Stoops a cup of coffee. "You look nice," he told Stoops as he set the coffee down. "Living with Organic Muffin must suit you."

"Thank you, you look nice yourself," Stoops said.

"Gay men always look nice," Bridge said.

After two compliments Chris walked away puffed up like a peacock.

"Why do gay men always look nice?" Stoops asked Bridge.

"It must be a competition thing," Bridge said. "Men can look like bums because there are more women than men."

"I start cooking at Bill's Restaurant and Libations this evening," Stoops said.

"It's a good thing I only drink there," Bridge said.

Stoops smiled. Being in love can take the sting out of comments by sarcastic friends.

"Have you seen a copy of Let's Turn Lost City Into A Political Hotbed this morning?" Stoops asked.

"I only read the paper when I want to get angry or throw up," Bridge said.

Stoops went to a table where Vivian gave away newspapers and brought back a copy and handed it to Bridge. On the first page was a photograph of Bridge with a caption - BRIDGE MCCOY - LOCAL AUTHOR, TELLS WOMAN HE LOVES HER. Then in a small paragraph it went on to explain that Bridge McCoy no longer walks two steps forward and one backward, but he walks like a bow-legged duck, and the woman he has fallen in love with owns the local coffee shop. It also mentioned Bridge's gallery was participating in the Chamber of Commerce Art Walk.

"Do I walk like a bow-legged duck?" Bridge asked Stoops, for some reason not offended he had made the front page.

"I've never seen a bow-legged duck," Stoops said. "But I do know that most ducks are pigeon-toed, which in all truth should be duck-toed."

Vivian came over to the table and planted a big kiss on the top of Bridge's head.

"If I was a woman, I'd be afraid to kiss him on the mouth myself," Stoops said.

"You look nice," Vivian told Stoops.

Stoops smiled.

"People keep telling him how nice he looks, we won't be able to live with him," Bridge said.

"Do you think I am ready for *GQ Magazine*?" Stoops asked Vivian.

"If there is a run for over the hill men, you might make it," Vivian said.

When one gets too many compliments there has to be a time when the bottom falls out.

"I start cooking at Bill's Restaurant and Libations tonight and I want you and Bridge to come over. I will cook you two dinner, on me," Stoops told Vivian.

"We'll be there," Vivian said before Bridge could open his mouth. Bridge was wondering what cooks cooked in prison, and he doubted it was steak or halibut with twice cooked potatoes. Plus, he had always heard that the biggest bitch convicts had was the food. I killed six people and got a life sentence, which really doesn't bother me, but they keep over-cooking my eggs in the morning. Doesn't anyone know what over easy means?

Stoops finished his coffee and said as he was leaving, "I'll leave you two lovebirds alone."

Vivian sat. "It was cute what Barbara wrote in the paper," she said.

"I wonder if I could sue them for defamation of character for comparing me to a bow-legged duck," Bridge said.

"I thought it was a compliment," Vivian said.

"Why do I love thee, let me count the ways," Bridge said.

"I think it is because Chris keeps giving you free coffee," Vivian said.

"If you tossed in some ham and eggs and toast, ours would be the biggest love in history," Bridge said.

"I wonder if Juliet cooked," Vivian pondered.

Bridge took another sip of coffee. He felt better, but he did not feel normal, which really did not bother him.

"Since you told me you love me do you feel any different?"

Vivian asked Bridge, giving him a serious look.

Little alarm bells went off in Bridge's head. What do I say? Do I lie? Do I, what? He remembered his ex-wife and her dreaded statement, "We have to talk." No man ever wins when a woman says, "We have to talk." What she is really saying is, "You have to listen."

What the man is thinking during all this is - 'I done screwed up somewhere. Really honey I didn't mean to leave the toilet seat up or look at that twenty-year-old with the cleavage down to her bellybutton. I will never look at another woman again in my life and I'll start pissing in the back yard.'

Since Bridge did not immediately reply, Vivian asked again. "Since you told me you love me do you feel any different?"

"I feel secure," Bridge said.

Satisfied with the answer, Vivian replied, "I wonder what Stoops is going to cook for us?"

Bridge stood and kissed Vivian on the forehead. "I'll meet you at Bill's Restaurant and Libations around seven," he said as he left, glad to be off the hook. Love has many complications.

Vivian watched him walk away. "I feel secure also," she said.

Chapter Forty-Four

Pill was the only person in the This Isn't Heaven Bar. His **THERE IS ONLY SIX BILLION YEARS LEFT FOR THE WORLD** sign was propped up against the bar. He had three empty beer bottles in front of him and was holding a full beer, which, at ten in the morning, is a good start on one hell of a drunk. Sad country music was blaring out of the jukebox. Gloria was at the end of the bar stocking the beer cooler. Bridge came in and sat by Pill. "Run out of peanut butter?" Bridge asked.

"How come everyone is falling in love and I can't?" Pill slurred.

Bridge wished he had gone to his store. So he did what most people do when put in a situation they cannot handle, he passed the buck. "Hey Gloria," he called. "Why can't Pill fall in love?"

"He smells like peanut butter all the time," Gloria hollered back. "Plus, from what I hear, he doesn't want to fall in love."

Plastic came in and sat by Bridge. "Why don't you sit by Pill," Bridge said. "He is feeling low and wondering why he can't fall in love."

"He smells like peanut butter all the time," Plastic said to Bridge, and then said to Pill, "No offense intended, but I hate peanut butter and I really don't give a damn if it is one of the best foods ever invented and, on top of that, I really don't care if there is six billion years left to the world or fifty."

"No offense taken," Pill replied, and then he told Gloria, "I never wanted to fall in love until yesterday."

Gloria brought Plastic and Bridge a Bloody Mary and said to Pill, "Do you know why yesterday was the day that made you suddenly want to fall in love?"

"It suddenly dawned on me that I am lonely," Pill sobbed.

Bridge and Plastic looked away. Men do not like to look at sobbing men. They also hate to look at sobbing women, because they know it is going to cost them something.

Gloria handed Pill a bar rag. Pill wiped his eyes and blew his nose. Bridge patted him on the shoulder. Plastic looked disgusted.

"What you need is some old hippie chick," Gloria said.

"I don't like hairy armpits and I would have to buy a teepee," Pill said.

"Scratch that idea," Bridge said.

"You could run an ad in the Let's Turn Lost City Into A Political Hotbed stating, 'Man who lives in his own truck in the wilderness, loves peanut butter, is building an ark with only a hatchet, and knows there is only six billion years left for the world is looking for woman, any age, who owns a nice travel trailer and has a lot of crackers,'" Plastic said.

A sudden transformation came over Pill. "Do you think it would work?" he asked Plastic like a little city kid who had just seen Santa Clause and thought Santa was going to bring him a horse.

"You never know," Plastic said.

"There are a lot of weird women in this town," Bridge said.

"You could also lie and say you are rich," Gloria said.

"I'll do it," Pill said with a big grin that would have made a chimpanzee jealous.

Berry walked in like only a man who has had a stroke can. "It would be a good bar if I didn't see you guys here everyday," he said.

"Screw you, up yours, go back to bed," he got for a three-way reply. Gloria abstained.

"Thanks," Berry said, and then looking at Pill, his eyes narrowed and he half laughed, "My God Pill, you look like a fucking smiling chimpanzee."

"Do chimpanzees smile when they fuck?" Bridge asked.

"Most of the monkey men I was with in my life grunted," Gloria said.

"I have never smiled or laughed when I was screwing," Plastic said.

"I think smiling or laughing could get you shot," Berry said.

Bridge kept his mouth shut. There are some things in life not worth contemplating, plus, Bridge figured most of the women he had slept with thought he was pretty funny.

Pill also didn't say anything.

Gloria brought Berry a Bloody Mary. "I like your picture in the paper," Berry said to Bridge.

"It doesn't take much to make the paper in this town," Plastic said.

"Do I really walk like a bow-legged duck?" Bridge asked.

"No," they all replied.

"Good," Bridge said - there was something about a bow-legged duck that bothered him. Vanity, it touches us all - sly little trickster.

"Rudolph and Rebecca got back together," Bridge announced.

"Too bad for Pill," Plastic said, "he could have got her on the rebound."

"Now, now," Gloria chastised Plastic.

Plastic, not chastised at all, just grinned.

Bridge finished his Bloody Mary. Without asking, Gloria gave him another one.

"I was thinking last night, and," Berry said but was interrupted by Pill, who said, "Thinking, you were thinking, that is novel."

"A novel is what a person writes," Bridge said.

"Shut up," Berry said. "As I was about to say, I was thinking last night that now that you walk one step at a time, Bridge, your shoes will last longer."

Pill, Plastic, and Bridge thought about the statement for a moment. They all nodded their heads in agreement.

Bridge finished his Bloody Mary. "It's time for me to go type more incomplete sentences," he said.

"You're good at those," Berry said.

While Bridge was leaving, they all watched him walk. "He does walk like a bow- legged duck," Plastic said.

"Let's Make Lost City Into A Political Hotbed is the only newspaper in the country that tells the truth," Pill said.

"It's very strange," Berry said, "but for the past few days I have felt very content and happy with my life."

"That's good," Plastic said.

"Real good," Pill said.

But for some reason the statement did not set right with Gloria. She looked at Berry closely then went back to filling the beer cooler, feeling apprehensive and a little afraid.

Bridge was about to open the door to the Why Am I Here when Organic Muffin stopped. "Stoops wanted me to ask you if you would like me to make your hors d'oeuvres for the art walk this weekend?" she asked Bridge.

A tiny jolt shot through Bridge. He felt his legs tingle. "I forgot all about it," he replied.

"Well do you want me to or not?" Organic Muffin questioned.

"I have to think about it," Bridge said, feeling a little faint.

Organic Muffin gave him a puzzled look and left.

Bridge went inside. He started to shake slightly. He felt cold and then hot. His breathing grew short. Old lampposts that were still good and were now living on a commune paraded through his mind. They had signs hanging from them that stated - Bridge McCoy, you are a traitor. Three paving machines roared in his mind. They were singing as they paved away, "Bridge McCoy, we love you." A Jaguar, a Mercedes, and a BMW filled with laughing realtors slithered through a gated housing development. A new art gallery was filled with abstract paintings from the East Coast. A tour bus stopped on the corner of Yankee Street and disgorged fifteen thousand cameras. Bridge jumped up. "What am I if I am not myself?" he hollered, waving his arms up and down like a little boy fresh out of diapers that had to pee pee but hadn't figured out a zipper.

Bridge looked out the window. A few tourists were on the street along with a few bikers, a few birds, a few stray dogs, and a few hippies. MeJoe was talking to himself. Lotus Blossom was sitting in front of her store working on a gourd. Gertrude was hanging up her open sign. Sergeant was talking to four of his sixteen girlfriends. Bridge visualized people in his store during the art walk. He could hear them talking. "I like this painting. I would have painted this in blue instead of orange. Why don't you write something about Lost City? I like your books, but I don't like the way you put your words together. This is such a nice little town. You artists are so different from the rest of the people we know. It's like you really don't know the world exists or maybe you just ignore it."

In a daze, Bridge went to his quill and inkwell. He pushed the on button. The little electric whatz a ma jiggets came to life. He brought up his novel. He wanted to close his eyes and say a few magic words and melt into the screen. He wanted to be a fiction character. And in the end they lived happily ever after.

He leaned back in his chair, took two deep breaths, and he started to laugh. He did not know if he was happy, or sad, or depressed, but he laughed. The old lampposts that were still working and living on a commune dropped their signs and started to laugh. The paving machines frowned. The realtors in the gated community looked around like they had never heard laughter. All the cameras getting off of the tour bus suddenly discovered their lenses wouldn't open. The people during the art walk looked at the sardines on their plates and made a face.

And then he started to type. It was a good day. The run-on sentences ran rampant. Adjectives and adverbs were put into positions they had never experienced. Semi-colons were non-existent - some things have no true function in life.

Pill was at the newspaper filling out his ad for the personal column. Somewhere in the world there is a lonely lady who loves men who smell like peanut butter.

Chapter Forty-Five

Vivian was radiant. Her dress was the color of every balloon that had ever been at a car lot, a circus, or a wedding. Her childlike eyes were skipping rope. Bridge had taken a shower at Vivian's, but he was not radiant - more the slightly used look. They were sitting at a corner table for two at Bill's Restaurant and Libations waiting for the meal Stoops was going to cook for them. Organic Muffin was waiting the table. Unlike the night Bridge had told Vivian he loved her, he could not force himself to drink wine and was drinking a beer. Vivian was drinking the house red. "This is fun," she said. "It's like we are on a vacation or we are kids and are playing grownup."

"I feel like a little kid around you," Bridge said. "You make my world a better place."

Vivian smiled. There was nothing to say.

They had salmon crusted with almonds on a bed of wild rice with a raspberry- infused side salad. For dessert they had chocolate mousse. It was all delicious. Bridge wondered what prisons Stoops had been in where he had cooked such over the top food. Maybe he cooked in the guard's kitchen?

When they were done eating, Stoops came out to the table. He had on a cook's hat and an apron. He looked proud. "It was wonderful," Vivian told him.

Stoops bowed to Vivian, looked Bridge directly in the eyes and said, "Thanks for all you have done for me," and went back to the kitchen.

"It's a strange life, isn't it, Vivian?" Bridge said.

"It's a good life if we let it be," Vivian said.

After dinner they walked around the art district holding hands. All the shops were closed. A few had dim lights on inside so people could see the artwork. "Have I changed you?" Vivian asked Bridge seriously while they were looking into Rainy Day's gallery, the Sunbonnet.

"I don't think so," Bridge answered, but he did not really know. Had he changed? Even though he now walked normal, and even though things that bothered him before did not seem to bother him as much, although they still did, had he changed? Had the war changed him? Had lost love changed him? Had being a hippie changed him? Had being a cowboy changed him? Or were people just what they were and everything changed around them and made them seem different?

"I don't want to change you," Vivian said.

"I don't want to change you," Bridge said.

Two stray dogs trotted down the middle of the deserted street. A police siren called from the distance. The siren was answered by the blaring of an ambulance. The ambulance grew closer. The two sirens blended into a scream and then stopped. Over the tops of the darkened buildings, the flashing red and blue lights lit up the night sky. "That's close to Berry's," Bridge said, feeling alarmed.

"Too close," Vivian agreed.

Vivian and Bridge hurried toward Berry's. When they got there, two cop cars, a fire truck, and an ambulance, all with their lights flashing, were parked in front of Berry's house. All the neighbors were standing in small groups outside. Bridge and Vivian went over to a man and woman. "Do you know what is going on?" Bridge asked.

"We heard a shot and I called the police," the lady said.

Bridge left Vivian and hurried over to a policeman. "I am a friend of Berry's, can you tell me what happened?"

Small towns are small towns. The police know everybody. It's their job and their business. "You're the writer, Bridge McCoy," the policeman said.

Bridge nodded his head.

"There's an envelope pinned to the wall for you, follow me."

Bridge followed the policemen. He felt like a shadow that

wanted to be invisible.

Blood was splattered on the wall, mixed with bone and brains. A sheet covered a body. By the body was a shotgun. Blood crept out from under the sheet like frozen dreams. Policemen and medics were talking - dead people do not need attention.

"This is McCoy," the policemen said to another policeman, who nodded his head. They went to the wall. Pinned to the wall with a red headed tack was an envelope. Written on the envelope was, 'For Bridge McCoy Only, You Fuckers.'

Bridge had to smile, a smile of futility. What else can one do with futility but smile at it?

"You can take it down," the policeman said.

Bridge took down the envelope, it was not sealed. He took out a single sheet of typing paper. It was folded neatly. He unfolded the paper. There was a one-hundred-dollar bill in it and written in a steady hand was - 'Bridge, you were a friend. I wanted to die happy. Call my sister at 520-456-4762. She knows what to do. Buy Pill, Plastic, Stoops, the Professor, and Gloria a drink on me. All you fuckers have a good life. Berry.'

"You want to read it?" Bridge asked the policeman.

"I have to," he replied.

Bridge handed him the letter. He read it. He handed it back and smiled. Bridge smiled. What does one say? Death is death. Pass the apple pie. If you see God tell him hello. If you see the devil tell him to eat shit. If you see nothing, ask the nothing why there is no God or no devil?

Bridge went outside. Vivian was standing by herself underneath a street lamp. Her arms were crossed under her breasts. All Bridge said was, "He died happy. What more could one ask?"

"He was lonely," Vivian said.

"He died happy," Bridge said.

They went to Vivian's house and Bridge called Berry's sister. Berry's sister did not cry. Berry's sister was a faceless stranger's voice. Berry's sister would take care of everything. Everyone needs a sister, even if she does not have a face.

Bridge and Vivian went to bed - a soft touch, an unseen tear, a sigh. Who needs words?

How many people die happy?

Chapter Forty-Six

It was a grand party for Berry. The jukebox was unplugged. Berry had hated loud music. Pill, Plastic, the Professor, Stoops, Bridge and Gloria were all drinking beer. Pill's sign was leaning against the bar. Gloria had put the closed sign on the door and would not let anyone else in. "The owner won't fire me," Gloria stated. "Who else would pull the day shift at this dump and put up with you jerks?"

The party had started at ten in the morning and it was now close to one. A hundred bucks buys a lot of beer, especially when Gloria was only ringing up about half of them. Connections in life are a good thing.

Berry had been toasted so many times if he had been real toast he would have had so much butter on him he would have felt like an English muffin. The five guys were now sitting at the bar slouched over, each with a half-finished beer in front of them. Gloria was leaning up against the bar with her pierced nipples so close to Plastic's nose he looked like he was a skinny bull tethered to her boobs. "If you ever go back to men, I want you to call me first," Plastic slurred to Gloria.

"If I ever go back to men, you're at the end of a very short list," Gloria said.

"This was a great party," Stoops said, "but I have to go take a nap so I can cook tonight."

He weaved his way toward the door.

"Responsibility has its price," Pill said.

"I'm going to take my broken heart home," Plastic said, untethering from Gloria's boobs and weaving his way toward the door.

"See your broken heart in the morning," Gloria called.

Pill put his **THERE IS ONLY SIX BILLION YEARS LEFT FOR THE WORLD** sign back on and headed for the door. He did not say goodbye - with only six billion years left there really is no time for goodbyes.

The Professor finished his beer. "Any money left?" he asked Bridge.

"About twenty bucks."

"Let's have another one, then," the Professor said.

"I think I could use a few more carbs," Bridge said. "I have one more day to get ready for the art walk."

Gloria brought two more beers and one for herself. "I got a letter from the Rock Lady," the Professor said.

"Was it carved in stone?" Gloria asked.

Bridge half laughed, it was a half laugh joke.

"She is getting married to a Baptist preacher," the Professor said.

"A Baptist?" Gloria and Bridge gasped at the same time. For some reason, Baptists can make a lot of people gasp.

"She said the fact they don't drink, smoke, or dance is the only way to true enlightenment," the Professor said, adding, "it seems crystals are as fake as the rock of rocks."

"I wonder how long the marriage will last?" Bridge asked.

"I wonder if I will ever fall in love?" the Professor asked, not answering Bridge's question.

"If Stoops and Bridge can find a woman who will put up with them, anyone can fall in love," Gloria said.

"Why don't you write a book about love," the Professor said to Bridge, seemingly content with Gloria's answer to his question, which Bridge didn't know if he liked or not.

"I don't think I can spell love," Bridge said.

"I'll really miss Berry," the Professor said. "We all need a grump around to keep things in perspective."

Bridge, Gloria, and the Professor clinked their beers together in a final tribute to Berry.

Bridge headed to the store. He was not drunk, but he was not sober. He wondered if bubbly Frauline and Berry were having a conversation, and if they were, what could a grump and a bubble possibly have to talk about?

Gertrude was standing outside of the Why Am I Here. "You haven't forgotten the art walk have you?" she asked, with a look in her eye that meant the answer had better be no I have not forgotten or yes I have not forgotten.

"Yes, I have not forgotten," Bridge said.

"By our calculations, there are going to be close to five thousand people here," Gertrude said. "Saturday morning a person will come by and give you balloons to tie outside your door. That way people will know you are a participant."

Bridge wanted to say he wasn't selling cars, but having half of a buzz on gave him the wisdom to keep his mouth shut, plus he really had to pee and didn't want to get into an extended conversation. A man peeing in his pants is only acceptable for a few years after birth and in the old folks' home - in the old folks' home it's par for the course.

After too many beers for breakfast and lunch, a pee is a very enjoyable thing - very simple and gratifying. After too many beers for breakfast and lunch, a nap is also a very simple and gratifying thing. Bridge lay on his cot. Bless the comforts of home. But at times sleep is not a comfort - dreams have a way of getting in the way.

Bridge's dream: Bridge was floating above the business section of Lost City. He felt tranquil, like he was a kite with just enough breeze to keep him in the air. Two ravens looked at him like he was the strangest bird they had ever seen in their lives, squawked twice, and continued on to wherever two ravens go, normally to the nearest dump. Below him cars zoomed everywhere. Masses of people trampled over each other to get into fast food joints, grocery stores, clothing stores, car part stores, movie rental stores, music stores, and stores that sold nothing at all but were just buildings that had the word STORE painted on them. Suddenly the wind kicked up and Bridge was tossed up and down violently. He flapped his arms in an attempt to stay stable, but the wind was so strong it drove him toward the ground. The ground raced at him like he was an Indy car doing three hundred miles and hour being driven by a man who had consumed sixty-five power drinks and had lost all reason. Bridge started screaming, "Help me! Help me! I thought I could fly."

Not one of the zillions of faceless people trampling each other to get into the stores looked up. Not one of the cars slowed down. Bridge was so afraid he could no longer scream. Just as he was about to hit the ground, an updraft tossed him back into the air. The sensation was so strong Bridge could not breathe. His stomach was going to shoot through the top of his head. Up he went up so high Lost City was merely a dot, and just as he felt like he would pass out, he was suddenly sitting on a telephone wire at the corner of Yankee and Texas Streets. There were so many people going in and out of the galleries it looked like the subway in New York. Every person was carrying a painting or a pot, one of his books, or had so much jewelry on they looked like a moving display cases. The gallery owners were standing outside their stores with fistfuls of cash and bewildered looks on their faces - they all thought they had died and gone to Santa Fe. The two ravens landed on either side of Bridge. "So this is what you wanted?" one raven said to Bridge. The raven sounded like Berry.

Bridge shook his head desperately.

"You have to be careful for what you wish for," the other raven said. The raven sounded like Frauline.

"I didn't wish for anything," Bridge pleaded. "I tried to stop this."

"You wished for fame," Berry raven said.

"You wished for love," Frauline raven said.

"You wished, you wished, you wished," they said in unison.

Just then an old lamppost that still worked, and was tired of living on the commune, marched down the middle of the street. "I'm tired of granola and bean sprouts and organic tacos," it shouted.

A huge paving machine, its grill turned into a sardonic grin, roared around the corner, sped up and smashed the lamppost. The dying words of the old lamppost were, "Maybe organic tacos weren't that bad."

A tour bus drove down the street. It was filled with realtors who were tossing brochures out the window informing the masses that real estate was going to go up twenty-five percent and the banks were going to raise mortgage rates. The tourists grabbed and punched each other as they fought over the flyers.

All the members of the Chamber of Commerce appeared on the sidewalk. They were holding copies of all the magazines in which they had advertised.

Then a crowd of at least five hundred people in military precision marched down the street. Each person had a different sign: **Make Lost City Into Santa Fe. High Rent Is Better Rent. Art Is Not For The Masses. Ten Dollar Margaritas. Lower The Minimum Wage. Bumpy Streets Have No Class. We Do Not Want To Be Different.**

As Bridge read each sign, he started to shake. As he read on he was shaking like he was an ice cube in a blender that really did not want to be a daiquiri. "No! No," he yelled.

"Yes! Yes!" the marching people yelled back at him with pompous grins on their faces.

Bridge woke up drenched in sweat. He sat up slowly - the living room, den, and bedroom came in and out of focus for several seconds. He stood, staggered to the front of the store, and looked out the window. To his surprise, two ravens were sitting on the telephone wire. Bridge stormed outside. Gertrude and Sergeant were talking. Bridge shook his fists at the ravens and hollered, "You two don't know what in the hell you're talking about."

The ravens seemed to laugh and flew off. Bridge went back inside muttering to himself. Gertrude said to Sergeant, "I think this art walk is starting to get to Bridge."

"Bridge had better start walking two steps forward and one backward again," Sergeant said.

Bridge did not type during the day. Each gallery owner in turn came by the store. Each in their own way was worried about Bridge. Artists are strange, but even artists don't talk to ravens, that is, unless they are on a spiritual quest. But a raven would not be able to tell them if there is a God or not. They might tell them that ravens are far superior to crows and blackbirds, but the God thing is beyond ravens. To answer the God question modern man has to go into a deep consultation with their computer.

Instead of typing, Bridge sat at the table and, with the help of his good angel and his bad angel, tried to figure out what he was going to serve for hors d'oeuvres during the art walk. Sardines - bad angel. Cheese and crackers - good angel. Vienna sausages - bad angel. Spinach dip - good angel. Beer - bad angel. Wine and flavored water - good angel.

By mid-afternoon Bridge was completely worn out by the

constant bickering between his good and bad angel and pondered how there could possibly be such a thing as a bad angel? If there is a bad angel, is there a good devil?

By four, Bridge had recovered enough from beer for breakfast and lunch, flying, bad dreams, hollering at ravens, and bad and good angels he headed for Bill's Restaurant and Libations. What better way to get over too many beers and weird dreams than to have another drink?

Chris was at Bill's. In Amarillo, Bridge would have felt weird sitting with a gay man at a bar, but since this was Lost City, he joined Chris. Bridge could not tell if Chris was feeling good or bad - however one can do it, Chris looked neutral. How is your day going? Not bad, I'm in neutral. Good thing there are no hills in town or you'd bruise your ass sliding downhill.

"I don't think I've ever seen you here," Bridge said. "I hope you are not going to order a cup of coffee."

"I feel like my life is in a rut," Chris said, which was definitely not a neutral statement.

"I'd figure you'd feel like you were stuck in a coffee bean grinder," Bridge said.

Chris tried to grin, but it did not work.

"My life has always been in a rut," Bridge said, "but, after so many years, what the hell, live in a rut, die in a rut. There has to be worse things."

"What?" Chris asked.

"Just off the top of my head, war, prison, having to listen to poetry every day."

Chris looked at Bridge seriously. Bridge continued, "For a few more things, poverty, hunger, ringworm, decaffeinated coffee."

Chris jumped up and hugged Bridge. The three gay owners of Bill's Restaurant and Libations smiled. "You are so wonderful at times," Chris beamed, sitting back down.

"I don't think anyone in my life has ever called me wonderful," Bridge said.

Organic Muffin came over to the table. "Let me buy Bridge a beer," Chris said.

"It's too bad about Berry," Organic Muffin said.

"He is in a better place," Chris said.

Bridge did not say anything. He didn't feel bad about Berry. He didn't feel sad. Life was a bad situation anyway. But he had always wondered about the statement, he or she is in a better place. If there is a hell, what if he or she went to hell?

Chris ordered a Mango Margarita, which to Bridge's thinking was a good drink for a gay man to order.

"I want to make your hors d'oeuvres for the art walk," Chris told Bridge.

First Organic Muffin and now Chris wanted to make hors d'oeuvres. Bridge wished they wanted to lend him some money. "I will even serve them for you," Chris went on.

"Do you have black slacks and a white dress shirt?" Bridge asked.

"Bridge," Chris said, seemingly exasperated, "I am a gay man. I have been a waiter in some very nice restaurants."

Bridge took the statement to mean Chris did have dress slacks and a dress shirt - in fact, probably more than one of each.

"Do you have serving trays and glass glasses?" Bridge asked.

Chris rolled his eyes back in their sockets, which in this case meant yes, but in some other cases could have meant no.

A book written only in body language would not be as easy as Bridge thought. "Ok," Bridge said. "It's all in your hands."

Chris jumped up, so happy he wanted to hug Bridge again. Bridge pushed him back down in the chair. "I've had my hug quota," he said.

"This is so exciting," Chris chirped. "I really have to do something besides make coffee. This will get me out of my rut."

Bridge decided there are some ruts that are a lot deeper than other ruts.

Organic Muffin brought the drinks. Bridge had to concede that the Mango Margarita looked pretty good. He just didn't know if he could get away with holding a glass with his little pinky finger sticking out at an angle or a stud in his tongue clinking on the side of the glass.

Chris only drank one drink and hurried off, explaining, "I have to go plan my menu, you will be so impressed."

"There are going to be a few sardines and Vienna sausages that are going to be depressed," Bridge told him.

Stoops came in. For as long as Bridge could remember, he had never seen Stoops look so happy. Organic Muffin hugged Stoops. Stoops waved at Bridge and went to the back to do whatever cooks do when they go on shift - maybe cut their fingers a few times or spit on the griddle.

For some reason, Bridge thought about the ceremony for the first person that had been killed in his unit. An altar had been made out of C-ration boxes. The man's boots were placed on the boxes along with his rifle and steel pot. All the men from the unit were in ranks. An artillery unit on their left flank shelled a distant target. Maybe women and kids? Maybe regular army? Maybe V.C.? Shells do not care. A priest read a few passages. Bridge had looked at the boots, and it was as though the boots were alive. The man who had worn them had only been an illusion, something the boots invented to give them meaning. Look at me, I am boots. I have heels and laces. It has been a good life, I have no holes in my soles. Then five F-150's had flown over and one peeled off - the salute to the lost pilot - the vibrations jarring Bridge to the center of his bones. The boots did not make him angry. The boots did not scare him. The vibrations did not make him embrace God.

Organic Muffin came over to the table. "You look like you are deep in thought," she said.

"I've been thinking about orange Jell-O salad with shredded carrots in it," Bridge said.

"I don't like it when they put pimientos in it," Organic Muffin said.

"I don't like boots with laces," Bridge said, put some money on the table and headed for the Wake Up Or Die.

Vivian was sitting at a window table. She was reading an article in the Let's Make Lost City Into A Political Hotbed. "What are you reading?" Bridge asked as he sat.

"I'm reading about the gray wolves they have reintroduced into the mountains," Vivian said.

Bridge could tell she was slightly agitated. "The ranchers want to kill them and the environmentalists want to save them," Vivian went on. "What do you think?" she asked.

"If I was a wolf I'd stay off of a rancher's land," Bridge said, "and I would teach my children to not eat beef or lamb."

"I also read an ad in the personal column that had to be written by Pill," Vivian said.

"He wants to find a woman," Bridge said.

Vivian set the paper down. "You don't want to marry me, do

you Bridge?" she asked casually.

How they got from wolves to Pill to marriage, Bridge didn't really understand. "Love is love," he said, which was an obscure answer, and had as much meaning as apples are apples or horses are horses.

Vivian smiled. "Good. I don't want to get married, and I don't want you moving in with me."

"Can I still ride in your car?" Bridge asked.

"Baby, you can ride in my car anytime you like."

A large group of people came in and Vivian went to help make frothy coffees.

Bridge headed for the Why Am I Here. He figured he should clean the store. He then remembered he had not told Chris what time to come to the store but decided it was no big deal - being Lost City, Chris already knew.

Bridge did his 'maid for a day' thing. He mopped the floor. He dusted the paintings, which seemed to enjoy it. He washed the windows. He straightened his books. When he was finished he went over to see MeJoe, thinking he might want to borrow his tie again. Hors d'oeuvres and a tie - that would freak out Gertrude.

MeJoe was sitting in the middle of his gallery blanking at one of the paintings. "You seem to be distressed," MeJoe said.

"How can you tell?" Bridge asked.

"Vibes, man," MeJoe said.

Bridge remembered when he had tried his career move at being a hippie. Hearing the words vibes and wow for the millionth time had finally shaken him out of his funk and made him into a cowboy. Cowboys don't say wow and vibes and groovy - they say shit and fuck a lot, and at the time, shit and fuck had more meaning - good fucking shitting vibes - wow, motherfucker - groovy my ass.

"I am distressed," Bridge finally answered MeJoe, pulling his brain back into his head.

"Telling a woman you love her is very distressing," MeJoe said.

"My world is crumbling all around me," Bridge said.

"That's what worlds are for," MeJoe said.

"I'm even walking normal," Bridge said.

"Get over it," MeJoe said, sounding like he was getting tired of talking about Bridge's distress.

"I want to borrow your tie again," Bridge said, also tired of talking about his distress - a man talking to men about their problems is only something that happens in the movies where men are supposed to care and feel. In all truth, if they want to care and feel, they should be gay.

MeJoe went to his living area and brought back a black tie and held it out for Bridge to take.

"I thought you only had white ties," Bridge said, taking the tie.

"I figured I should put some color in my life," MeJoe said.

Bridge started to leave, but then stopped by the door. "What would you do, MeJoe, if Lost City became a famous art town?"

"I try not to think about it," MeJoe said.

"If you don't think about something, does that make it not real?" Bridge asked.

"Bridge, none of us are real," MeJoe said.

"Thanks," Bridge said.

"Don't forget where you got the tie," MeJoe said.

Bridge went back to the Why Am I Here and turned on his quill and inkwell. Another day had gone to the trash can. Most paintings were still orphans, most books still unread.

Bridge punched up his book and started to type. Hemmingway, you dead boozer, eat your heart out.

Chapter Forty-Seven

It was close to closing time and only a few people were in the Wake Up Or Die. Vivian was sweeping. Chris was washing cups and had been telling Vivian about all the exotic hors d'oeuvres he was making for Bridge. He was so excited it was like he was a little kid that had gotten his first bicycle. Vivian hadn't realized the impact hors d'oeuvres had on people. She had heard that all the hotels and motels in town were booked full for the art walk. Already many people were walking around downtown peering into gallery windows like they were shopping for a puppy or kitten.

Vivian was tired. She felt like she had been a white blouse that somehow got thrown in the washer with a load of colors and now was a faded blue. She then had an idea. Maybe she should have a fundraiser for all the people who were in love. She could raise money so people could buy pills for anxiety, worry, depression, loss of appetite, libido, and how to say, "I really don't want to see you today," and not offend their love interest.

The remaining people left. Vivian put up the closed sign and locked the doors. She sighed. The silence when closing was both pleasing and sad. What is life without laughter and conversation and arguments? What is life without silence?

Vivian swept her pile of dirt into a dustpan and carried it to the garbage. Chris finished washing the last cup, steamed out the espresso machine, and started counting the money. "Lock the door behind you when you are done," Vivian told him. "I'm going to go to my room."

Vivian turned on the light, and the red, blue, green, yellow, orange, and purple fairies bounced to life. Fairies are like dogs, they are always ready to go. Ten in the morning, one in the afternoon, two in the morning, who cares, let's go, wag tail, oh boy, oh boy, oh boy. Life is good if you let it, go with the flow.

Vivian sat on the sofa. She hadn't smoked any pot in a long time, but she pulled her box and pipe out from under the sofa. She took two hits. The fairies coughed and wheezed a few times and got the munchies. The pot relaxed Vivian and seemed to put her wrung out feeling at bay. The fairies danced around, but Vivian's mind filled with questions. Now that I am loved, do I look different? Is life any different? I am still lonely at times. Will I live longer? Will I outlive Bridge and die sad? Vivian stood and started to spin around in a slow circle. She stretched her arms out from her sides. She shut her eyes. I have always spun through life, she thought. I have always been a big leaf that the wind has taken wherever it wanted to. I have always believed in causes and hoped life would get better for everybody. I have always been a dreamer. I dreamed about Bridge and now he loves me. Is Bridge only a dream?

Vivian grew dizzy and plopped back down on the sofa. The room spun around her. The fairies blended into one color.

Vivian stood, turned off the light and let the fairies go back to where ever fairies go when they cannot be seen, and went back into the shop. She sat at a table by a window. The street was empty. The pavement was sad that there were no feet using it. The street lamps looked lost, even though they were new. A lone car stopped at the light, the unrecognizable driver puffing on a cigarette - a lonely traveler at night or a happy person content with their solitude? The light changed and the car sped off. Vivian got up, unlocked the door, and went outside, relocking the door behind her. She looked down the street and could see light shining through Bridge's window. She started to walk toward her house but stopped and turned back toward the Why Am I Here.

Vivian peeped through the window of the Why Am I Here. The only light that was on was in Bridge's living room, den, and bedroom. She could see him sitting in front of his quill and inkwell. His face was serious. His brow was wrinkled in concentration. It was like he was gone from the world. He had abandoned the world or the world had abandoned him. Occasionally he would run his hands through his hair. Occasionally he would type a few words. Am I in your words? she questioned. Am I a young pretty lady of virtue who will be saved from the bad king by a lonely prince? Am I a comma that needs to be moved or a word that fulfills the complete paragraph? Am I a glow in the back of your mind that sends you to my door for more warmth?

Vivian tapped on the window. Bridge turned. He smiled. The smile flashed through the dim store like a sunrise after a month of dark, dank, days. Still smiling, he got up and opened the door.

"Maybe I should not have bothered you," Vivian said.

"You look like you need a hug," Bridge said.

Vivian stepped inside the store. Bridge closed the door. He held her like a little boy holds a dandelion he picked for his mother. Vivian did not hug him back. Her arms rested on his hips. Her head lay on his shoulder and she shut her eyes. "I never wanted to love you," Bridge said.

"I know," Vivian whispered.

"But now life would not be the same without you," Bridge said.

"Writers only need their words," Vivian said, but not sadly or trying to make Bridge feel guilty.

"A little playing never was a bad thing for inspiration," Bridge smiled.

Vivian stepped out of his hug. "Bridge, that is why I love you," she smiled.

"Why?"

"You are such a romantic."

Bridge kissed her on the forehead.

"Now, you who will never be on the best seller list, turn off that computer and come home with me," Vivian said.

"Are you going to cook me a late night snack?"

"No, there is something about an over the hill writer that really turns me on," Vivian said.

Bridge put his quill and ink well to sleep. Vivian and he held hands and walked down the middle of the street toward her house.

When they got there, Pill's truck was parked in front and he was sleeping in the back. The **THERE IS ONLY SIX BILLION YEARS LEFT FOR THE WORLD** sign was on top of the camper shell. They tiptoed around the truck.

There are really no words to describe two people in love making love.

Rolling, rolling, rolling, I mean really rolling, Oh God, Oh God, Ohhhhh God, Ohhhh Myyyyy, Oh my my my, in my sweet baby's arms.

Chapter Forty-Eight

The official art walk was scheduled for the next three days from four in the afternoon until nine in the evening. Bridge opened early. There would be no breakfast at the This Isn't Heaven Bar. He dusted again. He straightened paintings that did not need straightening and told them this might be their lucky day. He printed out more bios for his books. He then took his good set of clothes and MeJoe's tie and hurried to Vivian's, took a shower, changed clothes and hurried back to the store. Gertrude was standing in front of her shop and, seeing Bridge, was shocked. "I'll be," she said. "You clean up nice."

"It's disgusting, isn't it?" Bridge said.

From across the street, Lotus Blossom whistled and called, "Hey big boy, when you've got some time, come visit me."

Bridge waved, but he had to admit that wearing a tie did something for a man. For one thing it made him feel like he was choking and he had a morbid desire to buy a pair of loafers with tassels on the top and start carrying a briefcase stuffed with copies of *The New York Times*, *The Economist*, and guides to massage parlors in L.A. and Chicago.

On the corner, Jackson and The Open Doors were setting up to play during the art walk. Gallery owners were busy unloading things. A cloud of invisible anticipation hung in the air like some illegal chemical they still sprayed on crops in California while the environmentalists were taking a nap.

Chris parked in front of the Why Am I Here and carried in three boxes and set them on the floor. He was in a zone of whatever the zone is that a person who is going to serve hors d'oeuvres gets in. Chris gave Bridge a 'why are you here' look, didn't say anything, and went back to his car and brought in a folding table. Without asking Bridge where he could put the table, he set the table up, and out of one box he removed a white linen tablecloth and covered the table. Still without talking, and deeper in his zone, he placed cut crystal dishes on the table, arranging and rearranging them until they were exactly where he wanted them. Then he set out a stack of small serving plates, a silver container filled with toothpicks, and some very high-end plastic forks. He went back to his car and brought in a smaller table, complete with its own white linen tablecloth, and took out of another one of the boxes a crystal punch bowl and a silver ladle. He even had glass punch glasses. He then stepped back, put his hands on his hips, and surveyed his creations. "Perfect," he said with a proud and satisfied grin.

Paving machines started to roar in Bridge's head. "You are going to have background music, aren't you?" Chris asked like if Bridge was not going to have music he was completely without class.

Tour buses backfired in Bridge's head. "No," he answered, shaking his head like a wet dog with water in his ears, only it wasn't water, it was paving machines and tour buses.

"Do you need a Q-tip?" Chris asked.

"How much is this going to cost me?" Bridge asked.

"I will have to talk to my people," Chris said and hurried out, presumably to consult with his people.

Rainy Day from the Sunbonnet gallery came in, saw the setup, looked at Bridge, and said, "I thought you would never succumb."

"Do you think I am turning gay?" Bridge asked.

"Have you had a strange infatuation with eyeliner lately?"

"No."

"Do you find yourself looking at male models in magazines more than the flat chested women?"

"No."

"I don't think you have a problem."

Bridge felt relieved. Rainy Day left. The paving machines and tour buses in Bridge's mind went around the corner.

Bridge had to admit, the crystal looked nice. He didn't know about the plastic forks. When he got his bill, he would have to talk to Chris' people about that - some things were just not done in polite society. He would hate to have a Kennedy or Ted Turner drop by during the art walk and spread the rumor to all the high society shakers he was cheap. They would blacklist him from buying a house in the Hamptons, and he sure as hell wouldn't be able to join the country club in the Bahamas. In their sordid careers, plastic forks have ruined more than one life.

Bridge went outside. It was a great day. Nothing can spoil an art walk more than bad weather. An atom bomb could do a good job, but for most artists, bad weather is the main concern. Pill was walking down the street with his **THERE IS ONLY SIX BILLION YEARS LEFT FOR THE WORLD** sign on. With a supposed five thousand people going to be in town, Pill was in paranoid heaven. Roach was bonging on his bongos while Clip and Jackson plucked on their guitar strings to make sure everything was perfect for when the art walk started. Bridge wondered if plucking on guitar strings somehow derived from plucking a chicken. But he dismissed the idea as one of those questions in life that could never be answered and one that Aristotle never wasted his time on.

Bridge went into Gertrude's gallery. Three ladies were setting up tables for hors d'oeuvres while another lady was mopping the floor. Gertrude was looking at her paintings so intensely Bridge did not want to break her concentration and went next door to Sergeant's gallery, The Beginning Of A Rainbow. All of Sergeant's sixteen girlfriends were packed into the store. They were all arguing how Sergeant should rearrange his gallery. Sergeant was standing in the far corner with a pained look on his face. Bridge knew he had contact stomach cramps and a headache, and he wondered if he should go borrow a Midol from Vivian and bring it to him. But then he figured Sergeant had inflicted his own pain.

Bridge went to the Sunbonnet. Rainy Day had so many plein air paintings of sunrises and sunsets on the walls it almost blinded him. Rainy Day was standing in the middle of the room with sunglasses on. "What do you think?" she asked Bridge.

"Very bright," Bridge said, shielding his eyes with his hand.

Rainy Day smiled.

Bridge then headed for MeJoe's gallery, All Art Is The Same In The Dark. A pretty young lady was moving MeJoe's paintings around. Bridge wondered if she, in her off time, was moving MeJoe around - lucky old blind bastard. MeJoe came out from the back of the store. Bridge was not one into gasping, but he almost gasped. MeJoe was dressed in spit-shined black cowboy boots, red slacks, a black belt with silver dollars on it with a silver buckle about the size of a good-sized bluegill, a white shirt so starched a marine could have worn it, and a blue beret that any Frenchmen would have traded his mistress for. His normally white cane had been painted so it looked like a candy cane. "My God, MeJoe, you look like a flag," Bridge said.

"It's my new image," MeJoe said.

"He is so handsome," the pretty young thing gushed.

Bridge knew it did not take much for a pretty young thing to gush, so he was not too impressed.

"My tie blanks well on you," MeJoe said.

"How do you know I am wearing your tie?" Bridge asked.

"You have it tied so tight you are talking through your nose," MeJoe said.

Bridge headed for Lotus Blossom's Love Is Only A Painting Away loosening his tie just a tad as he did so. Lotus Blossom was her normal happy little pixie self. She had so many gourd masks with parrot feathers protruding from them hanging on the walls Bridge felt like he should cut off his leg, replace it with a stick, cut off a hand and replace it with a hook, and poke out his eye so he could wear an eye patch. But then he figured it would be hard to write a book if all he could say was shiver me timbers. But on the other hand he would only have one itchy foot and it would be easy to scratch his ass. "Do they have a hormone they give to parrots so they grow feathers quicker?" Bridge asked Lotus Blossom.

Lotus Blossom good-naturedly shooed him out the door. Bridge figured they did have a feather hormone, but it was illegal, as the feathers bulked up too quickly and it made parrots have to shave their beaks.

Bridge looked into the window to the End Of War gallery, decided it was a lost cause and headed back for the Why Am I Here. Roach was still bonging on his bongo and Jackson and Clip were still trying to tune their guitars by plucking. "Do bongos ever go out of tune?" Bridge asked Roach.

"Not really, but they change tone with dryness and humidity," Roach said seriously.

"Even a drum can get complicated," Bridge said.

"That's life," Roach bonged.

Jackson and Clip gave Bridge a dirty look that Bridge took to mean he was interrupting their plucking, which to a guitar player is not a nice thing to do. It was like telling a ballerina her tits are too big, or a country western singer that he really does have a good voice. Bridge decided to say hello to Rudolph and Rebecca in their cafe, Sally's. Rudolph and Rebecca were running around so quickly to get ready for the hordes of hungry people that if they would have been two little black Sambos they could have churned enough butter for every cafe in town.

Bridge went back to the Why Am I Here. He paced around the store like a wind- up train that only had one small oval track. In a distant corner of his mind was the faint rumbling of a paving machine. In another distant corner of his mind a tour bus was idling. In a small portion of the front of his mind, like a miniature TV set inside his brain, he could see two old lampposts that were still good and living on a commune. They were talking to each other in whispers. Bridge could not hear them, but he knew they were talking about him and what they were saying would not be good for his ego. "Talk louder," Bridge hollered just as the Professor came in.

"Good morning," the Professor hollered.

Bridge was about to say something snide and sarcastic when the Rock Lady came in and the Professor put his arm around her. The words froze in Bridge's mouth.

"We love each other," the Rock Lady said.

"I have loved her ever since she beaned me with those two rocks," the Professor said. "I just kept it to myself so none of you guys would laugh at me."

"What happened with the Baptist preacher?" Bridge managed to ask the Rock Lady.

"The only thing he could talk about was Genesis," the Rock Lady said. "I had the marriage annulled after two days by a born again evangelist."

"What can I say?" Bridge asked.

"Say life works out the way it is supposed to," the Professor said.

"Say life works out the way it is supposed to," Bridge said.

"I was only kidding, Bridge," the Professor said.

"I have a paving machine, a tour bus, and two lampposts in my head right now. It makes it hard for me to concentrate," Bridge said.

"Are they two of the old lampposts that still work that were torn down and replaced by the new lampposts that look like old lampposts?" the Rock Lady asked.

Too bewildered to say yes, Bridge nodded his head.

"I talked to them when I was lost in the desert on my search for the fake rock of rocks," the Rock Lady said.

"I think they are conspiring against me," Bridge said.

"Funny things go through your head when you miss breakfast," the Professor said.

"I wouldn't worry about it," the Rock Lady said, "living on a commune has made them mellow."

The Professor and the Rock Lady left.

No sooner had the door shut then Plastic walked in. He looked depressed. "I missed you at breakfast," Plastic said.

"It gave you some quality time with Gloria," Bridge said.

"It will never be the same, will it?" Plastic said.

"What do you mean?" Bridge asked.

"Berry is gone, Stoops is working, now breakfast will never be the same."

"Maybe it's time for us to start eating a real breakfast, you know, bacon and eggs, whole wheat toast and orange juice," Bridge said.

"That would be too radical," Plastic said.

"It would be a little over the top," Bridge agreed.

Plastic left without saying goodbye. A lot of people deep down enjoy their depression - it's the old positive and negative stimulus thing, for some reason they both work.

Bridge sat behind his table. He felt like he was a character in a novel - a not very well-developed character, but none the less a character. But at least a character that still had a lot more clout than a noun or an adjective. You're just a measly noun and I am a character and don't you ever forget it. But then Bridge could visualize all the nouns in the country getting together and forming a society that would begin by suing all characters for discrimination and asking the government for cheap loans to send their kids to school so they could become more than nouns. Then it would all snowball and even semi-colons would want to get in on the act.

Bridge couldn't take it anymore and headed for the Wake Up Or Die. He needed to look at some dogs.

There weren't the normal one hundred dogs outside of the Wake Up Or Die. There were about eight hundred - one hundred local dogs and seven hundred tourist's dogs. The dogs were having a merry old time getting to know each other and telling dirty little secrets about their masters. Dogs see people doing things that, if they could write, would make *The Joy Of Sex* seem like a cookbook. The dogs from California and Florida would corner the market in weird sex. The dogs from New York and Chicago would corner the market in sleaze. The dogs from the mid-west would have to be satisfied with true love stories and sex only on Saturday night. The dogs from the south could kiss the writing life goodbye, but they could make a good living smuggling the books into their states.

Bridge waved at Vivian through the window and sat with the dogs. "I wish my only problems in life were fleas and heartworm," Bridge said to a mutt dog that looked like a worn out mop with four skinny legs.

The dog barked.

"Life would be so much simpler if my complete mastery of language was growls, barks and yips," Bridge said.

The dog barked twice.

"I don't know if I could take those fake dog bones though," Bridge said. "I think I would be more of a real bone type dog."

The dog growled.

"I do know I would be a mutt like you. All those Lexus and Cadillac type dogs really give you real dogs a bad name. I bet they have so many write-offs they don't even pay taxes."

The dog farted.

Bridge rubbed the dog's head, which in return got him a long wet slobbery lick on the back of his hand. "I've had uglier things kiss me than you," Bridge said and went into the Wake Up Or Die.

The Wake Up Or Die was packed. If the building would have been made out of tin and had a pull-off roof, all the people could have been sardines. There were so many conversations going on Bridge felt like he was standing inside of a beehive. But most conversation is nothing more than a bunch of buzz anyway.

Chris was making so many frothy coffees, he looked overwhelmed, and Bridge wondered how he was going to take the strain of serving tourists hors d'oeuvres during the art walk. But he had volunteered, so that would teach him. Vivian was stuffing so much money in the cash register the cash register was going to get a belly ache and have gas for the next few days.

Bridge really needed a cup of Roast In Hell, so he got in the long line of people waiting for frothy coffees. Standing in line, Bridge noticed Pill sitting at a table with his sign **THERE IS ONLY SIX BILLION YEARS LEFT FOR THE WORLD** still on. He was talking to six women who were looking at him like he was the smartest thing since panty hose. Bridge wondered if they were ladies who had answered his ad.

Bridge made it to the front of the line. "You look funny in a tie," Vivian said to him, and then out of the corner of her mouth told Chris, "One Roast In Hell."

"I wore a tie the night I told you I love you," Bridge said.

"You looked funny then too," Vivian said, handing him a cup of Roast In Hell.

"When this is all over, let's move to the Cayman Islands and open up a bank only for money made from illegal coffee beans," Bridge said.

"Next," Vivian said.

"Did you hear about the Professor and the Rock Lady?" Bridge asked.

"It's old news. Next."

Not even love can get in the way of making some good money.

Bridge took his coffee outside to be with the dogs. He had never been one to think the inside of a beehive was a good place to live.

About five hundred dogs looked at Bridge like he was cheap and inconsiderate for not bringing them a cup of coffee. The other dogs were too busy trying to have an affair they couldn't care less.

Bridge sipped his coffee. Good, dark and bitter. Bridge took a bigger sip. He wanted to close his store, go buy a horse, make a set of clothes out of leather, and ride into the wilderness and live off of possum and chipmunks. Bridge finished his coffee, completely over his eating possum and chipmunk fantasy. He patted as many dogs as he could and headed back to the Why Am I Here. When he got to the store, six various colored balloons filled with helium were tied to the doorknob. Bridge got his staple gun out of his storage room, said hello to all his unplaced novels as he did so, and apologized for keeping them in boxes for so long. He stapled the balloons to the outside window jamb and had a sudden desire to walk up and down the block kicking the tires of cars and putting price tags on the windows.

Bridge then stood in front of the store. Sally's was doing a bang-up business. The outside tables were full and people seemed to be overjoyed as they drank iced tea and ate sandwiches with names so long they could have been South American countries. Bridge wondered whatever happened to the good old simple sandwiches: grilled cheese, cold roast beef, turkey, peanut butter, hamburger. Now we have grilled cheese with so many choices of cheese you have to take a cheese directory with you. Or roast beef with six choices of lettuce, ten mustards, bean sprouts, and twenty-two different types of bread. There is also turkey that can be turkey, pressed turkey, rolled turkey, turkey from Turkey, or vegetarian turkey. And the poor old hamburger. Lord help us Jesus, there are restaurants with fifty different types of hamburgers. No wonder the world is all messed up. No wonder an art walk tries to disguise itself as a car lot. Can you imagine years ago an Indian warrior after killing a buffalo telling his family with pride, "Now we can have fifty different types of buffalo burgers."

How did simplicity ever lose?

Even though the art walk had not started, a lot of people were walking around town. They were not going into the galleries, but they were looking in the windows. It was like it was taboo to go inside before the official time for the art walk to start, and if they did they would be turned into toads. It was ok with Bridge, he had always liked toads. Bridge went inside. The balloons hanging from his windowsill were giving him a headache.

Bridge looked at his books all lined up on the table. "Will a good person buy you and give you a good home?" he asked the books.

They shrugged their shoulders.

"I hope so," Bridge said. "I have not given you much of a life."

Bridge headed for his quill and inkwell. He had not gone three steps when four ladies came in - some people could care less about start times. They were all in their mid to late fifties and had a comfortable feeling to them. They saw the layout Chris had set up. "You are going to serve hors d'oeuvres," one of the ladies said.

"I thought about sardines and Vienna sausages," Bridge said.

"I like sardines," another lady said.

Bridge smiled.

All four of the women stopped in front of the books, and each picked up a different one. "You wrote all these?" one of the ladies asked.

"I've written thirty, and seven have been published," Bridge said.

"You like poverty," another lady smiled.

"She is good to me," Bridge smiled back.

"Are you crazed, a drunk, and do you want to kill yourself?" another lady asked.

"I don't think so," Bridge said, but the crazed and drunk could have been a possibility.

"Well you must be dedicated," the first woman said.

"Stupid is more the word," Bridge said.

The ladies smiled and continued to thumb through the books. Bridge hoped they did not bend any pages. Then he would have to sell the books at half price. Half price is what he had to pay for them, and even with no math skills, Bridge knew half of zero is still zero.

"We will each take a complete set," one lady said casually and started to walk around the gallery and look at the paintings. The other ladies followed her.

Twenty-eight books. Bridge would get writer's cramp from signing them, although it would be a happy writer's cramp.

"Just sign your name," another lady said. "We are all librarians from Oklahoma and will put your books in our libraries."

Bridge wanted to say, "I love you man," but it didn't seem appropriate.

"After we read them, and if we like them, we will tell other librarians at our convention in Vegas," a woman said.

I love you man, I really love you, Bridge thought.

A breeze bounced the balloons off of the window. The balloons seemed to say, "See, we work."

Snide balloons anyway.

Bridge went back and forth from his storage area until he had four neat stacks of seven books each. While the ladies walked around the store, he signed each one carefully, so carefully one could read his name.

The ladies, without having to be told Bridge did not take credit cards, all paid in cash.

Bridge put in each book a bio and an information card - all that capitalistic store owner's propaganda. He dug out four recycled bags.

The ladies signed his guest book. Being librarians, their writing was superb.

"Maybe one day you will have a best seller," one of the ladies said to Bridge as they were leaving.

"I don't think about it anymore," Bridge said.

"You don't have to lie to me," the lady smiled.

Bridge sat at the table. Twenty-eight books with a home.

Maybe one day I will have a best seller.

Chapter Forty-Nine

It was Close to three in the afternoon, Chris burst into the store like a dust devil. "Been snorting coffee all day?" Bridge asked him.

"I have never seen so many people in town who wanted frothy coffee," Chris gasped. "My life would be so much easier if people only drank black coffee like you do, but I wanted to stop by and tell you I will be here in thirty minutes."

"You're here now," Bridge said.

"Fuck you, Bridge," Chris said in the way a friend tells another friend to get fucked.

Bridge had never been told fuck you by a gay man, but he figured it was ok. Maybe not to Chris' significant other, but what the significant other didn't know wouldn't hurt him. Chris dust deviled out as fast as he had dust deviled in.

Bridge went to the bathroom, combed his hair and straightened his tie. Trying to look good is really a bunch of work.

When Chris came back, he had on black slacks that even Bridge could tell were expensive. His shoes were patent leather. His shirt had so many starched ruffles it would have taken an old Chinese man with an abacus two years to count them. "My God, Chris," Bridge said. "You could work at the Waldorf."

"It is beneath me," Chris said.

"Where are the hors d'oeuvres?" Bridge asked. The server looking good is one thing but, food is food.

"My creations will be delivered," Chris said like an artist who had made so much money he told inspiration what to do.

In less than five minutes, the creations were delivered by three gay men Bridge did not know, but figured were Chris' people. There were dates stuffed with imported cream cheese. There were mushroom caps stuffed with buffalo burger and sprinkled with some spice Bridge had never heard of and then layered with cheese. There were six different types of cheese, none of them yellow and wrapped in plastic. There was a fruit tray that would make a normal fruit tray weep. There was a salmon dip with four different types of imported crackers placed carefully around the bowl. The four men worked on the set up like they were working at the Governor's Ball.

Bridge had to admit he was impressed. The three men smiled at Bridge as they left, but a few moments later they came back carrying three boxes each. "More hors d'oeuvres," one smiled.

"When word gets out about my hors d'oeuvres, you will have people lined up to get into your store," Chris said with no lack of confidence.

The men put the other hors d'oeuvres in the storage room. Bridge wondered if the boxed manuscripts would drool all over themselves. The three men left again and returned with only one box each. There was a case of champagne, a case of orange juice, and a case of some imported wine with a name that had to be French or was made in New Jersey by some sneaky Italian with a French name.

They mixed the punch so carefully Bridge thought they might have been blending holy water.

When they were done, they all took delicate sips of the punch, nodded their heads like it was fine and shook hands. Bridge figured that, being gay, they should have hugged each other, but life is full of small revelations.

Then one of them left and came back with a small ice carving of a horse that floated on top of the punch.

Bridge did not know where the words came from, but he said, "It's beautiful. It is really beautiful."

He went over and hugged each of the hims, hers, or what-evers. Chris beamed like he was a two-hundred-watt light bulb.

The three hims or hers or what-evers left.

Across the street, Jackson and The Open Doors began playing. The balloons outside of the store, hit by a slight breeze, started dancing. Bridge reached for an imported cracker to try the salmon dip. Chris slapped the back of his hand. "We can eat whatever is left," he said sternly - one does not mess with a hors d'oeuvres chef.

"Can I try the punch?" Bridge asked, trying not to sound like he was begging -after all, he had missed breakfast.

Chris pondered the begging for a few seconds and then carefully ladled out two glasses of punch. "To making Vivian happy," Chris toasted.

"To old lampposts that still work and I hope are not mad at me," Bridge toasted.

The punch was divine, which is not a manly man word, but there are times manly men have to get off of their high horse. Thoughtfulness is a lot better than pride.

Bridge stood behind his table. Chris stood behind the serving table. Come one come all, see our wares, be a part of our dreams, the show is about to start. Buy a painting, buy a book, buy anything. How about some divine punch with an imported cracker and salmon dip? Trust me, you will love it, we can't feel sorry for salmon all the time. Hell, if he wasn't in the dip, he'd be rotting at the head of some cold river in Alaska.

And the people came. Bridge could hardly keep up with signing books he sold so many. Within two hours, there was a line of people waiting to get into the Why Am I Here to gorge on Chris' hors d'oeuvres. Chris was so happy he seemed to float around the room.

People, with salmon dip running down their chin, awed over the paintings. People so full of mushroom caps stuffed with buffalo burger were so impressed with the bead work they were ready to denounce being white and move to an Indian reservation. And still people bought books. And still people came. Bridge figured it was a good thing it was almost impossible to get drunk on wine punch.

Outside, the streets were so jammed Santa Fe was having a jealousy attack. People were carrying paintings, and pots, and every type of art imaginable.

Jackson and The Open Doors had to keep dumping the money out of their tip jar into a box. After one song, people were throwing so many dollar bills at them it looked like they were being attacked by fluttering green bats - fruit bats, not vampire bats, even though at times too much money can be blood sucking.

At nine o'clock, the official closing time of the art walk, the streets were suddenly empty. Gallery owners staggered out of their galleries. The female paintings took a deep breath and said to each other, "If someone only looks at my breasts again and not my eyes, I think I will scream."

The male paintings said, "My God, did you see that blond? I'd like to take her home and frame her."

Chris and Bridge stood outside. The gallery owners did not wave at each other or say hello. They were in people shock, and also wondering, since they had made so much money could they call themselves starving artists anymore.

"Two more days," Bridge said, sounding so tired he could have been a fast burning candle that was about to turn into a puddle of wax.

"You think what I served today was good, you just wait," Chris said.

Why is it gay men can always outdo what they have already done well and straight men can never get anything right two times in a row?

"Would you like a drink? I'll buy," Bridge asked Chris.

"Are you asking me out?" Chris asked with a sly smile.

"Chris."

"Just kidding. I'd love a drink."

An old veteran, ex-hippie, ex-cowboy, and a young gay man with a tongue stud and blue colored hair headed for Bill's. Life is good.

"What are you going to serve tomorrow?" Bridge asked as they walked.

"You'll see," Chris said.

"Will there be any sardines or Vienna sausages?"

"No."

"Have you ever had a dream about paving machines laughing in your head or old lampposts that still work conniving against you?" Bridge asked.

"No, but at times I have a dream an old time percolating coffeepot is chasing me around a room with a twelve-gauge shotgun."

"What do you do?" Bridge asked.

"Nothing. Thankfully as the coffeepot is about to pull the trigger I wake up."

"I'll trade you a paving machine for a coffeepot."

"No deal."

"I wouldn't do it either."

They stopped by the window to the Wake Up Or Die. It was still packed. People, after gorging on hors d'oeuvres all day, were now guzzling coffee like it was the elixir of life. Vivian was dressed in a dress with so many colors in it some of the colors did not even have names. She had a smile on her face that was so happy and contagious there was no one in the store who was not smiling.

"She is my rainbow," Bridge told Chris.

"You're lucky," Chris said.

"I know," Bridge said.

Bridge waved at Vivian through the window and motioned that they would be at Bill's Restaurant and Libations.

Pill came around the corner with his sign **THERE IS ONLY SIX BILLION YEARS LEFT FOR THE WORLD** on.

"I've had twenty-five replies to my personal ad," Pill said.

"That's good," Bridge said.

"It was very expensive," Pill said and ran down the street.

"What was that about?" Chris asked.

"You'll have to ask Pill," Bridge said - getting involved with someone else's love thing is more often than not a bad idea.

The Professor and the Rock Lady were sitting at a table in Bill's. They were looking at each other like Cupid had run out of arrows. "Getting beaned with a rock has a way of making a relationship stronger," Bridge said to Chris.

Bridge and Chris pulled up chairs to the Professor's and the Rock Lady's table. Sitting with people that are in the first stages of love is rude, but what the hell, they might need a break to get their feet back on the ground.

Plastic came in and pulled up a chair to the table - being rude had never been of any great importance to him.

The Rock Lady and the Professor straightened up and looked around nervously like they had been caught trying to have sex in a public place.

Organic Muffin came over to take the drink orders. Chris ordered his normal Mango Margarita. Bridge his normal Tecate and a lime with a glass. Plastic ordered a shot of whiskey - he was having a mild depression over Gloria's nipple rings - not the fact that she had them, but the fact she wouldn't let him polish them. The Professor and the Rock Lady still had full drinks in front of them -

people when they first fall in love have a tendency to not eat or drink for a few weeks, which for the Professor was a good thing, as he was starting to get a little chubby. The Rock Lady on the other hand needed a few pounds - being married to a Baptist preacher for two days seemed to have leaned her out a little.

"Everyone in town is talking about how good your hors d'oeuvres were," Plastic told Chris.

"It was nothing," Chris said, which was a statement that really meant he was fishing for more praise. Human beings are like dogs - we never get enough praise. For dogs, it is easy though. For humans, at times, it is hard to tell the difference between true praise and buttering-up bullshit. Chris did not get any more praise, which Bridge thought was a good thing, because any more praise might have puffed him up so much he would think about running for President.

Organic Muffin brought the drinks. Bridge, since he had sold so many books and was now a rich author, paid for the round. Nobody said thanks, which for a bunch of rude people that would butt in on two people who have just fallen in love was normal. "How's Stoops doing?" Bridge asked Organic Muffin.

"He's back in the kitchen cooking away like some little Iowa farm girl who got an A for the best pot roast in Home Economics."

"When I was in school they wouldn't let me take home economics," Chris said sadly. "They said it was only for girls."

"But you are a girl," Plastic said.

"Exactly," Chris said.

"I bet you could take it now," the Rock Lady said.

"Not even if they paid me," Chris said vehemently, which no one believed - name one person, excluding Jesus, who would not take a payoff.

Organic Muffin headed for another table where she knew the tips would be better.

"To all your book sales," Chris toasted.

"To Gloria coming back out of the closet," Plastic toasted.

"To the Rock Lady and the Professor," Bridge toasted.

"To all you rude bastards," the Professor toasted.

"Second that," the Rock Lady toasted.

They all drank, which in polite society is the proper thing to do after toasting.

"How's your sex life?" Plastic asked the Rock Lady.

"Up until last night it was very boring and too religious," she replied.

The Professor swelled up like a Russian Thistle bloom about to burst and spread a new crop all over Nebraska in its quest to ruin the hay crop.

"How's your sex life?" Plastic asked Bridge - this nipple ring thing really had Plastic on a roll.

"Rolling in my sweet baby's arms," Bridge replied with a twinkle in his eye.

Nobody wanted to ask Chris how his sex life was, and nobody really cared how Plastic's sex life was going, so the topic was dropped.

"I heard that there are more people in town for the art walk than ever before," the Professor said.

An old lamppost slammed Bridge on the inside of his skull and a cackle from a paving machine tried to give him an earache.

"If it was like this everyday all the people from Santa Fe and Sedona would move here," Plastic said.

"Then we could move up there," Bridge said while rubbing his head with one hand and sticking a finger in his ear with the other. Pesky lamppost and cackling paving machines - they are almost as bad as the black flies in Maine, and for sure as bad as the chiggers in Missouri.

"Bridge had to have sold at least a hundred of his novels today," Chris said, which was a breach of conduct, as profit margins are normally kept secret. At any given time, an IRS agent could be sitting within earshot.

The Rock Lady looked impressed. No one else seemed to really care. Bridge was used to it. Unless they are famous, writers get about as much respect as sparrows, and the only encouragement or advice they get is how they are throwing their lives away.

Vivian came in. She looked frazzled. There are only so many dollar bills one can stuff in a cash register before it starts getting to you. She pulled a chair up to the table without Bridge getting up to help. Vivian did not like Bridge to do things for her unless she asked. She explained to him once, "I have feet," which Bridge really didn't understand how the statement had anything to do with people doing things for each other. Ninety-nine percent of all the people in the world have feet, and for that matter eyes, hands, noses, and faces.

Organic Muffin took Vivian's order, which after a day of

handling cash was upgraded from two shots of cheap tequila to two shots of Cuervo Gold, Cuervo not being the most expensive tequila in the world, but anyone who spends more than ten bucks for a shot of booze should be roasted with an apple crammed in their mouth or move to Aspen where they can bitch about the lousy help and the sad decline of ski wax.

The shots came. Vivian drank them so quickly they didn't know if they had ever existed.

"Vivian, how's your sex life?" Plastic asked.

Vivian popped Plastic on top of the head just hard enough to rattle his brain a little, what little brain he had.

"That good," Plastic said with a slightly stunned smile.

"All I heard in the coffee shop today was how delicious your hors d'oeuvres were," Vivian told Chris.

Now Chris will run for President, Bridge thought. But as Bridge rolled the idea around in his mind, he decided it might be a good idea. If Chris were President, it might make the Arabs try to discover more of their female side and get over all that two- thousand-year-old revenge stuff.

Chris did not reply to Vivian, but he smiled at her.

Sergeant came in with all of his sixteen girlfriends trailing behind him. At times, finding a table for two is a pain, but a table for seventeen - Lord. There were no tables, so they stood along the wall, several of the women arguing over who could stand by Sergeant.

"You could write a book with a character that has sixteen girlfriends," Plastic told Bridge.

"Who would believe it?" Bridge asked.

"You might get great sales in Utah," Chris said.

"Is the Mormon god a polygamist?" the Rock Lady asked.

No one knew the answer, but it did make Bridge wonder if angels had a sex drive.

Organic Muffin stopped at the table. Chris did not want another Mango Margarita. "I have to go create my creations," he said, which everyone figured meant he was going to make more hors d'oeuvres. Chris pranced off wondering if he should run on the Democratic or Republican ticket. He knew the Libertarians and other parties would never have a chance in hell.

The Rock Lady and the Professor did not want another drink. They figured trying to have sex in a public place was way beyond their capabilities and they should go to the Professor's house.

Plastic didn't want another shot of whiskey. He wanted to go home and watch TV and try to figure out a way to make Gloria go back into the closet.

Vivian ordered two more shots of Quervo and Bridge another beer. "I saw a lot of people carrying your books around today," Vivian said.

"I hope they read them," Bridge said.

Lotus Blossom and Gertrude came in. They looked like they had been stranded at the Denver Airport for sixteen hours and, besides all the bathrooms being out of order, all there was to eat or drink were Egg McMuffins and Diet Coke.

Lotus Blossom and Gertrude sat with Vivian and Bridge. I guess all our advertising worked," Gertrude said to Bridge.

"The Chamber of Commerce could rival Florida for promotion," Bridge said.

"I sold almost half of my masks," Lotus Blossom said.

"I wonder why so many people want to hide?" Vivian stated more than asked.

Organic Muffin half dragged herself to the table. The waitress thing is really not what it is made out to be. Especially in an art town where most of the people are alcoholics and the bars are always full. Lotus Blossom and Gertrude ordered the house red wine, which, as things go, is really the proper artist drink. It's hard to talk about inspiration while drinking beer - beer is more belching.

Organic Muffin brought Lotus Blossom and Gertrude two glasses of wine each instead of one. "My feet are killing me," she explained. "I thought I would save a trip."

It was a good thing she brought two, because Lotus Blossom and Gertrude did not swirl, smell, and then sip their wine. They guzzled their glasses like two Texas Longhorns at a watering trough that had not had a drink of water in fifteen days. Art walks to artists are really stressful and tiring experiences. It is very hard for artists to smile at people all day, especially when, according to most people, they are supposed to be depressed and suicidal.

Rudolph and Rebecca came in. "Five thousand people really eat a lot of food," Rudolph said. "We made more money today than we have ever made."

"If your hors d'oeuvres would not have been so good, I bet we would have doubled what we sold today," Rebecca said to Bridge. Women always have a way of dwelling on the bottom line - it might be one reason they outlive men - it might also be the reason men don't really want to outlive women.

"Take it up with Chris," Bridge said, "he was the one who nixed my idea of sardines and Vienna sausages."

Rebecca, having been a waitress for years, and being at heart a very nice person, went to the bar and ordered drinks for her and Rudolph. She brought back two gin and tonics. Bridge was out of toasts. Vivian was out of toasts. Gertrude and Lotus Blossom were halfway done slurping their second glasses of wine. So they all just drank. Toasts can only go so far.

Barbara, the lead writer for Let's Make Lost City Into A Political Hotbed, came in. She had had so many scoops for the paper during the day, she looked like a wet newspaper. Bridge got up and let Barbara sit. He was not quite as dumb as most people thought he was and knew that it was always good to keep the press on one's side. Ask any politician from any party if this is not a true mandate.

Bridge waved at Organic Muffin, who, seeing Barbara, brought over two glasses of the house red wine. Barbara also did not smell, swirl, or sip the first glass, she drained it like it was a shot of Nyquil and she had the worst runny nose in history, along with congested lungs and infected ears. She then took three deep breaths, exhaled like she was checking her breath, and said, "This is the most excitement this town has seen since Geronimo and his men killed fifteen men, raped twenty women, and rode off into the wilderness trying to figure out why his men had crabs."

"Can you really get them from a toilet seat?" Lotus Blossom asked.

Vivian, having had crabs twice in her life, the flower child bit in California in the 1960s was not really all that great, decided it was in her best interest to keep her mouth shut.

In fact, no one answered her question - silence normally being a main ingredient to guilt.

"You tell Chris that I want to write an article on him. His hors d'oeuvres have made him famous," Barbara said.

"You'd better catch him quick," Bridge said. "Right now he is practicing saying, 'for the American people,' and wondering what suit he should wear when they swear him in as President."

"Do you think someone who is gay, and has a tongue stud, and blue hair could get enough votes?" Gertrude asked.

"The people elected Reagan and Bush and Trump," Vivian said.

"He'd be a shoe-in," Lotus Blossom said.

Bridge suddenly felt like he was in the middle of a high school debate. He winked at Vivian, who knew it was his 'get me out of here I think I am going to puke' wink. They got up, said goodbye, and went to the bar and Bridge paid. If I keep paying, this wealthy author bit is not going to last too long, Bridge thought. Oh the price of fame.

As they went out the door, Jackson, Roach, and Clip were about to go in. After plucking all day on the guitar, and bonging all day on the bongo, and going to have to pluck and bong for the next two days, they only nodded their heads as they went by.

Vivian and Bridge held hands as they walked to her house. They did not talk. They sat on the back porch and drank a beer and still did not talk. They drank another beer and still did not talk. They went to bed, kissed, and slept. Love is being comfortable with silence.

Chapter Fifty

Of course, Chris outshone himself the next day. There are hors d'oeuvres, and then there are hors d'oeuvres. Chris served baked English walnuts sprinkled with spices so exotic they did not have a name, some type of fancy cheese wrapped with thinly cut imported ham that was so good there really was no way it could have been pork. There were prawns that were baked in a sauce that was so scrumptious a vegetarian would swear off green things forever. A punch that was so unique Chris and his people made Bridge go outside as they mixed it. And to top it off, a chocolate truffle that good old King Louis would have traded one of his mistresses for.

And there were people, and more people, and still more people. The galleries were selling art like it was a sidewalk sale. Jackson and The Open Doors had trouble shutting the trunk to their car they had stuffed so much money in it. By the end of the day, there had been so many people in the Why Am I Here Bridge felt like he had been a float during the Rose Bowl parade. He sold five paintings and double the books he had sold the first day. He had autographed so many books he wondered if he should have a rubber stamp made with his name on it and just stamp his signature. But Chris nixed the idea with, "Fame must experience pain."

Bridge was going to ask him why, but he decided not to, as he really didn't want to piss off the cook. Cooks are about as bad as artists when it comes to mood swings.

At nine o'clock Vivian came by the Why Am I Here. All she said was, “I love you. I am going home,” and left.

It had been an, ‘I served too much coffee’ day. Chris left a few minutes later to go make hors d'oeuvres to outshine himself one more time.

Bridge was relieved to be alone. He left all the lights to the store on and looked around. The empty places on the walls, where the paintings he had sold had hung, seemed lonely. Bridge wondered if the ghosts of paintings haunt the bare spots of walls where the painting had spent so much time. He went through his book inventory and found he only had five copies left of each of his books. He would have to call the publisher. Maybe since he had sold so many he would ask for a bigger discount? Numbers are power. Plus, publishers don’t really care about words, they care about numbers, good old money numbers. Kind of degrading, isn’t it? It puts artists in the same boat as bankers. Bridge thought about starting a bank, The First National Trust of Inspiration, interest will be paid in paint, brushes, beads, clay, gourds, printer ribbons, and tying paper.

Bridge went into his living room, den, and bedroom and sat looking at his quill and inkwell. He did not turn it on.

Bridge leaned back in his chair. Two paving machines chugged in his mind. Twelve old lampposts were sitting around a barbecue pit discussing how much time they would have to do in jail if they went through town jabbing knives into tires that were on cars with out of state plates. A tour bus was driving recklessly and belching out so much diesel smoke Bridge felt like he had a lit Cuban cigar stuck in his ear.

Bridge went outside. He sat on the curb. None of the stores had their lights on. The lights from the Why Am I Here penetrated a portion of the darkness. Bridge sat halfway in the dark and halfway in the light. The street was littered with paper cups and napkins. Garbage is the legacy of mankind. The way most people toss their garbage on the ground, garbage cans should be outlawed.

On Bullard Street, the lights from the new lampposts seemed to mock Bridge. The asphalt patches in the streets were like festering sores. The buildings with their new coats of orange, red, blue, and oatmeal paint were trying their best to scratch off the paint. It was like wearing an all-wool shirt without a T-shirt. Several blocks away, a police siren screeched. Humanity needs police, we cannot police ourselves, scum would win if we did.

Two homeless people high on something stumbled across the street - the land of the free and the home of the brave. A stray cat rattled through the garbage can on the corner. The jukebox blared from the back door of the This Isn't Heaven Bar. The press for the Let's Make Lost City Into A Political Hotbed would be running, churning out the latest scoops, and horoscopes, and advertisements for realtors, and praising the Chamber of Commerce and the Arts Council for the masterful job they did bringing the masses from out of town to attend the art walk. And now more masses would be coming.

Stoops came around the corner, saw Bridge sitting on the curb and came over and sat next to him. "A long way from home, soldier?" Stoops asked.

Friends don't have to ask what mood another friend is in.

"Does anyone ever stop being a soldier in life?" Bridge asked.

"We all fight a lot of battles," Stoops said. "Some we win and some we lose."

"I'm happy for you and Organic Muffin," Bridge said.

"I'm happy for you and Vivian," Stoops said, stood and added, "I'm going home to cook a late night snack for Organic Muffin."

"Enjoy."

"Are you ok, Bridge?"

"I'm trying to figure out how to tell a bunch of remodeled stores I'm sorry while at the same time telling a paving machine to get lost."

"Fill the diesel-loving bastard's tank with gas," Stoops said and disappeared into the darkness.

Bridge looked at the buildings. He looked at the patches on the street. He looked at the new lampposts on Bullard. "I don't think I can really tell you I am sorry," he said to them and went back to his living room, den, and bedroom.

He turned on his quill and inkwell. Bring forth the nouns and adjectives and adverbs. Bring on the incomplete sentences.

Bridge typed for several hours. He then went to bed. Before he fell asleep he thought, I am rolling in my sweet baby's arms even if we are not together. Love is more than I. Love is more than me. Love is we. We love. Cupid, you winged bare-assed adolescent, how sly and wonderful you are.

The next day, Chris once again outdid himself with hors d'oeuvres. It's one thing to outdo ones self once, but to do it twice is almost worth a Pulitzer Prize in hors d'oeuvres.

The hors d'oeuvres were so fancy Bridge did not even bother to ask what they were. But they smelled so good it made him salivate so much he felt like a dog with rabies, only he really didn't want to bite anybody - maybe Vivian, but that would only be a love nip.

The punch was so good it made people smile, and several ladies wanted to know how to make it. Chris told them they could go to his website and then buy the recipe through PayPal.

Once again the people poured into the art district. The streets were packed like the main drag of Tijuana - only there were no sailors, or marines, or students, no cheap silver jewelry, no leather goods, no bars and whorehouses, or undercover cops trying to sell dope, or over the hill porn stars selling tickets to the donkey show.

The people bought art and ate. They bought all of Bridge's last books in stock. Bridge wondered if he could run out and photocopy some of his unpublished novels and sell them. Discounted - this book is on sale because it does not want to have a cover on it. It thinks if it did have a cover the Chinese would steal it and you could buy it in Hong Kong for a nickel.

An hour before the art walk was to officially close, all of the hors d'oeuvres were gone. Only a few stragglers walked the streets. Jackson and The Open Doors looked so worn out Bridge wondered if they would ever plunk or bong again.

Bridge sat behind the table by the front door. All day the paving machines, and the lampposts, and the tour buses had only been a slight buzzing in his mind. But with no people to distract him, they started to rumble. If someone could have heard what was going on inside of Bridge's head, they would have thought he had gas in his mind. Mind gas is a very serious thing. It can cause a person's brain to blow up and stink up close to three square blocks.

Chris brought Bridge's chair from behind his quill and inkwell out into the store and melted into the chair. "My God, Bridge," he exclaimed. "Three days of hors d'oeuvres is almost as bad as making frothy coffee for a living."

Rumble, gurgle, went Bridge's mind. "If this went on everyday it would be a nightmare," Bridge said.

"It would be like working on a cruise ship," Chris said.

Bridge glanced at the punch bowl. There was enough left for maybe three or four glasses. "Will this batch get you pie-eyed?" he asked Chris.

Chris sadly shook his head.

"Why do people drink if not to get a buzz?" Bridge asked.

"It's a social thing," Chris said.

"You'd think people would want to get pie-eyed because they had to be social," Bridge said.

Gertrude walked by the window. She looked like she had been standing behind a cargo plane propeller. The plane was so big it could carry twelve tanks, ten thousand soldiers, and ten tons of Geneva Convention cards that soldiers could use to start fires or pick their teeth with.

Bridge and Chris both went outside. The new lampposts on Bullard Street had just come on. Automatic sensors in life have a place. Sergeant was leaning back against his gallery, The Beginning Of A Rainbow. It looked like the building was holding him up. He waved at Bridge like he was too tired to raise his arm.

Rainy Day staggered out of her gallery, the Sunbonnet. She had sold so many paintings of sunrises and sunsets, she was thinking about doing a series on the moon.

Across the street, Lotus Blossom had one of her masks on and was dancing around in circles. She looked like an old hippie at a Blue Cheer concert who needed another hit of acid. She was chanting voodoo curses that were guaranteed to keep tourists away for at least a week. Tourists that dared to deny the gods of voodoo would have their tongues turned into credit card receipts and would have uncontrollable urges to dance around like a chicken. Traveling salesmen, UPS and Fed-X, beer, and food delivery people were exempt - also George, who brought in the weekly supply of pot.

MeJoe was sitting outside his gallery, All Art Is The Same In The Dark. He started waving his cane around madly, screaming at the same time, "Fuck all you fucking motherfuckers, fuck heads."

His mastery of the English language reminded Bridge of a master sergeant he had had the bad experience of serving under in the army.

Rudolph and Rebecca were sitting on the curb in front of their restaurant, Sally's. They had mustard and mayonnaise, bits and pieces of cheese, sliced pickles, onion, and lettuce all over their clothes. With two huge slices of bread they would have made a great sandwich.

Gertrude came back, still looking like she had been hit by the backwash from a prop engine cargo plane. She had a twelve-pack of beer. "Gertrude," Bridge said, "I would have never thought."

"Sometimes wine just won't do the trick," Gertrude said, going into her gallery without even offering Bridge or Chris a beer. Chris was not offended - Mango Margarita people are pretty much stuck on one drink. Bridge, being the true beer drinker in the art community, at first thought it was rude on Gertrude's part but then had to smile, even Chamber of Commerce people at times get too much chambering and too much commerce.

Chris' three people drove up and parked in front of the Why Am I Here. True professionals that they were, they loaded the serving pieces and the tables without Chris having to go into the store or say a word. What are a person's people if they have to be told what to do all the time? If your people have to be told what to do all the time, you need some different people.

Chris, without warning, hugged Bridge, kissed him on the cheek like some dumb ass Frenchman, and said, "I will give you your bill within a few days," and jumped in the car with his people. The car sped off like if it ever saw the art district of Lost City again it would be too soon.

Bridge looked around. There was no one remaining on Texas or Yankee Streets. The lampposts on Bullard Street started laughing at him. The paving machines started to taunt him. The remodeled buildings started to weep and cried out, "Bridge, you lied to us. This is not retirement."

The old lampposts that still worked were having a secret meeting. One of them wanted to go to Mexico and buy a dozen fully automatic M-16's and attack Lost City. There were a few who were not so radical. They only wanted to go to all the grocery stores and piss in all the bottled water.

In Bridge's mind, the street with all its new patches started rolling up and down like an ocean wave.

Bridge grabbed his head and hollered, "I'm sorry. Will you ever forgive me?" He ran into the store and locked the door behind him. The words from the old buildings sledge-hammered in his mind, "You can run but you can't hide."

He leaned back against the door and frantically looked around the Why Am I Here. The paintings that had not sold were sobbing like fifty-year-old women who had just discovered they had cellulite on their butts.

None of Bridge's published novels could cry or bitch. They had all been sold, but the bookstands the books had rested on were feeling lonely. From the storage room, Bridge heard his unpublished manuscripts scheming. Unpublished novels are not to be trusted, even if they are error free and set up in *Chicago Manual* style. They normally, by subtle and treacherous means, and over a period of time, make their writers commit suicide, and the police blame it on depression. What, me? An unpublished book kill? Never. I am just a gentle pussycat. I loved my writer. It's just that he could not take rejection, and you know what years of exposure to computer screens can do to brain cells. Now would you leave me alone so I can enjoy my box? Then after the police completely exonerate them, they throw all their money in together and self publish themselves - their reasoning being that at least they have one shot in a million of getting read.

Bridge staggered toward his living room, den, and bedroom. The room was whirling like he was sugar that had been tossed into a cotton candy machine. He bounced off a wall. He almost fell. He made it to his living room, den, and bedroom. He turned on his quill and inkwell. The electric thing a ma jigs shot out of the black screen at him. They were microscopic balls that were all mouth, but even microscopic, their teeth were the size of sheep shearing scissors. The electric shears snapped at him, yelling at the same time, "Traitor, traitor, since you betrayed buildings and streets and old lampposts that still work you will betray us."

"No, no," Bridge begged, prostrating himself like he was suddenly a Muslim and had forgotten his noon prayers. To top it off he had really liked the born again Christian centerfold in the new *Playboy.*

Bridge struggled to his feet and staggered to the front door. With all his strength, he managed to yank the door open, slamming it shut behind him. He ran down the middle of the deserted street toward the Wake Up Or Die. Vivian could save him. Vivian could beat the shit out of lampposts and paving machines and tour buses. She might have a hard time with the unpublished manuscripts, but if they really became a problem, Bridge could burn them.

Bridge, after his run, was slightly composed. There were a few dogs outside of the Wake Up Or Die. Trying to catch his breath, he petted each of the dogs, who, sensing that he was a desperate man, and out of the kindness of their hearts, licked him until saliva was dripping off of his hand. Dogs have a way of sensing weird people and knowing what weird people need - normally a hand full of slobber.

Bridge went inside and, to his surprise, Chris was behind the counter making a frothy coffee. The espresso machine sounded like a steam shovel to Bridge. There were only a few people in the store, but by the slovenly way they were dressed, Bridge knew they were not tourists. Pill was talking to a lady in the corner. He was wearing his sign **THERE IS ONLY SIX BILLION YEARS LEFT FOR THE WORLD**. The lady had on a sign that read **YOU HAD BETTER BELIEVE THERE IS ONLY SIX BILLION YEARS LEFT FOR THE WORLD.** Every cake mix has a mixing bowl.

Vivian smiled at Bridge, but then gave him a funny look. A look that said even though she knew it was Bridge she really didn't know him.

Bridge tried to smile at her, but it felt like his lips were stuck together with super glue and his smile came out looking like he had a cherry pit stuck in his throat. Chris quickly poured Bridge a cup of Roast In Hell and brought it to him. "What are you doing here?" Bridge managed to ask, holding the coffee like it was the Holy Grail.

"I discovered while making and serving hors d'oeuvres my true calling in life is making coffee," Chris said.

"A calling must be followed," Bridge said, sat, wiped the dog spit off his hand on his trouser leg, and took two huge swallows of coffee even though it was hot enough to soft boil an egg in two minutes instead of four - depending on the elevation of course.

The caffeine raced through his body. It was so strong the paving machines, the lampposts, the tour buses, and the streets took off. Strong coffee is not something to mess with. It has a kick-ass jab and one hell of a right cross.

Bridge took two more big swallows, set the coffee down and wilted into the chair like a dandelion after it has been sprayed with weed killer.

Vivian hurried over and sat. "Lord, Bridge," she said. "You look like someone has kicked you in the balls."

"Paving machines smashed them," Bridge replied.

"Are you ok, Bridge?" Vivian asked, so concerned her own voice frightened her.

Bridge told her the truth, "No, Vivian, I am not."

"Let's go home," Vivian said.

"We don't have a home," Bridge said.

Vivian took him by the hand. "Wherever we are is home, Bridge."

"Come by the store after you close up. There are a few things I have to do," Bridge told Vivian. He took several more swallows of the coffee and left.

Bridge saw the Rock Lady and the Professor sitting at a window table at Bill's. Organic Muffin was waiting on them. He knew Stoops was cooking away in the kitchen. He saw Plastic talking to a lady he had never seen in front of the This Isn't Heaven Bar. He did not call to Plastic - he might break up Plastic's train of lying. What man tells a woman he has just met the truth? Please.

Bridge went back to the Why Am I Here. He turned on his quill and inkwell. The little thing a ma jigs had gotten over their ferocious thing. He punched up his book. He liked the book he was working on. It was different from most of his other stuff. So what if the west was shrinking? So what if ranchers couldn't hold on? That's kind of how life is. Nothing stands still. Bridge sat back and had a thought - Arts Councils and Chambers of Commerce were not bad things, and money is nothing more than a potato, a head of lettuce, or a pig. Bridge went outside and looked at the buildings on Texas and Yankee Streets. "Don't tell me that at times you don't enjoy your new life," he hollered.

The buildings tried to look the other way.

"Come on, fess up," Bridge demanded.

The buildings reluctantly nodded.

"Ok, from now on you leave me alone," Bridge said. "I was wrong, so get over it."

MeJoe came out of his store. "Bridge, what the fuck are you hollering at, you fucker?"

"I'm having a conversation with the buildings."

"Well make it quick. I'm trying to sleep."

"How do I convince the buildings to get off my case?"

"Tell the stupid fuckers that if they don't, you will tear them down, ship their carcasses to L.A. and put them back up."

"Do you hear that, Texas and Yankee Streets?" Bridge demanded.

The buildings started to shake. Even buildings have a fear of California - it's something to do with earthquakes.

MeJoe went back inside his store.

Bridge walked to Bullard. All the new lampposts that looked like old lampposts were shining away. "What the city did to the old lampposts was not right," Bridge told the first lamppost he came to. "We know, Bridge," the new lamppost replied. "But that's how life is. The old lampposts are starting to enjoy their life on the commune now. They've got an organic garden going and are going to sell their produce at the farmers market. They play softball, and a few of them are even growing pot. They told us they really don't care if they get busted. They are so old they can't keep them in jail for long."

"I'll be," Bridge said.

"Most things turn out for the best, Bridge," the wise beyond his year's new lamppost said. "One day we will be put out to pasture also."

Bridge walked down the middle of the street. "And what about you, street?" he asked.

"These asphalt patches are really pretty nice," the street replied. "A pothole to a street is like a toothache to a person."

"Never thought about it that way," Bridge replied.

"You are not a street," the street said.

"I don't want to be a street," Bridge said.

"Who does?" the street said, but it really didn't seem to bother him.

Bridge headed back to the Why Am I Here. "Tour buses would be fine," he mumbled. "Vivian would sell more coffee. I'd sell more books."

Bridge stopped walking. His legs felt strange. Luckily the strange feeling did not hurt. "Let new gallery owners come in and bring art from the East Coast and West Coast," he said. "Who cares if they don't think western art is art."

Bridge took a step. His legs felt really strange. "People can come to Lost City from everywhere," he said. "Lost City can have a New England suburb, a Florida suburb, a California suburb. Each group can sit around in their suburb and talk about where they came from."

Bridge took a step with his left leg, but when he tried to move his right leg, it wouldn't budge. He moved his left leg back. The right leg moved forward by itself. His left leg moved one step forward and one backward and his right leg moved one forward. "Lord help me Jesus," Bridge hollered.

Two steps forward and one backward. "Pass the collection plate," Bridge hollered again.

Two steps forward and one backward. Bridge tried to walk three steps forward. He couldn't do it. Bridge two-stepped forward and one backward to the Why Am I Here. He sat at his quill and inkwell. He brought up a blank page and started to type a new book about a weird art town. "No one will believe it," he said. "No one will ever believe it."

After Bridge had typed about ten pages, Vivian came in the store. She saw the empty spots where paintings used to be and the empty bookstands. "You did good, Bridge," she said.

"In my older years capitalism suits me," Bridge said.

He turned off his quill and inkwell and two-stepped forward and one backward toward Vivian. "My God, Bridge, you're back to normal," Vivian shouted with happiness.

"I don't know if I am normal, but at least I walk normal again," Bridge said.

Vivian hugged him in one of her bear hugs so hard he did fart. There is nothing like a good fart-producing hug. It gets right to the essence of life.

"I am going to rename my store," Bridge said after squirming out of Vivian's hug. A fart is one thing, but having the shit hugged out of you is an entirely different matter.

Vivian said what she was obviously supposed to say. "What are you going to rename it?"

"I am going to rename it, I Know Why I Am Here."

Bridge turned off all the lights to the store and he and Vivian went outside. Bridge locked the door. "You know, the art walk was fun. It was tiring, but it was fun. I have some ideas for the Arts Council and the Chamber of Commerce next year to make it better."

"Why don't you just stay with being a writer? That is what you do best," Vivian said.

Bridge and Vivian held hands and they walked down the middle of the street toward her house. "You know to a street a pothole is like a toothache," Bridge told Vivian.

"Where do you come up with some of this stuff?" Vivian asked.

"I started a new book," Bridge said. "What would you think if I ended it differently?"

"What do you mean?" Vivian replied.

"Instead of The End I put, They Lived Happily."

"That is not an end," Vivian said.

"Exactly," Bridge smiled and kissed Vivian's hand.

****

I, I, I, I, I, I, Lo, Lo, Lo, Lo.
We are only smoke.
Make me a child.
One, two, three, turn, glide, twirl.
Homogenize the planet.
Ambition can be a virtue.
Am I a rock?
Love is not salvation. It is a helping hand.
Bong, bong, bong, bong.
Whatever happened to black coffee?
There is only six billion years left for the world.
Every kettle has its own soup.
Toss the homeless a turkey leg.
True art is a hug.
Peanut Butter and Jelly - if only life could be so simple.
My saint of the rainbows.
Two steps forward and one backward.
There is always hope.
Identity, form, and substance are only temporary illusions.
Dogs don't mind a little bird shit on them.
The homeless don't have a take home container.
How quickly time flies.
It's a man man, man woman, woman woman thing.
There is no center to the universe - there is only off center.
The rock of all rocks is hollow.
Life is good even if we are all full of shit.
Rolling in my sweet baby's arms.
At times quickies solve a lot of problems.
Sometimes birds have to learn to fend for themselves.
Bloody Marys for breakfast are a good thing.

The old ticker is a time bomb.

I know God needs someone to bring him a drink.

Cupid, you winged bare-assed adolescent, how sly and wonderful you are.

All grumps have a heart.

Straight men hugging gay men is not a bad thing.

There is always a lifeguard.

Bubble, bubble, bubble.

Somewhere in the world is a lovely lady that likes peanut butter.

Everyone needs a sister even if the sister does not have a face.

Waiters that smile make good tips.

Even run-on sentences have a place in life.

There are red, blue, green, yellow, orange and purple fairies that don't need light to glow.

If you do what you love, futility takes a back seat.

Happily ever after has no end.

How many people die happy?

A pothole to a street is like a toothache to a person.

Boots with laces are not really boots.

What do a grump and a bubble talk about?

Old lampposts like communes.

We are all an illusion.

Maybe one day you will have a best seller.

If there is a bad angel is there a good devil?

Flirting is a nice thing.

Thoughtfulness is a lot better than pride.

Love is being comfortable with silence.

I love you Vivian.

I know why I am here.

Bless the silence of friends.

Love is more than a spoken word.

And last but not least, please, do no harm that is hateful.

THEY LIVED HAPPILY

FOR MORE NOVELS BY ROBERT K. SWISHER JR VISIT
swisherbooks.com

www.ingramcontent.com/pod-product-compliance
Lightning Source LLC
Chambersburg PA
CBHW021749110726
47902CB00006B/1462

9780997909654